D0907302

Fairyville

EMMA HOLLY

BERKLEY SENSATION, NEW YORK

THE BERKLEY PUBLISHING GROUP
Published by the Penguin Group
Penguin Group (USA) Inc.
375 Hudson Street, New York, New York 10014, USA
Penguin Group (Canada), 90 Eglinton Avenue East, Suite 700, Toronto, Ontario M4P 2Y3, Canada
(a division of Pearson Penguin Canada Inc.)
Penguin Books Ltd., 80 Strand, London WC2R 0RL, England
Penguin Group Ireland, 25 St. Stephen's Green, Dublin 2, Ireland (a division of Penguin Books Ltd.)
Penguin Group (Australia), 250 Camberwell Road, Camberwell, Victoria 3124, Australia
(a division of Pearson Australia Group Pty. Ltd.)
Penguin Books India Pvt. Ltd., 11 Community Centre, Panchsheel Park, New Delhi—110 017, India
Penguin Group (NZ), 67 Apollo Drive, Rosedale, North Shore 0745, Auckland, New Zealand
(a division of Pearson New Zealand Ltd.)
Penguin Books (South Africa) (Pty.) Ltd., 24 Sturdee Avenue, Rosebank, Johannesburg 2196, South Africa

Penguin Books Ltd., Registered Offices: 80 Strand, London WC2R 0RL, England

This is a work of fiction. Names, characters, places, and incidents either are the product of the author's imagination or are used fictitiously, and any resemblance to actual persons, living or dead, business establishments, events, or locales is entirely coincidental. The publisher does not have any control over and does not assume any responsibility for author or third-party websites or their content.

First edition: September 2007

Library of Congress Cataloging-in-Publication Data

Holly, Emma.
  Fairyville / Emma Holly.—1st ed.
    p. cm.
  ISBN 978-0-425-21705-4
  1. Young women—Fiction. 2. Fairies—Fiction. 3. Arizona—Fiction. I. Title.

PS3608.O4943F35   2007
813'.6—dc22   2007014538

PRINTED IN THE UNITED STATES OF AMERICA

10   9   8   7   6   5   4   3   2   1

To the real-life mediums
who share their stories.
Many thanks.

One

Zoe Clare saw dead people.

This wouldn't have been bad if dead people were all she saw. In this day and age, a person could make a decent living talking to ghosts. But Zoe's gift had come with an eccentric extra—a tiny, annoying extra that was, even now, tugging at the covers she'd pulled determinedly over her head.

"I need my sleep," she said, her eyes screwed shut against the bright Arizona morning. "It's important for a medium to recharge her batteries."

The tugging changed to a weighted prickle on her scalp, between the corkscrew curls of her long black hair. One of the fairies who'd been her constant companions since childhood (much to her parents' dismay) was standing on Zoe's head.

"Wakey-wakey," it said, like a DJ on helium. "It's a beautiful day in Fairyville, and your batteries are as charged as they're going to get."

"Your mother was a toadstool," Zoe retorted, her eyes still closed.

The avoidance was ineffective. Her tormentor shone clearly in her mind's eye, complete with diaphanous gown and dragonfly wings. Like many mediums, Zoe saw the other world better without her physical sight. Although the different fairies' voices sounded the same to her, this one's iridescent purple wings and gaudy yellow tiara proclaimed that she was Rajel, queen of Zoe's personal flock. She flashed her tiny white teeth in a twinkling grin, Zoe's insult having slid right off her.

Serious fairies, apparently, had little hope of rising through the ranks. Only the most persistently positive could be queen.

"It's time to rise and shine," Rajel cooed. "You know you hate to be late to work."

This was usually true, but today was the day after the full moon. Spiritually, this affected her not at all. Personally, it made her stomach sink to her toes.

The full moon was when her landlord-slash-manager, the painfully scrumptious Magnus Monroe, indulged in his monthly sexual debauch. The day after the full moon was when Zoe had to watch him stroll into her office, all loose-hipped and jovial, and know that—yet again—she wasn't the woman who'd put that smile on his face.

She wondered who his partner had been this time. Every month was different, and he didn't seem to have a type beyond female and breathing. She suspected the lucky lady was Sheri Yost.

Sheri was the waitress at Zoe's favorite steak house, where she and Magnus often ate lunch. Magnus flirted the way some men inhaled oxygen, but over the last week, Zoe thought she'd noticed an extra bit of zing in his and Sheri's repartee. If Sheri had been his "chosen one," Zoe's lunch was destined to be as hard to stomach as going in to work. The women who slept with her manager always had a glow afterward, an I've-been-screwed-six-ways-to-Sunday-and-I-loved-it glow.

Remembering how many times she'd seen that sensual female smirk made Zoe sit up growling in disgust. She shoved her tangle of long black curls away from her face. Now that her physical eyes were open, Rajel was a sparkly purple sphere, no bigger than a penny, hanging in the air in front of her. Most people wouldn't have seen her, but Zoe could see her and more. Rajel's fairy court bobbed behind her, a cloud of at least a dozen snickering rainbow glows.

It was a larger gathering than usual.

"Well, well," Zoe said. "The gang's all here. Must have been a slow night for parties."

The fairies giggled in agreement and whizzed off in different directions.

"Dibs on helping Zoe with her hair!" cried one.

"I'm picking her jewelry!" said another.

"I'll talk to the toaster!" announced a third.

"No!" Zoe whipped out her hand to grab the last fairy, but the little bugger was too fast. "No talking to the toaster! You guys keep shorting it out."

The darting rose-pink sparkle paid her no mind. "Stop her," Zoe begged Rajel. "I'm tired of cold cereal."

"Oh, I couldn't discourage Florabel." Rajel brushed a bit of fairy dust from her gown. "She's only trying to communicate with the machinery. It does have a primitive form of consciousness, you know."

"Great," Zoe mumbled, throwing off the covers and stumping toward the shower. "I guess until Florabel figures out the toasters' 'primitive consciousness,' I can kiss my morning bagel good-bye."

*   *   *

Cold cereal aside, if a person had to go to work, Fairyville, Arizona was the place to do it, especially on a cool, bright morning in July. The sky was a deep, saturated blue, and while the temperature might climb toward ungodly as the day went on, for now it was as pleasant as a baby's smile.

Zoe's fairies swooped off somersaulting into the ethers, chasing bees or showing off. Zoe couldn't begrudge them their high spirits—or their abandonment of her. No matter how many times she'd seen the local red-rock cliffs against that deep blue sky, the sight never failed to catch at her breath.

You just couldn't forget the power of Mother Nature here.

A definite beneficiary of that power, Fairyville lay north of its more famous sister, Sedona, but shared the same awe-inspiring landscape of buttes and spires—and the same reputation for mystical oddities. Zoe's home had been a virtual ghost town fifty years ago, a copper mine gone bust in the Great Depression. It had been revived by a carefully calculated tourist scheme, devised by the then-desperate residents, who decided to tout it as the "Number One Fairy-Spotting Capital in the U.S.A." Today Fairyville was divided into two camps, the "real" Fairyvillers and the "normals." Being a real Fairyviller had nothing to do with how long you'd lived there. You became one by having a psychic gift, by treating those who had psychic gifts with respect, or by being so Looney Tunes everyone figured you had to be touched by *some*thing.

Normals were the folks who thought the real Fairyvillers were "colorful."

Zoe grimaced at how much local color she herself represented and parked her classic white VW bug at the end of Canyon Way, well beyond the spots the tourists would be fighting over once they rolled out of their B&Bs. Even at this distance, her walk would be reasonable. Fairyville's carefully restored historic district was, at most, a ten-minute stroll from end to end. Zoe knew every inch of it, from the mix of Old West storefronts to the rock shops to the Spanish adobe restaurants.

She'd lived in or around Fairyville all her life and considered herself lucky this was the case. Her parents, normals down to their toes, had tolerated her claims of being visited by dead relatives. This was, after all, a mainstream sort of weirdness. When she refused to outgrow her fairies, however, they'd drawn a line. Dead people existed. Fairies were delusions. It was time Zoe admitted she'd made them up.

Fortunately, the psychologist they'd insisted she see while she was in high school was a real Fairyviller, too. Dr. Sweetwell ended up being—unbeknownst to Zoe's parents—her spiritual mentor. In truth, it would have been hard for Catherine Sweetwell to avoid it, seeing as how *she* liked to call in angels for consults. She'd guided Zoe to the best teachers to hone her gifts, even covered for her when she went to workshops.

"Thank you, Doc," Zoe murmured as she forced her reluctant sandals past the Navajo rug store. She felt in need of counting her blessings. The gallery in which she did her readings was only a few doors down, a restored brick two-story building from 1910. From where she stood, she could see the potted prickly pear cactus that guarded the entrance, the last of its lush hot-pink flowers drooping off. Magnus loved that cactus. He called it "Gorgeous" and said hello to it every morning. The first time Zoe had heard him do it, her heart had clenched.

Magnus was sweet to women no matter what their species.

You can handle this, she told herself. *Every month you see him do the same thing, and every month you survive.*

But the pep talk didn't help. The "Open" sign in her gallery window sent her pulse into a panic. Magnus was already there, probably lazing back in her chair with his long, strong legs propped on the desk she used for paperwork. He looked good in cowboy boots, Magnus did, a man's man with a sensually handsome face. The memory of how his faded Levis cupped his basket made her whole body flush. He always looked mellow the morning after, as if he'd just lie back and let a woman ride.

Chickening out at the last moment, Zoe ducked into The Fairyville Café one door short of her own storefront. Her first client wasn't due for fifteen minutes. She didn't have to torture herself by spending every one of them pining after her well-screwed landlord.

Metaphysically speaking, that wouldn't do anyone any good.

The café's owner was Teresa Smallfoot. A mix of Native American, Anglo, and six-foot-tall goddess, she'd been a friend of Zoe's from the day she opened, trading free coffee for the occasional free reading. Since Teresa's troubles were of the mild romantic sort and the coffee was hot and strong, Zoe considered the exchange a fair one. Plus, Teresa's departed relatives were well behaved. Not a pesterer in the bunch. Considering some of her clients' connections showed up hours ahead of schedule to jabber inanities, Zoe valued the ones with restraint.

Teresa was watching her customers from behind the coffee bar today. The decor was Western Victorian, with little round antique tables and sepia photos of long-dead people hanging on the walls. Teresa leaned forward as soon as she saw Zoe.

"Girlfriend," she said in a low, excited tone. "You should have heard the ruckus from next door last night! There was such a caterwauling coming out of Sheri's bedroom windows, you'd have thought a pair of cougars had been locked inside!"

Zoe fought a wince. She'd forgotten Sheri Yost was Teresa's next-door neighbor.

"Great," she said, pouring herself some coffee from the carafe of dark roast on the counter. Teresa used real cups, mismatched china she picked up in junk stores. "Just what I was hoping to hear."

"I know, honey," Teresa crooned sympathetically. That lasted about two seconds, or until Teresa's love of good gossip had her grinning again. "I'll be surprised if Sheri comes to work today. In fact, I'll be surprised if she can walk. That manager of yours is a *luuuvv* machine. Every time I thought he must be wrung dry, they started up again. If I didn't know you had a thing for him, I'd throw myself in his path out of sheer curiosity."

Zoe took such a big swig of coffee, she nearly scalded her throat. "Don't let me stop you," she said through her coughs.

"Oh, right. Like you wouldn't want to gouge out my eyes if I slept with him. I know the girlfriend rules."

"At least I could see why he'd go for you. Sheri Yost is a whiny bore."

Teresa flipped her long black locks behind her shoulders, her expression indicating pleasure at the compliment. "Sheri Yost is a whiny bore who isn't smart enough to make change. You, on the other hand, are beautiful, sweet, and wise. Clearly, Magnus has no sense."

"Unfortunately, you can't force people to have sense—as I've learned from my many years of giving advice." Zoe turned her cup between her hands. "I just don't understand him. Why would a guy with his looks and charisma restrict himself to having sex once a month? And why does it have to be a new woman every time?"

"Maybe that's the secret to his stamina. Abstinence plus variety. I mean, he can't be the only man who'd like to be able to perform like that. Without Viagra, I mean."

With a rueful cluck, Teresa interrupted the conversation to serve another customer.

"He's a freak," Zoe said when her friend returned, though she should have let it go. "I have no idea why I like him."

"How about because he's a hunka hunka burning love, and you've got eyes? Plus, he's nice."

Magnus was more than nice. Magnus was considerate, charming, funny, and had the sunniest disposition of any human being she knew. Nothing got him down—not hundred-degree weather, not dents in his SUV, or the evening news. His only flaw (and, to be fair, it was only a flaw to Zoe) was his refusal to look at her in a sexual way.

Teresa set her elbows on the counter. "Couldn't you ask your little friends what his story is?"

Zoe's mouth quirked. Teresa was open minded, but she'd never liked saying the word *fairy*. "I have asked them. They're keeping mum."

Weirdly mum, in fact. Zoe's fairies tended to air their opinions about everything.

"Well, what good are they then?"

"They aren't my slaves, Ter. They hang with me because they think I'm fun."

"Fun on every topic but one."

This tease was a bit too close to the mark. Some days Zoe thought if she didn't get over her crush on Magnus, she'd turn into a lifelong grump.

"I don't know what's wrong with me," she grumbled into her empty cup. "I never used to like guys that tall."

Teresa reached out to pat her arm. "Oh, face it, honey. It's not the height you like, it's him."

It is *him*, Zoe admitted, though she only pulled a face at her friend.

She was debating buying a chocolate muffin as consolation when a flicker of gray in her peripheral vision reminded her of the time. The ghost was one she knew: Mrs. Darling's late husband, Leo. Once he'd finished materializing, Leo nodded to her and smiled. He was one of her favorites, as gentle in death as he'd been in life. In spite of her sour mood, it cheered her to know he'd be her first job.

"Gotta go," she said to Teresa. "My special guests are starting to line up."

"Brr," Teresa responded, pretending to shiver as she hugged her arms.

Leo tipped his Stetson to Teresa, but Zoe was the only living being who saw.

Zoe gave her readings in the front room of the gallery. The furnishings were as homey as she could make them—secondhand chairs and sofas, with nicked tables set between. A beautiful Navaho rug hung on one wall, her biggest decorating splurge. The light from the wide front window filled the space with gold, glinting pleasantly off her assortment of crystals and stones.

The fairies had insisted she buy them to "cleanse the atmosphere." They were her only mystical bric-a-brac. Most of her clients felt more comfortable without too much woo-woo stuff, though tourists sometimes asked why she didn't use tarot cards. Zoe knew such touchstones worked for others, but she'd never wanted to be dependent on objects. She needed nothing to jump-start her gift except an open heart and a focused mind.

Even that seemed unnecessary with a contact as clear-spoken as Leo Darling. As usual, Ada Darling's weekly appointment went smoothly. She liked to share her news with her disincarnate spouse and get his advice on the decisions of daily life. Her husband was always patient with her concerns, letting her know which handymen she could trust, reminding her she didn't need his permission for anything.

Mrs. Darling never seemed to doubt the authenticity of these interactions, but she also never seemed to realize they might inspire deeper thoughts. The soul survived death, and the dead still loved those they left behind. That was Big, as far as Zoe was concerned; that was a message she suspected she'd never tire of delivering. Although Mrs. Darling was a sweet old lady, sometimes Zoe wanted to shake her out of her mundane world.

Heaven loves you, she longed to say. *What does it matter if your best friend cheats at bingo?*

When her hour was up, Mrs. Darling counted out her payment in cash like she always did. Her old, arthritic hands made each bill seem as heavy as a volume of *War and Peace*. Every time Zoe watched her do it, she had to bite her tongue against telling her to keep her money. Zoe performed a service, and she performed it well. This was her sole source of income. Even more important, if she didn't charge Ada Darling, Zoe suspected the woman would come in ten times a day.

Mrs. Darling sighed with satisfaction once the painstaking ritual was complete. "Thank you, dear," she said, handing over the fee. "You've put this aching old heart to rest."

Zoe smiled in spite of her impatience. "That's why I'm here."

Mrs. Darling nodded, her usual reluctance to leave showing itself. She really didn't like facing her life without "dear old Leo" to hold her hand.

"You'll be fine," Zoe said, reaching out to squeeze her plump but fragile arm. "Leo watches over you all the time, not just when you talk to him here."

"But you're the one who makes me feel him," said Mrs. Darling. Her faded blue eyes teared up, though she waved off the tissue Zoe offered her. "You're a good girl, Zoe. I hope you find a man like Leo yourself someday."

"So do I," Zoe admitted, and then had to clear her throat.

Without warning, Mrs. Darling cackled out a laugh. "Ask those fairies of yours to fix you up. Then you'll be set!"

"You hear that?" Zoe said to the apparently empty air above her head.

No piping voices answered, even after Mrs. Darling left. A prickle at the back of Zoe's neck told her why. Magnus was standing in the door behind her, the one that led to her office.

From their first meeting, Magnus had struck her as more man

than most. He was tall, for one thing, at least six five—though you didn't notice how big the various parts of him were until you stood up close. With half a room between them, he simply looked in proportion. At five foot six Zoe was no pygmy, but she wasn't fooled. Toe-to-toe, Magnus could make an Amazon feel delicate. His looks were as dramatic as his size. He had dark, beautiful hair—not long but a little shaggy—smooth, high-colored skin, full kissable lips, and eyes as green and clear as a mountain stream. If he hadn't exuded masculinity, he'd have been pretty. Instead, he came off as unbelievably sexy. Zoe had known him two years, and she still had to swallow at the sight of him.

No matter how cool she wanted to act, he was hard to look away from.

Now his face held something uncertain, something she hadn't expected to see on this of all days. She wondered how much he'd heard of her conversation with Mrs. Darling. She could only hope not a lot. Zoe might be psychic, but she wasn't a mind reader. The images she caught from people now and then weren't conscious thoughts. They came, she was almost certain, from the part of them that shared the same nonphysical territory as the deceased: the high, wise angel of their better selves.

As far as she could tell, Magnus's high, wise angel didn't have a peep to say to her.

"Your hair looks nice," he said, waving one hand in her direction. "Shiny."

Zoe couldn't help touching it self-consciously. Left to itself, her hair had a tendency to devolve into a long black snarl. "I had help this morning."

He nodded without his usual trademark smile. Like most of the locals, Magnus knew about her fairies. He also knew, because she hadn't figured out how to keep it from him, that they avoided him like the plague. She had only to think hard about

Magnus, and they'd disappear into whatever dimension fairies hung out in when they weren't in hers. Zoe had no idea why they did this—unless they simply didn't like his effect on her moods.

In all her life, only one other man had provoked a similar reaction from her "little friends" . . . but that was a ghost Zoe preferred not to resurrect.

"I don't suppose they're still around," he said with an uncustomary tinge of wistfulness. His Western-style shirt hugged his chest just right, and his big, tanned hands were thrust into his front jean pockets. The faded patches in the denim, where his cock and balls habitually rubbed, pointed out how very well hung he was. Sadly, none of these things were encouraging Zoe's eyes to stay where she wanted them.

"I think the fairies are outside playing," she said. She shifted from foot to foot, caught off balance by his strange mood. "I didn't expect to see you here this late."

Magnus owned a number of properties in Fairyville, where he also acted in a managerial capacity. From the day he'd invited Zoe to set up shop here, she was always his first stop, though half an hour was generally as long as he stayed.

He didn't respond right away, and she was soon sorry she'd forced her gaze to his face. He was looking at her steadily, as if whatever he was thinking was serious. She would have given her right arm to have him look at her like that in bed. Unable to stop the reaction, Zoe felt a bead of sweat trickle down the small of her back. If he'd figured out she had a yen for him, she was going to die.

"You received some more requests to speak," he said at last. "I was trying to see if I could organize them into a tour."

"A tour?" she repeated, praying the words wouldn't strangle on their way out. He *had* figured it out. He was trying to get rid of her.

"You could go in the fall. Get your name better known. You deserve that, you know. You're a princess, Zoe, not a girl wrapped in a donkey skin."

Zoe blinked at this odd reference. Realizing her eyes were threatening to overflow, she dropped her gaze to his feet. The sight of his shoes momentarily blanked her mind. He wasn't wearing his usual cowboy boots, but a pair of high-topped yellow sneakers with Wile E. Coyote painted on the sides. With an effort, she pulled her concentration back.

"I'm not sure I want to travel. My friends are here. I . . . I feel more comfortable at home."

Her voice was low and husky, and all the curses in the world wouldn't erase the emotion that gave away. Magnus crossed the room before she could step back. He didn't touch her, but the heat from his body was distracting. Magnus's appeal was based on more than his looks. His energy always seemed twice as high as other men's.

"Zoe . . ." he began.

Zoe knew she had to stop whatever he was going to say. "I hope you're not unhappy with what I'm earning," she interrupted hurriedly. "I could advertise for more clients. Maybe put a site on the Internet."

"Zoe." He gripped her shoulders in his hands, the tingling warmth of his hold like hot molasses running down her skin. She struggled not to shudder with enjoyment. "I'm not unhappy with what you make. I want this for you. Because you deserve it. You can't imagine I'm looking forward to you being gone."

She did cry then, horrible, sniffly sobs that had her gasping into the tissue Mrs. Darling had refused. Completely mortified, she tried to struggle out of Magnus's hold, but he wasn't having that. He pulled her close instead, tucking her head under his and enfolding her in his arms.

He'd never held her like this before. She had to use all her self-control to stiffen instead of melt.

"Shh," he said, then swore softly into her hair. "Zoe, Zoe, Zoe. You had to go and make this harder than it was."

"Oh, God," she cried. "You're turning me out!"

He clucked his tongue in exasperation, then tipped her head back and held her face. "I like you, Zoe. I'm not turning you out. I enjoy having you around."

She mopped the last of her crying jag from her nose. She was light-headed from her outburst and probably not thinking straight, but she knew she'd never find the nerve to ask this again.

"If you *like* me," she said as deliberately as he'd been addressing her, "why haven't you made a move on me?"

His green eyes darkened a second before his face followed suit, a flush washing up his chiseled cheeks. She'd thought his smile could knock a woman flat, but the intensity of this expression stole her power to think. His gaze burned down at her from his greater height. He looked like he was angry, but she was pretty sure that wasn't it.

She was certain when his lips covered hers.

His kiss might have been soft, but it sure wasn't wasting time. She felt his tongue push into her mouth and heard her own knee-jerk moan of excitement. The rest of the world disappeared as that hot, wet flesh speared deep. His heat, his scent, his pounding heart became her universe. Suddenly, his arms were wrapped hard around her, one hand forking through her curls to cradle her head. He angled it to suit his pleasure, while his second hand crushed her left butt cheek. She was wearing a gauzy, printed skirt, and he gripped that buttock like he owned it. His long, hot fingers stretched farther forward than she let most men get on a second date.

She had no urge to stop Magnus, and it wasn't just because

it had been longer than she could remember since she'd had any date at all. At the first intimate contact of his fingers, her body jolted with an erotic shock so powerful it surprised her—even with the time she'd spent hankering after him. No wonder women dropped like ripe cherries around this man. His hands conveyed an energy that fairly buzzed. A flood of moisture ran into the folds he'd brushed, then overflowed them in a heated rush.

Boy, it had been too long since anyone had touched her. If the mewls she kept spilling into his mouth hadn't clued him in already, Magnus had to know what he'd done to her.

Right that moment, it didn't seem to bother him. Feeling the evidence of her arousal, he made a low, rough noise and kissed her harder, his hunger a savage, wonderful thing. His body moved in a slow undulation, his erection grinding against her belly.

God, it was big. Big and hot and—

Magnus tore his mouth away from hers.

"This is . . . not the plan," he gasped.

Dizzy, Zoe stroked the pulse throbbing in his neck. She had to touch him, had to feel his skin against her palms. His tendons were tight, his skin dark with the blood rushing under it. She felt starved for him, for this. Going on tiptoe, she tipped her head up for another kiss.

"No," he said, very firm but still breathless. "You're not thinking like yourself."

Zoe's head cleared reluctantly. If thinking like herself meant stopping, she didn't think she wanted to. Magnus had kissed her. Magnus had eaten at her mouth like he'd been lusting after her every bit as much as she'd been lusting after him. His big, broad chest went up and down with his labored breathing. Then he let his hands slide to her elbows and stepped back.

Zoe dropped onto her heels like a balloon with the air let out.

"I'm sorry," he said. "This isn't how I want it to be with you."

Hurt and anger had her eyes sliding to his groin. She might not be the queen of the sex parade—her oddball calling saw to that—but she remembered the difference between a man who wanted her and one who didn't. Magnus's erection shoved starkly against his jeans, its outline almost too thick and long to be real.

"This isn't how you want it?" she repeated in disbelief. "I'd say one large part of you would disagree."

"I'm easily aroused," he said with an odd, defensive dignity.

Zoe folded her arms across her breasts, uncomfortably aware of how sensitized they were. "Well, that explains why you only fuck once a month."

Her sarcasm called a shade of purple into his face. The contrast made his eyes blaze like emeralds, in spite of which his voice was calm.

"Don't be crude, Zoe. It doesn't suit you."

Her temper, which she almost always had under control, abruptly snapped. "How about this? Is this too crude to suit me?"

She slapped her hand around the bulge of his big erection, squeezing hard enough to feel the give of his balls through the worn denim. It was possible she'd meant to hurt him, but she forgot to be angry in her enchantment. She might as well have taken hold of a python; his cock felt that substantial, that alive. Magnus moaned, agony and pleasure mixing in the sound. His hand jammed over hers, completely covering it.

It took a second to register that he wasn't pulling her away.

"Don't do this," he said through gritted teeth, his hips beginning to circle into the cup their locked hands had formed.

Zoe's jaw dropped as she watched him writhe. Maybe he *was* easy to arouse. He did seem to be having trouble controlling himself. Teresa had said he'd gone all night, and now he was pushing at her so hard her fingers were going numb. His palm was actually sweating. When he spoke again, he sounded desperate.

"You know you won't appreciate being the next notch on my bedpost. You know you're too good for that."

She looked at him, her soul gone cold. "You're saying I wouldn't be any different than the others?"

"I'm saying you *couldn't* be."

Failing to see the distinction, she wrenched her hand out from under his. She would have stepped away, would have salved her pride somehow, but he brushed her cheek with his fingertips. The tenderness of the gesture arrested her.

It was pathetic, really, how badly she wanted to believe he cared.

"Be my friend," he said. "Be the friend I've always hoped you'd be."

His tone was gentle, his expression genuinely fond. She didn't say she couldn't be his friend, that she cared too much in a different way. That would have been a lie. Magnus meant so much to her, she suspected she could be his friend even if her heart cracked in two.

She did, however, have too much self-respect to admit it.

She blew out her breath instead. "You're even weirder than I am."

That inspired one of his dazzling smiles. "High praise, coming from a real Fairyviller."

She should have been grateful he was still comfortable enough to tease. Unfortunately, she was too busy fighting memories. The sad truth was that Magnus wasn't the first man she'd loved who'd pulled a number like this on her.

Two

When Lizanne Pruitt entered the investigative offices of
Goodbody & McCallum, first thing Wednesday morning, she
didn't look like the oddest client they'd ever had. With her five-
year-old son in tow, she looked like any harried suburban mom
they might have run across in a Scottsdale mall.

From his seat behind their broad walnut desk—the one that
told clients they were solid—Bryan McCallum watched his aptly
named partner, Alexander Goodbody, usher Mrs. Pruitt in. He
and Alex had run this eight-man firm for the last four years, and
they'd been college roommates before that. Being so familiar
with each others' strengths made responsibilities easy to divvy
up, though it wasn't as simple as brains and brawn. Bryan wasn't
stupid, nor Alex weak, but Alex was the more polished of the
two. He did the gentlemanly niceties, pulling out Mrs. Pruitt's
chair and helping her to sit.

Bryan did his bit by sizing her up.

Mrs. Pruitt had been pretty once upon a time, in a pink-cheeked, former cheerleader way. She wasn't unattractive now, just ordinary and tired and plump. Her outfit, a coordinated powder-blue dress and cardigan—one hair short of country-club chic—was nice enough to suggest she could afford their fees. Her eyes, blue like her dress, held a hunted look. Bryan would have bet this was a cheating spouse case if it weren't for the kid's presence. It still could be, he supposed. Some parents liked to get a head start in the battle for their children's sympathies.

"Coffee or tea?" Alex offered in his surprisingly raspy voice. The way he looked, it should have been as smooth as sherry. Instead, it came out as rough as a rock star's.

Mrs. Pruitt responded to the aural stimulation with a touch of flusterment. She blushed when Alex leaned down close enough to hear her faint request for tea. Bryan knew she'd probably gotten a whiff of the cologne beneath Alex's business shirt.

When you added *Pour L'Homme* to Alex's natural smell, you got a guaranteed wet panty.

The effect wasn't deliberate. Bryan's partner was no flirt; his manners were too reserved for that. But Alex *was* unnaturally good looking—a tall, lean, sun-streaked blond with eyes the color of a Caribbean cove. The sleek gray suits he favored took nothing from his sex appeal. In Bryan's experience, the women who met Alex tended to fall into two camps: those who wanted to mother him and those who wanted him in the sack. It didn't take a genius to figure out which Mrs. Pruitt was, or that she was uncomfortable with her response.

Join the club, Bryan thought, at which point her son looked up and laughed.

"Oscar," scolded his mother, though the five-year-old couldn't have meant any harm, or even known what he was laughing at. "Go sit in the corner and be quiet."

The boy obeyed her without objection, clambering into the extra chair where he sat grinning and swinging his short legs. His shoes were bright yellow high-tops with some sort of cartoon figure printed on the canvas. He was a cute kid, as lively as his mother was worn down. Something in his expression, maybe the joie de vivre in his eyes, made Bryan grin back at him.

"I'm sorry," his mother said. "I had to take him out of pre-school."

"Not a problem," Alex assured her as he handed her the tea. Rather than take the chair beside Bryan, he perched his narrow runner's butt on the desk's front corner. Bryan had entertained fantasies about that butt that he couldn't repeat in public even to himself. "I can see that . . . Oscar is a nice young man."

Oscar seemed to think being called a *nice young man* was hilarious, though he didn't make a sound as he somersaulted over in the chair, ending up with his head and hands on the ground and his feet wiggling manically in the air.

"Oscar!" his mother said, her voice gone sharp. "Stop that this instant!"

"Why don't we leave Oscar to entertain himself?" Bryan suggested. "Since he seems to be good at it. And then you can tell us what this is about."

Mrs. Pruitt turned back reluctantly, clearly torn between controlling her son's high spirits and her own concerns. After a moment, her own concerns won out. "Raymond Lederer said your firm was the best in Phoenix."

Raymond Lederer was a defense lawyer for whom they did skip-trace work, tracking down potential witnesses and the like. "Raymond didn't lie," Bryan assured her. "You can count on our competence. And our discretion."

Discretion didn't seem to be the issue. Mrs. Pruitt had a death grip on the handles of her designer purse. "He said you could find anyone anywhere."

Bryan began to revise his assumption that she was worried about her husband's extracurricular activities. He resisted exchanging a glance with Alex, though he knew his partner was probably jumping to the same conclusion. "Finding people is one of our specialties. Who is it you're trying to track?"

"My son," said Mrs. Pruitt. She leaned forward over her purse and dropped her voice. "My *real* son."

The hair on the back of Bryan's neck stood up as his crazy meter started going off. This was so not what he'd expected. He looked at little Oscar, right-side up now and, except for his pleasant smile, the spitting image of the woman who seemed to be denying he belonged to her.

"You mean you gave up a son for adoption?" Alex tried hopefully.

Mrs. Pruitt shot him a glare Bryan doubted Alex had seen the likes of very many times, at least not from female eyes.

"No," she said crisply. "Oh, I know this one looks like me, but he's not mine. Oscar." She snapped her fingers at the little boy. "Do one of your tricks for these men."

For the first time Oscar looked less than content with his circumstances. He slid out of his chair and onto his feet with a thump. "You told me I'm not supposed to, Mommy."

"Well, this time I'm telling you you should."

Still unsure, the boy stuck his index finger in his mouth.

"Come on," his mother said.

Oscar gave Alex and then Bryan a worried look. Bryan responded with a smile, trying to reassure him they knew his mother was a few cards short of a deck. The message failed to communicate. Oscar didn't stop looking scared.

"A little trick or a big one?" the boy whispered.

"Just do it," his mother snapped.

The boy closed his eyes, and all at once the air in the office changed. It was cooler and thicker, and now it wasn't just the hair at the back of Bryan's neck that stood up. His whole body prickled as a rustling noise met his ears, like a dozen heavy books having their pages flipped. Movement caught the corner of his eye, and then—with a jolt like a mule kicking adrenaline into his chest—Bryan noticed that the contents of their inbox had begun to levitate. He stared in amazement as, one by one, invoices and memos slid off the stack and flowed around their office in a conga line. It would have been funny, if it hadn't been impossible.

Caught off balance, Bryan gasped for air as his heart pounded with something deeper than shock. He couldn't believe what he was seeing, but he couldn't disbelieve it, either.

This little kid was making paper fly.

"That's enough," said his mother, and every sheet dropped to the floor.

In the silence that followed, Bryan's breath sounded in his ears like a thunderstorm.

"I can put them back," Oscar offered in a small, guilt-stricken tone.

"That's okay," said Alex, then cleared his throat, his voice having come out raspier than usual. Bryan's partner was stroking his tasteful silver tie like a worry stone, up and down, up and down, as if stopping might pose a threat to his sanity. "That was . . . quite a trick."

Alex was by no means a kid person, but he put his hand on Oscar's wheat-colored head. "That was fine. You did good."

"You see what I mean," said Oscar's mother as Oscar fled back to his chair and curled up. "He isn't normal. People like him don't get born to people like me. My family is normal. My husband's family is normal. For heaven's sake, we go to church!"

Alex looked at Bryan, an obvious and unprecedented plea for help.

"Um," said Bryan, not about to let him down. "I know your son's gift is a little odd, but surely these things can pop up in any family."

"The hospital switched them," Mrs. Pruitt said, the insistence in her words hard to listen to without wincing. "One of those weird Fairyville families has my son."

This time Bryan couldn't resist his urge to glance at Alex. Having given up on fondling his tie, he was now gripping the edge of the desk so hard you'd have thought he was bracing for an earthquake. It was a challenge for a lifelong Arizonan to look pale, but Alex was giving it a shot.

"You're from Fairyville?" he asked carefully.

"Of course I'm not!" Mrs. Pruitt huffed. "I was passing through on my way from Santa Fe to Phoenix when I went into early labor in that freak show they call a town. I *had* to go to their hospital, and that's where they stole my boy!"

Bryan was fighting a serious compulsion to apologize to Oscar on his mother's behalf, or at least remove him from the room. "I assume you've had genetic testing done. To confirm whether or not Oscar is your son."

Mrs. Pruitt twisted her mouth in scorn—as if genetic testing were on a par with casting horoscopes. "Those doctors stick to-gether. They're not going to admit one of their own snatched my boy. Please." She choked the handles of her purse again. "You have to find out what happened to my child. My husband and I hardly sleep for worrying what this one's going to do next. I don't dare send him to school anymore, and I'm too embar-rassed to bring him to family parties. We used to be so close to my relatives, and now he's ruining our lives!"

Mrs. Pruitt dissolved into quiet tears, no doubt grieving over missed barbecues. Oscar regarded her solemnly. He didn't look half as upset as his mother, but Bryan still strode across the room and lifted him onto his hip.

The boy stared up at him, trusting but surprised. Bryan could see he wasn't used to the idea of being protected.

"Let's go out and meet our secretary," Bryan said. "Charlene has a boy about your age, and I'm pretty sure there's a fire truck in her bottom drawer."

Bryan stayed in the reception area long enough to ensure that Oscar was comfortable with Charlene. Bryan's expression must have been strange, because two of their interns did a double take as he passed their desks. Bryan ignored them. This particular interview wasn't going to be discussed with them.

When he returned to the office he and Alex shared, Mrs. Pruitt wasn't just recovered, she was radiant. Bryan walked in as she was clasping Alex's right hand in both of hers.

"Thank you," she said, her entire body vibrating with gratitude. "I can't tell you how this sets my mind at ease."

Bryan's mouth fell open, but the event that couldn't be happening apparently was.

"We'll do our best to find the truth," Alex said. "That much I promise you."

He escorted Mrs. Pruitt out, pointedly avoiding his partner's incredulous stare. The second he returned, Bryan's protests burst out.

"You can't have taken this case! It's totally without merit!"

Alex shrugged out of his suit jacket, draped it over a chair, then bent to pick up the trail of fallen paper Oscar's trick had left. To Bryan's surprise, his crisp striped shirt was damp under the arms. "She wrote a check for our retainer. If it clears the bank, the case is ours."

"Oh, well, as long as her money's good, who cares if she's nuts!"

His hands full of memos, Alex straightened and gave Bryan a level look.

"She's crazy," Bryan insisted. "She's got a perfectly nice little boy. Okay, that floating paper thing is strange, but she's treating him like he's defective. She needs counseling. She needs to count her goddamn blessings. She doesn't need a private detective!"

"I was born in Fairyville."

Alex's voice was matter of fact, but Bryan noticed his eyes were showing too much white.

"You what?" Bryan said, completely flummoxed now.

"I was born in Fairyville. Grew up there. Left when I was seventeen."

"I thought you were born in Tucson."

"I know. I didn't want to talk about my background."

Bryan knew Alex liked his privacy. All those weekends they'd spent drinking in college, it was always Bryan spilling his life stories. Still, this was taking reserve to new levels. Who the hell cared if Alex grew up in some town with a funny name?

Bryan rubbed the throbbing center of his forehead. "What does you being born in Fairyville have to do with us taking this case?"

Alex stared at the wall that held their licenses, his preternaturally chiseled profile stirring things inside Bryan he'd learned not to pay attention to. "Fairyville is . . . different." He shook himself and met Bryan's eyes, the directness of his sea-blue gaze a small but palpable shock. "Fairyville is like Sedona. Vortexes and spirits and all that mystical crap."

"Which presumably you don't believe in."

Alex shrugged—not the confirmation Bryan was expecting. "I know no one's taken Mrs. Pruitt's theories seriously, not even her husband. If we check them out—talk to the hospital, see what's what—maybe we'll find something to reassure her, something to help her accept the son she has."

Alex referring to Oscar as *the son she has* wasn't striking the right note for Bryan.

"You can't believe what she says is true. That boy is her spitting image. Do you honestly think some family in Fairyville stole her son? And why? So they could raise a son who's normal? If Fairyvillians are so freaky, that's the last thing they'd want."

"Fairyvillers."

"Huh?" said Bryan, convinced his head was going to explode.

"They call themselves Fairyvillers, not Fairyvillians. Look, I'm not saying I believe her. I'm saying maybe something out of the ordinary happened. Don't you like to know the why of things? Doesn't it calm you even if it can't change what is? I can go alone, if this makes you uncomfortable."

Normally, Alex wouldn't have thought twice about handling a job this size solo. The fact that he'd been assuming Bryan would come made Bryan think he really was shaken.

"I can go," he said after a pause to hide his thoughts, most of which involved sharing hotel rooms. "We've got nothing on deck right now except that mountain of background checks for Burrough's new hires. The other staff can handle that."

Alex blew out his breath and set his stack of collected papers into their inbox. "Good," he said. Not *thanks*, not *glad to have you*, just *good*.

Bryan mentally rolled his eyes. Polished manners or not, Alex could, on occasion, be an abrupt son of a bitch.

"Crap," Alex said now, tugging impatiently at his tie. When he yanked it off, the sight of his strong, tanned neck was enough to make Bryan swallow. "I'm sweating like a pig. Have Charlene make reservations while I grab a shower."

Bryan and Alex had a private bath attached to their office, a luxury neither of them apologized to the staff for, because they liked to run on their lunch hours. Actually, Alex ran on his lunch hour—as if his long, gold legs were made of Olympic springs. Bryan jogged and huffed. It was a pain, but it was worth it. Bryan liked his pizza, not his pizza gut.

"Reservations for tonight?" he asked, his trousers tightening at the thought of water streaming down Alex's hard body. The erection was so sudden he had no chance to head it off.

Luckily, Alex didn't turn as he stopped at the bathroom door. "Tonight," he agreed, sounding as grim as Bryan had ever heard him. "We'll take my car."

"Works for me," Bryan said as lightly as he could.

He realized he was excited for more reasons than Alex being naked one room away. Bryan's friend had always been something of a mystery, but maybe if he tagged along to his old hometown, Bryan would figure out the why of him.

Alex shut the door behind him with shaking hands. Too rattled to undress, he leaned over the sink and let his head hang like a dog's. He didn't want to go back there. Didn't want to see those people and dig up his sins. Most of all, he didn't want to see Zoe.

Christ, he still got hard just to think her name. Sweet, black-haired Zoe with her apple breasts and her soft gray eyes that no one could read but him. He'd wanted her to near insanity when he was younger. Even now, he didn't know how he'd kept it zipped. Yeah, she'd only been fifteen—and a fragile fifteen, at that—but she'd adored him with all her heart. She'd been his fruit to pluck, and he'd burned so hot for her he should have set his pants on fire a dozen times a day.

"Crap," he said, the ache in his chest as bad as the one in his slacks.

He didn't mean to put his fist through the wall. His field of vision simply went red, and his arm cut loose. The next thing he knew he was shaking plaster off his scraped knuckles. The reaction shook him, the loss of control. He couldn't even pull himself together when Bryan opened the door in concern.

"Jeez," he said, looking from the wall to Alex's hand. "You all right?"

"I can't go back there."

The confession was completely raw. Bryan furrowed his brow. "Well," he said, pretty calmly, considering Alex had never done anything like this in front of him before. "I'm not the one who's making you."

Alex cursed and sat on the closed toilet. "I have to go. No one else is going to take this case seriously."

He propped his head in his hands, as Bryan hunkered down beside him. The other man's nearness—simple, patient, affectionate—was more comforting than he'd ever guess. Bryan had no idea how deeply Alex valued his friendship—which was, in a way, part of the problem with going back to Fairyville.

"You're going to hear things about me," Alex warned. "Things that might make you feel differently about the man you've been friends with these last ten years."

Bryan's hand gripped Alex's knee. It was a gesture the most committed hetero couldn't have taken offense at, and Bryan was pretty much a master of those things. "Everybody has a past."

Alex blew out a bitter laugh. "Everybody doesn't have a past that's going to make you, personally, feel betrayed."

"Me?" Bryan's voice still wasn't cautious, just confused and kind.

Alex weighed whether telling him now or letting him find out later would be worse. If Bryan came with him, Alex knew he'd hear the stories. No way had people forgotten how Fairyville's favorite quarterback fell from grace. Briefly, Alex considered leaving Bryan behind, then dismissed that option as the worst of all. Alex liked to think of himself as stoic, but being hated with the intensity that most Fairyvillers hated him was more than he could face alone.

His own scorn for himself was hard enough to take.

He lifted his head and met Bryan's near-black eyes. Bryan was

Italian on his mother's side, his olive skin darkened by stubble, his mouth cut like a statue. He looked rough and mean and had as good a heart as anyone Alex knew. Alex trusted him. He just wasn't sure Bryan ought to trust him back.

Unused to the scrutiny, Bryan shifted in his crouch.

"I know how you feel about me," Alex said. "I've known almost from the start."

This was a bombshell Bryan wasn't prepared for. He opened his mouth, shut it, then tried again guardedly.

"It occurred to me once or twice that you might." The fists his hands were making on his knees belied the mildness of his tone. "But I always knew you didn't swing that way. To tell the truth, I appreciate you pretending not to know. It made it easier to be friends."

Alex shook his head. Bryan so wasn't getting this. "Do you know I can hardly go two days without having sex? Do you have any idea how many times I've come into this bathroom to jack off because I couldn't last?"

A flush swam up Bryan's swarthy face. "I'm not sure I need to—"

"I've got news for you, Bryan. Your business partner is a sex addict. Have been since I was fifteen. I've been working on it lately. My control, that is. Two whole weeks, this time. Two whole weeks without a partner or a release." Just saying it made his body tighten with restlessness. Alex stood up from the toilet, forcing Bryan to rise and back away.

Something about the retreat compelled Alex to follow.

"Hey." Bryan's hands raised to fend him off, but Alex didn't care if he was crowding him.

"What happened today, the hell I'm going to face tomorrow, is barely a distraction. I stay off the stuff for two weeks, and I'm ready to climb the walls."

Bryan was breathing harder, though he probably didn't want

to be. They were both nearly the same height, and when Alex slapped his hands on the wall to either side of Bryan's face, it brought them nose to nose. Bryan squirmed against the tile, as if he were hoping to miraculously dig himself a hole and get more space. He could have saved himself the trouble. Alex couldn't miss how blazing hot his body was.

"Uh, you know, Alex," Bryan said, trying to laugh it off. "For a man of my persuasion, this position you've got me in might be considered a come-on."

Alex kissed him, hard and deep, his tongue shoving against Bryan's as if he meant to fuck him with that. He didn't let him go until he'd tasted all of him.

"Jeez, Alex," Bryan gasped, his face beet-red. "If you know how I feel about you, you shouldn't be—"

Alex kissed him again, longer and slower, pushing his body into Bryan's until the other man moaned helplessly.

"Don't play with me," Bryan said, his eyes taking on the glitter of angry tears.

Alex put his hand between Bryan's legs, squeezing the erection he knew was there. It was a good one, firm and thick. Alex let the deftness of his fingers prove he knew how to bring it higher. Soon Bryan had filled out the front of his pleated khaki's, his hard-on straining the smooth cotton.

Starting to breathe hard himself, Alex rubbed him all the way up and down, curling his grip over the crown to give those nerves the extra friction they'd be screaming for. The way the cloth stuck to that bulging knob told him Bryan was liking that.

"Christ," Bryan said, squirming for a whole new reason. He licked his lip, clearly wanting another kiss. Alex leaned in closer.

"I don't only fuck women," he said, his voice low and harsh. "I let you think I was completely straight, but I've been fucking men all along."

Bryan went very still.

"Remember Eric Stedtler?" Alex said, perversely wanting to turn the knife, though whose chest he'd sunk it in was hard to say. "From the lacrosse team?"

"Noo," Bryan breathed, his eyes like plates.

"He was my second male partner."

"Well, damn, who was your first?"

Alex's temper jumped again. He ran the heel of his palm hard down Bryan's shaft. "You want a recitation of my sexual history or a piece of what you've been wanking off to for the last ten years?"

Bryan pushed at his chest, the anger Alex had been expecting finally coming to the fore. His panting breaths sounded like a train. "Fuck you, man!"

"Oh, I was thinking it would be the other way around."

"You were—" Bryan stopped, mid-tirade. His eyes narrowed. "You're serious."

"As a heart attack. Now are we going to do this or not?"

Bryan paused for two seconds.

"Hell, yeah," he said and pulled his pine-green polo shirt over his head.

His heavily muscled chest was worth admiring, but Alex had his own priorities. He had Bryan's zipper down while the shirt still covered his face. Liking the way this left his partner trapped, Alex eased his cock out with both hands. Nothing could have stopped him from stroking it right away, or from feeling anything but greedy as it grew bigger.

"Shit," said Bryan, finally wrestling free of the shirt. His stomach jerked as Alex wrapped his base and pulled. "I didn't lock the door."

Alex was too far into his lust to do any more than *shush* him. He went to his knees, his focus on what he held. He licked the shining head even as he rubbed it round and round with his thumbs. Such delicate skin this was, so sensitive. Bryan tasted sweet as honey, his little slit leaking clear fluid. With a moan of pleasure, Alex pressed the meaty thickness between his lips.

Bryan fisted Alex's hair and groaned, half ecstasy and half panic. "I'm gonna go too soon if you keep that up. Oh, God, Alex, your mouth is sweet."

Alex had never qualified as any sort of mystic, but he did have one gift. He always sensed how long he could tease his partners before they came, often better than they did. He liked Bryan's edge of panic, but it didn't worry him. Bryan was still rising, not on the brink. Alex sucked him, firm but slow, letting himself enjoy the act, letting himself love the melting smoothness of this rigid flesh.

Now that he had what he'd been denying himself, some of the tension in him eased. This moment was what he lived for. To want someone. To be wanted back. To lose himself in desire. He gentled his motions, giving Bryan a chance to trust he wouldn't get him off right away. Then, just in case that was too easy, he dug his hand into Bryan's trousers to fondle his balls.

Oh, they were fun to play with, ripe and heavy against the cup of his palm.

"Alex," Bryan moaned, his hips beginning to answer Alex's rhythm. "Fuck. You don't know how much I've wanted this."

However much he'd wanted it, he was being too careful for Alex's taste. He needed his partners to go as crazy as he did. Determined, he dug his fingers into Bryan's buttocks hard enough to bruise, which forced his cock closer to his throat. If Bryan thought Alex couldn't match his longing, he had no idea just how bad his partner's urges got. Hell, feeling Bryan start to shove in earnest had his own cock so hard it hurt.

He sank into the act as long as he could, but finally he had to let go and swallow. When he did, he realized he really couldn't wait anymore. Bryan's groan at being released came from a distance. A haze was filling Alex's head, one that would take over if he didn't give his body what it demanded. Alex didn't want that. He'd turned rough in the past when he let himself get that bad, and just because his partners hadn't complained didn't make it right.

He rested his cheek against Bryan's groin.

"Do you like to be fucked?" he asked into Bryan's hipbone. "Because I sure would like to take you now."

For a second Bryan didn't speak. When he did, he had to gasp for breath between the words. "Jeez, Alex. Even if I didn't like it, I'd let you."

Alex stood and held Bryan's face. "You do like it, though?"

"Oh, yeah," he said with all the heartfelt hunger Alex could desire. "I like it as good as being sucked off."

Alex smiled, so savagely pleased he should have been baring fangs. Too close to getting what it wanted to be contained, the dominant in him shoved out of its cage.

"Take off your clothes," he ordered.

Bryan shivered at his tone. "You've got protection?"

"Buddy, I've got better. I've got lube, too."

Bryan watched him pull both out of his wallet, feeling as if his world was turning upside down. Alex wanted him. Alex was going to fuck him here and now. As Bryan shucked his pants and underwear, Alex began stripping, too. Bryan hadn't expected him to get naked and couldn't help wetting his lips. The barest he'd seen the object of his obsession was in running shorts. Good though that was, it wasn't the same as the full Monty. Bryan watched in fascination as Alex shoved his trousers down. His cock bounced out in full erection . . . and kept on bouncing with the blood that pumped through it. It was thicker than Bryan expected, and as hard as if *he'd* been getting sucked. His thatch was honey-brown, the only part of him that wasn't bleached by the sun.

Bryan's fingers itched to explore all of it.

"Turn around," Alex ordered in that same harsh voice that had ramped through Bryan like a lick of sound. Bryan couldn't move. Alex's hands were racing up the buttons of his own shirt. He wrenched it off his lean, muscled chest. "Do it, Bryan. I want you to grip the sink."

Bryan shook his head, his gaze arrested by all that flexing, flushed bounty.

"Bryan," Alex said, bringing his eyes to his face. "I know you want to touch me, but I really can't wait for that."

He folded his shirt and threw it on the closed toilet seat, meticulous even in his impatience. His eyes were strange, their blue intensified by his lust. Bryan wasn't sure he bought Alex's theory that he was a sex addict, but his expression held a definite hint of menace as he came closer. He looked as if not being able to wait meant something different to him than it would to Bryan, something dangerous. Bryan's cock jolted higher and began to throb. He'd never thought he'd like rough sex, but he sure was hoping for it now.

"Turn," Alex said, even lower than before. He took Bryan's shoulder, guiding it where he wanted. "You can touch me all you want later."

"That's a risky promise," Bryan tried to joke.

Alex kicked his feet apart.

He gave Bryan no warning when he started with the lube, using two fingers to shove it in with quick hard strokes. A tingle started deep inside him. Alex's hand was hot, his fingers long and narrow, and every insertion felt like sheer heaven. He rubbed those outer, nerve-rich reaches with arousing skill, leaving Bryan in no doubt that he had indeed been fucking men.

Fortunately, Bryan was way too excited to be upset.

"Good," Alex said, feeling the ring of muscle relax.

And then he was there, his hairy legs pressing between Bryan's, his prick hot and insistent against the opening. Bryan's pulse went into double-time.

He liked being fucked. He'd just never done it this fast.

"It's okay," Alex said, his hands tight and sweaty on Bryan's hips. "You're ready. Just breathe out nice and slow."

He must have known better than Bryan. He pushed as Bryan exhaled, gliding in without a hitch, though the glide took a good long time. Bryan had to bite his lip to hold back a moan of delight. All they needed was some intern hearing them and breaking in. The tweak of anxiety was more arousing than Bryan needed. God, Alex was big—big and hot and better than any dream he'd jacked off to.

Alex seemed to like being clamped so closely. He groaned and pressed his face into Bryan's back. His hands ran up Bryan's chest, twanging across his erect nipples before closing on his shoulders. His cock stirred inside Bryan's body, satin wrapped around a core of fire. Alex really must have been hard up. His whole body was shuddering with need.

"God," he said, an edge of fear in it. "Oh, God, that's good."

Bryan pulled one of Alex's hands to his cock. Sometimes his erection faded when a partner took him anally, but not this time. This time he'd stayed full enough to burst. Alex gripped his swollen base like holding on to it was all that kept him from doing something stupid.

Since Bryan suspected "something stupid" was giving in to what he really wanted, he wasn't about to preach caution.

"Go," Bryan urged instead. "You feel good to me, too."

Alex's curse held a hint of apology, but that didn't stop him from uncoiling into swift motion. He shot from zero to sixty in two seconds, his cock pounding into Bryan like he'd gone insane.

Bryan would have lost his footing if the sink hadn't held him up, and even then he had to grip it for dear life. It wasn't just the force of Alex's thrusts that robbed him of strength, it was the incredibly sweet pleasure. Bryan hadn't known he was a size queen, but every bulge of Alex's big erection rubbed every spot that needed it, as if Alex had a periscope in there that told him where to go. His technique was so effing perfect, it seemed unreal—and the speed! That was like jumping off a cliff straight to orgasm. No buildup, just a drop as scarily intense as defying death.

"Yes," Bryan panted, trying to thrust back for more.

Alex grunted, bent his knees, and got an even better angle.

Fireworks went off in Bryan's prostate, and somehow Alex knew.

"That's it," he said, his hand abruptly moving on Bryan's cock, the motion rough but effective. "That's it. That's—"

He plunged in deep and stiffened, and Bryan's ejaculation just about exploded from his prick. He actually heard his semen hit the sink pedestal. The orgasm was so good he had to shove his forearm in his mouth to keep from crying out. When another peak of feeling welled at the end, his legs threatened to buckle.

"Don't stop," Alex said. "I need another."

Bryan could hardly believe it, but those three words were enough to harden him again.

Alex's second sprint to orgasm was as quick as the first, too quick for Bryan to follow. He bit Bryan's shoulder when he came that time, probably the sexiest love bite he'd ever had, because he knew for sure Alex hadn't meant to lose it like that.

"Shit," Alex said, coming to enough to see the mark. "I knew I'd hurt you if I made myself wait that long."

Bryan began to laugh. He turned around and wrapped Alex in his arms, kissing his reassurance into Alex's sighing mouth. To Bryan's delight, Alex didn't pull away for a long, long time.

His skin was velvet on Bryan's chest, as preternaturally perfect as his cock had been.

"Okay," Alex said at last, a bit breathless. "I guess you don't hate me after all."

"That's your conclusion?" Bryan teased. "That I don't *hate* you?"

Alex averted his gaze. "I know you feel more than that."

Bryan snorted at his embarrassment. "Alex, I'm not expecting you to marry me because we fucked."

Alex flushed up to his hairline. "I'm honored that you care about me. Really. That's why I—I didn't want to screw up our friendship."

"You haven't screwed it up."

Alex's mouth twisted. "There's plenty of time for that."

"Right," said Bryan. "In Fairyville."

The wryness of Alex's expression just might have slanted into a smile. Still not looking up, he slid his hand down his friend's belly, his fingers skating through his black pubic bush. It was a gentle, intimate gesture, one Bryan hadn't expected. "I didn't finish you."

His palm had an interesting tingle as it wrapped Bryan's shaft. His erection had been subsiding, but that little surge of whatever it was brought him up.

"Oh, no worries," Bryan said, his voice a fraction higher than before. "I'm perfectly happy to let you make it up to me now."

Three

Bryan and Alex were cruising north on I-17, halfway to Sedona, when they had a fluke accident. Bryan didn't see it happen, but somehow Alex caught the sole of his shoe on the gas pedal, and the thing peeled off like the top of a sardine can.

Fortunately, Alex's reflexes were quick. The wheels barely squealed before he was able to pull over onto the sandy verge. In the distance, a lone saguaro cactus raised beseeching arms to the sapphire sky.

"How the hell did I do that?" Alex demanded, pulling the remnants of the loafer from his bare foot.

His mood had not been cheery to begin with, but he frowned in genuine affront at the ruined shoe. As a rule, PIs learned to expect the unexpected. Subjects rarely did what suited their convenience. Bryan had noticed, however, that Alex didn't like it when the things he believed he *could* plan didn't go according to.

"I can take the wheel," he offered, without a single objection to driving Alex's beautifully kept, dark-brown, eight-cylinder

Audi. His own two-year-old Buick looked more like ten—and that was before you considered the fast food trash. It had never run as smoothly as the Audi, not even when it was new.

"That's okay," Alex declined. No surprise, since he was kind of a control freak about his car. "I saw a sign for Target at the last exit."

When Alex came out of the store, at least twenty minutes after going in, Bryan couldn't contain his amusement. Alex's face was storm-cloud dark.

"Don't. Say. A word," he ordered, sliding grumpily back into the driver's seat. "These were all they had in my size."

"Yeah, 'cause thirteen is such a freakish shoe size for men." Totally cracking up, Bryan craned to get a better look at the glory that clad his partner's feet. The shoes were neon-yellow high-tops with—oh, Lord—was that Wile E. Coyote printed on the side? Tears of laughter began to squeeze out from the corners of Bryan's eyes.

"Shut up!" Alex said, but Bryan was having too much fun.

"They're rad," he choked out between gasps for air. "I'm sure they're all the rage with the high school boys."

Alex covered his face, finally beginning to laugh himself. "I swear, I searched every shoe in that freaking store. This was the only thirteen they had."

"Well, they go great with your navy sport coat. Very preppie casual."

"Asshole," Alex said through his grin. He put the car into gear and backed neatly out of their spot. Witnessing the deft maneuver, Bryan could hardly blame him for wanting to drive. Alex was a genius behind the wheel. Now he narrowed his eyes at Bryan. "You just wait till we get to Fairyville. Then you'll see this weird shit happens all the time."

"Can't wait," Bryan promised, relaxing back in his seat. The happiness that rose inside him had been a stranger far too long.

Meeting his laughing gaze, Alex reached out briefly to squeeze his hand. It was a boyfriend squeeze, sweet and spontaneous. It surprised Bryan enough that he had to turn his face to the window, to hide how his own eyes pricked.

Don't get ahead of yourself, he warned his budding optimism. He and Alex had only had sex once. In Bryan's experience, this was no guarantee of a great romance. Alex had slept with a lot of people. In fact, he'd slept with more than Bryan had suspected, considering he'd only guestimated the female ones. Bryan wasn't sure he could count them all without a calculator. Alex had dates most weekends—sometimes more than one. That little hand squeeze could be nothing more than a friendly bit of afterglow.

Determined to play it cool, Bryan curled his fist on his thigh.

As luck would have it, Alex glanced at him just then.

"I'm glad you're here," he said in his perpetual bedroom voice.

The acknowledgment was too much, the little extra rasp of sincerity. Every shred of Bryan's caution tore loose in the highway wind.

It wasn't unusual for a being of Magnus's persuasion to enjoy sexual release numerous times a day. The fey were a lusty lot, and sex was like food to them: something to be enjoyed with gusto, not life or death serious. In the decade since Magnus had stolen, unsanctioned, into the human realm, he'd enjoyed countless such tasty meals.

All that had ended when he met Zoe—or it had ended as much as it could.

The terms of his magical visa were simple: Win a woman's heart under each full moon, seal the deal by climaxing inside his partner, then return the heart afterward. Nothing said he couldn't have sex more often, and certainly he wanted to, but to do so with Zoe watching didn't strike him as the best way to keep her regard.

Unfortunately, given the amount of satisfaction he was wired to crave, it was nearly killing him to restrict himself to having sex once a month. He could pleasure himself, of course, but to his kind nothing compared to the delicious skin-to-skin contact of intercourse. He needed that like Phoenix needed water, and without it he felt himself approaching a state that, for a naturally cheerful person like himself, resembled surliness.

Zoe had no idea how she'd upped the difficulty of his life by breaking into tears this morning and forcing him to kiss her. Now he'd tasted her sweetness. Now he'd felt her eager embrace. Now—damn it all to the nether realm—he knew what he was missing!

In spite of the arousal that still goaded him like a lance, Magnus chuckled at the cloudless sky. He sat beneath an awning in the little courtyard across the street from her gallery, waiting patiently for her to emerge for lunch. Sun-sharp shadows shifted slowly around the circle of adobe shops, different but every bit as beautiful as his home.

He could hardly claim to have been *forced* to kiss her when he'd been wanting to do it for the last two years—ever since he'd spotted her giving readings in the little park the locals called Tourist Square. All sorts of artists and prognosticators set up booths there on summer weekends—and Zoe hadn't been the only friend to dead people there. Nonetheless, a line ten-deep had snaked back from her table, mostly women fanning themselves in the blazing heat, clearly determined to speak to no psychic but her—even if they melted in the meantime.

Magnus had taken one look at the reason for their patience and had known he wasn't going to move on to Colorado like he'd planned. Zoe was worth sticking around for, even if it meant remaining where his mother could get at him.

Stable portals between the human world and Fairy were hard to come by, and just as hard to open if you weren't a queen. Sadly, Magnus's mother was a queen, and the door to Fairyville was as old and stable as they got. Titania could come and go as she pleased, with one disadvantage. Should she ever step into the human realm, she'd have to leave the bulk of her magic behind.

Titania didn't want to do that, not even if it improved her chances of retrieving her unruly son. Full-strength fairy magic was a drug without which she couldn't function, the blood that kept her power-loving heart beating. She'd try every way she could think of to reel Magnus back, so long as she didn't have to come into this world.

Imagining how many ways Titania would think of—especially once she realized he wasn't going to tire of his "rebellious phase"—had been behind his plan to change states; at least, until he'd laid eyes on Zoe.

Zoe had been a vision in that park, as if one juicy little person could unite the glitter and buzz of Fairy with the comforting solidity of humanity. Her curly hair had rioted like silk around her slender shoulders, a rich blue-black that made her soft gray eyes shine. In her bright gauzy skirt and skimpy summer top, she'd resembled a sexy butterfly—lean and lithe with breasts the size of oranges. Her smooth, tanned skin had made him want to nibble her all over, to sample every inch of those sun-kissed curves, but even then he recognized his reaction as more than lust.

She'd smiled at her clients, nodding at their troubles and patting their hands. Some had shed tears as she'd shared messages from their dear departed, and all the while that soft, sweet smile of hers had not wavered.

This one knows, Magnus had thought. *This one knows there's more to life than most people see. This one knows there's truly nothing to cry about.*

He'd been tempted to get a reading for himself but hadn't dared, for fear of what she would discern. Her magic was a perfume swirling through her aura, a pulse of deeper, more vibrant life. He'd watched her for days before he'd concluded she could not read minds, days during which he'd realized he couldn't sleep with and forget this one. Instead, he'd proposed she join his string of protégés, the human artists whose shops and studios he funded, whose careers he gently oversaw and took commissions on.

She'd been surprised by his offer but not shocked. He'd been pleased to discover she knew how good she was. Confidence was a kind of magic by itself. Though it hadn't been his primary goal, he'd known his investment in her would pay off.

That she had a private coterie of fairies had been an unexpected plus. Magnus hadn't had a close-up encounter with his diminutive cousins since they'd slipped from his mother's iron grip two human centuries ago. He'd been looking forward to the reacquaintance. As fellow escapees from Fairy, they had much in common. He hadn't realized the little fey were going to flee in terror whenever he came near.

That hiccup in his ambitions should have told him his simple desire to enjoy Zoe's nearness wasn't going to stay simple long.

He wanted her heart and body, and he wanted both for keeps. Sadly, this was a luxury the very magic that allowed him to be near her forbid. The only thing that pained him worse than not claiming all of her was knowing how his monthly ritual bruised her feelings. That, more than anything, prevented him from taking extra partners. No amount of temporary gratification was worth hurting her.

But who said sex was all that could gratify him? Magnus straightened as Zoe's door opened, the glass pane flashing like a mirror. Seeing it was her, he waved his arm to catch her attention and jogged across the street.

It wasn't the few seconds of exercise that had his heart pumping hard. An unfamiliar nervousness battled with the physical excitement that always hummed through him in her presence. Magnus couldn't read human thoughts, but he sensed their earlier kiss hadn't left his friend in an ideal mood.

"I thought we'd have lunch today," he said, putting all his fairy power into the smile he turned down at her. This was nothing to the power he could have called on if he'd still lived in Fairy. The denseness of the human realm muted all glamour. All the same, he knew the flash of teeth was persuasive.

Zoe rubbed her forehead perplexedly. "Today?"

"Sure. My treat."

It wasn't an unusual invitation. They ate together several times a week, under the pretense of it being casual—though Zoe was the only protégée he did this with. Now she looked down the street toward the Longhorn Grill, where they usually went. The words *oh, no* swam into his mind. Until that moment, he'd forgotten the existence of Sheri Yost. He might not know all the ins and outs of human romance, but he was pretty sure having lunch in the restaurant that employed his previous night's lover wouldn't count as considerate.

"I didn't mean for us to go there," he said, trying to recover.

Zoe kept looking down the street, her eyes squinted and resigned. The sun turned their gray to silver: old soul eyes, temporarily tired of life.

"I don't think so," she said. "I think today I'm going to see if Teresa's free."

Something uncomfortable twisted in Magnus's chest, something he didn't think he'd ever felt before. It was more than hurt at being turned down. It was . . . insecurity. It was, just maybe, a little loss of hope.

"Sure," he said, trying to swallow the feeling down. "It's not as if we had definite plans. Perhaps tomorrow."

Zoe wriggled her feet in her flat leather thong sandals. Her toes were painted cherry-red, a fashion choice that seemed to fascinate her now.

"Sure," she said. "Tomorrow would be fine."

The listlessness in her voice didn't make him feel better. Always when they were together, Zoe gave him her attention. Always he sensed her enjoyment of his company. Sometimes, when he didn't do what a human would, she thought him funny, but she always looked at him fondly. He hadn't known how much he relied on that. It was, truth be told, a big part of the reason he was happy here.

Bored with his long life in Fairy, and increasingly leery of his mother's plans for him, Magnus had tricked his way into the human realm in search of new adventures. He'd loved the challenge of doing magic in a place where it took focus, where the things he wanted didn't fall into his lap with a thought. Every day he'd been here, he'd embraced the drama of human life, and every power he'd managed to recover was a thrill singing through his veins.

In that moment, though, watching Zoe walk away and not look at him, he'd have sacrificed every one of those pleasures to see her smile again.

By the time they pulled into the Desert Spa Hotel two miles outside Fairyville, Alex's laughter had worn off. It was too hard to forget how much he didn't want to be here, nor did his old hometown waste time reminding him. Charlene had booked their rooms without a hitch, but it came as no surprise—at least not to Alex—that no trace of their reservation could be found.

"I know our secretary didn't screw this up," Bryan said in the gruff, menacing tone he used to make lowlifes sweat. With his thick New Jersey accent, he sounded more like a mob enforcer than a licensed P.I.

The young male desk clerk in the light pink golf shirt did him the courtesy of going pale. "I'm sorry, Mr. McCallum, but every place in Fairyville is booked up with this 'Meet Your Animal Guide' conference."

Bryan looked ready to introduce the clerk to *his* animal guide.

Before he could do more than snarl, Alex took his elbow and pulled him aside. "Forget it, Bry, it's not his fault. It's just more Fairyville shit."

"*Towns* don't lose reservations. People do."

"Let it go. I know an inn on Canyon Way that almost always has an extra room."

As soon as he said it, Alex rubbed his face, adrenaline surging through him unpleasantly. He'd been counting on a little distance in this swank new place where the staff barely knew each other, much less who'd lived in Fairyville fifteen years ago.

"You're sure about this?" Bryan asked in an undertone. " 'Cause I'm willing to bet if I leaned on that desk clerk, I could make him cry."

Alex laughed dryly. "I'll keep that in mind in case we have to come back."

He knew they wouldn't, though every parking slot behind the Vista Inn was full.

"This is nice," Bryan said, taking in the lobby's antique log-cabin atmosphere. "Comfortable."

"Glad you think so," Alex muttered and braced himself to handle the woman behind the reception desk. She was about his mother's age, stocky and silver haired. Her soft beige sweater declared her as noneccentric as Fairyvillers got. Alex didn't recognize her, but that was no guarantee that she wouldn't know him.

He'd been this town's hero once upon a time.

The woman greeted them with a friendly smile.

"We'd like a room," Alex said, doing his best to smooth out the distinctive rock-star rasp of his voice.

"Oh, honey." The woman flattened one hand on her trussed up bosom. "I'm afraid we're all booked up."

"We'll take four-ten," he said curtly.

Her brows went up. "Adventure seekers, are you?"

"We read about it in the guide book," he said before she could ask how he knew about the Vista's special attraction. "We were curious."

"Well, it's available," she said, reaching behind her for the key. "But I have to tell you, nobody stays there more than a night."

Alex said nothing, just took the old-fashioned metal key and handed her his credit card. It was the firm's card, with Goodbody & McCallum imprinted on the front. His own name was on it, too, of course, and her motions slowed as she ran it through her machine, the tumblers in her head beginning to fall into place.

Alex scrawled his signature on the credit slip as illegibly as he could.

"Enjoy your stay," she called with a definite lilt of question as he stepped away. "Let me know if I can help you find your way around."

Alex ignored that minefield, already striding up the broad, carpeted stairs. His face was hot, his breath coming in too-short rushes. He knew he couldn't run away from facing this, but his body sure as hell wanted him to try.

Bryan caught up to him at the first landing. "You want to tell me what that was about?"

Alex set his jaw and kept climbing.

"At least tell me why she called us adventure seekers. I have to admit, right at this moment, I'm kind of hoping for a mirror on the ceiling and a big, round bed."

Alex stopped, his palm on the peeled log handrail, his heart wishing he could respond to Bryan's humor with the appreciation it deserved.

"We're not staying in the room with the big, round bed," he said. "We're staying in the room with the ghost."

"Oh," Bryan responded . . . and said not another word after that.

Despite his annoyance at the change of plans, Alex enjoyed watching Bryan's wide-eyed scan of their perfectly ordinary-looking haunted room. To judge by the way his head was swiveling, he expected some grisly specter to jump out of a corner in broad daylight.

The only object that seemed to fascinate him more was the room's king-size bed, which he was trying not to eyeball too obviously. Alex wondered if Bryan realized there was no chance in hell he wasn't getting laid tonight. The lid was off that particular Pandora's box and, for better or worse, Alex had no intention of forgoing his favorite method of stress relief.

Keeping his amusement to himself, he emptied his suitcase, set out his toothbrush, and picked up the phone. Somewhat to his surprise, he got lucky with his first call. The hospital informed him that the intern who'd been named in Mrs. Pruitt's now defunct malpractice suit was having her day off. Alex worked a little magic on his laptop and, within minutes, had Dr. Alisha Kerry's home address.

"You want to call ahead?" Bryan asked. "Make sure she's there?"

Though they hadn't been here longer than half an hour, Bryan's half of the room already looked messy. Evidently as organized as he was going to get, Bryan parked himself on the bed a foot away from Alex. The distance was carefully calculated—

familiar but not presumptuous. Alex considered the small open stretch of mattress, then smiled directly into Bryan's eyes until the other man flushed slightly.

The response inspired a pleasant heaviness in his groin. Yes, indeed, Bryan was on the menu for tonight.

"No calling ahead," Alex said. "She'll only avoid us if she gets a chance."

Alex was convinced he'd made the right decision when he saw the good doctor's home. It was a modest, single-level ranch, whose yard was overgrown with bear grass to the point where the clumps were swallowing a small birdbath. In Alex's experience, this was not the mark of someone who'd welcome uninvited visitors. The windows were dark, increasing the abandoned look, but an old blue Honda Civic sat in the cracked driveway.

It seemed Dr. Kerry hadn't upgraded her circumstances since her days as a broke intern.

"TV," Bryan said, pointing to a flicker on the front window.

"Oprah," Alex replied after glancing quickly at his watch.

They grinned at each other, realizing things were looking up. Oprah fans were favorite targets for interrogation. As long as you appealed to their emotions, you could almost always get them to talk.

They needed the advantage. When Bryan knocked and began to explain who they were, Dr. Alisha Kerry turned fury-red.

"That crazy bitch needs to let this drop!" she snapped—once she'd stolen enough breath back from her anger to speak.

Alex caught the door she was trying to slam in their faces. She was better looking and better kept than her surroundings led them to expect. Slim, thirty-ish, and tidy, she wore a pair of jeans and a crisp white T-shirt, which she filled out generously. Her dark brown hair was brushed back into a shining ponytail.

Her eyes were blue and, beneath their glare, desperate for understanding. The minute Alex saw them, he knew the interview had a chance.

"Our job isn't telling our client what she wants to hear," he said, holding her gaze as steadily as he held the door. "Our job is telling her the truth. Frankly, we're concerned about her inability to accept Oscar as her son. For his sake, we'd like to settle this once and for all."

"Fuck," said Dr. Kerry, but it was a curse of resignation. She stepped back from the threshold to let them in. "I've told this story a thousand times. Why not a thousand and one?"

Bryan and Alex followed her into a darkened living room that smelled of stale takeout. Two open cartons waited on the coffee table: rice and teriyaki steak. Dr. Kerry switched off Oprah, and they all sat down—Alex and Bryan on the old plaid couch and Dr. Kerry in a big armchair. She sat forward on its cushion, her body canted over her knees. Hollows deepened beneath her eyes as she played with her fingernails.

The controversy surrounding Oscar's birth seemed to have cast a long shadow.

"I was an intern," she began with a heavy sigh. "First year. Pediatrics. Oscar Pruitt was practically my first case. He had a heart defect, a murmur. It made him turn blue periodically. Hearts were my thing then, and, damn, I was sure the problem was serious. The attending surgeon, Dr. Lopez, was sure of it, too. He ordered an echo . . . an echocardiogram," she explained when Bryan made an inquiring sound. "Lopez told me to inform the mother. I assumed he meant for me to warn her that her kid might need surgery, or even die, so that's what I told her. I thought she had a right to know."

Alex turned his most soothing look into her defensive eyes. "Of course you did. I'm sure most mothers would want to be told."

"Damn right they would." Alisha Kerry stared at her nails again. "Lopez had no call to tear my head off the way he did, or to put that reprimand in my record. He was the one who didn't explain clearly. The thing was, when the tests came back, the baby's heart was clean. No murmur whatsoever, benign or otherwise. That's when Mrs. Pruitt started up her racket about the baby being switched. She said he didn't *feel* the same as when she'd held him for, like, two minutes after he was born.

"I swear to you, though, nobody could have taken him. Even if the DNA hadn't come up a match, he couldn't have been stolen. Those neonates aren't left alone. There's always someone watching them."

"And none of the nurses or other interns had a history of mental imbalance? Nothing you might have seen that someone else would miss?"

Bryan had asked the question, and Dr. Kerry shifted her gaze to him. Alex noticed she did this reluctantly. In the time he and Bryan had known each other, he'd never understood why women seemed to prefer him. To his mind, Bryan's roughness was more attractive—ironically, more masculine. On occasion, Alex had seen his partner respond to women just as he would himself: with automatic sexual speculation. How would this one look naked? What would she be like in bed? So Bryan wasn't giving off unavailable vibes; he was giving off vibes that said he'd be a challenge.

But it wasn't a challenge Dr. Kerry was rising to. She shrugged sardonically. "Every intern is imbalanced those first few years. Believe me, though, no one at Fairyville General was insane enough to snatch an infant. Shit, I can hardly take care of my plants. If you ask me, Mrs. Pruitt had a bout of postpartum depression that she hasn't gotten over yet."

Alex brought her attention back to him by the simple act of flipping a page in his notebook. "Did you notice anything odd? Anyone who might have spoken to Mrs. Pruitt? Either to witness her acting strangely, or maybe someone who could have given her the idea that her real son was gone?"

Dr. Kerry leaned back in the armchair, apparently not having thought of that. After a moment, she shook her head reluctantly. "It was a quiet night except for Mrs. Pruitt coming into the ER in early labor. FG isn't like a big city hospital. We had a patient die that night, but that was just old age. They'd transferred him the week before from a nursing home." She rubbed her lips, her eyes focused five years ago. "I think that lady who talks to ghosts was sitting with him, the one who's got a shop in town. We see her now and then, helping patients 'cross over.' " She made the quote marks with her fingers. "Honestly, though, I'm not sure that counts as odd in Fairyville."

Goosebumps prickled down Alex's arms. "Do you remember the woman's name?"

"Chloe something. No. Zoe. Zoe Clare, like clairvoyant. But she's nice for one of those weirdos. She told me my Grandma Ellen was watching over me. She sang the little song Grams used to put me to sleep with." Alisha's eyes went misty. "I wasn't even paying her. She just said Grams had asked her to pass it on. I don't think a woman like that would be putting crazy theories into Mrs. Pruitt's head."

"No doubt you're right." His throat gone tight, Alex closed his notebook and tucked it into his breast pocket. "Thanks so much for being patient with our questions."

Alisha Kerry looked surprised to see him rising from the couch, and maybe even disappointed. "You sure I can't offer you some ice tea before you go? It's hot out there."

Alex was sweltering where he was, despite the ranch's powerful AC. "We're good, but thank you for asking. We'll contact you if we have more questions."

"You can have my pager," Alisha said, scribbling the number on the corner of an old magazine.

Alex accepted the scrap of torn paper.

"Thank you," he said, not meeting her eyes this time. She wasn't being obvious, but he still knew what he'd find in her expression, and it had nothing to do with Oscar Pruitt's parentage. If he'd met her in a bar, he'd probably have encouraged her. Alisha Kerry was his type in a lot of ways. Smart, pretty, hungry for human connection. Most of all, she didn't seem to have a lot of expectations. She was the kind of woman he could spend a weekend with, the kind who might wish he'd stick around, but who wouldn't bother crying when he left.

Alex always left. That was a constant you could take to the bank.

His lip curled in self-contempt as he and Bryan escaped into the bright sunshine. Sweat immediately popped out beneath his clothes, but it felt better than being inside that gloomy house. When he opened the door to the Audi, the metal handle nearly burned his skin. The interior was too hot to get in.

"Well, that didn't get us very far," Bryan observed across the Audi's roof. "She confirmed what we suspected. Lizanne Pruitt is nuts."

Alex stood in the street with the car doors open, a hook of memory tugging at his consciousness. A red-tailed hawk floated on a thermal high above the slightly shabby suburban homes. The memory was something to do with babies being expected to die but then recovering.

He pulled out his cell phone as it came to him.

"I have to call my mother," he explained to Bryan. "I'll be done in a few minutes."

Amanda Goodbody lived in San Diego. She'd moved there after her youngest son had been metaphorically run out of Fairyville on a rail. Though she loved all her boys, Alex was her baby. His behavior fifteen years ago might have disappointed her, but she adored him no matter what. She'd had a hard time forgiving people who couldn't find it in themselves to forgive him.

She picked up after the second ring.

"Sweetie!" she cried. "How lovely to hear your voice!"

"You haven't heard it yet," he teased, turning slightly away from Bryan. Taking the hint, though it hadn't been deliberate, Bryan got into the sun-baked car.

"I saw it on the caller ID! Thanks again for my phone. I'm really enjoying it. I'm in the garden talking to you!"

Alex felt his heart well up with love for her, picturing her among her beloved peonies. "I'm glad you like the present, though I don't know how I'll top it for your next birthday."

"You don't have to," she assured him. "I'll still be grateful for it then. Your father says I spend so much time talking on it, he thinks I've been reborn as a teenager."

"Good." Alex propped his hips back against the hot metal of car. "Mom, I have a question I need to ask. You used to tell me a story about when I was born, about how I got sick in the hospital."

"Lord, yes," she said. "That was a terrible time. You were a preemie, and that Fairyville General wasn't the showplace it is today. You picked up some sort of antibiotic-resistant infection: nosocomial something or other, they called it. I remember sitting by your incubator hour after hour, knowing it must be bad because the nurses didn't kick me out. You were just a quivering, hairless kitten, too weak to cry, and me praying and praying until I thought my pray-er would fall off."

"But I got better."

"Yes, you did, and to this day nobody quite knows why. I remember nodding off with your tiny fist clenched around my pinkie, and then when I woke up you were all right. The nurses thought it was wishful thinking, but when I finally convinced them to check your vitals, they were crying right along with me."

"So you actually thought I would die."

"Yes, I did, and I suspect that's part of the reason you're precious to me now."

Alex shoved his hand through his hair, unsure where to go with this next.

"Why do you want to know, sweetie?" his mother asked into the pause. "I hope your doctor hasn't found something wrong."

"It's a case," Alex said. "Just a thread I wanted to track down. I'm healthy as a horse, like always."

"Well, I'm sure you'll solve whatever it is. You tell that nice Bryan fellow 'hello' from me."

Alex smiled, because Bryan was always that 'nice Bryan fellow' to his mom.

"I will," he promised, then said "I love you" and hung up.

His hands were shaking just a little when he slid the key into the ignition.

"Everything all right?" Bryan asked.

"Yeah," he said. "Just a weird coincidence."

Except his gut was telling him it was more than that. He thought of his older brothers: Jason, Mark, and Steve. None of them had caused his mom the trouble Alex had. All of them had played sports, but none had excelled to the extent that Alex did. They were TV warriors now, every one slowly going soft. They'd all settled down with nice, cookie-baking wives, whom they seemed to have no trouble being faithful to. Alex doubted they'd kissed a man on the cheek other than their father, much less gone adventuring the way Alex had. Hell, the idea that Alex worked for himself was exotic enough for them. Alex loved his brothers, but there were huge portions of his life that were as alien from theirs as the Milky Way.

I'm different from them, he thought, his stomach clenching uneasily. *Probably as different as Oscar Pruitt is from his relatives.*

"Where to now?" Bryan asked, his tone carefully light.

Alex considered swinging by the hospital to see if they could track down more former staff. His other choice was to find Zoe. See what she might have noticed with her "extra" senses on the night Oscar was born.

These ideas had barely run through his mind before he dismissed them—the latter because he wasn't ready to face his old high school flame, and the former because he didn't hold out much hope for it paying off. This case was already steeped in Fairyville weirdness. His mother's confidence notwithstanding, they'd never solve it by following the book. No, they'd have to rely on subtler forms of guidance.

Like maybe praying for a decent lead.

He shook his head at the thought. His focus was all over the place today. He needed to get himself together before they tackled anything.

"We're going back to the inn," he decided. "I need to think for a while."

He glanced at Bryan just as the other man turned his face to the window. Bryan's elbow was on the armrest, his hand covering his sensual, half-Italian mouth. Despite the barrier, Alex could tell he was smiling. The knowing expression made Alex realize he was warm from more than the near-century temperatures. His zipper was clutching his cock a good bit tighter than it had before.

It seemed Bryan had guessed what his partner needed besides "thinking."

Four

Magnus lived in what humans colorfully termed an "earth ship." It was a small one-bedroom house with its backside dug into the ground, built with recycled materials like automobile tires and cans. Solar panels enhanced the energy conservation of the three-foot walls, but living green hadn't been his incentive for buying it.

His incentive for buying it had been the unobstructed view of the town's red rocks. Fairy was a lush, green cradle, cloying in its sweetness. This landscape reminded him he wasn't there, reminded him, too, that the Earth itself was a power object.

Tonight he was more pleased than ever that nothing stood between him and the stark formation called the Giant's Teeth—nothing except the scrub and dirt of national park land.

He watched both through the single window that ran the length of his home, drinking in the beauty of the sunset until the last blood-red glimmer disappeared and the land went black.

When it did, he couldn't restrain a shiver. His soul felt as if a similar shadow had snapped over it.

"You won't lose her," he said quietly, his fingers pressed to the sun-warmed glass. "She's still your friend."

He shut his eyes to the darkness. He'd known for some time that he loved Zoe, but he hadn't known how deeply until she turned away today. Friendship truly wasn't enough to ease the ache inside him, but it was better than never seeing her again.

"Stop," he whispered, feeling the first tinge of hopelessness beginning to stain his spirit, like an octopus's ink clouding a sun-lit sea. He knew the basic laws by which all realms operated, Fairy or otherwise. Hopelessness drew more reasons to lose hope as surely as magnets drew iron filings. Joy was its only cure, but sometimes—like now—joy needed help to bloom.

Knowing he couldn't reach for it on his own, he turned to the simplest magic, the one that demanded no rituals or spells, the first and purest any child of Fairy learned.

"Send me sweeter thoughts," he murmured to the Will-Be. "I am the child of your maker, and I am willing to receive."

The Will-Be wasn't a being or a realm. It was a sphere of influence, discrete unto itself but overlapping the worlds of matter and spirit. The Will-Be was the nonplace where wishes first began coming true. Magnus pictured it as a limitless metaphysical storehouse for possibilities that hadn't yet taken form. Every desire—assuming its birth had been intense and focused—existed, ghostlike, in this not-quite-real domain, waiting for its summoner to welcome it. The way its summoner did this was to embrace two things. The first was faith in the mechanism that brought desires into being. The second was belief that the summoner was worthy of the gift. So long as these qualities could be sufficiently sustained, no desire was too big for the Will-Be to gratify.

In Fairy, as long as the request didn't oppose an edict of the queen, the process was quick and easy. In the human realm, coaxing wishes into manifestation took more time than most beings had patience for. Magnus was still working on his ability to wait gracefully, but he knew frustration slowed the magic, and despair shut it down entirely—because what did that emotion represent but a lack of faith?

Magnus couldn't afford to despair over the prospect of losing Zoe's friendship. Yes, his fear would take time to appear. Everything happened slower in the human realm. But feeding it even a little would lead him in a direction he didn't want to go. Far better, and far easier, to stop the dread when it was small.

"I am clever," he said, determined to head off his gloom. "I have wooed many women and won their hearts. Surely keeping one woman's fondness isn't that different. I love Zoe, after all, and love is a good, strong magic, perhaps the oldest magic of all. Caring for her need not lower my spirits, not when it's so clearly an advantage."

His breath came easier with the soothing, and his heart didn't feel so heavy in his chest. Opening his eyes, he noticed a field of energy wavering outside the window, a heatlike shimmer in cool, moon blue. Magnus smiled at the sign that he was making progress. As he did, a tendril licked against the glass. The Will-Be was coming close enough to taste his thoughts.

"Just an idea," he petitioned politely. "A little help getting Zoe to feel easy with me again."

The Will-Be gathered against the glass, taking on a shape Magnus recognized.

"Perfect!" he exclaimed, delight tugging at his lips. "That's even better than I asked for."

Zoe floated naked in the hot tub on the deck behind her adobe house, her arms and neck draped limply over the padded rim. She didn't fear being spied on. None of her neighbors were close, in addition to which, Fairyville had an ordinance against commercial lights shining after ten. Left undisturbed, the stars were twinkling crystals on a field of ebony. Coupled with the sea salt she'd thrown into the roiling water, the view of the undimmed heavens acted as a balm. She felt her upsets drain away—at least, as much as they were going to.

No amount of sea salt could tell her what to do about her sexy manager.

It didn't seem she could forget him. Magnus called to her emotions and her body too much for that. Being friends had already proven painful, and yet the thought of not being friends appealed to her even less. At lunch, Teresa had suggested she try to seduce him, just go for it and get him out of her system. On the face of it, this appeared to be her best option. Magnus had kissed her—more than kissed her, strictly speaking—and surely a seduction had a chance of success. The problem was, even if she did succeed, she was far from certain one night with Magnus would put her itch to rest.

She'd heard the wistful sighs of Magnus's former lovers. Although none spoke of him resentfully—an accomplishment she attributed to his sunny charm—she couldn't doubt he was a hard act to follow.

Regrettably, she couldn't convince herself she'd last any longer than Magnus's previous one-night stands. Even ignoring his warning, her history wasn't reassuring on that subject. She hadn't held on to Alex when they were kids, and she wasn't so insecure that she didn't know he'd wanted her quite a bit.

Her toes curled beneath the water at a memory: her and Alex making out in the back of his mother's hideous wood-paneled station wagon. As she recalled, it had been the night before a big game. They'd been dating six months then, starting a week and two days after she'd been assigned to tutor him in calculus. He'd been a typical I'll-never-use-this jock, whereas she'd been grades ahead. The match had been perfect—in more ways than one.

Other boys before Alex had thought that hanging with a psychic was cool . . . until they realized she wouldn't, or couldn't, tell them which teachers were going to give pop quizzes. The dead came to Zoe with their own agendas, so hungry to communicate with their loved ones that they'd gravitate to anyone who could hear. Most boys, no matter how brave they thought they were, were creeped out by the idea that Zoe didn't just see ghosts, she drew them—a teenage pied piper to the deceased. Boys like that wanted a normal girl they could take to dances. They wanted a girl they could get to second base with without wondering if their Aunt Ida was watching from the Other Side.

Alex was the first boy Zoe met who was more interested in her than in what she could do. Oh, her gifts were what had sparked his curiosity, but it was *her* he called on the phone each night to talk for hours. All the extras she could do and see he simply took in stride. To Zoe, this was a miracle of the highest order: not to be doubted or viewed as a freak. Alex could have been ugly and obnoxious, and he'd still have earned a friend for life. That he was the hottest boy in school, a championship quarterback over whom Zoe had been struggling not to sigh, earned him her devotion almost before he'd known he wanted it.

Happily for her, his attraction hadn't taken long to catch up to hers. The three-year age difference had bothered him from the first, but he hadn't been able to resist her bumbling overtures. Naturally, him having to fight his honorable intentions had made the relationship all the more romantic to her.

He'd been very careful not to "despoil" her, as he'd put it. They'd kissed—a lot—and he'd touched her breasts under her bra, but the closest they'd come to actual sex was grinding against each other with all their clothes on. This had gotten them so excited, they'd both been able to climax, a feat Zoe could only marvel at today. None of her partners since had managed anything like it.

That night, though, like most nights when she was fifteen, Alex was the only male in her world. That night in the beat-up Ford Country Squire, she'd made up her mind to touch his penis with her bare hand, a decision he was trying to argue her out of between their usual deep and desperate French kisses.

"It's too much," he'd gasped, his lower body pressing hers insistently into the station wagon's thin carpet. "If you take it out, I'll want to put it inside you."

"I won't let you," Zoe promised, though when his teeth scraped lightly over the skin beneath one ear, she wasn't quite as sure.

"You're wearing a skirt tonight. That's only panties between you and me."

"I'll stop you," she said more firmly. "I just want to see it. I want to feel what happens to it when you come."

Alex groaned into the neck of her pink-and-white-striped spandex halter, the one she'd worn to persuade him to go along with her idea. It clung to what breasts she had with formidable faithfulness, but so far it wasn't living up to the hopes she had for it.

"I probably shouldn't before a game anyway. The coach said we should refrain."

"The coach isn't you. Remember what happened the last time we 'refrained'? You fumbled twice on important plays."

She wasn't certain Alex heard her. He was licking her nipple through the halter's stretchy cloth, which instantly hardened it. Then—as if this evidence of her responsiveness was too much for his control—he groaned and sucked most of her breast hard into his mouth.

It was a rough thing to do, and not his usual style, but Zoe couldn't have loved it more. Her back bowed off the cargo area's floor as she thrust her hands into his sun-streaked hair. A line of fire had ignited between her nipple and her sex, tightening the sensations welling there. He groaned again and tugged at her more fiercely. What he was doing felt so good that, for a startled second, she thought she was going to come from that.

When he let her go, her moan of protest was sincere.

"I didn't refrain that night," he panted in his dark, rough voice, the voice that made him sound like a full grown man. "I got so crazy not doing it with you that I jacked off five times in a row as soon as I got home."

Fresh heat flushed through her to her toes. She had to swallow before she could make her own confession, and that was only in a whisper. "I've done it five times in a row myself, but I didn't know boys could get off that often."

Alex's breath caught at her words. Clearly, he hadn't thought about her needing release, too. He stared at her, his eyes burning in the soft illumination of the dome light.

"Jesus," he finally said, forgetting she'd asked him not to curse in front of her.

The bulge in his jeans pressed snug against her panties, so huge it frightened her. She was more excited than afraid, though, and she laid her palm gently over it. She'd never touched him that directly before. He jerked, but didn't jerk away.

"Let me take it out," she coaxed softly. "Aren't you tired of driving home with sticky underwear?"

"Zoe . . ."

She heard his resistance crumbling. "Who else is going to let me? All the other boys think I'm weird."

His face went hard as steel. "You stay away from other boys."

"Make me. Prove you want me more than they do."

His jaw ticked at her dare, and then he practically tore his zipper open, shoving her hand inside his briefs. He moaned with pleasure the instant her palm touched skin, a sound that made her go liquid. She'd never felt anything so silky, so hot and alive and hard as his bare penis. She tried to explore him, but when he rasped "tighter" in a pleading tone, she strengthened her grip.

It took four squirming thrusts through her inexpert hold to bring him off.

"No fair!" she remembered crying. "I didn't have a chance to pay attention!"

She chuckled at the memory now, because he'd let her do it again—grudgingly at first, and then with all the groaning, gasping, curse-laden enthusiasm she could have wished. Going once had barely made a dent in his need. She'd felt like a goddess when he exploded that second time, an honest-to-goodness woman coming into her power.

He'd dragged her panties down her legs not thirty seconds later, ignoring her embarrassed protests to sink sweet, tonguey kisses into her sex.

"I can do this now," he explained, his mouth wet and hot against her. "It's safe for me to do it until I get hard again."

He hadn't taken long to figure out what she liked, or to demonstrate just how spine-wrenchingly good an orgasm could be. He'd also known not to leave it at just one, sucking her clitoris even harder between his lips and tongue for the second peak.

"Where did you learn that?" she remembered asking after she'd caught her breath. She should have been jealous, but was too stupefied that an eighteen-year-old boy could be so uninhibited.

"I learned it from you," he'd said, seeming surprised that she had to ask. "Your body told me what I needed to know."

Her amusement faded as she remembered what had happened two short weeks later. Yes, indeed, Alex had wanted her. She simply hadn't been the only one he was on fire for.

She sighed, and as if on cue, one of Rajel's junior fairies popped into existence on the edge of the hot tub. It was a boy fairy, dressed like Robin Hood in forest green. He wasn't really a boy, of course. Fairies only looked like children. For all she knew, this one was hundreds of years old.

"Whatcha doin'?" he asked, his little tighted legs swinging in the steam. "Trying to make Zoe stew?"

Zoe laughed, which was probably what he'd intended. "Better be nice, or I might decide to make fairy stew instead."

"I'm too quick," bragged the fairy, fluttering off his perch before she could pretend to nudge him. "I'm Samuel the Swift, fastest fairy in Arizona!"

He whizzed around her to prove it, a jet trail of green fairy dust twinkling in his wake.

"Why did the chicken walk across the road?" Samuel demanded, moving so rapidly the question sounded like it came from both sides of her head at once. "Because he was too slow to fly!"

Zoe was about to tell him this was the lamest chicken joke she'd ever heard, when Samuel came to a hovering, midair halt. His tiny body quivered with attention as he peered down the quiet road that led to her house, his wings beating so quickly they were nearly invisible.

Zoe saw nothing but the shapes and shadows of the night.

"Oh, no!" he gasped, both hands pressed to his mouth in horror. "Anything but a k-k-kitten!"

Zoe assumed this was another joke, but Samuel let out a tiny shriek, disappearing so abruptly that his fairy dust was left hanging in the air. Zoe could only wonder what had set him off.

But the fairy's eyes and ears were sharper than hers. It wasn't long before two bright headlights appeared over the gentle rise of her street. The distinctive throaty purr of the engine told her whose car it was.

The arrival of Magnus's red 4Runner felt like a sorrier joke than the chicken one. Her manager would drop by tonight while she still pulsed with thoughts of all she'd never gotten to do with Alex, while she was—conveniently enough—undressed for a seduction she hadn't yet decided she should attempt.

What was it the women of Fairyville said? Better to have loved and lost Magnus than to have never had him in your bed.

She scowled to herself as Magnus parked his vehicle in her driveway. Magnus used it for his weekend adventures—white river rafting on the Colorado, hang gliding in the Grand Canyon—trips he took alone and came back glowing from. Zoe was no daredevil, but she wouldn't have minded camping out with him if he'd asked. He hadn't, though, and now the car's door opened and shut. She heard him whistling a passage from *The Magic Flute*. Magnus loved music almost as much as he enjoyed exploring Mother Nature's more dangerous corners. He was a man who grabbed life with both hands, and his incessant happiness was an undeniable aphrodisiac. Against her will, Zoe's body tightened on itself.

He must have heard the bubble of the hot tub, because he didn't try her front door, but came around the walk to her deck in long, sure strides.

Every footfall made her sex tense more.

"It's an Irishman bearing gifts," he called, holding up a bottle and two glasses in his right hand. His left was cradling something dark against his chest.

Whatever Zoe was going to decide, she knew she'd better do it soon. His eyes went a little wider, his smile and his footstep faltering when he noticed her bare shoulders. Tonight, there were no bathing suits in this tub.

"Oh," he said, suddenly sounding dazed. "Maybe I should have called."

An extra flush of color rose in his cheeks, making his already sensual face look as if he'd just rolled out of bed. He'd stopped at the edge of her cedar deck, and he was staring at the place where her breasts would be beneath the water. When his tongue came out to wet the curve of his upper lip, Zoe's inner rebel gave her a shove.

So what if Magnus thought she wouldn't be any different from his other partners? The least she could do was show him what he'd be missing. As to that, the least she could do was show herself.

If he was going to grab life with both hands, he might as well be grabbing her.

"Is that chilled?" she asked, nodding at the bottle.

"What?" He dragged his eyes to her face.

"The wine. Is it chilled?"

"Oh." He licked his upper lip again. "Yes. It's your favorite Chardonnay. The one you order sometimes at lunch." He stepped onto the wooden platform, the movement cautious. "I . . . brought some company, in case you're not in the mood for mine."

He held up the object he'd been cuddling in his second arm. It wriggled and let out a *mew*. It was exactly what Samuel had predicted: a yellow-eyed, black-furred kitten with white feet. Its tiny pointed tail, also tipped in white, stuck straight down as it dangled from Magnus's large, tanned hand—utter cuteness held by a big, strong man.

"Aww," Zoe said, helpless to keep the croon inside. "How did you know I've been wanting a cat?"

"Lucky guess." He cleared his throat. "I meant it as a peace offering."

Zoe smiled in spite of herself. "How could you need one? I don't think any woman could stay mad at you. There's a box near the sliding doors that ought to hold him. Set him in it and hand me my robe. I want to say hello without parboiling him."

"Right," said Magnus, fumbling slightly with the wine glasses. "I'll just set all of this down."

His nervousness decided her. Magnus was rarely nervous, and never because of a woman. She didn't give him a chance to hold up her robe or to avert his eyes the way a friend might do. No, she stepped out of the water in all her glory, and let the object of her affections get a good eyeful.

Magnus knew he should look away, and Magnus's aching cock knew it even better. He'd turned aside to set down the wine and the kitten, and when he turned back she was simply there.

His prick punched against his jeans, hard as iron in a single breath.

Zoe was a nymph in her nakedness, streaming wet and shining in the soft porch light. She'd twisted her curls into a single cable and pinned them atop her head, leaving every inch of her body bare. Her legs were long and perfectly muscled, her hips almost boyish in their leanness. His mouth went desert dry at her breasts. They were round and high—silky, curving handfuls whose swollen nipples begged to be rolled against his tongue and sucked like candy. Their centers stiffened as he stared, the relaxation they'd undergone in the hot tub reversing now.

"Zoe," he said hoarsely, his pulse jumping in his throat.

"Magnus," she answered and skimmed a sparkle of water droplets from her waist. Her belly was a gentle curve between her hipbones, which in their turn framed an inky triangle of curls. Her pubic hair was so black her skin glowed next to it.

One shapely leg swung forward and took a step toward him.

Magnus was certain she wasn't far enough away for that to be safe.

"Please," he said with a hint of panic.

"Please what?" she teased as she stalked closer.

She wasn't a nymph then, she was a siren, full of confidence and devilry. Magnus had never seen her like this, and he wasn't prepared for it. She was just so . . . *naked*. His eyes slid down her endless legs again. Her cherry red toenails stopped an inch away from his shoes. Heat crashed across his skin in great humid waves. When she put both damp hands on his shoulders, forcing his gaze to hers, his knees threatened to give out. She seemed to look straight into his soul, her smile a softness in her eyes.

"Come on, Magnus. Don't you get tired of sleeping with women you barely know? Wouldn't you like to try it with a friend?"

"Oh, God," was all he could say, trapped by her gentle question. She had no idea how much he wanted what she was offering, or how dearly he'd pay if he accepted. Her hands slid down his chest and up again. He was wearing a lightweight Western shirt, and the touch was more than he could stand. His cock throbbed behind his zipper like a marching band.

"I know I get tired of watching you sleep with everyone but me," she continued in that silky tone. "Especially since I suspect you really are as good as they say." She looked down between them, to the ridge of flesh that was shoving thickly out from his groin. "I liked touching you this morning, even though I know it was rude. I liked kissing you, too. It's been so long since anybody kissed me, I forgot how nice it can be."

"I want to," he gasped out, his hands gripping hers to stop them from drifting into the danger zone beneath his waist. "I want to kiss you and kiss you until you forget what other men taste like."

Her eyes were dark as they locked on his, a stormy gray he wanted to drown in. She went on tiptoe, her pointed nipples just barely grazing his shirt. The pulsing warmth of her body almost made him cry.

"It's been two years since I had a date," she whispered. "Don't you think it's cruel to kiss me and leave it there?"

Magnus's lungs forgot how to work. Two years was how long she'd known him. Two years and twenty days. She'd been saving herself for him even if she didn't recognize she was doing it.

He couldn't just stand there in the face of that. Urges too basic to be denied had him lifting her off her feet and hugging that slender, curving body against his own. The sexy sound she made when his mouth met hers was enough to call a groan from him. He wanted her so badly he could barely think. He reached behind him for the sliding door, yanking it open and carrying her backward into her house.

Magnus's magical abilities might have been dulled by coming to this realm, but he was still stronger than most humans. Zoe weighed next to nothing in his tightened arms, a sleek and sexy nymph who felt like she would break at the first good thrust.

Or maybe not. She wasn't making it easy for him to remember what lay at stake. Her thighs came around his waist and squeezed, stronger than he expected, putting her pussy not quite where he wanted it but damn close. He nearly tripped over a sofa, then had to catch himself on its back.

She was tugging up his shirt even as she kissed him, her hands slipping greedily beneath its front to reach skin. When the heel of her palm rubbed a circle around his nipple, it felt so good he nearly bit her tongue.

Humans released oxytocin when they touched each other, but the fairy version of the pleasure hormone was many times stronger. Magnus felt it tingling through him and knew he really ought to end this now.

"Sorry," he mumbled, promptly kissing her even deeper. He couldn't stop himself. He'd been wanting her too long, and this morning's taste had only whet his appetite. One hand slid brainlessly down her naked spine, pausing when it reached her sweet, round bottom. That was too good not to admire all over.

"Oh, God," he moaned, loving the way her muscles gave beneath the pressure. "I could fuck you every day for two months straight."

"Do it," she said, pressing a string of kisses along his jaw. "Do it, Magnus. Lock the door and keep me under you."

He growled at the images she was raising, feeling her wetness against the muscles of his belly where she'd rucked up his shirt. She was flowing with cream, the musky scent tightening his cock to the point of pain. The arousal had to have come on her quickly, only since she'd stepped from the tub, for that would have washed all the signs away. Knowing he had to feel her or go insane, he slid two fingers into her from behind. He'd thought maybe only one would go in, but the husky cry that tore from her throat thrilled everything male in him.

She was ready. She was twitching and creaming and clutching at his penetration like she couldn't pull it deep enough. Her fluids spilled down him hot as fire. When he began to work his fingers inside her, pressing them outward just a little to test her size, her head fell back to bare her throat.

She said his name like she was singing it. "Magnus. Oh, Magnus, I want that to be you. I want your cock inside me. I want to feel you come."

She writhed on his hand, stealing what little sense he had left. He wanted to shift her down and impale her, to feel those urgent motions against his cock. All his fairy instincts screamed at him to do it. He was born to revel in the sexual act, was meant to seek release so much more often than he'd been doing. What he felt about her just intensified the need.

Groaning at the torture she was inspiring, he bent his head to nip her shoulder. He knew she was close to coming, knew, too,

that bringing her to pleasure quickly was the only thing that
might save him.

If he took her the way he wanted, heart and body, he'd have
to give both back when the moon was full; have to return the
sweetest, dearest prize he'd ever won.

He wasn't sure either of them would recover if he did that.

"Omigod!" she cried, stiffening without warning. "The cat!
We left my kitten outside!"

He panted like one of Tryon's flying horses as she wriggled
out of his hold. It took a couple of tries before he could form
words.

"I'm not doing this right if you can think of that."

"You were doing it perfectly," she assured him, patting his
arm a second before she tugged it excitedly. "Oh, Magnus, look!
The fairies have come back."

They had come back. Magnus could see them clearly as they
both peeped through the sliding doors, though Zoe probably
didn't know that. A crowd of at least a dozen were clustered
around the box that held the kitten, darting back and giggling
when it reached for them with its paw. They must have been
making sure it wouldn't try to leap out.

"Can you see them?" she whispered. Her fingers curled into
his as naturally as if they'd been holding hands for years, instead
of this being the first time. "They might look like fireflies to you,
but in different colors."

"I see them," he said.

His voice was rough. Zoe lifted his knuckles for an impulsive
kiss, her hand still warm with sexual excitement. "That was so
clever of you to bring him! Kittens are like catnip to fairies. I bet
they couldn't stay away when they saw."

He couldn't utter a word. Her pleasure in his pleasure—without ever guessing how much it meant to him—closed his throat.

For millennia, the little fey had served his world's ruling

families—happily, so they thought. It was their nature to delight in helping others' dreams come true. They had not, however, delighted in doing it as slaves, or at his mother's whim. One by one they'd slipped through the cracks between the worlds, hitchhiking on their larger cousins' trips back and forth. The last of his tiny kindred had disappeared when he was a boy. Since that time, he hadn't seen a single one until tonight.

When Zoe's gaze found his, alight with her happiness over this privilege she was sharing, he couldn't have looked away to save a million magical visas.

Her fingers tightened meaningfully on his. "The kitten seems to be fine. Lots o' babysitters. Maybe we could continue where we left off?"

A bashfulness she hadn't shown a scrap of when she climbed naked from that tub had crept into her voice. Blood surged harder through his groin. He knew no male in Fairy could have resisted her blend of shyness and availability. Everything in his highly sexual nature told him to claim her, hard and fast, for himself alone. He knew he needed to step back now, while his sanity was still intact. Except, if he left her when she sounded this insecure, he doubted she'd forgive him a second time.

Feeling more solemn than he ever had in his life, he cupped her lovely face between his hands.

"I think we should slow down, sweetheart. Maybe not go 'all the way,' as the kids put it. What you're offering me is a precious gift. I want to take my time unwrapping it."

Zoe pulled his clasp away from her.

"Oh, boy." Her voice was breathless . . . and not in a good way. "This is sounding sickeningly familiar."

"Zoe—"

"No." She stepped back and shook her head as he reached for her. "Far be it from me to rush any man."

He didn't understand her reaction, but knew it couldn't

bode well for him. He scrambled in his head for something to say that would make it better, but only got as far as drawing breath when her kitchen phone began ringing.

"Saved by the bell," she said bitterly.

He had the stomach-dropping sensation that she believed the bell was saving him.

Five

Bryan had spent many evenings in Phoenix in overloud country-western bars, waiting for some cowboy to give him The Eye. Despite these numerous assaults on his eardrums, his hearing was fine. He caught more of Alex's conversation with his mother than he suspected Alex intended. Why Alex had been rattled by the information, Bryan didn't want to speculate.

Alex couldn't be thinking he'd been switched as a baby, when Oscar Pruitt was so obviously exactly who the hospital said.

That Alex was rattled was undeniable. Bryan's partner didn't take a "thinking" break from a case before they'd barely gotten under way. Bryan also had the impression that Alex was avoiding making his presence known in his old hometown. It was nearing sunset, late this time of year, and guests were coming back from dinner. These weren't people likely to recognize him, but Alex chose to enter the Vista Inn via a side door, handily skirting the public lobby.

Equally suspicious, they took the rickety elevator to the

fourth floor, riding it alone and in silence. Alex's face was tense, maybe a little flushed. Though this might just have meant his partner was upset, Bryan found his body hardening.

If Alex was a sex addict as he'd claimed, it seemed likely he'd be wanting to have it soon. Bryan had been pretty sure he'd had a boner back in the car. And possibly being on edge, for whatever reason, might increase his need. For motives that, admittedly, weren't unselfish, Bryan was more than ready to be Alex's therapeutic sex object—repeatedly, if required.

He'd been wanting him way too long to have exhausted that appetite.

Alex had the key out and entered the room first. Bryan made up for that advantage by kicking the door shut behind him and pulling off his shirt.

The slamming door spun Alex back. A flicker of irritation crossed his face, but the appearance of Bryan's chest erased it. That his disrobing also darkened Alex's cheeks brought Bryan's erection to its most demanding proportions. In that moment, he thought *he* might go crazy if it wasn't seen to soon.

"Bed first," he said firmly, kicking off his shoes. "Brooding later."

Alex didn't say a word, just took two steps toward him and grabbed his face for a quick, deep kiss. Bryan fell back onto the king size bed almost before he knew he'd been pushed. Alex was on top of him in two seconds, on his knees, and heading straight for Bryan's belt.

He got it off so fast, Bryan's waist should have had whiplash.

"Hey," he said as Alex started wrestling off his pants as well. "Give me a chance to get my hands on you this time."

Alex looked up. His eyes were the same intense blue Bryan had noticed back in the firm's bathroom. Whatever caused the effect, it had to be the sexiest expression he'd ever seen.

"Be quick," Alex said. "I'm not in the mood to wait."

"Are you ever?" Bryan asked rhetorically.

He sat up to make short work of freeing Alex from his business shirt, then gave in to temptation to lick his nipples. They were pink and flat but sharpened at the first wet touch, his velvety skin taking on a sudden taste of sweat. Alex's arms came around his shoulders, tight and hard. For just long enough to make Bryan's heart skip, Alex clutched him close, like what he needed from Bryan was more than sex.

Then Bryan bit the nipple he'd been licking, and Alex's fingers dug into his back.

Oh, yeah, he thought. *You like to get it as rough as you give.*

Encouraged to test his limits, Bryan shifted to the meat of Alex's pectoral muscle and nipped that. Alex jerked, sucked in air, then let it out as a moan. Adrenaline flooded Bryan, aching along his skin. He knew as surely as he'd known Alex wanted him in the car that this encounter wasn't going to go slow.

"The rest," Alex demanded on a rasping breath, as if they'd been engaged in foreplay longer than two minutes. "Take off the rest."

Getting their clothes off was like a battle, with each wanting the other naked so he could examine every part that came into view. Bryan couldn't get over the perfection of Alex's skin—so addictively smooth Bryan simply couldn't keep his hands in one place. He didn't deliberately get in Alex's way, but Alex had to fight him to keep up.

For once, Bryan had an edge over his partner. His one sport in high school had been wrestling, and he hadn't forgotten how to maneuver. Used to being in charge physically, Alex lost his patience when both were down to their briefs. Bryan had squirmed down to kiss his knees and knead his calves, putting him temporarily out of reach.

"Enough," Alex said, using sheer strength rather than technique to pull Bryan up him full length.

Bryan couldn't claim to be sorry. The bed had what he thought of as granny covers—chenille, he thought it was called. The stuff was nubbly, and when Alex hauled him up it, the texture felt delicious against his skin. As soon as Alex had them level and was able to run his own hands over Bryan, they writhed together like teenagers, their pricks bumping and rubbing through the cotton of their underwear.

It was difficult to say which one of them was more eager.

Images flashed through Bryan's mind of the first time he'd "experimented" with another boy. The forbidden thrill of it had been piercing, the sense that being with another male was what his body had been born for. For reasons he couldn't have defended even if he'd wanted to, the idea that Alex didn't always do it with men made his fervor for doing it with Bryan even sexier.

This was probably the closest Bryan would ever come to sleeping with a straight man.

He groaned at the power of that particular fantasy—which was enough to crash Alex through the last of his ability to hold off.

"The lube and rubbers are in the bathroom," he said, his hips grinding against Bryan's with astounding force. "But I am so not moving from this bed until I come."

"Not a problem," Bryan assured him, almost as raggedly. "There are more things than fucking that I want to do with you."

Happy to demonstrate, Bryan shoved his hand down Alex's briefs, finding him hot and full and long. Alex's breath hissed inward a second before he returned the favor. If Bryan's hand felt half as good as Alex's, Bryan understood why the other man shuddered hard. One of Alex's thighs jerked between his, the hairy muscle pressing his balls. Bryan's briefs were bunched around his testicles, holding up their fullness like a sling. His shaft was throbbing in the open air. The sensation of Alex fisting it made his own hand tighten on what it held.

"Yes," Alex urged, his leg hooking behind Bryan's to lever

them closer. "Rub me against your belly. Rub my dick next to yours."

Bryan grunted and shifted his body until their pricks were perfectly aligned. The technique of rubbing head and shaft together like boy scouts starting a fire was one he'd known well once upon a time, a throwback to the only sex he'd had the nerve to try as an eighteen-year-old. Revisiting his old standby pushed his buttons enough to need to bite his lip for control. Alex really knew how to crank him up, if only by accident.

Fortunately, Alex was just as ready. They squirmed their cocks up and down, slightly crosswise so that the best bits got plenty of pressure, each alternating directions in short, rough thrusts. All that smoothed the increasing friction was the sweat and pre-ejaculate dripping down their skin.

The closeness of their heights was perfect for what they were doing, maybe too perfect. The position was more intimate than Bryan was used to, especially since Alex didn't seem to know the meaning of self-consciousness. Once he got going, he threw himself into sex, as if the thought of being shy about going straight for what he wanted was foreign. He didn't seem to care who was what size or where they touched each other, didn't seem to mind what sounds their bodies were making, or want to ask permission to go as hard as he could. Not quite as unbuttoned, Bryan buried his face in Alex's shoulder, rather than expose how much he wanted him back. This, of course, meant he heard every catch in Alex's breathing, every groan of pleasure and half-swallowed cry.

The noises Bryan was making were a little too embarrassing to describe—unless he wanted to admit he could whimper.

When the noises started coming faster, Alex clamped his free hand over Bryan's buttock. His hold was so determined Bryan was pretty sure his palm was going to leave a mark. The way their other hands were trapped between their frantically rubbing pricks was a mixture of inconvenience and ecstatic pain. The bones of their fingers were too hard to be comfortable, considering the force they were using, but the edge of hurt didn't slow either down. Bryan might not have been at ease with meeting Alex's eyes, but he sure as hell was good with what was happening. Alex was lost to pleasure and controlling the proceedings at the same time. The combination was enough to bring a fresh flow of pre-come spilling over Bryan's knob.

Alex curled his thumb over the brimming hole. "Do this to me," he ordered, the directive like sandpaper. "Feel me come."

Bryan made a low, hungry sound he couldn't have held back to save any amount of pride. Urgency swelled inside him, pressure and tropic heat. He fumbled to get his thumb positioned like Alex's. The tip of Alex's cock was wet with arousal. As Bryan pressed, its slipperiness increased. That one small change was a surge of lightning whipping through his groin—and maybe Alex's as well. A second later, both were groaning, their seed squeezing out against the pads of thumbs that ground down as hard as they could and couldn't possibly have kept the stuff dammed up.

Bryan didn't think he'd ever come like this. He climaxed with a concentration of feeling that stole his breath, and still every flutter of Alex's ejaculation registered in his brain.

This wasn't just a good orgasm; this was epic.

The last contraction came for both at the same time. As the near unbelievable pleasure receded, Bryan felt as if he'd come up for air after being tumbled in a huge ocean wave. The veins in his head were throbbing, his hand and belly spattered with seed. When he rubbed it gently into Alex's silken skin, Alex's hard-on stopped softening.

Alex drew back and smiled at Bryan's gasp of astonishment, their gazes meeting for the first time since they'd begun. Alex's eyes were dark and knowing and hot.

"You *are* insatiable," Bryan said.

"Uh huh," Alex agreed. "Want to choose what we do next?"

"I want to take you," Bryan said without hesitation, the glow of climax having loosened his tongue. "And then I want to suck you off."

Alex rolled away from him, flopping onto his back in wordless offering. He stretched from fingertip to toe against the white granny cover, a quivering display of just how beautiful and hard and golden his body was. By the time he'd finished, his cock lay thick and ripe against his admirable abs, not just fallen there but upright. The head was so close to his navel that Bryan wondered if his desire to go down on him weren't biting off more than he could suck.

He honestly wasn't sure how many inches Alex was.

"A three-fer," Alex mused. He grinned and stacked his hands behind his head. "That sounds about the right speed for me."

It was hard to fuck a man who preferred being on top as intensely as Alex did. They managed by lubing up Bryan's condom and having Alex lower himself onto him in a crouch. The position didn't demand a lot of Bryan except that he enjoy the show. Alex put on a good one, every muscle in his legs highlighted by the effort of raising himself up and down. His strength was great enough that he didn't need his hands for support, but used them to tweak the nerves of Bryan's body in places he hadn't known could feel good.

The tendons under his arms were tingling from Alex's massages, his Adam's apple hummed from his kisses, and the back of his knees had gone sensitive from a stray caress. Alex had a knack for tightening his inner muscles around Bryan's prick that just about spun stars in front of his eyes. If Alex hadn't been groaning himself, Bryan would have accused him of being too unselfish, but Alex clearly got as much pleasure as he gave.

His enjoyment was inspiring to watch. When Alex brought Bryan off for the second time, the climax was as phenomenal as the first.

Bryan was done for the night then, his prick limp and satisfied. He didn't, however, have any objection to keeping his promise to suck Alex off. He'd been wanting to run his tongue all over that melting skin ever since their first time. No amount of sensual exhaustion was going to interfere with that.

"Lay back," he said, his tone telling Alex it wasn't a choice. "You can let me take charge this once."

Alex opened his mouth to protest.

"No," Bryan insisted, pinning him to the bed by his narrow hipbones. "This is my show."

Alex's breath came faster, telling Bryan he'd made a better choice than he knew. Maybe Alex had been wanting someone to take charge of him. With that in mind, Bryan didn't play it conservative. He pulled out all the tricks he knew, whether they came from previous lovers or porn movies. Alex writhed and groaned over every one, his reactions too abandoned to be anything but sincere. It was like making love to someone you simply could not displease, and knowing how much Alex was enjoying what he was doing was enough to bring Bryan up again.

"God, you're good," Alex said, about ten minutes into it. "Oh, yes, suck me just as hard as you can."

Bryan didn't just suck him hard. Bryan grabbed his balls in one big hand and gently twisted their now-tight sac. This wasn't something you could do without a hint of pain, but Alex's reaction confirmed his suspicions. He gave a whimper of pleasure that could have been torn from Bryan's own throat, his back arching high off the bed. Alex was helpless to resist the rough stimulation, his cock stiffening in Bryan's mouth like it hadn't known what hard was before.

His shaft felt huge, its blood pulsing madly with urgency. Bryan let the crest bump his throat with each digging thrust. He knew he wouldn't have to tolerate it long. Alex was practically throwing his hips off the bed with his need to come. Not wanting to be overwhelmed, Bryan put his weight behind his forearms, trapping Alex's upper thighs.

Then he rubbed his tongue fierce and hard over the sweet spot beneath his rim.

Alex's cry of pleasure sounded pretty close to a scream.

His own erection twanged when Alex shuddered into his mouth, as sympathetic as it could get without coming, too. Alex's climax was nearly dry this time but not shorter because of that.

"God," he finally sighed, his spine subsiding against the mattress. "I needed that."

Bryan crawled up beside him and collapsed on his back. Holding Alex down had taken a lot of strength. If this relationship was going to continue, Bryan might need to renew his gym membership.

"Man," he said, his side brushing Alex's. He rubbed his aching jaw. "Maybe I should have suggested a threesome instead of a three-fer. I'd have had a better chance of keeping up with you."

Alex squeezed his hand. "You were fantastic. I feel much better now."

"Better," Bryan muttered, "but maybe not completely done."

Alex rolled onto his side to face him. "You're not worried, are you? I'm this way with everyone. I mean, sex with you was great, but I always need to go more than once."

Hearing Alex try to be reassuring was kind of funny. "You don't have to flatter me. I could tell you had a good time."

"It's not flattery. That was out of the ordinary good. I hope . . . I kind of lost it there at the end. I hope I wasn't too rough."

Bryan grinned and laid his hand flat on Alex's chest. Alex really was in Olympic shape. His heart was barely pounding hard anymore. "As long as I don't have to scream in the next few hours, my tonsils ought to recover."

Alex winced and put his hand on Bryan's wrist. "Were you serious about a threesome? Because I have to admit I like them."

Bryan hesitated, in part because he wasn't certain how cool he could be about sharing the object of his longtime crush with another man. He noticed the question had been tentative, as if Alex feared he'd be judged for this secret wish.

"I think I'd be game," Bryan answered as honestly as he could. "It would depend on who the third person was."

"What if it was a woman?"

Alex was completely still, completely focused on Bryan's response. Bryan's cock got a few ounces heavier. Even if he'd been averse, it would have been hard to pass up an option that so obviously floated Alex's boat. He could hardly imagine what it would be like to see him more turned on than he'd been tonight.

"It would still depend on who it was," he said slowly.

"You're attracted to women?"

"Sometimes. I'm just not ready to give up men to be with one long term, and that's what most of them seem to want."

Alex's face lay inches from his on the pillow. He was holding Bryan's hand against his chest, and now his heart rate had picked up. Bryan suspected that if he looked down between their bodies, he'd find Alex's former steel-hard stiffness recovering. As it was, Alex's pupils were as big as dimes.

"You *really* like this idea," Bryan said.

"Oh, yeah." Alex's voice was soft. "One of each is something I've never managed to arrange."

"Two of either?" Bryan asked, his interest piqued.

Alex threw his head back on a quiet laugh. "Two men," he

admitted, his eyes dancing. "And four women once. That was fun. They were curious lesbians."

"Get outta here," Bryan said, his jaw dropping. "You seduced four lesbians?"

"They seduced me. I think they wanted the crowd for moral support."

"Don't tell that story to a straight man. He'll want to strangle you on the spot."

"As long as you don't want to strangle me."

"No," Bryan assured him, pausing for a jaw-cracking yawn. "I just want a good, long nap."

He felt himself sinking under almost as soon as he closed his eyes. If he hadn't been so tired, he might have stopped to wonder whether he and Alex were actually forming a more-than-friend bond. He also might have wondered whether anyone but a masochist would waste his time hoping that was true. Fortunately for his peace of mind, he was too relaxed to give either worry his attention.

By the time Alex and Bryan's interesting postcoital conversation had wound down, it was black outside, the kind of black you could only find in a town where the sidewalks rolled up at ten. The sole light in the room came from the cheap clock dial.

Alex discovered he didn't mind sharing the bed with Bryan. His partner was easy to be with, no matter what they were doing. Considering what he knew about Bryan's feelings, this surprised him. Alex would have thought he'd feel awkward after his lust had been slaked. But maybe Bryan's crush was wearing off, now that he'd finally had what he'd been longing for.

Alex shifted on the covers, a frown he wasn't sure what to make of pulling at his lips. He debated getting under the sheets. The room was cool, now that they weren't so busy trying to suck all its air into their desperate lungs. The atmosphere felt thick against the sweat drying on his skin. It reminded him of something he couldn't put his finger on.

Oscar Pruitt, he thought, *right before he made paper fly.*

His eyes snapped open in time to see the bucket-size boulder hovering above their heads.

"Rock!" he yelled, which wasn't the most informative thing he could have said, but at least he had the presence of mind to grab Bryan's shoulders and roll with him off the bed.

"Whuf?" Bryan grunted as they crashed to the floor.

The boulder fell with an impressive thump.

It was followed by a hailstorm of fist-sized rocks.

"Hey!" said Bryan. "Who punched a hole in the roof?"

Alex yanked him, still half asleep, into the lee of a tall bureau. "It's not the roof. I think it's a poltergeist."

"I thought you said this room had a ghost."

"Yeah, well, ghosts don't throw rocks."

The rocks weren't just being thrown; they were materializing out of thin air.

"Sheesh," said Bryan as one missile chipped a splinter off their impromptu shelter's door. He wasn't panicking, but his body was all cold sweat, his pulse racing inside his elbow where Alex's hand had clamped onto him. "Maybe we should say a prayer or something."

"Be my guest. I'm going to turn on the light."

The switch shot sparks when he dashed to it and flipped it on, but the overhead fixture worked. As if confused by the burst of illumination, the rocks stopped falling and just hung.

Bryan goggled at their motionless state, forgetting his prayer in awe. "No wonder people only stay one night."

"I don't think this is usual." Not taking any chances, Alex crouched beside Bryan again. Still the rocks hung in the air. Alex was panting with adrenaline, but not quite ready to flee. This was a mystery, and solving them was their job. He cocked his head at a strange, low sound. It was almost too deep to hear, like a whale calling to its brethren beneath the sea.

Assuming, of course, that a whale could sound evil enough to make skin crawl.

"Do you hear that?" Bryan said, suddenly twice as breathless as before.

"I hear it," Alex answered grimly, "and I think it's time we got out of here."

The rocks resumed their pelting mere seconds after they did.

Zoe couldn't immediately identify who was on the phone. She was still fuming at Magnus and his idiotic blather about her offer to sleep with him being a "gift." If she wasn't sexy enough for him to go all the way with, he should just come out and say it. Being nice didn't make things better, it made them worse. It *encouraged* her to keep hoping. She could have kicked herself for thinking she could seduce him, and could have kicked herself even harder for letting that blessed kitten interrupt.

He'd brought her to the edge so fast it was shocking, as if his fingers had powers her favorite vibrator lacked. If she'd just let him continue what he'd been doing for ten more seconds, she could have had her first non-self-induced orgasm in the last two years. That, at least, would have been slightly less pitiful to share with Teresa—or not share, if she'd decided to be a lady about the thing. Now, whether she told Teresa the truth or not, there'd be nothing but pitifulness inside her. Stupid, maudlin, pitifulness.

"I'm sorry," she said to her caller, pressing her palm to her forehead in an attempt to get her brain to follow a single track. "I'm afraid I didn't catch what you said."

Mrs. Fairfax from the Vista Inn was on the line, her voice so frantic and high that Zoe realized her lack of concentration wasn't the only reason she hadn't understood.

Mrs. Fairfax drew a gusty breath, obviously trying to pull herself together. "You have to come to the inn," she said, her pitch now at a level beings other than dogs could hear. "There's something wrong in Room 410. I think the ghosts have gone mad."

"Gone mad how?" Zoe felt Mr. "Let's Take This Slow" move up behind her and fought an urge to cover her breasts. Somehow, talking on the phone in her kitchen with all the lights on made her nakedness seem a lot less appropriate.

"They're flinging stones at the guests!" Mrs. Fairfax cried. "And I'm not sure they're ever going to stop!"

Zoe rubbed the side of her face. She'd "read" the infamous room 410 for a local TV station doing a piece on Arizona hauntings. Four spirits were connected to it that she knew. One was a nondescript "white lady" whose origins no one could ascertain. Another was a gambler from Fairyville's heyday as a mining town. He'd been shot in his sleep by a rival card cheat. The third and fourth ghosts were abused siblings from the 1950s, who'd run from their guardians only to die of exposure in the then-abandoned shell of the inn. Zoe had helped the children cross into the light, though now and then they came back to visit, perhaps just because they could.

None of the ghosts were malevolent, though the white lady and the gambler probably suffered from the spiritual equivalent of OCD. No matter how many guests ran screaming, they never tired of rattling the headboard or playing with the lights. That, however, was strictly ghostly footsteps phenomena, unnerving but harmless.

Most definitely none of the four had the juice it took to throw stones.

"It sounds like you've either picked up a prankster or a poltergeist," Zoe theorized to Mrs. Fairfax. "How old is that grand-daughter of yours?"

Zoe wasn't sure she bought the theory that poltergeists were the products of the turmoil inside adolescent female minds—though pranks certainly could be.

"She's fourteen," said Mrs. Fairfax. "But it can't be Candice. She's with her mother now. Please come get rid of whatever it is. My guests won't think this is colorful."

"All right," Zoe said, already looking around for her purse. "I'll be there in ten minutes with the big guns."

"I'll drive you," Magnus offered after she hung up. Interest lit his handsome face, the eagerness to embrace new experiences that was as natural to him as breathing.

If he'd been anyone else, she knew she could have stayed mad at him. Hell, she *was* mad. She just wasn't mad enough to be mean.

"Fine," she said, "but you stay in the lobby until I'm sure it's safe."

This seemed to amuse him. "No problem . . . as long as you put on more than your birthday suit before we go."

Six

Zoe was certain she'd have remembered to put clothes on without Magnus's reminder. She'd remembered the kitten, after all, whom Queen Rajel was insisting was named Corky.

Naked no more, Zoe carried Corky inside, snuggling him—now sleeping—against her nose. She settled him in a cardboard box nested with an old flannel shirt and some newspaper. Rajel and her court cooed quietly over him, utterly besotted with his fuzziness. Samuel the Swift, Rajel's boy fairy, was making grand, whispered pronouncements about the hordes of mice Corky would catch.

It was just as well her fairies were occupied. They'd never been much help laying ghosts. If the spirits were stubborn, they were too likely to laugh at a fairy's order to be gone. Oh, the fairies had sufficient mojo to make them sorry; their power was not proportional to their size, but experience had taught Zoe it was better all around if a spirit decided departing was the wisest choice.

Left to her own resources, she prepared by meditating in the car. Happily, Magnus was driving and did nothing to distract her. Perhaps because she'd deliberately pushed her conflicted feelings from her mind, she was struck by what restful company he could be. Not only did he keep his mouth shut, but his aura was calm and clean, as if he'd been meditating, too.

She felt safe with him, which was odd. She hadn't known she felt *un*safe before.

In hardly any time, she'd attained a deep state of receptiveness. She felt positively floaty by the time he parked across the street from the inn. No fear marred her concentration, no doubts that her skill wouldn't be enough. The angels she called her "big guns" were gathering already, their presence signaled by subtle changes in the atmosphere—as if the air were pressing tighter around her head. Zoe didn't see angels like she saw ghosts, but her old mentor, Catherine Sweetwell, had taught her how to tell they were there.

Calling them was the easy part. Angels came to anyone who asked. A person didn't even need to know their names for that. The challenge lay in releasing resistance to letting them work their magic on her behalf. That took faith and a little practice, but in an emergency almost anyone could do it.

"We're here," Magnus said, opening her door for her.

She was wearing sneakers, but he helped her down the step from the SUV anyway. His touch was as quiet and reassuring as his company had been. It was as if he knew exactly what she needed to be at her best—though he'd never mentioned any metaphysical leanings. Because the fairies had always avoided him, she'd assumed he had none. Then again, he'd seen her fairies tonight. Not everyone could do that on the first try.

Evidently, as she mulled this over, she spent too long staring up at him.

"What?" he asked, his smile gentle and warm. He appeared

to have forgotten they were at odds, and that might have been the most disconcerting thing he'd done yet. An argument didn't seem to keep him from liking her, not even a little bit.

"Nothing," she said, shaking herself. "Thanks for driving."

He offered his elbow to lead her in, a courtly gesture she couldn't bring herself to refuse. She was grateful for the support the moment they stepped into the inn's lobby. Magnus's energy was a boulder in a pool of chaos. At least three babies were squalling, and it looked like half the inn's capacity had left their rooms to huddle on the lobby chairs. Most seemed grumpy rather than afraid, but their presence said that more than headboards had been rattled.

A spirit had to make a lot of noise to empty so many rooms.

Mrs. Fairfax circulated among the crowd, trying to put a calm face on the disruption while looking frazzled herself. She rushed to the door as soon as Zoe and Magnus came in.

"Mr. Monroe!" she exclaimed, taking his hand as fervently as if he'd been the one she called. "How good of you to bring Zoe. I swear I don't know what I'm going to do if this doesn't stop."

Zoe fought a smile. Even a hysterical, ghost-plagued woman couldn't ignore Magnus's appeal.

"Where are the guests from 410?" she asked, hoping to get a preview of what she was up against.

"They're in the fourth floor hallway, making sure no one else goes in."

Zoe's brows shot up. "That's brave of them."

"They're nice gentlemen," Mrs. Fairfax said, her forehead furrowing as if some part of her wasn't sure of this. "Very handsome and polite. I can't imagine why the ghosts, or whatever this is, would take offense at them."

"Well, I'll go see," Zoe said. "You'll take care of Magnus while I'm gone?"

"Oh, absolutely," promised Mrs. Fairfax, then blushed a little bit.

It was good to approach the coming task with a grin. Humor was a big part of the angels' nature. The more Zoe could match their joyous vibration, the easier accepting their help would be.

She took the stairs rather than the elevator, not sure what electrical devices the purported poltergeist might affect. She was breathless when she reached the fourth-floor landing, which made it all the easier to see her exhalations puffing white in the air. The floor was frigid, as if an entire ghost convention had gathered there. Zoe could hear the rain of rocks from where she'd paused to gather herself. She understood why guests had been disturbed. It would have taken quite a talent to sleep through that racket.

Room 410 was a left turn from the landing, at the end of a narrow, wainscoted hall. The two men Mrs. Fairfax had mentioned waited outside the door. One was bundled in a sheet, and the other in a fringed coverlet. Their bare feet suggested they were naked except for that.

Zoe wondered if the poltergeist had interrupted these two in the act. Even from a distance, they had the flushed and rumpled look of lovebirds. Opposites must have attracted, because one man was blond and lean, and the other dark and muscular—like a runner and a wrestler thrown together by the hand of Fate. The thought of them working out their differences between the sheets caused her tender bits to heat, despite her many excellent reasons not to be aroused by the thought of two buff males getting it on.

She pressed her temples between her thumb and fingers. It was perfectly understandable if she had sex on the brain right now, but she needed to let it go. The perversity of her personal kinks was not the issue at hand. She continued down the hall in what she hoped were confidence-inducing strides.

"It's okay," she said when the fair-haired man moved forward to intercept her. "I'm the ghost buster."

Her heart knew before her eyes did. Her sneakers slowed on the flowered carpet, her face suddenly too hot for the icy air.

"Zoe?" said the fair-haired man. "Zoe, is that you?"

His palm was pressed to his chest, like a prince about to swear an oath. Zoe took in his appearance with a single blink. To her dismay, he hadn't lost his hair or grown a beer gut. He wasn't shorter than she remembered or less handsome. Truth be told, he looked better than he had when he was eighteen. More adult. More *male*. His eyes were still the blue of a tropic sea, and they still begged better than any eyes she knew.

"Alex," she said, his name coming out too hoarse for comfort.

"Uh, I can go," said the other man. "If you two want to be alone with the rocks."

She remembered what she'd assumed when she first saw them and abruptly knew it was true. Room 410 had one bed, not two, and Alex's color was way too high for them to have been sharing it as friends. Come to think of it, that wasn't just a flush on his face, that was a whisker burn.

Her old pain rushed back with stomach-turning force. That she hadn't been enough for Alex. That no matter what he said, he hadn't truly loved her. She thought she'd moved past this, but it seemed not. Her humiliation might have happened yesterday, instead of fifteen years ago.

The thing was, on this day, she had no right to be hurt or angry about who Alex took to bed.

"There's no reason to leave," she said, her vocal chords thankfully under control again. "Unless you'd rather not stick around while I work."

"Oh, I'd love to watch," Alex's lover said, his smile diffident but charming. "Lately, I've been getting quite the education in supernatural phenomena."

Alex wasn't watching him. His gaze was running over her somewhat haphazard outfit: bright green silky short shorts, running shoes with no socks, and a belly-baring white tank top with a moth-eaten, pink crocheted sweater dragged over the top. Not having expected an audience, she hadn't put on a bra. She was small enough to go without one . . . except when she really wished she were covered up.

Her gratitude that she'd shaved her legs this morning wasn't something she wanted to think about.

"We got you out of bed," he said dazedly.

Zoe didn't bother to contradict him, because the hint of judgment in the flattening of his mouth made her pride bristle. Let him think she'd been yanked from just as warm a pair of arms as he had.

"If you didn't want to disturb anyone," she said, "maybe you shouldn't have taken room 410."

The set of his mouth turned sheepish. "I didn't think it would be this bad."

She almost snapped something about other decisions he hadn't thought through any better, then blew out her anger on a breath. She'd forgiven him for her sake, for her own peace of mind. Now was not the time to be forgetting that.

"It shouldn't be this bad," she admitted, her voice still a little clipped. Then, preferring to avoid bumping against any more of their ancient history, she reached for 410's doorknob.

Alex caught her arm before she could turn it. The warmth of his hand was an unwelcome shock, as was the way his heat slid over nerves he shouldn't have been able to excite after all these years. "Those rocks are big, Zoe. You might get hurt."

She wished he didn't sound so caring. It dissolved her anger too handily. She turned her eyes to the worn carpet. "It's all right. I can do whatever I need from the hall."

Reluctantly, he released her. He rubbed his palm down the coverlet, as if touching her had been equally uncomfortable for him. "There's something else in there, something . . . not nice."

Zoe nodded, not telling him she'd already sensed it. "I'll be careful," she said.

She drew a deep, slow breath to center herself before opening the door. A few, small pebbles were all that were falling now, but the entire floor and most of the bed were covered in a layer of gray rocks. If she'd known how to whistle, she would have. She'd never seen a disembodied spirit accomplish anything like this.

Curious, she turned her inner vision around the room, wondering what the white lady and her buddies thought of this incursion into their space. But the usual specters weren't about. More surprisingly, she sensed none of the purposeless anger that was a poltergeist's calling card. The "not niceness" Alex mentioned had what she could only call a professional feel, as if someone had sent this energy to wreak havoc.

"There's a noise," Alex's friend volunteered helpfully. "Like the buzz from an electrical transformer."

Zoe had noticed it. Now she tried to listen with her nonphysical ears. There were words in the low, hair-raising vibration, but she couldn't make them out. She wished she'd thought to bring her tape recorder. If this sound was an EVP, an electronic voice phenomenon, the tape might pick up details her ears could not.

Since that option was out, Zoe took one last look at the rather interesting materializing pebbles and sank into a lotus position in the doorway. The posture served the same purpose for her as a bell did for Pavlov's salivating dog. Calm fell around her like a blanket of angel down.

"I call on Archangel Michael," she said, the words firm and sure. "Cleanse this room of violence. Heal whatever fear or anger is troubling this being's heart."

The icy hall immediately warmed, enouch that sweat broke out on her brow. She smiled just a little. Michael was a warrior angel, a being of fire. One of the surest signs that he was around was things heating up. Encouraged by the quick response, she continued.

"Michael, we thank you for clearing this room of lower energy. Banish any who wish its occupants harm. Love is welcome here, and any spirits who are kind. All others we send back to the field of illusions from whence they came."

"Hey!" said a gruff male voice so close to audible sound that it startled her. "I am NOT an illusion. Or a lower energy. I'm just delivering a message."

"Messages are fine," Zoe told it, "but violent acts are not acceptable."

"Hah! This is an open spirit vortex. Anyone can come here who has the juice. I have as much right to be here as a ghost. I'm—Ack!"

A huge rustling of wings, invisible but somehow glowing, told her Archangel Michael was looming over their visitor. He wasn't fighting him, just pressing against him with all his angelic will. The spirit said *ack!* again, and Zoe had the distinct impression that it was searching for an opening to wriggle free. Michael wasn't letting it find one, and in less than half a minute, the thing gave up.

"Hold on to your feathers, Mr. Bigstuff," it grumbled ill-naturedly. "I'm going!"

Zoe's ears popped as if they'd been stuffed from landing too quickly on a plane. Without opening her eyes, she knew that whatever had been haunting the room was gone.

When she did open her eyes, the rocks had disappeared as well. "Rats," said Alex's friend. "I was going to take pictures."

Magnus had always liked small hotels. They made him think of tourists and weekend sex, of warm, appreciative women he'd probably never see again. He'd have given a great deal to be staying in this one with Zoe. He couldn't remember what it was like to be completely satisfied, not just physically but in his heart. He wanted to wake up soft for once instead of aching, with a woman he cared about snuggled to his side. Zoe was right about him missing that. She simply didn't realize how much.

Frustration aside, he was glad she'd let him come along tonight. It said that she was warming to the idea of having him in her life in a bigger way. Yes, maybe their sex life was destined to be eccentric, but men and women could have other fun in bed besides intercourse. Magnus knew he had the skill to pleasure her creatively. Conceivably, he could string out unwrapping her "gift" indefinitely.

Right, he thought sarcastically to himself. Zoe wasn't going to put up with him putting her off forever, and she really wasn't going to tolerate him continuing to sleep around. At the time he'd worked the spell that got him out of Fairy, the monthly carnal offering had seemed a small price to pay. Now, he was screwed every which way, except the one he wanted most.

He shoved his hands into his jeans pockets, glum and aroused at once. He knew he'd better stop dwelling on what he could and couldn't do to Zoe. A full-blown erection wasn't easy for a man his size to hide, and Mrs. Fairfax was already hovering a bit too close. Women her age usually responded to fairy charm with mothering and not flirtation. While Magnus didn't mind his women seasoned, Mrs. Fairfax unnerved him. She was candy-sweet instead of earthy. And her undergarments creaked.

"Oh, Mr. Monroe," she said with the plaintive sigh that was beginning to wear on him. "I do hope Zoe will succeed."

"I'm sure she will, Mrs. Fairfax. She's very good at her job. And you might start a pot of coffee in the meantime. Give your guests something to keep them occupied."

"What a wonderful idea," she gushed, beaming up at him. "It's so comforting to have a levelheaded man around."

Magnus answered her beaming look with a shoulder pat, then sighed in relief when she scurried off. He needed breathing room to tune his radar onto Zoe, to make certain she was safe.

As amped up as her focus was, he found her easily. Another energy curled over hers, blending at the edges in a shimmer of midnight blue. Sensing no threat, Magnus concluded it was one of the beings she called angels. The sheer might of it amazed him, unwavering strength meeting absolute love in a form so huge he wondered that the inn could hold it.

It didn't hold it, of course. No man-made structure could contain a consciousness of that magnitude.

Fascinating, Magnus thought. Angels weren't a force in Fairy, and he'd never thought of studying them, but when in Rome . . .

Before he could follow this train of thought, his senses picked up something far more familiar and far less nice. The back of his neck crawled with memory. An elemental was at the inn, a bogeyman for fairy children that his mother sometimes used to run her nastier errands. Elementals were only half physical. They could move between realms wherever supernatural occurrences had thinned the veil. They were vicious creatures, with little conscience regarding how they used their power. If Zoe was tangling with one of them, Magnus had no business waiting in this lobby!

He took the steps three at a time, so intent on saving Zoe that he ran straight into her on the second landing.

He caught her before she could fall over, then hugged her tight. "You're all right!"

"Of course I am." She pushed a curl from her face, laughing. "I don't know what was dropping those rocks, but Michael got rid of it just fine."

"Michael?" He narrowed his eyes at the two hastily dressed men coming down the stairs behind her.

"The archangel? Tall? Big, flaming sword?"

"Right," he said, pulling himself together. Humans knew about angels, and human was what he was supposed to be. He could leave his warnings about his mother's evil minions unmentioned. "I'm glad you were successful."

"No biggie," Zoe assured him. "The stone throwing was impressive, but Michael did all the work."

The men had stopped on the landing beside Zoe. Magnus's hackles bristled. Something was wrong here, something that made his fairy warning lights go off.

"Oh," said Zoe, craning around at them. "This is, um, Bryan McCallum and Alexander Goodbody. They were staying in 410 when the incident began. Alex and I knew each other in high school."

They more than *knew* each other. Their energy was tangled up like old lovers. Magnus put his arm around Zoe's shoulder.

"Nice to meet you," he said coolly. "I'm Zoe's friend, Magnus."

The one who hadn't been her lover offered his hand. "Nice to meet you, Magnus. Your girlfriend has quite a gift."

"Oh, we're not—" Zoe started, then shut her mouth.

Like hell we're not, Magnus thought, shaking Bryan's hand.

The other one, Alex, didn't offer his. He was gazing at Magnus as coolly as Magnus was at him. He was very handsome, very smooth and golden and buff. He crossed his arms with perfect superciliousness across his chest. "You and Zoe know each other long?"

"Two years," Zoe answered before Magnus could. "Magnus is my manager."

"Among other things," Magnus added, his fingers sliding slowly to Zoe's wrist. Her pushed-up sleeves left her forearm bare, and he fed his personal magic into her skin, letting it curl low in her body, where the nerves bundled thickest inside her sex. He made the magic lick her where he wished he'd had a chance earlier, right over the swollen tip of her clitoris.

The energy had exactly the effect he'd intended. Zoe gave a little gasp as her nipples tightened violently. She immediately yanked her sweater closed over her flimsy tank top. She tried to pull away from him, but Magnus wasn't having that.

Alex's sea-blue eyes narrowed down to slits. "Her manager and more. How very ethical of you."

Magnus's vision flashed red with rage, a reaction that came to him straight through his mother's blood. His father would have been ashamed, but in that second, he didn't remotely regret the maternal half of his heritage.

"Hey." Zoe pushed at his chest as he stepped forward. Her voice was husky from his secret touch, and a primitive satisfaction, every bit as potent as the rage, swelled in his chest. She was his, and this Alex couldn't get in the way. Magnus had at least four inches on her old boyfriend and who knew how many pounds of muscle. He'd smash him into a pulp before he used that smirking tone again.

Magnus leaned closer, maybe looking like he was going to try something, because the force of Zoe's shove increased.

"What the hell is wrong with you?" she hissed. "You never treat people this way."

Magnus felt his upper lip curl back from his teeth. His awareness of Zoe's nearness was all that kept his snarl silent.

"Magnus," Zoe said, changing tack to stroke his upper arm. Her words weren't nearly as conciliatory as the caress. "Just say hello to the man and shake hands. Alex, you stop glowering and pull out the manners your mom taught you."

Oh, Magnus did not like hearing that she knew this man's mother. In the human realm or in Fairy, meeting parents was serious. With an effort, he forced his jaw to unclench.

"Sorry. Force of habit. I tend to be protective of my friends."

Alex's hooded eyes seemed to hide a smile. He put out his hand. "I understand. Friends like Zoe are worth protecting."

Magnus took the hand, fully intending to exert some fairy strength on its human joints. The moment their palms slid together, he knew that wasn't going to work.

Hellfire, he thought, his own hand getting squished in his slack-mouthed horror at the surprise.

Alex was a fairy, too. Not only that, Alex was Magnus's cousin on his mother's side. The signature Murphy energy was impossible to mistake, though Alex's genetics—and thus his features—had been altered to match whatever human had traded realms with him. Now that Magnus thought about it, he'd met Alex's human opposite at one of his friend Tryon's flying hunts. Magnus's Aunt Elena had been terribly proud of her adopted son, said he had a head for spells most humans in Fairy lacked.

All of which boiled down to Zoe's old boyfriend being a changeling.

No wonder Magnus's territorial instincts had gone into overdrive. The Monroes and Murphys were royal lines, closely matched in power. Magnus wasn't facing off against a human, he was in a pissing contest with a full-blood fey, a preternaturally seductive, sexually insatiable full-blood fey. Worse, being a changeling gave Alex permanent green card status. He actually *couldn't* return to Fairy unless his counterpart agreed to return. Which meant Alex could screw Zoe senseless without losing his right to stay.

The only bright spot was that Magnus's competition didn't have a clue what he was. The Murphy magic was in him, but his human parents wouldn't have taught him what do with it. Fair or not, that was the way the exchange worked.

"We should go," Zoe said, pointedly separating Alex's hand from Magnus's. "You two need someplace else to stay."

"Someplace to eat," Bryan corrected, his hand pressed to his stomach. "After that rain of rocks, a few lights turning on and off aren't going to scare me away."

"We also need to talk," Alex said, sounding like he meant just him and Zoe. Zoe must have looked reluctant, because he held up one hand. "Nothing personal. You might have information about the case that brought us here."

"That's right," she said. "Your mom mentioned you'd become a private detective."

"She stayed in touch with you?"

Zoe smiled with the gentle understanding that had made Magnus fall for her. Seeing that warmth directed at another man caused his hands to curl into fists. "Christmas cards, complete with pictures of your older brothers and their kids."

"I'm sorry I didn't—"

"No," Zoe said. "I never expected you to write." She shrugged as if that could end the trip down memory lane. "I'd be happy to answer whatever you want over food, though I'm afraid it's going to have to be take-out pizza. My larder is bare, and that's the only thing that's open this time of night."

"Pizza is not a problem," Alex laughed. "Left to himself, I'm not sure Bryan here would eat anything else."

He slapped his companion's shoulder, causing a curl of energy to flare between them. To Magnus the link looked new, but definitely sexual, and it was equally strong in both directions. Bryan's gaze dropped to the floor. From the tension that had just ramped up in Zoe's body, she'd picked up on the connection, too.

Well, well, Magnus thought. *Isn't this getting complicated?*

Whether the complication was good or bad he didn't know. Historically speaking, Murphy men had always had sufficient charm to collect harems.

Seven

Zoe's legs were even better than Alex remembered, curvier, with more muscle in the thighs and calves. He couldn't take his eyes off them as she preceded him and Bryan down the stairs. Knowing Bryan was watching made him feel vaguely guilty, but Zoe had haunted his self-torturing fantasies for so long he couldn't stop himself.

Zoe was the one who got away.

Hell, Zoe was the one he'd thrown away in his stupid teenage hormone fog. He'd never stopped wanting her, not for one single day, and the idea that—theoretically—he could have her now was driving him insane.

When that lunk who managed her had tried to claim her as his girlfriend, Alex had wanted to crush his knuckles into dust. The pity was, Magnus had barely noticed. That was the problem with men that big: They didn't have the decency to wince when you were giving them your best power handshake.

"Hey," said Bryan, elbowing his ribs as they threaded through the crowded lobby. "Check out the shoes."

Alex wasn't in the mood to be entertained, but he looked in the direction Bryan pointed. Magnus was talking to Mrs. Fairfax, the woman who owned the inn, no doubt assuring her that her guests could go back to bed because his "girlfriend" had saved the day. Annoyed by the reminder, it took a moment for Alex's eyes to slide to Magnus's feet.

"Shit," he said. Zoe's manager was wearing the same stupid fucking yellow cartoon high-tops Alex had been forced to buy on the drive here. Alex had switched them for a pair of sandals first chance he got, but this man didn't seem to realize the things weren't standard adult wear.

Bryan had started to snicker, but the minute Alex turned his glare to him he stopped. Most men would have kept up the ribbing once they knew it bugged him, but Bryan's eyes went soft.

"I get it," he said with almost too much understanding. "This particular coincidence is just between you and me."

He couldn't have turned the screw on Alex's guilt any better. Bryan liked Alex, and Bryan had finally gotten into his bed, in part because Alex was too freakishly horny to do without. It didn't matter what Bryan said about his lack of expectations; he didn't deserve to watch Alex squaring off with this tower of muscle over someone else.

"Bryan." Alex put his hand on his friend's shoulder.

Looking back later, he decided everything was context. Mrs. Fairfax had known Alex looked familiar when he checked in, but until she saw him in Zoe's presence *and* with another man, two plus two hadn't equaled four.

Once it did, she sucked a shrieking gasp that echoed through the room.

"I know you," she said, her grandmotherly face quivering with rage. "You're that perverted Goodbody boy, the one who ruined Coach Vickers's life. How dare you come back after the heartache you caused this town? Tom Vickers was a good man. The least you could have done was stick to your own kind!"

Her outburst shouldn't have shaken Alex. It was only what he'd heard a hundred times before, what he'd expected before he came. All the same, he had to swallow a lump the size of Mitten Butte before he could speak.

"Believe me," he said as levelly as he could, "I wouldn't be here if I didn't have a job to do."

"A job!" Mrs. Fairfax's cry drew every eye that hadn't been on her already. Parents began to hug their children to their sides. "You don't deserve a job! Trash like you deserves prison!"

She was closing the space that separated them, her hand coming up to strike like she was in some damn catfight on a soap opera. Alex didn't know how to stop her and wasn't sure he wanted to. His face felt like it was frying with self-consciousness, his feet frozen to the ground. *Let her slap me,* he thought. There just wasn't a good way to defend yourself against a woman your mother's age, especially when you knew her accusations held a lot of truth.

And then Zoe was between them like a Fury, straight-arming Mrs. Fairfax's shoulder so she had to stop.

"You are so not doing this in front of me," Zoe said.

Mrs. Fairfax wasn't the only one whose jaw dropped. Alex had never heard sweet Zoe Clare sound like this. Her declaration had been so deep and angry it was a growl.

"Zoe," Mrs. Fairfax protested. "How can you defend him?"

Zoe put her fists on her hips. "I can defend him for three very good reasons. First of all, Coach Vickers probably was Alex's 'kind' all along. Loath as this town was to admit it, men don't turn homosexual overnight. Second of all, Alex was a teenager, which ought to cut him slack by itself. Third of all, even though he was a teenager, and could have stayed nice and cozy as everybody's poor victim, he chose to come forward and tell the truth.

It wasn't his fault people were angry because he wasn't the perfect golden hero they made him out to be. They built that pedestal, not him. He chose to do the right thing."

"The right thing! But he hurt you worst of all."

Mrs. Fairfax's astonishment had turned to pleading. She'd obviously been sure her stand against the depravation Alex represented would be approved, but Zoe didn't back down an inch.

"He was a kid, Mrs. Fairfax, and aside from Coach Vickers's involvement turning it into a public stink, what he did was no worse than kids do to each other every minute of every day. If I can forgive him, I see no reason why people whose hearts weren't broken can't do the same."

Her voice had a ringing clarity. One of the teenage guests, a boy with a nose stud and a Nine Inch Nails T-shirt, began to clap. He was quickly shushed by his parents, but the brief offering of approval tipped Alex into a welter of emotion from which there was no turning back. His eyes went as hot as his face had been a minute earlier. Zoe forgave him. His knees began to shake in reaction, like he might fall if he didn't sit.

"Shit," he whispered, and grabbed the edge of an end table.

Mrs. Fairfax was murmuring a flustered apology and backing off. As she disappeared somewhat huffily into the office behind the reception desk, Zoe thrust her hands into her curls. Her hair had been skewered messily atop her head, and her elbows stuck out on either side. As she stood there, the other guests began to drift away. She exhaled loudly and turned to him.

"Sorry," she said, her expression wry. "Didn't mean to cause a scene."

He couldn't help it, he smiled at her, then felt his heart turn over when she smiled back. Those gray eyes of hers were sweeter than spring rain. "I don't think you need to apologize."

Their gazes held a beat too long, heavy with history. Predictably, Alex's groin began to tighten, and the history became a mutual flare of heat. That was all it took to shove him tight against his slacks: the idea that, just maybe, his chance with her wasn't completely lost.

Zoe turned away before he could. "Come on," she said, waving him along from over her shoulder. "Let's get pizza."

There was no question Magnus had an arrogant streak, but when he'd imagined losing Zoe, it hadn't been to another man. He'd never heard her speak of this Alex, not even once. Unfortunately, her reticence might mean Alex was more important, rather than less.

His face felt stiff from his uncustomary frown as he held the lobby door for the others. Zoe was laughing with the second man, Bryan, doing her sweet Zoe best to put him at ease, as if she hadn't just shot metaphysical laser beams into his lover's eyes. Right about then, Magnus wouldn't have minded watching both men dematerialize.

He'd wanted to finish this night alone with Zoe, to get a chance to mend his earlier missteps, to pleasure her in a hundred delicious ways, preferably until he heard her scream with orgasm. Now he was stuck in this ridiculous love quadrangle, at least for the space of a meal and maybe more. For all he knew, she'd be offering to host the haunted visitors in her home!

This doleful possibility transformed his frown into a glower. They were walking around the inn to its parking lot, dropping Alex and Bryan off at their car before returning to his. Magnus was trailing behind the trio with heavy steps when the Will-Be, his fickle friend, decided to give him more of what he was dwelling on. Despite his super fairy coordination, a tiny crack in the asphalt caught the toe of his wonderful yellow sneaker and sent him sprawling flat on his face.

The Will-Be wasn't trying to hurt him, just to remind him that his current thoughts were not creating in the direction of his true desires. Despite knowing this very well, he still cursed up a blue streak when he felt the scrape on his cheekbone.

"Magnus!" Zoe cried, rushing back to him.

Far too annoyed with himself to be pleased by that, he cursed a few colors more.

Zoe crouched to help him sit up. "What's the matter with you tonight? The way you're acting, I feel like I ought to be checking you for spirit attachments."

He held her hand harder than he had to. "Aren't I allowed to be in a bad mood?"

"Well, yes, but—Magnus, nothing gets you down." She stroked his hair off his forehead, wincing when she saw the scrape. "Your cheek is bruised. You should go home and put some ice on it before it swells."

Oh, he should go home and let her have her fun eating pizza with her high school flame. Magnus *loved* pizza. It was, he thought, a creation of profound human genius. Being bothered that he wasn't going to eat it with her tonight was not terribly adult, but in truth he felt like he was five years old, his feelings hurt by an older playmate, and mulishly determined not to cry. It seemed to take all his strength to unlock his jaw.

"Zoe," he said, his hand cupping her warm, soft cheek. "Do you know how much you mean to me?"

She let out a laughing sigh. "Magnus, I'm not sure any woman could figure that out."

It was a comeback he didn't have an answer for, at least not with an audience. When he did nothing but make a speechless fish mouth, Zoe pulled away from his touch.

"Go home," she said. "I'm sure we'll both feel better in the morning."

Huh, Magnus thought. Good thing one of them was sure.

*   *   *

Zoe's fairies fled the instant Alex came in the door.

She thought she heard one cry *Traitor!* as it disappeared, but the imprecation was too squeaky to be certain.

Corky, at least, had no objection to her guests. The kitten woke up long enough to lap some milk and practice his nascent pouncing skills on a bottle cap. Zoe's kitchen wasn't big, but it had a homey ambience, with vintage appliances and old-fashioned wood cabinets painted white. Alex looked right at home crouched on the terra cotta floor, where he spun the bottle cap for Corky, his laughter low and masculine when Corky overshot it or fell over on half his tries.

Finally exhausted, Corky plopped down on his tummy and fell asleep.

Alex rose with his lips quirked sexily. "I hate to break this to you, Zoe, but I think your cat is a klutz."

Zoe scooped up the kitten protectively, delighted to find him purring beneath her chin. "He's not a klutz, he's just little."

He was also a good excuse to pull herself together away from Alex's too-familiar grins. Back when they'd dated, those lazy, wolfish smiles had been her undoing. Trying to shake off the old effect, she settled the kitten back in his cardboard box, while Alex and Bryan spread their not-so-gourmet meal across the booth-style table in her breakfast nook.

When she returned, three meat-laden pizzas fought for space with a dozen Mexican beers. The men had taken one bench and left the other for her. Even without the food, they filled up her kitchen in a way women never could. Both Alex and Bryan were six-footers, broad-shouldered and muscular. Polite enough to wait until she was back, they fell on the food like they were starving, though Alex managed to relate the story of why they were in Fairyville between slices.

By that point, the men had decimated a pizza each and were beginning to pick at hers. The amount of food males could consume always amazed her, which was probably a sign she didn't spend enough time with them.

If she had, she might not have been so backward about relationships.

Grimacing to herself, she tipped another swallow of Dos Equis into her mouth. She sat crosswise on her bench, her back to the wall and her bare feet up on the cushion. She was trying to make sense of what she'd been told, and of this new responsible business person Alex seemed to have grown into.

His partner, Bryan, had only spoken up a few times, but he struck her—ironically enough—as a likeable guy's guy, more at home at a baseball game than an art museum. He certainly had enough testosterone to make her girly hormones come to attention, in spite of them having little chance of being gratified by him. His five o'clock shadow was a heavy, blue-black demarcation on his handsomely thuggish face. He had great eyes, dark and snapping, with lashes so straight and long she couldn't help imagining all the places they might flutter over Alex's anatomy.

Or her own, for that matter.

She cleared her throat of its inappropriate tightening and set down her beer. If she was starting to fantasize about both of them, she'd had enough alcohol. "You say this little boy made paper fly?"

"He made it dance a conga line around our office," Alex confirmed.

Zoe pinched her lower lip. "I've heard that children these days are being born more psychic, but that kind of telekinesis really takes control."

"Can you float things?" Bryan asked curiously.

Zoe let out a quiet snort. "Not me. My gift is more about seeing things most people can't. Of course, lots of young kids see ghosts or angels. That isn't rare at all. We simply forget how to do it as we get older."

"I never saw spirits," Bryan said.

"You might have when you were a baby. Remember, if I see an infant chortling and flapping its hands for no apparent reason, I know who it's waving at."

Bryan shook his head in wonderment. "It doesn't scare you to see that stuff? I mean, tonight, somebody tells you a poltergeist is raining rocks, and you just come, no questions asked."

"I didn't notice you screaming in terror."

"Couldn't." His lips fought a grin. "Alex was watching."

"Whatever the reason, staying calm was a good decision. If you're not afraid, there's very little that can hurt you in the spirit world. In fact, I'm not sure there's anything that can. You'll see far worse in a horror movie than any ghost will show you, and people survive watching horror movies every day."

"Were you ever afraid? Say when you were little?"

Zoe smiled. "The first time I saw a ghost I was four. It was my Nana Sonia, the day after her funeral, and she wasn't going to scare me. She was a nice, nice lady. Always room in her lap for a grandkid. She wanted me to tell my mother she was all right. When I did, my mother insisted I was lying. I pitched such a fit, she had to send me to my room. Nana Sonia was the one who comforted me. She told me she was proud of me for sticking to my guns."

Zoe had to laugh. "If Mom had known the long-term effect that one bit of praise would have, she'd have put Nana in the ground herself. To answer your question, though, you could say I learned early who to be afraid of—and who not to."

Bryan thought about this. "I guess it would be cool to see the world the way you do, to know there's more to life than the day-to-day ordinary stuff."

"Sometimes it's cool. Sometimes, like when I've got six ghosts lined up and yammering in my ear at the grocery store, it's a serious pain in the butt."

"It's not easy being green?" he suggested, quoting Kermit the Frog and flashing her a teasing smile.

"Yeah, but it's better being green than hiding who you are."

She could see in Bryan's eyes that he liked her for what she'd said and that he knew she wasn't just referring to her own differences. The rapport between them was surprising but nice. She enjoyed knowing Alex's lover was a man she could have been friends with. In her experience, it was almost always more pleasant to like a person than to hate them—or to be jealous. Considering she still seemed to feel some lingering sort of something for her old boyfriend, jealousy was a danger. So it was better that she liked Bryan. Better all around.

It was Alex who reminded them they weren't here to socialize. "Speaking of gifted children," he said, leaning forward across the table.

His forearms had a thicker fuzz of golden hair than she remembered, his muscles flexing as they took his weight. His fingers played up and down the bottle he was holding, graceful and sensitive. When Zoe had been fifteen, she hadn't appreciated how truly beautiful his hands were. Now, as they caressed the glass, she was mesmerized. The shape of the beer was phallic, a firm, thick, upright cock. The motions of his fingers, however, were more suited to stroking tender, feminine things. Watching his well-tended nails draw those tiny patterns made it hard to breathe, like the air was heated sugar instead of oxygen. Alex seemed unconscious of what he was doing, but what if he weren't? What if he was jealous of that moment she'd shared with Bryan? What if, consciously or not, he meant to turn her erotic fascination back to him?

From the corner of her vision, she saw Bryan looking at Alex, so maybe he thought Alex's behavior was deliberate, too. Her nose flared at a scent she hadn't noticed before, not pizza, not beer, but something hot and musky and masculine. It wasn't the scent she remembered from her and Alex's long-ago make-out sessions—or not only that.

It was, she couldn't help thinking, the mingled arousal of both men.

In the time it took her to think this, her nipples went tight as nails. Lord, she should have taken two minutes to throw on a bra when she put Corky down. The urge to check if the men were looking was hard to resist, but she didn't dare. The best she could do was ignore how wet her panties had become.

"Speaking of gifted children?" she repeated, trying not to sound breathless but aware the pause had dragged out.

She did lift her gaze then, and, boy, she shouldn't have. Alex's laser-blue eyes were narrowed—maybe knowing or maybe suspicious—but definitely zeroed in on her. Already primed to react, her pussy creamed with a vengeance. If her body kept this up, her silky short shorts were going to have a wet spot.

"Speaking of that," he agreed, his eyes still on hers. "The intern we questioned remembers you being at the hospital the night Oscar was born. She said you were helping an elderly man cross over. I know five years is a long time, but anything you recall might help."

"If you give me the exact date, I'll check my calendar."

Alex gave it to her. Having no bonafide home office, she dug in her "business" drawer until she found the old Day-Minder. As she moved, her fears were confirmed. Her shorts were sticking to her panties at the crotch. Deciding some distance was called for, and careful not to show the men her back view, she leaned against the Spanish-tiled counter to flip through the pages.

"Okay," she said, thankful to have found the date. "April second was the night Mr. Marshall died. I remember sensing a lot of spirit activity around the hospital, but that's not unusual. I've never seen anyone transition without a good escort."

"Can you, um, summon this Marshall guy?" Bryan asked. "Maybe see what he remembers?"

Zoe laughed, liking him more and more. "It's very open-minded of you to ask, but I'm afraid it doesn't work that way for me. The spirit world comes to me because they want to talk to their loved ones, not because I ring them up. You know, though, now that I think back, something odd did happen that night. When I got home, there was a light show going on out by Fairy Falls: orbs of light in different colors dancing around. I could see them glowing all the way from my deck."

"Any idea what that means?" Alex asked.

"Not a clue. Fairy Falls is supposed to be a power vortex, but I've never noticed anything except how pretty and peaceful it is. I chalked up the light show to plain old Fairyville weirdness. I can ask my fairies, though, after you're gone."

Bryan's eyes went round. Apparently, Alex hadn't shared the "extra" aspect to her gift. To his credit, Alex's partner didn't say a word. He didn't even roll his eyes.

"Maybe we should go now," Alex said, rising awkwardly from the cluttered table. "Before Mrs. Fairfax locks us out."

"You . . . could stay here," Zoe offered hesitantly.

"No," both men said in unison.

"That's nice of you," Alex added, "but we don't want to put you out."

The fact that Alex had refused so quickly increased her sureness that they should stay. As long as both men were here, being a couple, she and Alex couldn't get into trouble on their own. Otherwise, trouble was exactly where she was headed. She couldn't have sat across from him for the last hour, struggling not to squirm each time he looked at her, and not know that.

"At least for tonight," she said more firmly. "You've both been drinking, enough that you shouldn't drive back to town. My guest room's clean, and it's got a bath. Plus, I can guarantee you a ghost-free night."

"No ghosts in the medium's house?" Bryan asked with a crooked smile.

"Nope. The angels and I clear 'em out. I like to unplug the switchboard when I come home."

"In that case, we'd be grateful to stay," Alex said. "For tonight."

His eyes were as blue as the jets beneath her gas burners. She couldn't count the times she'd watched them blazing down at her like that, sure in the knowledge that she'd say yes to whatever alternative to going all the way he'd decided he was going to let them try that night. She'd watched them burn even hotter over acts he'd longed to try but hadn't had the nerve to, for fear his control would snap. They'd flown close to the flame in those days, but never as close as either of them wanted.

Seeing that look again, feeling it turn her insides to molten lava, she had to wonder how she'd managed to stay a virgin for more than ten minutes after they'd met.

"I'll . . . just get fresh sheets," she said, too aroused to hide the huskiness in her voice.

"Thanks," Alex responded, his always gravelly baritone sunk to a level that sent chills rippling down her spine.

He wasn't unaffected by their lingering looks. He was thinking about unfinished business, too.

She was glad for the excuse to leave, blushing furiously as she was. To her surprise, both men turned to watch her when she passed the breakfast nook, their eyes like big, warm hands slipping down her skin. She'd been assuming Bryan was gay instead of bi, but perhaps she'd misjudged.

Oh, boy, she thought. Maybe having them stay here together wasn't the safest choice after all.

Eight

Zoe's guest room wasn't the personality-free box Bryan expected. On either side of the window, two mismatched iron bedsteads sat. They were draped with colorful antique quilts, each stacked with sufficient pillows for three people. A round braided rug lay on the hardwood floor, faded enough to have been washed many times. On the warm patina of the adobe walls an assortment of Native American baskets hung, their simple artistry offset by a rusted "Nu-Grape" sign. In the corner a skirted table held a sewing machine, evidence of what Zoe did in here. That one indication of functionality pointed up the truth even more.

This was a guest room for visitors she liked.

Oddly touched, Bryan propped his shoulder on the edge of the deep window, watching Zoe and Alex dress the beds in new sheets. Amusingly, both were blushing, both pointedly not asking whether they only needed to dress one. Seeing them practically vibrate with lust should have hurt him, should have reminded him of all those times in college when he'd watched Alex get hot and bothered over some girl. Instead, he felt a bit roasty himself.

He was staying tonight, and Zoe would leave. She wasn't going to creep in here at 2 a.m. and steal Alex away, because she wasn't that kind of woman. She knew he and Alex were together—though probably not how temporarily—and she was going to do her damnedest to respect that.

Suspecting this was going to drive her as crazy as it was driving Alex sent his blood thumping to his groin. Zoe was a hottie, as tempting in her way as Alex was. Those legs of hers were spectacular, those boyish hips and that high, tight ass. And—Lord—when she bent over to tuck in the sheets, he saw what Alex couldn't from the other side of the bed. Her silky green shorts were damp, right where the cloth stretched over her pussy.

It was enough to make Bryan's mouth water, to make his fingers curl into his palms with an urge to cup and squeeze her juicy little mound. If a woman like that wouldn't have asked him to swear off men, he'd have gone for her in a second. Heck, he'd have gone for half a dozen just like her and done his best to break Alex's record for female partners at one time.

He was smiling faintly at the thought while she made flustered hostess noises: mentions of fresh towels in the bathroom . . . if there was anything they needed . . . and she was afraid they'd be on their own for breakfast, because, apart from coffee, her pantry really was empty.

"We can drive into town to eat," Bryan assured her. "And, thank you. Everything is wonderful."

She nodded and wet her soft pink lips, her gaze sliding—probably against her will—to the bed Alex was standing by. "Well," she said, "have a good night."

And then it was just him and Alex and the heavy sensual tension Zoe's presence had left.

"So," said Bryan, his hands shoved into his back jeans pockets, his eyes on the now-closed door. "I'm surprised you two didn't set the sheets on fire making that bed."

"Shit," said Alex. "I didn't mean to— I just never got a chance to get over her."

"Hard to forget your first."

"She wasn't—"

Bryan turned in time to catch the rawness of the longing in Alex's face. He'd come around to the near side of the bed, the one Zoe had been tucking under.

"She wasn't my first. She was only fifteen when we were going out. I was eighteen, and my momma raised me to treat girls nice. I didn't think it would be right to take her, so I . . . refrained."

The word twisted his mouth, a bitter humor in his expression. Suddenly, Bryan did feel a pang tighten in his chest. "She's the one you think of when you want a threesome."

Alex sat heavily on the mattress. "I think of her all the time. I've never gotten over losing her." His shoulders sagged with weariness, his face too sad to bear.

Bryan swallowed, then said what he knew he had to. "She's not fifteen now, buddy. You want me to step aside?"

Alex shook his head. "It wouldn't matter. I want you, too."

Bryan released the breath he'd been holding, wondering if hearing Alex say this made him feel better. He sat beside his friend and colleague on the narrow bed, letting the brush of his arm warm the other man's. "I'm glad you want me, I really am, but you can't spend your whole life hating yourself for having different needs from other folks."

"I hate myself for hurting her. I loved her so much. I just don't understand how I could have done it."

Alex's confession sounded as if it hurt his throat. Bryan took his hand and held it loosely against his thigh. Unable to resist, he ran his thumb over the knuckles. Alex's palm was as smooth as if he scrubbed it with a pumice stone. "I think you should tell me what happened with this Coach Vickers. I think you need to get it off your chest."

Alex sighed. "I wish it were that easy, but I guess you might as well hear the tale from me."

The temperature had cooled enough to leave the windows open. Alex wanted nothing more than to close his eyes and forget everything in the soft, juniper-scented breeze.

"Lie back," Bryan said as if he knew. "It's easier to talk in the dark."

Alex kicked off his sandals and let Bryan turn off the lights. The bed was narrow, especially for two grown men, but it felt good to have Bryan stretch out beside him. Alex was on his back, his fingers laced on his belly. Bryan rolled onto his side and covered them with one hand.

"Whatever it is, I'm betting the statute of limitations has expired."

It never would for people like Mrs. Fairfax, but Alex began anyway. "I played football in high school. Quarterback. I could take a hit if I had to, and I had good instincts for how to use the rest of my team. When you play for a town called Fairyville, winning cuts down on a lot of teasing. I knew how to win, and since I was more outgoing then, I was popular."

"I can see how that would be the case." Bryan scooted down to settle his head in Alex's shoulder. It wasn't his usual careful gesture. It was trusting and relaxed, and it made a part of Alex relax as well.

"My friends had a nickname for me. They called me the Super Outer."

"The Super Outer?"

"A couple times, guys on the team who were . . . conflicted about their sexuality came to me for advice. I think it was partly me being a big brother figure, and partly because they hoped I'd admit I thought about guys that way myself and might offer to initiate them."

"And did you think about guys that way?"

Bryan shifted beside him, lying heavier against his side. The slight increase in pressure had Alex's ever-willing cock weighing heavier, too. Alex blew out a laugh.

"From the first time I gave myself a hand job, which was—I don't know—maybe at thirteen, it seemed like I thought about every erotic possibility under the sun. Everything was sexual to me: guys, girls, new leather seats in cars. Luckily for me, I looked more mature than I was. By the time I hit fifteen, girls were throwing themselves at me—older girls especially. My mother would have died if she'd known, but I was having regular sex with girls, more than once a week, at sixteen. It seemed easier to leave the nonstandard options to my fantasies."

"And then you met Coach Vickers?"

"Not quite. Then I met Zoe." Arousal spurted through him at the memory, changing his cock from heavy to stiff. Trapped by the cloth of his trousers, the head began to push down his leg. He lifted a knee to give it room, this sort of adjustment second nature to him. "The guidance office assigned her to tutor me in some stupid math crap I couldn't pass, and, God, I fell for her hard. She was cute and weird, and every time I looked at her, she blushed beet red. She'd barely kissed a boy before I met her. I knew she was too young for me, and way too innocent, but I couldn't make myself turn away from how much she liked me. It was one of those can't-eat, can't-sleep, can't-think-of-anything-but-you crushes. Just seeing her smile at me was a drug."

"So you gave up your harem for her."

Alex snorted. "I suppose you could call it a harem. Romantic genius that I was, I thought true love would cure me of wanting those other girls. I knew Zoe wouldn't believe I loved her if I kept seeing them, that she'd be so hurt if she heard about me cheating that she'd probably run away. The way she looked, she should have been tripping over would-be boyfriends, but she was too much of an oddball. I had no competition. There was nobody to keep me from having her but me."

Restless, Alex turned to face Bryan, their hands tangling together on the quilt. "We did everything I could think of short of intercourse and oral sex—well, short of oral sex on me."

Bryan chuckled. "You performed oral sex when you were in high school? I'm impressed."

"I would have done anything to make her happy. I didn't want her dying of frustration the way I was. The funny thing was, I was actually getting off more than usual, but nothing we did seemed to be enough. I was obsessed with going all the way—with getting my dick inside her pussy. I started looking at other girls again, started noticing everyone who gave me any sort of an eye. And *that's* when Assistant Coach Vickers hit my radar."

"He was gay?"

"He wasn't supposed to be. He was engaged to another teacher at the school, some pretty English teacher who'd started chasing him as soon as he got the job. I guess he wanted to be straight, because he let her get her hooks in, but the closer the date for the wedding came, the more I noticed him watching me. Tom was fresh out of college. Couldn't have been more than twenty-two. He was a good coach—a good guy who wasn't ready to admit what he was. He didn't do anything overt, just a little too much eye contact. When he offered to oversee a new weight-training regimen to increase my upper body strength, I knew his reason wasn't just to give his winning quarterback a stronger arm."

Sighing, Alex let his chin rest on Bryan's head. "I don't even know who made the first move. One minute he was spotting me at the players' gym after-hours, and the next we were rolling around the floor mat like animals, trying to rip off each others' clothes. I'd never done it with a man before, but—by God—Tom wasn't going to let me stop once we started.

"I remember him saying nothing but 'fuck me, oh God, fuck me' for at least five minutes, and it took that long to get me in. He was like, 'Just spit on it. Just push harder.' It was exciting to see anybody that desperate, and even with both of us being clueless, the sex was great. We blasted off like we were never going to have that kind of sex again—which was probably what Tom was afraid of, what with the wedding looming over him.

"I don't know how many times we did it that first night. I mean, we had to take a towel to the mats afterward. When we were both wrung out, Tom looked at me real intense and said, 'I'm going to be here again tomorrow night. You can meet me or not. It's up to you.'

"He never forced me, Bryan. Never made what was happening between us about my spot on the team. He just said, 'You can do this or not.' "

"And you wanted to do it?"

"At the time, it seemed the perfect solution. If anyone would keep what we did a secret, it was him. I could have a consenting partner to take the edge off what not quite having Zoe was doing to me, and Zoe wouldn't be hurt. I knew it was cheating. I just thought it was the lesser of evils."

Bryan wriggled upward until his face was on the pillow opposite Alex's. Their knees bumped together, and a thrill Alex didn't know how to quash slid up his thighs. His guilt didn't have much influence over his libido. He was so hard from telling this story he was aching.

"Somebody caught you."

"Somebody was bound to. We went at it like freaking bunnies once we broke the ice. We even did it a couple times in Tom's office, during school hours. I guess he thought he was going to get wanting men out of his system, and then be able to get married, but it didn't work that way. The more he had, the more he wanted and, Jesus, it felt good to have someone as crazed for sex as I was. I was finally getting all I needed. I was finally feeling relaxed.

"But you can't be that intimate with someone—even if you're only screwing—and not give off signals people can read. There was one kid on the team, kind of a borderline player who spent a lot of time on the bench. He was always half a minute late to practice, as if he wanted to be reprimanded so he could gripe about how unfair the coaches were. I had him pegged as a potential outee, but I think he was too jealous of my status to come to me. He spotted what was going on between me and the coach and decided he was going to get back at us both.

"He did a good job of it, too. One night he surprised us in the weight room, with a camera, no less. Then he got his outraged parents to bring a complaint to the school board that Coach Vickers had molested him."

"And you knew your coach couldn't have done it?"

"Oh, yeah. The kid gave times and places that the supposed incidents had occurred, and each time I knew Tom had been with me. This kid was lying through his teeth to get even. I don't know if he liked presenting me as Tom's victim, too, but I guess he figured I wouldn't admit I'd been willing. I was king of the school, in his mind. Why would I give that up?

"I'm ashamed to say that for a while he was right. I was terrified of what would happen to my life. My family was going to know. And Zoe. I didn't think I could face it. But people started talking about Coach Vickers deserving to go to jail or worse. I could see the lynch mob forming. His own players, guys he'd been really good to, wanted to beat the crap out of him. And Tom was protecting me. He wasn't saying what had really happened. He wasn't using me as his alibi. I knew I had to come forward."

Alex's eyes filled with tears at the memory. "My mother got me through it. I'd never known how strong she was until I told her the truth. She wouldn't let my brothers say a word. Not to mock me. Not to be pissed. She just said, 'We're a family, and we're going to help your little brother do what's right.' I think my dad was kind of stunned by how fierce she was."

"You were lucky to have her."

"Yes, I was."

Bryan was quiet for a moment. When he spoke, his thumb swept back and forth across Alex's hand. "I think I have to agree with Zoe. I don't understand why the town hated you. Yeah, they might have been freaked that their golden boy liked guys, but you did the right thing. The rest wasn't their business."

"Small towns think everything is their business, and they needed someone to blame. It didn't seem enough that Tom's career was ruined. People started to remember how lucky I was with women, how nobody seemed to be able to turn me down. I'd insisted the relationship had been consensual, and they got it into their heads that I was the aggressor, that I'd seduced a formerly heterosexual male and had infected him with my perversity. I went from golden boy to scapegoat within a week. My teammates were so angry about what they saw as my betrayal that I had to quit. And maybe they were right. Maybe Tom would have married and lived happily ever after if it weren't for me."

"Alex." Bryan's scold held a hint of laughter. "I know you're hot, but come on. Even if your coach never came out of the closet, he wouldn't have lived happily ever after. He'd simply have lived a lie that was more comfortable for everyone but him."

"Zoe never lied. I kept remembering that through the worst

of it. Zoe always was who she was, ghosts and fairies and all, no matter how uncomfortable that got."

"Alex, there are people in this world who are born with parts of their truth very clear to them. Trust me, though, everybody—even Zoe—struggles with something."

Alex couldn't speak. He could only hug Bryan tight to his chest. There was no softness to Bryan's muscles, no comforting give, but his hardness was exactly what Alex needed.

"Shh," said Bryan, rubbing his back.

"I don't want to hurt you," Alex choked out. "I don't deserve you any more than I did her."

Bryan kissed his ear and laughed. "Why don't you let me worry about that?"

Emotion swelled inside him in a great hot flood. He couldn't keep from turning his head, couldn't keep from claiming Bryan's mouth and kissing him deeply. Bryan's hold on him shifted to his butt, their groins sliding together as their legs found a tangled fit. Alex moaned at what the contact revealed.

Bryan was full and ready behind his jeans.

"Oh, thank God." Bryan broke free of the kiss with a breathless laugh. "I don't know if I should admit it, but that story made me really hot."

Not the least offended, Alex was already shoving Bryan's metal waist button through its hole. "Tell me what you want," he said, his cock practically screaming at him to hurry up. "Tell me how you want me to get you off."

Bryan gasped as his hand dug deeper and found skin. "Take me in the shower. I want to pretend you're coaching me."

Lust blazed through Alex in a searing wave, paralyzing him for a second before it jolted him into quick motion.

"I hope you mean that," he said, rolling off the bed to help Bryan up. " 'Cause right this second, I could 'coach' you straight through the tile."

Nine

The guest room was on the opposite end of the house from Zoe's bedroom, both the living room and kitchen lying between. There should have been privacy aplenty, but with the windows open and the night so clear, Zoe couldn't help but hear the escalating masculine groans.

Her guests were in the shower. Zoe knew this because the pipes in her sixty-year-old house always sounded like Niagara Falls. Sadly, the torrent wasn't loud enough to drown out the moans of rising pleasure-pain. Those were the kind of cries people made when they really, *really* wanted release. Given the somewhat twisted nature of her kinks, she didn't know whether to burrow under a pillow or listen harder. Alex and Bryan were screwing in her house, despite her and Alex's history, either so inconsiderate that it didn't occur to them to be quiet, or so overwhelmed by their needs that they'd forgotten to.

Zoe's hands clenched on the sheets like she meant to rip them, her own needs coiling tight inside. She was not going to let this get to her. She wasn't so pathetic that she was going to do herself while her old boyfriend did his lover. She didn't care how long it had been since she'd had a man. She was not turning Alex and Bryan into her masturbation aid.

Groaning, she turned onto her belly, her eyes screwed shut against the images in her mind. Was Alex as big and smooth as she remembered? Could Bryan get his friend's erection all the way into his mouth? Did Alex like being on top as much as he used to? She pulled a pillow over her head, then shoved it off as someone began to come. *Bryan*, she thought. She remembered how Alex sounded, and that wasn't it. Then Alex's strangled snarl split the darkness, and she knew she'd guessed correctly.

No more than a minute later, the noises started up again.

With a muffled curse, Zoe flopped onto her back. Kinks be damned. No way were Alex and Bryan spending another night.

A tap on her window had her sitting up with a gasp.

"Magnus! What are you doing here?"

The casement was open to catch the breeze. Her manager pushed up on his arms and swung one long leg inside, his yellow shoe just missing her houseplants. Zoe's heart began to beat faster as she yanked the sheets over her breasts. All she had on were a short-sleeved cotton T-shirt and clean panties.

A wish flew through her mind that she were wearing something small and slinky and feminine. She squashed it down with sheer force of will.

"I don't recall inviting you in," she said coolly.

"Well, lucky I'm not a vampire and you don't have to."

He was in her room then, him and his sullen attitude—which, considering how he'd treated her, showed a lot of nerve. He crossed his arms over his powerful chest. "You sent me home tonight because you didn't want to talk our problems through."

"And if I still don't want to?"

She must have been seeing him with more than ordinary

sight, because his eyes abruptly seemed to flare, green as phosphorus in the shadowed room.

"Fine with me. I'd rather show you how I feel."

For such a big man, he was unfairly fast. He moved too quickly for her to evade him, bounding onto her bed and pulling her to her knees. The sheet fell down her body with a hiss. She thought he'd kiss her, but all he gave her was a little shake.

"Your guests are rude," he said, "and obviously idiots."

"Yeah, well, *they* were invited."

He did kiss her then, and it was hot and angry and absolutely spine-melting. She knew she should have been madder than she was. Only a masochist would let him start this up with her again, especially with the reminder of a very similar mistake getting lucky in her guest bathroom. But when he kissed her with those heated satin lips, when he wrapped that incredible energy of his around her, her resistance shredded like tissue.

The things he did with his tongue, the way he downright fucked her with it, made her moan with hunger and grab his back. The arm he'd wrapped around her waist felt like it was all that held her up, but—oh—did it feel good doing it! He was pressing her against all his hardness—chest, groin, thighs—and if she hadn't been so weak-kneed from his exploration of her mouth, she'd have climbed high enough to rub more than her belly button against his target zone. The size and heat of his erection went to her head. It *was* a freaking python, and she wanted every inch of it. When he finally released her lips, the room was spinning.

"You're wearing your sneakers on my bed," she said faintly.

"Zoe." He made her name a synonym for exasperation. "Exactly how long do I have to kiss you before you forget to pay attention to things like that?"

Her heart was pounding hard enough to shake her breasts, her pussy aching with the need he'd twisted into something truly ferocious. Still, she tried to gather her pride. "I need more than kisses to forget how you left me hanging earlier."

He shook her again, his hands so large a tremor that wasn't exactly fear ran across her shoulders in an aftershock. Oh, she so didn't want to know he could get to her in more ways than he already had.

"I care about you Zoe," he said. "Whatever else you doubt, don't doubt that."

"I thought you didn't want to talk. I thought you wanted to show me." She tossed her head, and her hair fell out of its pins in a curling mass. What she could see of Magnus's face went grim.

"Oh, I'm going to show you, Zoe. I'm going to show you until you scream."

"Yeah?" she said. "You've had two years to show me. All I'm hearing now are more words."

He made a noise like a growl, which streaked straight from her ears to her sex. Then, with a swiftness that left no room for protest, he ripped her T-shirt up her body, over her head, and down her arms. Zoe was left gasping into her fallen hair. By the time she got it behind her again, Magnus's big, hot hands were covering her breasts. Her body stilled as he squeezed the small rounded flesh, whatever snippy retort she'd meant to fling forgotten in the pleasure of his energy tingling down the nerves that led from her nipples.

"So beautiful," he said in a tone of awe as he caressed her. "So fucking beautiful."

Her pussy creamed for him, overrunning her tender folds and ruining her fresh panties. Sadly, her pride wasn't any harder to dissolve.

"Magnus," she sighed, her voice all breath.

He lifted his gaze for one tight-wired, glittering perusal of her face before his seal-black lashes dipped again. He squeezed her nipples between his fingers, hard enough to make them pulse sharply. Then he bent to lick one tip slowly. His tongue felt like it was painting her in fire and ice, tickling, teasing, until every molecule of air sighed out of her lungs.

"Sighs are good," he breathed into her shivering flesh, "but I think you can do better than that for me."

She did better as soon as his mouth covered one aching peak. That wrenched a whimper from her throat. He was too damn good at this. She'd always been sensitive, but what he and his energy did to her was unreal. He rolled her nipple against his teeth and licked it, first around the areola and then the tip. He sucked her breasts like they were perfect, and he'd never tasted anything so good. His breath rushed damply against her skin as he mounded both within the circles of his hands, turning from one breast to the other as if he couldn't settle on his favorite. The greedy sounds he made had her squirming uncontrollably. Finally, he flicked her so quickly with the point of his tongue that her clit twitched wildly with sympathy.

The sensation almost tumbled into orgasm.

"My God, you're sexy," he said, breaking free to gasp and lower her to the covers. Since every muscle she possessed was in the process of going limp, his timing couldn't have been better.

He really was enough to make a woman lose her head, and Zoe was swiftly losing interest in keeping hers. Moaning, she thrust her hands into his thick black hair.

Her clutching him closer seemed to be his signal to advance. His right hand left her breast. She heard buttons popping and a zipper's rasp—*his* zipper. He grunted as he worked to tear off his shirt and jeans without releasing her.

Her heart rate jumped into higher gear. The sound of him wrestling from his clothes had to be the best thing she'd heard all night.

Determined to meet him on the other side of naked, she

wriggled out of her panties. He paused for a second when he realized what she was doing, then helped her pull them down her legs, his suckling now twice as strong as before. He was taking more of her in his mouth, was scraping her with the wider flat of his tongue.

Yes, she thought, arching helplessly toward him. *This is more like it.* She was on the edge again, so close to coming that the suspense was like a pre-climax.

The only problem was that her eagerness had discombobulated him. His funny yellow high-tops hung him up enough to curse against her breast. It seemed he'd forgotten to remove them before his jeans. Grinning at this sign that he was human and not a perfect sex machine, she slid one hand from its grip on his hair to his bare shoulder. She'd intended the caress to reassure him that he could take his time, but as soon as that smooth warm skin met her palm, she couldn't resist touching more.

Oh, this was a good male back. This was shifting muscle and hardness. This was velvet skin and big, strong ribs that expanded to fill his lungs. She slid her fingertips down his spine with a purr of pleasure, stopping only when she reached the rounded muscles of his clenching butt.

She needed both hands to admire that.

"Zoe," he said with a throatiness that delighted her. "You're distracting me."

"Mm," she said, not at all apologetic. "You feel so good."

She pulled his kiss up to her mouth again. He groaned when he obeyed her urging, his tongue tangling with hers, his hand moving down the length of her side. He'd been hovering over her, but now his palm flattened on the mattress as he eased his lower body down. Both his legs straddled one of hers, their hair and muscle a stark reminder of his maleness. She jerked when the heat of his erection met her thigh. He was naked. And huge. And throbbing like half his blood had run to his cock. He settled his balls against her carefully, and the intimacy of that one movement made her sigh blissfully.

"Oh, boy," she said. "Am I ready for you!"

His hand cruised up her body to mold her breast again, then changed direction to drag a trail of fire down her front. She could tell he was up against the edge of craziness with her. He was breathing like a steam train, and, God, his aura was strong. She felt like he was touching her even after his hand had passed.

Where his caress was headed was just as good. His fingers combed through her pubic curls, sliding deep between her legs to cover all her mound. That big hand of his was enough to make any female feel small. Maybe he liked the contrast, too, because first cupping squeeze drew a groan from him.

"You have no idea," he said, the words a match rasping on stone, "how long I've been ready for you."

His hand trembled when he said it, but he was lost in shadow above her. She wanted to believe him so much it hurt.

"Turn on the light," she said, giving in to the urge. "I need to see your face when you tell me something like that."

He hesitated, then reached past her for the bedside lamp. The bulb wasn't bright, but he took a moment to lift his head. For a second, all that hit her was how freaking beautiful he was. And then she saw. His eyes were sheened with tears, honest-to-goodness, ready-to-spill-over tears.

He was telling the truth. He had been yearning for her.

A shock ran through her to see it, along with wonder that he could feel so much without her knowing it.

"Why?" she asked, her hand rising to his cheek. The bruise from his fall was fading, the skin around it only slightly hot. "Why would you wait so long to be with me if you felt like this?"

He closed his eyes. "Please don't ask me that. Please just trust that I want you to be happy."

"Magnus . . ."

"Please." He kissed her, his lips as gentle as a dream on hers. His hand moved back to cup her pubis. The length of his fingers pressed just a little between her lips. Knowing how wet she was made this a tad embarrassing, but his hold felt oddly protective. "Please trust me."

She couldn't trust him, not quite, but she also couldn't turn away. If it was true . . . If he did care for her . . .

She gave her head a little shake. It would have been better if he hadn't turned serious. She could have kept her guard up, could have stayed just a bit angry.

He's going to break my heart, she thought, but she wrapped her arms around him anyway.

Quite possibly Magnus had been insane when he convinced himself to crash Zoe's party. He'd spent an hour pacing down his house's long window, fuming about her old boyfriend. Not once had he tried to calm himself. Not once had he asked the Will-Be for help. Decisions made under those conditions were bound to be rash, but he hadn't given a damn. He couldn't leave his beloved alone with two men, not when one of them was a changeling who knew more about what pleasured her than Magnus did.

Now he wondered what his rashness had gotten him into. Yes, it was wonderful to feel her hold him and to be spoken to sweetly again, but neither of these boons resolved anything.

The only promise he could give her was pleasure. The knowledge that she longed for more than pleasure nearly broke his heart. Of course, he couldn't doubt she wanted what he could offer. Her body wept for it, the pearly sleekness running into his cupping palm. Praying physical gratification would be enough, he returned his mouth to her small, ripe breasts—gentle, tender— and slid one careful finger into her channel.

She moaned for him, her spine rolling strongly with arousal, her hips coming up to drive him deeper. She was soft inside, was wet and swollen and tight. The feel of her was more than Magnus's fairy instincts could tolerate. Swollen to its limit, pain speared through his cock with its next hard throb. He clenched his jaw and ignored it. He couldn't risk sliding inside her even for a minute; other parts of her, but not this, not with her so blessedly ready to love him, not with her precious heart swimming in her eyes. He would spill himself the instant she came, and from the hungry kitten noises she was making, that wasn't going to be long.

"Shh," he whispered around her nipple. "Let's try a soft climax first."

He moved his finger inside her, searching blindly for the places where her energy burned strongest. Those would be nerve centers. He could feed his aura into them until the pleasure that sang through her swelled to a symphony.

She squirmed as he found the first bright spot, a sound of yearning breaking in her throat. Her nails dug into his back in a sort of panic. She probably wanted him to massage her clit, but he resisted the obvious. His intent wasn't to tease her, only to ease her into what he hoped would be a long, hot night of climaxes. With that in mind, he pressed a second finger inside her. The fit was snug enough to make him grit his teeth. God, what she'd feel like around him, creaming and twitching like she was now! Encouraged by her responsiveness, he sent a tendril of energy to connect what his mouth was doing at her breast to what his hand was doing in her pussy.

He knew the moment the circuit closed, because Zoe groaned and twisted her hips like she meant to screw his fingers right off his hand.

Yes, he thought, and as easy as that her orgasm broke.

She went for a good half minute, gasping for air as he coaxed her pleasure out and out. Her clear surprise at how strong the climax was delighted him. He smiled against her flushing breast, stroking her through her shudders, optimism spreading through him like sunshine. He could do this. *They* could do this. It was going to be all right. As her body calmed, he released her breast to whisper in her ear.

"How about another, love? I believe you mentioned you've got some lost time to make up for."

Lost time didn't begin to cover what Zoe had to make up for. She'd managed not to scream so far, but it had been close. She shook with pleasure, great, earth-shaking quakes as Magnus brought her to one aching peak after another. After so many orgasms, her need should have been exhausted, but it only built. Magnus's touch was magic: sweet and slow and unbelievably intense. He paid attention to everything, learning what she liked with a swiftness that was frightening. She was panting too hard to kiss him except in glances, but every part of him tasted good.

He jerked when she nipped the muscle of his bicep, and she knew she simply had to get him under her.

"It's time to finish this," she said, trying to push his big, beautiful body back onto the sheets. "I think I've still got a box of condoms in the bedside drawer."

He caught her wrist before she could check. "Touch me while I'm bare. I want your hand on my skin."

The plea halted her. Through all their play, he'd evaded her touches there, pleasuring her but taking little in return. She'd thought it might be because he had a quick trigger, but perhaps he simply liked to draw his lovemaking out. Perhaps restraining his own release was the secret to his sexual feats.

"Just my hand?" she asked slyly.

He leaned back cautiously, his shaggy, glossy hair spilling

onto her pillow in an arc of black. His long, tanned fingers slid up her arms. "Your hand is fine to start with. After that I'd like to run my cock all over your creamy skin."

She couldn't contain her anticipatory shudder. "Don't you ever want to come?"

His eyes darkened. "Oh, yes, but only after I've pulled every scrap of ecstasy out of you."

Magnus thought he could control himself. His kind were nothing if not sexually determined, and he'd had centuries of practice. Despite his lengthy experience, when her warm little hand wrapped his straining thickness and began to pull, he wished he'd let her cover him in the rubber.

It wouldn't have kept his magical contract from activating; all that required was releasing a burst of orgasmic energy inside her sex. The latex would, however, have prevented him from feeling every whorl of every fingerprint drag along his nerves. All fairies were susceptible to skin hunger, and Magnus had reached the state of arousal where the flutter of an eyelash was as potent as a sucking tongue. When Zoe gentled the palm of her hand around his testicles, he actually hallucinated, actually saw himself pushing her thighs apart and spearing her.

The vision was so vivid he could feel the Will-Be shivering. The dream would become reality if he didn't distract himself. The Will-Be would make him a puppet to his own desires.

"You're so big," she murmured as he jerked beneath her careful strokes, her thumb tracing the route of a thickened vein. "I know it sounds cliché, but I honestly don't know how you're going to fit."

Cliché or not, the words were sufficient to give him another technicolor flash of taking her. He could hear the sounds she would make, could feel the press of her heels behind his buttocks as she'd struggle to pull him in. He tried to push the image away, but she was bending toward him in truth, was softly pressing her lips to his weeping tip. Her mouth formed a circle around his rim, beginning to draw, beginning to create suction against the very nerves that could least stand it.

"Stop," he croaked as her tongue came out.

"Magnus?" she said, her voice very strange.

He'd blacked out for a second. He had to shake his head back into reality. When he returned, he felt as shocked as she looked. His hand was on her throat. It only held her off from going down on him, but it was in the same position as if he'd meant to strangle her.

"Sorry," he said, panting it. His cock was pulsing like a rabid animal inside her hand, his vision of taking her threatening to rise again. "Sorry." He forced his fingers to release her. "I wanted to be inside you, and I . . . Do you have any lubricant in that drawer?"

She stared at him, maybe sensing his evasion, maybe just amazed by his behavior. Her gaze was steady but wide. She should have been frightened, but he didn't think she was. She was breathing raggedly, shallow puffs of air that made her little breasts tremble. Her pupils were swollen, her cheeks stained red.

She looked like what he'd accidentally done had excited her.

If it had, she wasn't ready to discuss it. He wasn't either. Fairy males were naturally controlling. The idea that Zoe might enjoy letting him take charge of her in bed wasn't one he could afford to contemplate just then.

"Lubricant . . . sounds smart," she said breathlessly. "As big as you are, you might need a little help."

As wet as she was, he doubted it, but he wasn't intending to get inside her the way she thought.

"Give it to me," he said when she found it. "And

please—" He swallowed, meaning the *please* to soften the harshness of his request. "Please turn onto your stomach and wait for me."

She didn't argue. She turned and stretched her arms upward, wrapping her hands around the wrought iron vines and leaves that formed her headboard. The design reminded him of a garden his Aunt Elena had once spelled together for an orgy. Seeing Zoe lock her hands to the cold metal, playing submissive nymph to his satyr, had his cock jerking. Her curls were the ultimate in femininity as they spilled down her slender back, the image triggering reactions he could not control. His breath came faster as she turned her head over her shoulder and gazed at him knowingly.

Her soft gray eyes seemed to hold the keys to a hundred realms' mysteries.

"You'd like to tie me here," she said.

The guess was good enough to spur a shiver.

"Just keep your hands where they are," he said hoarsely. "Don't let go, and let me do as I please."

"You're finally going to please yourself?"

"Yes," he gritted out.

"Good," she said with great decisiveness. "I'm looking forward to feeling you go."

She meant this when she said it, and once she had, she really couldn't begrudge him whatever he wanted to do. All the same, she couldn't restrain a squeak of surprise as he nudged her body rather more rearward than she'd been planning on.

"Shh," he said, his hands gently parting her bottom cleft. "Trust me to make this good."

It was hard not to, considering the skill he'd shown so far, but Zoe felt quite the neophyte as his thumbs pushed lubricant into her ass. *He knows what he's doing,* she told herself. *This is going to be fine . . .*

"Pull your knees up," he said. "You're going to want to give me room to work."

Lord, even his arrogance was arousing. She let him guide her into position, each leg bent up and angled to the side. The change immediately allowed his thumbs to slide farther in.

Okay, maybe this was going to be more than fine. Her hands clenched harder on the iron headboard as her breath rushed out. The sensation of him massaging those outer inches was much more pleasurable than she'd expected.

"You've never done this before," he whispered, and she could only shake her head.

The idea of being her first didn't seem to daunt him. He lowered his head until his parted lips brushed her shoulder.

"Good," he said, deliberately echoing her. "I need to claim some part of you tonight."

He could claim any part of her he wanted, but she didn't get a chance to tell him so. He'd slipped his thumbs free just then and put his sheathed cock behind her instead.

Oh, God, she thought as she felt the intimidating broadness of the head, and, *Oh, God, yes* an instant later.

She groaned as he began to push, her neck arching back against him helplessly. He was so big, not just the part of him that was breaching her, but his entire body. She felt overshadowed—both protected by the shield of him and vulnerable to his strength. This man could crush her, but he was acting like he didn't want her to break. The sounds he made, grunts of effort and enjoyment, caused her sex to liquefy anew. He slid his forearm between her and the mattress, surrounding her pussy in his hold. When one long finger slid inside her from the front, the combination of his snug warm grip and the more traditional intrusion demolished her resistance.

Every part of her relaxed at once.

"Oh, yes," he said as his cock suddenly sank into her all the way. "Oh, yes, love, that's what I want."

The instant he reached full penetration it was exactly what she wanted, too. The sheer size of him conquered her, the pressure on that tingling interior skin. When he began to move, his strokes were so protracted she felt as if her nerves were being hypnotized. The front of him bore close against her with every roll of his hips, his velvet skin enthralling her, his free hand smoothing over her wherever it could reach. He was taking her with so much more than his cock, like a cat rubbing against her, skin and energy and tiny hairs prickling.

She began to gasp in time to his thrusts, her tension tightening until it hurt. He didn't have to speed up to increase the torment; he just pushed her and pushed her up against that wall of excitement without letting her slide back. Her clit became a separate entity, tortured by the very blood that caused it to distend. She felt him begin to tremble, but his shakes were nothing compared to hers. Desperate to go over, she wrenched her right hand from the headboard and wrapped it over his.

"Please," she said, pushing his fingers between her lips. "Please."

He made a sound, pained and harsh, and then he did move fast, so fast she suspected he'd been dying to all along. He came almost all the way out of her with each rough stroke and then all the way back in. Oh, she loved his size then, with a fervor that truly shocked. The swollen flare of his cockhead scraped all the nerves whose charm she was even then gaining respect for.

When his spearing finger moved in tandem with his cock, and his thumb found her aching clit, she couldn't help but fly apart. Pleasure was bombarding her from a thousand aching-sweet points at once. She cried out and crashed through the edge, the violence of her climax jerking her like a rag doll. The spasms tightened her around him as his body slapped hers harder and harder and at last stiffened like a board.

Electricity surged through her as he came, as if his aura were penetrating her in ways no physical body could. Her orgasm peaked higher as emotion welled. She felt such love, such gratitude and overwhelming joy. Magnus was beautiful beyond beauty, was kinder than kind. Nothing about him needed changing. He was perfect just as he was. Her skin felt like it could melt away beneath the blaze of her admiration. They would merge together in this pleasure. They would lose their bodies and truly be one.

"Zoe," he gasped against her neck.

The sound returned her to herself—or as close as she was getting in that moment. His hands were clenched possessively around her, one on her pussy and one on her breast. His breath sobbed in and out of him.

"It's all right," she slurred, her sensual lassitude nearly preventing speech. "Magnus, it's all right."

She expected him to collapse on her, wanted him to in the deepest, most nurturing part of her soul. Instead, he drew himself carefully away, hanging above her on hands and knees.

Fortunately, she was still glowing and couldn't mind. She wriggled around until she could look up at him from the cage he'd formed. He was bathed in sweat and shaking like a weary dog. She soothed his chest with her own trembling hands, loving every sign he carried of what they'd done.

"You didn't hurt me," she said. "I enjoyed that."

"Zoe." His voice was soft as her touch trailed to the limpness dangling between his legs. She rolled off the condom, heavy with his seed.

"You came a lot," she said, strangely aroused by the volume of his ejaculate. "Is this what happens when you hold back?"

She smoothed the wetness that remained on his skin, exploring him in this new state. His balls hung low now, loose in their sac, and his penis was so silky it seemed unreal. Her fingers could meet around his shaft now that he was smaller. She pulled the ring of them gently down his length, not wanting to hurt him if he was sensitive.

He said her name again, a little groan in it this time.

"I'm sorry," she apologized with a laugh. "I can't seem to stop touching on you. I could go again if that makes it better. I'm not sure I'm capable of coming anymore tonight, but I'd really, really love to have you in my pussy. I'd really love to feel you come inside me that way."

He pulled her hold from him, but not before she felt a fresh spurt of stiffness roll through his cock.

"Zoe," he said. "I can't do this with you now."

His cock seemed to think it could. He had leaned back from her onto his heels, and her view was clear. His erection wavered higher even as she watched, a miracle of human pneumatics.

She wriggled onto her elbows. "What do you mean, you can't?"

"I mean I'm not ready to have intercourse with you."

His expression was absolutely serious. Zoe felt her temper begin to rise. "You mean emotionally ready, right? Because the rest of you is looking like it's in the mood."

He closed his eyes for a long heartbeat. "There are things about myself I can't explain to you."

"And I guess that's because I'm so untrustworthy?"

"Zoe—"

"No, don't bother feeding me more lines." She sat up and hugged a pillow to her front, abruptly in need of the shield. "I know you haven't got vagina-phobia. As much as the local rumor mill blabbers about you, someone would have mentioned that."

"Zoe—"

"I'm your friend, Magnus, or I thought I have been for the last two years. Yes, I've been stupid enough to want more, but that doesn't mean I'll tolerate being treated like someone who can't be confided in. You know who I am. My character isn't a mystery. If your issues, whatever they are, are too intimate to share with me, you can just bundle them up and go."

His mouth opened again, but this time she interrupted him before her name could come out.

"I mean it. I think something special happened here tonight, but no amount of special is going to excuse you still holding back. I've had enough of men wanting to hide half of themselves from me. Come back when and if you're ready to get over that."

He swallowed, his Adam's apple jerking in his throat. She was glad to see she'd shaken him—though her satisfaction was premature.

"I need to think about this," he said, adding insult to an injury she'd thought was plenty deep enough.

"Fine," she said. "You go think."

She didn't call him back when he pulled on his clothes and climbed out her window, not even when he sent one last searching glance over his shoulder. Maybe he was sorry to be leaving, but that didn't fix what was wrong.

Growling with frustration, she threw her pillow across the room. What was wrong with her that she kept falling for these conflicted men? There seemed no point in guessing what Magnus's problem was. This whole mess only underscored how near to a stranger he really was. She'd never met his family or heard him mention their names. He'd never told her where he'd grown up, or gone to school, or what he'd done for work before he took up managing artists. Apart from knowing that he was cheerful, fabulous in bed, and possessed of occasionally odd taste in shoes, they might as well have met a week ago. Oh, she knew she held a higher place in his interest than his other protégés, but did having lunch a few times a week truly constitute friendship?

Right then, it didn't feel like it. Right then, it felt like she'd been deluded about everything.

The house was silent, lonelier somehow than if she'd been in it alone. Bryan and Alex were probably asleep, curled up together in sensual exhaustion, neither of them available to talk to her—even if confiding in them had been a good idea.

I want my cat, she thought, pushing out of bed to get him.

The irony that her one present comfort had come to her from Magnus wasn't lost on her.

Ten

Zoe's morning didn't seem destined to lift her mood. Yes, it was sunny and, yes, the heat index was reasonable, but the fairies were sulking over her having welcomed their two least favorite people into her home. Aside from a shimmer of presence around Corky, they didn't appear at all. Without their assistance, Zoe's hair did scary things when she blew it dry.

Alex and Bryan were long gone by the time she shuffled into the kitchen. Whether they were embarrassed by the noises they'd made the previous night or the ones she had, she didn't know. Their absence wouldn't have been so annoying if they'd left her more than a drip of coffee that wouldn't keep a flea awake. Half a stale bagel languished in her bread box, but of course her toaster was still on the fritz from Florabel's linguistic experiments.

"Love you, too," Zoe muttered to her absent friends.

Corky stretched and mewled as she tucked him into her handbag with what supplies she could scrounge up for him. He seemed to find his new container fascinating, sniffing at the woven straw with great interest.

"At least you're no trouble," she said to the now wide-eyed cat. He had, to her relief, already figured out the purpose of his newspapers.

She'd almost gotten on her way when Samuel popped into visibility before the door. He was still dressed like Robin Hood and had clearly come to her in a snit. His hands were planted on the hips of his leaf-green tunic, and his wings beat so fast the tiny feather in his tiny cap threatened to blow off.

"What's wrong?" she asked in exasperation. "None of your compadres want to talk to me, and you drew the short straw?"

"I gave you my name," he huffed. "And now you do this!"

"This?" Zoe attempted to sound more patient. A fairy's name was a sacred trust. Theoretically, it could be used to summon them against their will—though she wasn't sure the old lore applied to fairies as willful as Rajel's flock.

True or not, Samuel was milking her supposed betrayal for all it was worth. "Kittens don't need to go to work!"

"Kittens need to be fed, Samuel. By someone who can actually lift a box of kibble. And kittens need to bond with their owners, not just their fairy guardians."

"Your workplace is a bad environment. All sorts of riffraff go there!"

"I doubt Magnus will show up today, if that's what you're getting at."

Samuel could fit an awful lot of disapproval into a face no bigger than her fingernail. He did not, however, disappear at the mere mention of Magnus's name.

"You could come to work with us," she suggested, sensing an opening. "I'm planning to shop for Corky on my lunch hour."

"Petsmart?" Samuel breathed, his reverent tone suggesting this was akin to visiting the Louvre.

"With my credit card. Corky will be needing toys."

Samuel trembled with his inner conflict, obviously bursting to come along. Shopping, toys, and kittens were practically the Holy Grail of fairy fun. If you added music and dancing, you could win their loyalty for life.

"I'll join you at noon," Samuel finally snapped. "Possibly with a friend."

Well, that's progress, Zoe thought, and rubbed noses with Corky to celebrate.

As Zoe had predicted, Magnus wasn't at the gallery when she arrived, which left her both irritated and relieved. Since that snag in the fabric of her life was put off indefinitely, she settled Corky in her office with a pillow and a spool of thread she'd brought as a stopgap toy. The kitten seemed to think it was just as good as the store-bought kind, chasing it across her office like a small dervish. Seeing that he was happy, she composed herself for her first client.

Today that was Teresa Smallfoot. Blowing in with her usual brilliant smile, the café owner made herself even more welcome by plunking two tall mocha espressos on Zoe's reading table.

Since Teresa was a friend, Zoe allowed herself to moan with pleasure as she grabbed the closest container and took a slurping hit. The caffeine ran into her like liquid gold. "Teresa Smallfoot, you are a lifesaver."

"Not me." Teresa sat in the opposite armchair and smoothed her denim skirt down her knees. At her waist, a handmade turquoise and silver belt showed off how curvy her figure was. Her hair was perfect, as always, a straight and shining fall of black. Zoe suppressed a twinge of envy. She knew better than to think that if she'd looked more like Teresa and less like herself things would have ended any differently with Magnus.

"Well?" said Teresa. "Aren't you going to ask? Or is whatever happened to your hair this morning—which I only mention as a caring friend—affecting your usually sparkling wits?"

Zoe's hand flew to the ball of frizz she'd tried to minimize by braiding it. "My little friends went on strike this morning. This was the best I could do."

"The coffee," Teresa prodded patiently. "Aren't you going to ask about the coffee?"

"What about the coffee?"

Teresa laughed at her confusion. "The coffee comes to you courtesy of two secret admirers."

"*Two* secret admirers?"

Zoe hadn't known she had any admirers, but Teresa grinned in acknowledgment. "One blond, one dark, both tall and yummy. They came into my café this morning. Asked if I knew the woman who worked next door. When I admitted that I did, they said they owed you coffee."

"Oh, *them*," said Zoe, her cheeks going a little hot.

"You're blushing!" Teresa exclaimed. "This must be better than I thought. Just tell me you're not interested in the dark-haired one. You know I love bad boys."

"Actually, I think he goes for bad boys, too."

"Well, shoot," said Teresa with a full-lipped pout. "That wasn't showing on my radar. I was going to have Grandma Rose scope him out for me."

Zoe started to explain that Bryan might have no problem swinging Teresa's way, then shut her mouth. She told herself it was nothing to do with her niggling attraction to the man. Bryan was gone on Alex, and nobody—least of all her—needed to get in the middle of that.

"What?" said Teresa. "Not going to lecture me on asking dead people to run my life? I know they're not necessarily smarter than we are, but you gotta admit Grandma Rose's record is good."

"Your Grandma Rose probably gave good advice when she was alive. And she can see more from where she is. People who are nonphysical always have a broader view."

"So I *should* ask her for the inside track."

Zoe smiled at her friend's teasing. "She'll only tell you the same thing I'm going to. Right now, Bryan is too interested in Alex to play around."

"Alex," Teresa mused, leaning back in the comfy chair. "You mean *your* Alex? The one from high school who seduced the coach? Oh, my God. *That's* the devil's spawn Mrs. Fairfax was muttering about this morning! Thank heaven they didn't come in at the same time. That would have been a scene."

"We had the scene last night at the inn. When I went to banish Mrs. Fairfax's poltergeist."

"Do tell," said Teresa, now back on the edge of her seat.

"Don't you want your session?"

"Oh, no," Teresa said. "Your life is sounding way more interesting to me."

"It was interesting all right. I yelled at Mrs. Fairfax in front of a lobby full of her guests."

"You yelled at Mrs. Fairfax? That, um, fakely sweet old lady?"

"She's okay most of the time. She just hit a nerve for me last night. Alex didn't seduce that coach, not like people say. He's a decent person. The rest is none of their business."

Zoe knew how defensive she was acting when Teresa's expression turned sober. "You say that like you still have feelings for him."

Zoe grimaced. "I'm not sure what I feel about anyone today."

"Poor baby," Teresa crooned, her sympathy quick and free. "I take it things didn't go well with Magnus, either."

Zoe blinked to calm her burning eyes. The last thing she wanted was to talk about that. She wasn't certain Teresa would understand. As to that, she wasn't certain she did. "Let's just say it wasn't the seduction of the century."

"Men are creeps," Teresa declared. "All right, they're cute creeps, and they're handy for opening jars and kissing, but other than that, they can all go hang."

Zoe had to laugh at that. "This from a woman who'd fall in love every week if she had the chance."

"Being in love is great," Teresa admitted, then reached over to pat Zoe's hand. "At least Mr. Magnificent knows he has competition. He does know, right? That your old flame is back in town?"

"Oh, he knows," Zoe said. "And doesn't like it one bit."

"Well, that's good."

"Maybe. And maybe it just means everybody is going to get weird."

"This is Fairyville," Teresa reminded her. "If things didn't get weird, we wouldn't know what to do with ourselves."

Late that afternoon, as Alex approached Zoe's storefront, butterflies danced in his stomach. He knew his nervousness was a sign of trouble. He'd had all day to gird himself to face her—and never mind how gratifyingly eager Bryan had been to exhaust his "tension" the previous night. They'd slept the sleep of the dead afterward, waking refreshed and early to track down more hospital employees for interviews.

Those had all been dead ends, though a janitor had remembered Zoe being there. "That Miss Clare is a sweet, sweet girl," he'd said. "Before she passed, my momma had the Sight like she does. One night, Miss Clare and I sat in the cafeteria trading stories for two whole hours. My supervisor nearly fired me for coming back on shift so late, but I didn't care. Laughing with that Miss Clare made me feel like a boy again."

Alex didn't feel like a boy, or at least not like the boy he'd been. He was used to being confident with women, used to knowing most were happy with his company. With Zoe, he wasn't sure where he stood, or if he should care. He only knew the simple thought of seeing her had him breaking into a sweat.

Bryan wasn't there to act as buffer. He was hunting for a hotel that could put them up, both of them having decided that discretion was the better part of valor when it came to the Vista Inn. Bryan's absence increased Alex's anxiety *and* his arousal. If this went the way he hoped, he and Zoe would be alone together soon.

Don't be an idiot, he told himself as he yanked her street door open, causing a brisk jingle. *Just because she's forgiven you doesn't mean she'll hop into bed. Or that you should be considering inviting her to.*

Fifteen years was a lot of water under the bridge. Zoe had experience now, and a possible boyfriend, which could also be said about him.

Alex's face twisted. This thing with Bryan wasn't turning out as casual as he'd expected, certainly not on his side. He was forced to acknowledge—and not happily—that both Bryan and Zoe had his cock sitting up to beg. He was thickening as he stepped into the quiet, air-conditioned space, as if he were expecting to get lucky here. A murmur from behind the closed office door told him Zoe must be with a client. Considering the bitterness his expression probably held, it was just as well she wasn't out front to greet him.

He took a moment to compose himself and look around. Zoe's Reading Gallery, as the lettering on the window declared it, was as welcoming as her home. The antique floorboards were silver beneath his feet, the walls hung with local crafts and desert photographs. The old-fashioned junk shop furniture looked as if ghosts and clients would feel equally comfortable "sitting a spell" in it.

Alex smiled at that. This was a well thought out business. His little Zoe, once Fairyville's biggest misfit, had come into her own.

The sound of a door opening behind him turned him around.

"Hey," Zoe said from the threshold of her office. "I didn't expect to see you this afternoon."

She was cuddling her black and white kitten beneath her chin, the little fuzzball purring loud enough to hear across the room. It was a reaction Alex understood a bit too well; those were nice breasts Corky was snuggled up against. As if to add to the Norman Rockwell flavor of the moment, a ray of sunlight slanted in the window to strike her face, firing up a halo of dust motes around her head. The sight of her smiling softly between Corky's ears, the essence of who she was shining in her eyes, drew every drop of blood closer to his skin.

Alex knew the truth then. He would never get over being in love with her. Never tire of that hint of wryness in her sweetest smiles. Never stop yearning to connect with her. She was his first real love, and it was never going to be over.

His lungs went hollow at the revelation, and his voice broke slightly when he tried to speak.

"I . . . thought I'd see if you were free to visit Fairy Falls. So far the rest of our leads aren't panning out."

Zoe bit her lip for a tempting second, the pressure of her teeth on that plump pink cushion making him want a bite of it himself.

"I'm free," she said. "I just finished a phone consultation, my last appointment for the day. I'll get Corky's stuff together, and we can go."

"Great," he said. "I have a feeling this is going to help."

She raised her brows at him, a brief sardonic quirk that let him know she'd heard the things he hadn't meant to say as clearly as the things he had.

Magnus decided it was time to remember who and what he was, i.e., not a helpless human.

He'd gone on his usual rounds, checking in on his artists to make sure all was well with them. He loved his protégés. Their creativity amazed him, and he enjoyed nothing better than guiding them to shine a little brighter in the public eye—whether that meant underwriting new equipment or helping to arrange a show. As far as he was concerned, they did the deepest magic—for what was magic but creating something out of thin air? Some days, letting them know that was all his job required. Today, his heart hadn't been in the usual friendly exchanges. Today, his attention had been sucked away by the one gifted person he wasn't checking on.

He had nothing to say to Zoe he hadn't said last night, nothing to do that he hadn't done. Changelings weren't unheard of in the human realm. On any day, Zoe's world might harbor a few hundred. They fit in, more or less, because they didn't know what they were. But Magnus was something else. Magnus was an illegal alien, one with secrets. He didn't know what would happen if humans discovered his kind lived among them, or if they learned the trick to opening Fairy's door. Magnus trusted Zoe not to repeat anything he said, but his paranoid and power-hungry mother had only to fear humans might obtain this information, and extreme measures were the least of what she'd attempt.

Titania's ability to scry outside her realm might be iffy, but that was no reason for her son to throw caution to the winds. He wasn't exactly on her Most Trusted list since he'd escaped.

It was his misfortune to be the queen's only son, her only

hope of turning her line into a dynasty. Magnus's father had been an extraordinary power. Titania had married him to unite their formerly separate realms. When they'd divorced, Jovian had split the realms apart again, taking his people and his magic into what humans would have called an alternate universe. Ever since, Titania had dedicated herself to pressuring others—Magnus foremost among them—to compensate her for the loss.

The idea that he'd share his secrets with a human for the purpose of convincing that human to let him do what he needed to stay here for good would drive Titania insane.

Assuming, of course, that she wasn't insane already.

Magnus pressed his aching head between his palms. He stood barefoot in a special structure he'd added to his property several years ago. From the outside, it resembled a traditional sweat lodge. From the inside, it was a small round bunker lined over every surface, including the floor, with fluorite and amethyst. Magnus had more respect than Zoe for the power of stones. In his experience, they were wonderful focuses for intent. What he'd devised for this hideaway was a psychic shield, one that would bar even his mother's minions from entry.

He was glad for his foresight now. He didn't think it was co-incidence that an elemental had shown up at a local inn, especially when it had done so during another fairy's stay. Magnus knew the visitation had something to do with his mother, though precisely what he couldn't guess.

Leave that be for now, he told himself, trying to push away his concerns. Titania would show her hand eventually, and when she did, he'd figure out what to do.

Sufficient unto the day were the challenges thereof. Magnus couldn't scry into Fairy from the human realm at all; the magical ethers here were too thick. He could, however, peer into any place on Earth. Right now, he needed to know Zoe's state of mind, to understand what she was choosing before he could do the same.

It was trite perhaps, but he'd found a crystal ball worked best. Rolling his favorite clear quartz sphere over the fingers of his right hand, he sank to his knees on the fluorite floor. Once there, he folded his feet flat, turned his toes slightly in, and sat on his heels. The flashlight he'd laid beside him, a heavy model used by spelunkers, shot a beam of light that broke into a thousand shards against the purple walls. It was the perfect atmosphere for allowing one's mind to drift, for allowing one's eyes to play tricks and see what wasn't there.

He cradled the scrying ball between his palms, letting its weight rest on his thighs. His breath fell without effort into a calm rhythm. Almost at once, a rush of energy streaked up his spine, and a tingling like a funnel made of static opened in his head. He let his focus soften as he gazed at the ball.

"I wish to see Zoe Clare," he told the Will-Be.

Figures moved inside his crystal. A cat carried in a handbag. A woman. A tall man with sun-streaked hair. Zoe and Alex were walking outside her gallery, down the touristy stretch of Canyon Way. They looked like people who knew and liked each other well. The swing of their legs matched as if timed by a metronome.

Hellfire, Magnus thought, which caused the images to waver. Knowing he couldn't afford to lose his concentration, he blew away his anger.

"I am willing to be shown," he insisted, though he knew he might not like what he saw.

Liking it didn't matter. One lesson he had accepted from his mother was that information helped a person set an effective course. If Magnus hoped to keep Zoe, he had to understand what he stood against.

Eleven

They took Alex's nice brown Audi to Fairy Creek Canyon, parking at the overlook where, for as long as Zoe could remember, high school kids had made out. Today, all the slots but theirs were empty, horny teenagers apparently having better things to do while the sun was up. A broad hiking trail led them down into another world. Alex followed Zoe, the emergency blanket from his trunk slung over one arm—protection against the poison ivy that was the bane of this lush, green place.

"God," he said as they descended into cool, moist air. "I forgot how beautiful this is."

Compared to the scrubby pine woods or desert that covered most of the land around town, Fairy Canyon was an exotic oasis. The creek that ran through it was fed by the local aquifer. It narrowed during the summer but did not dry up. As a result, oak grew here and cypress and maples that would turn to flame in October. Moss padded the ground like fairy stepping stones. Zoe had to remind herself this wasn't a romantic date. They'd come to see what readings she could get off the falls, to see if she could shed light on the mystery surrounding Alex's client's son.

The falls announced their nearness with the steady rushing sound they made plunging down the rocks. Fairy Falls was no Niagara, but for Arizona it was tall and wide, booming slightly over the hollows that undercut the striated red sandstone. A poison-green pool met the waters' misty culmination, the color the result of a vigorous algae content and a lot of silt being stirred up. Only the bravest souls swam here, because the pool was known to be home to snakes and leeches, and the rocks were slippery enough to defeat experienced hikers. The caves behind the water also remained unexplored, being prone to rockfalls. Fairy Falls was strictly for admiring by eye—not that this was a great hardship.

"Wow," Alex exclaimed as they emerged through the veil of trees for their first clear look. "You can see how rumors started that this was the spot to scope out fairies."

Zoe could see it, though she'd never met a fairy here herself. Despite her own flock not seeming to like the place, the effect of the sun slanting through the leaves to strike rainbows off the misting water was magical. Birds and insects set up a steady chatter among the trees, their pleasant noise underscoring the peaceful stillness that lay beneath. A heron stalked farther down the stream, partially hidden by the bank's tall reeds.

Good hunting, Zoe thought, wishing him a meal he liked—a nice plump lizard or a juicy frog.

Alex startled her by tugging at her hand. The warm length of his fingers inspired a shiver of déjà vu. She'd loved holding hands with him when they were dating. Walking down the halls at school. Feeling for a little while as if she fit in.

"Sit," he said. "I've got to enjoy this for a few minutes. I missed this nature stuff in Phoenix."

He'd spread the blanket on a grassy spot near the pool. Zoe

set her purse beside it, which allowed Corky to bounce out like a jumping bean. Fortunately, she'd thought to buy him a teeny-tiny harness on her and Samuel's lunchtime shopping spree. Florabel had come to Petsmart as well, so perhaps there was a fairy romance in the offing. Zoe smiled as Corky chased a small white moth across the grass, losing his prize—and falling over—when he came to the end of his bright blue leash. Zoe was glad she'd already attached it to her purse handle, and gladder still that the purse was too heavy for the kitten to pull.

"Corky's fine," Alex said, tugging her hand again.

With a trepidation she couldn't avoid, Zoe accepted his help to sit, careful to smooth her skirt beneath her before she did. Alex's hand held on to hers a moment longer than it had to, seeming to pull away reluctantly. Heat slid through her, uninvited but unstoppable. Disconcerted, she pressed her lips together and looked at the falls.

She was here to work, and so was he. He had a boyfriend, and so did—well, she really didn't, but that was beside the point. Determined to do what she'd come here for, she blew out her breath and closed her eyes, trying to sense any remnants of supernatural events. She cast her memory back to how the falls had looked that night five years ago. Only the top of the canyon had been visible from her house. The colored spheres had danced in and out of the chasm, flirting with the stars. They must have been huge for her to see at that distance, maybe as big as cars.

Tell me, she thought to whatever spirits were listening. *Tell me what this has to do with Oscar Pruitt.*

Her insides got very quiet, the silence opening in her head and spreading out. She felt a pulsing beneath her thighs, coming up through the blanket from under the ground. The cadence was slow and steady, thick as honey but clear as sunshine. It carried a scent like wet leaves and earth, and its warmth seeped into her flesh, making her aware of how big this planet was. Perhaps it was an illusion, but she had the sense of tree roots reaching deep for water, of flowers straining toward their bees. She understood then that every living thing wished to grow in some way— to be taller or stronger or more fruitful. The thrumming of that universal drive coiled unexpectedly in her sex, the sudden unexpected tightening making her so wet so fast she gasped.

"What?" said Alex. "What did you see?"

Zoe blinked her eyes open and hoped her voice wouldn't sound too husky. "Um, there's a lot of earth energy around here."

"What does that mean?"

"That the Sierra Club should be really proud of us."

Alex swore under his breath.

"I can try again in a few minutes. Narrow my focus more on Oscar. That was just kind of unsettling. Maybe this spot *is* a power vortex."

And maybe reaching out for answers had activated it.

"Earth energy, huh?" Alex peered at her. Knowing she was flushed and unlikely to grow less so with him looking at her, she struggled not to evade his perusal too obviously.

"So," she said, hoping to nudge his thoughts from where she feared they were veering. "You remember Johnny Thurman?"

Alex leaned back on his hands, his legs stretched out in starched khaki trousers, his head turned to consider her. He wore a beautiful, European-styled business shirt. Even with the sleeves rolled up and the collar open, it fit so well it must have been custom-made. Alex had never been a slob, but his new adult polish increased her sense that she was out of her depth with him. Clearly, he was no hand-to-mouth PI. An expensive-looking Tag Heuer circled his left wrist with perfect casualness. The bone it rested on looked strong.

You're really losing it, she told herself, *if some man's wrist is pushing your buttons.*

When she began to think he was just going to stare at her, Alex finally spoke. "You'd be referring to my best friend and running back, Johnny Thurman—until he decided I was the devil incarnate who needed to be frozen out of my team."

"That's the one," Zoe said, relieved that he remembered what she was talking about. "He owns a firing range outside of town."

"Oh, great." Alex snorted. "Now I have to watch my back for a new reason."

"Everybody isn't like Mrs. Fairfax. I think he feels bad for helping run you out of town. He asks about you now and then. What you're up to. If you're okay. I tell him I only know what your mom tells me, but that seems to satisfy him."

Alex sat up straighter. "Johnny Thurman asks *you* about me?"

"Crazy, I know. Unlike you, I wasn't his favorite person."

"He hated your guts. I almost lost him as a friend when I started dating you."

Embarrassed, Zoe rubbed the side of her face. "That was because of what I did to him my second week of school."

"What did you do?"

"I'm only telling you because these days I don't think he'd mind if you knew."

Alex laughed softly at her foot dragging. "What did you do?"

"Actually, it was more what his dad did."

A funny look crossed Alex's face, superseding his amusement. "Johnny's dad was dead by the time we got to high school."

"Five years when I met him, according to him, and every day of those five years he'd been looking for someone who could give a message to his son. I spent my first week of freshman year being yelled at by this colonel guy whose son I'd never met, who I was pretty sure didn't want to hear from lowly little me. But the more I tried to ignore him, the louder he got. It was no wonder my classmates thought I was spacey. I barely heard a word anybody said until I gave in."

"What did he want you to tell Johnny?"

Zoe smiled at that. "To stop being a bully. Which I could have lived with, except the colonel told me all this other stuff about his son that I knew Johnny wouldn't want me privy to. Most ghosts are more considerate, but I guess Johnny's dad wanted to be sure his son couldn't blow me off. He didn't, either. Once Johnny knew his dad was watching everything he did—and I do mean *everything*—I never heard of him beating up another person. I think he hated me because that felt better than thanking me for bullying him into doing what he knew was right."

"Huh." Alex scratched the fine gold stubble on his jaw. "I always wondered what made Johnny straighten up. I have to admit I thought I'd finally gotten through to him about leaving the nerds alone."

"His dad did like you," Zoe was happy to say. "He thought you were a good influence. In fact, the colonel told me he tried to talk to you for a while. He thought you might be sensitive enough to hear."

Alex gave a shiver that was only part exaggerated. "Now you're giving me the willies."

"It's not an insult. You were sensitive enough to see I wasn't just a freak, despite most of your friends thinking that you were nuts."

"I'm not convinced I deserve much credit for that. I fell for you too hard to care what they thought."

He grinned as he said it, his lazy, wolfish smile, but Zoe wasn't sidetracked. "You always were hard on yourself. You never wanted to give yourself credit for being a good person."

Alex's smile faded. He drew a circle on the dull blue blanket between their hips. "I wasn't very good to you."

"Yes, you were. The bad part was only the end. The good parts were some of the best times I ever had. My own parents never made me feel as loved as you."

"Zoe, I—" He stopped, turning toward her like she'd turned to him, their knees bumping lightly through her gauzy skirt. Color suffused his down-turned face, rising up his strong, tanned throat. Zoe felt as if some power outside herself were tugging at her gaze. When it hit his groin, she couldn't miss how turned on he was. His erection looked like it was ready to tear right through the placket of his nice trousers.

She made an involuntary noise—hunger or apology. Alex looked up, his eyes a dark, swimming blue. For a second Zoe felt like she was falling.

"I can't talk to you like this," he said hoarsely. "I can't just . . ."

"Just?"

He shook himself, the motion turning into a shudder that ran across his broad shoulders. "I can't act like this is just you being nice and trying to help me let myself off the hook for being a shit to you. I don't feel nice with you next to me. I don't feel nice with all your sweetness shining in your eyes."

The pulse started up beneath her again, the earth's own heart reverberating in her pussy. "What do you feel?"

His pupils swelled at her hoarse whisper. "Like I want to push up that skirt and fuck you so hard we dig a trench in the grass. Like I want to do every fucking thing we didn't get a chance to when you were fifteen. And then I want to repeat them all about a thousand times. I want you, Zoe. There hasn't been a day—"

He broke off, his hands clenched on his thighs with white-knuckled force. "Look at me, Zoe. *This* is what I feel."

His fists framed his erection, and as she did what he asked, as she looked at him, she saw the straining arch swell thicker.

Instinct took over, not right or wrong, just pure primal reasoning. This was fair. He'd waited long enough, and this was fair. She bent to him, and he didn't stop her, just hissed in a surprised breath as she pressed her lips to that raging pole—gently, softly, treating his hard-on like a boo-boo her kiss could soothe.

"Zoe," he said, her name strangled. He hadn't moved—not to touch her, not to get away—as if the fate of the world hung on his muscles staying locked where they were. She braced her hands on his knees and kissed the bulge again, adding a dragging brush to her lips' soft press.

"Zoe, don't do that unless you mean for me to—"

He couldn't finish. When she sat back on her heels, a muscle ticked in his jaw.

"I mean for you to," she said.

He gasped for air like he'd been drowning, then grabbed her shoulders and pushed her onto her back so fast she got dizzy. Her legs sprawled as she toppled, and his knees found a home between them almost before she spread them wide enough.

He kissed her, his jaw pressing hers open for his tongue's smooth plunge. His weight came down hard into the notch of her thighs. Him being there felt so good, so right, that she didn't argue when he lifted off her far enough to tear off his belt. He yanked out his shirttail a second later, making short work of the buttons so he could strip it off all the way. His chest was gorgeous, hairier than she remembered, with a six-pack that could have graced the cover of *Men's Fitness*.

"Back pocket," he said, returning to grind that other steely hardness against her crotch. "Condoms in my wallet."

She had a second to change her mind, but she let it pass. He groaned as she pushed her hands into both back pockets, scratching her nails up his butt to pull the wallet out.

"Hurry," he said. "I'm working on fifteen years worth of dying here."

He had four condoms in his wallet, lubricated and extra thin, all of which spilled out of her hold when his hips found the perfect spot to roll against between her legs.

"Wow," she panted, fumbling to gather them back up while her pussy sang a thanks for the treatment it was getting. "That's . . . quite a stash you've got."

He groaned again and pivoted harder. "It's not enough for you. I swear I'm going to use them all."

She couldn't tease him for his ego. His face was too serious, his flush so dark his eyes appeared to glow. Still watching her, he reached between them to ease down his zipper, wincing at the task of working the teeth over that much pressure. Zoe's insides tightened in reaction.

Yes, you are going to use them all, she thought. *And I'm going to let you.*

He knew she was going to let him, not just because she didn't contradict him, but because a small, feminine smile was curving up the corners of her kiss-flushed lips. That smile sent such a whip of heat through his groin that he ripped down the last inch of his zipper and nicked himself.

"Shit," she said, though she rarely cursed. Her hand reached for the little spot of blood on his flange.

"Don't," he said, jerking back.

"But—"

"Don't. If you touch me, I'm going to go. I am too fucking close to the edge. Just hand me the condom and wait a sec."

He sat up to open it. On her elbows, she bit her lip and watched him roll it carefully over his throbbing length. He was too sensitive to play with himself at all, though women usually liked to watch him do that. He cursed silently as he struggled not to make it worse. This was as bad as he could remember being in a long time, his dick so hard and swollen it was trying to stand vertical. The rubber was a larger size, but it didn't cover him all the way.

"You grew," she said and pressed trembling fingers to her rosy lips. For a second he worried she was afraid, but then she said, "Oh, God, I'm going to enjoy this."

"Jesus," Alex said, suddenly so hot he feared the top of his head—make that both his heads—were going to come off. "Maybe you shouldn't talk too much, either."

Zoe laughed at that, obviously pleased by his desperate state. "You want to rip my panties, or should I pull them off?"

Another wave of heat seared through him.

"Pull them," he ordered when he caught his breath, flashing on the image of her wriggling them down her perfect legs a second before she actually did it.

"Oh, man," he moaned, his hands following hers down those silken muscles. "Oh, man, I need a case of condoms for you."

"How about if I do this? Will that mean you need two?" She pulled her skimpy eyelet top over her head, leaving nothing but a strappy white undershirt for modesty. The thin ribbed cotton wasn't modest now, clinging to every curve and hollow of her perky breasts. Her nipples were dark and swollen, peaked hard with arousal. Alex had never seen them that big. In fact, she looked lusher all over, her breasts like little hills instead of ripe peaches.

"Pull that off, too," he said, jerking his chin at the undershirt.

She blushed, but she did it, and then he absolutely had to lick his lips.

"One kiss," he said, his voice like gravel. "One kiss before I fucking have to get into you."

Her breasts were smooth as cream under his tongue, as warm as if she were fevered. She moaned at his first light pull, and he remembered how sensitive her nipples were. It was one *long* kiss then, one long, sucking kiss that made her squirm like an eel and dig her fingers into his hair. Her nipples got longer inside his mouth, rewarding every greedy flick of his tongue.

"Oh, now," she said, arching closer. "Please, Alex, come in me now."

He couldn't drag it out any longer. He rose from her, breathing hard, and fit his hips into the cradle they'd been dreaming of nearly every time he jacked off. For a moment, he let his cockhead rest against her labia.

That heated, slippery softness was a joy to take his time over, but even as he ground his teeth at the bliss of it, the weight of his erection sank him deeper into her folds. Her flesh gave way for him, her cream welling around him, her skin molding naturally to his crown. He felt her entrance beneath it, his aim truer than he'd known.

"Meant to be," he murmured as he shifted his angle the tiny bit it needed to go in. His entire body gathered for a good, hard shove.

"Wait!" she gasped, her hand coming to his breastbone to hold him off.

Alex shook with his effort not to do what every fiber of his being had been prepping for.

"Wait?" he said once his jaw unclenched. "I've been waiting fifteen years for this!"

"I just . . . it's been a while since I've had actual sex."

Her confession struck him as odd, but he wasn't sure he wanted an explanation of *actual sex* right then.

"Maybe," she suggested, "you could go in slow."

Clearly, Zoe had some idea of the difficulty of what she asked. Her cheeks had turned a shade of pink that neared red.

"And *after* I go in?" he growled.

Zoe's squirm of embarrassment did nothing to make obliging her easier.

"Maybe you could go slow for a few more strokes," she pleaded. "It's my favorite part. When a man pushes into me all the way. I want to feel it with you."

"If *that's* your favorite part, you've been sleeping with the wrong men."

He knew he sounded surly, but Zoe smiled.

"Try," she said, stroking his face. "Try for me."

He kissed her wrist, then nipped the skin lightly.

"I'll try. Now pull your knees up and give me room."

He should have known doing what she asked would kill him, but he wasn't sure it would have mattered. He loved pleasing Zoe, he always had. If she wanted a slow first thrust, he was damn well going to give it to her. Of course, he moaned before he even had the head inside her, a long, pained trail of sound. One inch went in, then two, and Zoe's hands began to push up his back.

Her touch made him shiver deliciously.

"Oh, yes," she crooned, stroking his straining muscles. "Oh, just like that."

She was slick around him, tight but welcoming, her inner muscles flickering without stopping him.

He moaned her name when he hit four inches, finally beginning to feel like he was inside her. Five made his neck arch, and six pulled his breath from him in a rush. He was really doing this. He was really sliding his aching dick inside Zoe.

At seven he started to have to work for room, but Zoe's fingernails were dragging tingling tracks up and down his spine, and he was highly motivated to keep going. Eight finished him, nearly in more ways than one. He was shoved in her to his root, throbbing tightly against her walls while her heels dug into the upper slopes of his ass. His balls were so ready to shoot it felt like they were trying to crawl into his abdomen.

They opened their eyes in the same instant. Zoe's were soft and glowing in their frame of black.

"Wow," she said, writhing slightly under his weight. The wriggle seemed part discomfort at his size, part eagerness to savor every inch. "That was worth waiting for."

"It's not over yet."

Her slow, hot smile might as well have been an injection of Viagra. Alex winced as he swelled to a state of hardness he hadn't known he could reach. "You promised me a few slow ones."

"I didn't promise, I said I'd try. And anyway, you could say please first."

She shook her head, outright grinning now. "You're such a control freak, I'm afraid you'd like me begging too much."

In all his fantasies, he hadn't expected her to make this fun. It occurred to him that she was teasing him like they were still friends.

"Okay," he said, his voice husky for more reasons than being insanely aroused. "I just want you to know my sex drive wasn't built for restraint."

Though this was truer than Zoe knew, he couldn't complain. Her groans of pleasure made the effort more than worthwhile. He managed to give her six slow strokes: six killing, breath-stealing strokes. He was up on his arms, his elbows locked to keep them from trembling. When she moaned "Oh, God" and started panting, he knew he'd reached the end of his rope.

"Can I go faster now?" he gasped.

"Oh, yes," she said. "And, please, go harder, too."

He barely had breath to laugh at her politeness, but he sucked in more before he let his body explode into the fucking it so badly wanted to give her.

She wailed at the first strong thrust, but it was an *oh, God, keep doing that so I can come* sort of sound. Alex clenched his jaw and kept going, pumping his thickness high against her passage, bumping her clit with each downstroke. He was hoping force of habit would keep him from hurting her, because his control was pretty much shot to hell. His body drove him faster, harder, ignoring her jerky rhythm to keep its own. Pleasure rose like a flood tide, until he didn't know how he could hold more. It felt like someone had turned the dial to maximum on his nerves. Every sensation was sweet and sharp: the squeeze of her pussy around his cock, the dig of her heels on his buttocks, the almost cutting prick of her nails. He nearly died himself when she came and her eyes went blind.

"Alex," she gasped, her body quaking, and he immediately wanted to send her up again.

Though he wanted to come bad enough to scream, he set his knees in the blanket and kicked his hips faster.

"Oh, God," she said, round-eyed and throaty voiced.

"Put your feet down," he snapped. "Let me take over."

She was too startled not to do it. He pulled her hands from behind his back, catching her wrists together and stretching them over her head. Her breasts arched higher on her ribs, shaking with his near violent thrusts. Her rosy nipples were making him crazy. He lowered his chest, braced on one forearm so the hot little pebbles could scrape his hair. He couldn't doubt she liked the hard treatment. Her belly jerked with her excitement, with her gasping, ragged breaths. He tightened his grip on her wrists, and the breaths got faster. Her eyes were wide, almost frightened but not quite. His blood surged like a dam breaking.

This was his fantasy. Her at his mercy, shaking helplessly with pleasure, letting him take her and take her until the beast that drove his body felt like fury as much as lust. He hadn't known the fury was there, but he could guess why. The Zoe he'd fallen in love with had let him go. He'd loved her with all his heart, and she'd let him go. It hadn't mattered what he'd done; he'd wanted her to fight for him. He wanted her to fight now.

"Alex!" she cried, almost screaming it as she came.

"I love you," he said, the words tearing from his throat. It was what he wanted her to say, but it was coming from his own mouth. "I love you. I love you."

He lost it completely with his next heartbeat. One second he was sobbing for breath and straining for the edge, and the next he was rocketing through the gates of bliss. The orgasm squeezed from him in jets of fire, over and over, like his whole body was trying to empty out. He held tight inside her, as far as he could reach, gasping at each spasm until he just plain couldn't come anymore.

He was dripping sweat, and her hands were stroking his hair, her lips pressed tenderly to his cheek. She kissed him like she loved him, but he knew better. Zoe Clare was the original open heart. If she'd felt what he did, she would have said it back.

"Hey," he said, striving to make light of his embarrassment. "I think we scared your cat. He crawled back into your purse."

Zoe didn't look away from him to check.

"Alex," she murmured, her lips reaching for his mouth.

He couldn't stop himself from kissing her. He should have been pulling out, getting a little distance, but he couldn't stop. Her hands were so sweet, so kind, her incredible legs coming back around his waist so that he started to swell again.

It was high school all over. He'd never get enough of her.

Shit, he thought. *I am so fucking screwed.*

They used all Alex's condoms in quick succession, barely pausing long enough for him to roll them off and on. The intensity with which he took her was undiminished, though he didn't say he loved her after that first time. Instead, he humped her with a fervor that was breathtaking. Admittedly, Zoe liked aggressive lovers, but nothing he did seemed truly rough to her. Yes, he enjoyed positions where he had control, but he didn't neglect her pleasure. In fact, he seemed to love pushing it higher. That said, he always reached a point in the final shafting part of the act where she knew it was all only about him. He went hard and fast then, completely focused on his drive for release.

He seemed to need each orgasm equally.

Zoe didn't think finally having her as his partner was the only reason. This felt like a puzzle piece she hadn't known to look for when she was fifteen. This was telling her that Alex really, *really* liked a lot of sex.

He let her roll him beneath her for the final bout, riding him so forcefully any other man would have protested. Alex simply gripped her hips and pulled her down harder.

Even when she was on top, he stayed in charge.

"Is this okay with you?" he panted. "Is this good?"

She was too busy coming to reassure him, her blood roaring in her ears, her body taking what it wanted with an abandon she didn't think she'd ever experienced.

He grunted, feeling her contractions, his face going grim and tight like it had every time right before he climaxed except the first. Then his face had been open. Then it had been both tender and furious.

What lay behind the change came to her clear as crystal. He was sorry he'd said he loved her. He regretted it because she hadn't said it back. She hadn't known what to make of his confession, thinking it was the heat of the moment talking. Now, though, seeing that her silence had caused him pain, her conscience jabbed at her to tell him she loved him, too.

No, she refused, swallowing the words. She wasn't going to do this, not with him and not with Magnus. She'd opened herself to Magnus last night only to have him reject her—the man she'd thought was different from Alex, the man she'd thought, at the least, could be trusted if he ever fell in love with her.

But neither man could be trusted. They were more alike than different, unable to give their hearts to any one person.

She cried out as Alex did something wicked with his fingers

on her swollen, cream-drenched clit. He'd found the little spot on the side that made her crazy, the one he'd discovered all those years ago in the back of his mother's car, the one so sensitive that rubbing it too early almost felt like pain. But it wasn't too early now. No, it was screamingly perfect.

"That's a . . . girl," he gasped, his fingers stiff with the closeness of his own climax. "One more time . . . with me."

His head jerked back on the rumpled blanket, his lips pulled snarling from his teeth. His hips snapped up and locked inside her as his cock grew thicker and began to pulse. Zoe's sex contracted around him at the same instant, as if their separate pleasures were being detonated by a single switch. It wasn't just energy that exploded inside her, but emotion, the same irrational burst of—well, *love* was a pale word for the adoration that swept through her—that she'd felt for Magnus the night before. In that moment when her orgasm blinded her earthly eyes, she knew that Alex was perfect just as he was. That she only had to love him, just as he was, and everything would turn out all right.

She was crying silently when she came out of it, two long, hot trickles running from the corners of her eyes. She swiped them away before Alex could see, easing her weight down carefully on his hips. He was still inside her, still hard, though not as hard as before.

He looked serious when he opened his Caribbean eyes— serious and wary.

Her heart gave a little spasm for the wariness, which she tried her best to ignore. She couldn't love him again, she couldn't, but she feared it would be easy. The slightest wavering of her guard, and she would be lost.

I am a stupid, stupid woman, she thought.

"You okay?" His palms slid carefully up her arms.

She nodded as steadily as she could. "Tired," she said. "That was quite a hurricane."

*   *   *

A hurricane was nothing to the storm that ripped through Magnus. His fists were trembling, the scrying ball fallen from his hold.

The fairy bastard had taken her—not once but four hard times—until she'd wept with pleasure at her last climax.

Alex had been shoved deep into her pussy, shoved by the strength of Zoe's own hips and thighs, shoved in that tight velvet sheath of flesh she'd been keeping—perhaps unknown to herself—untouched for Magnus for the last two years.

Magnus's prick should have been where Alex's was. Magnus was the one Zoe had a crush on, and Magnus loved her more than life itself. He would have been true to her had his fortunes allowed, would have made love to her and no one else. She had no idea how hard it was for one of his kind to have sex only once a month, but—to spare her feelings—he'd done it without complaint.

And now some other fairy knew how she felt inside. *Alex* had felt her sex clutch and cream around him. *Alex* had spilled his energy into her core. Barely two days after blowing back into her life, he'd done what Magnus would never, ever be able to.

At least not without losing her.

Magnus had been at war with his sexual requirements for far too long. He'd chained them with love and caring, but now he heard the sound of metal squealing with strain. His eyes glowed in the darkness, the furious burn of green the literal embodiment of his envy. He couldn't even tell Zoe the truth of what he'd done for her, for fear that knowing would endanger her. He had nothing to fight with, nothing to hope for.

Worst of all, he'd put himself in this position by invoking the particular magic he'd used to steal into the human realm. He couldn't even soothe his spirits by blaming someone else.

He threw his head back, roaring his frustration until his throat was raw, until the points of the purple crystals that lined the ceiling chimed the sound back to him.

He knew the tantrum wouldn't impress the Will-Be, but— just then—anger seemed a hell of a lot better than the helplessness he could have felt.

Twelve

Titania, Queen of all Fairy, strode through the pitch black cave with nothing but her glorious aura for radiance. Water roared behind the enchanted lapis lazuli wall ahead, an earth stone twisted from its natural state to guard this valuable portal.

In a moment, Titania would step through it, would leave her beautiful Fairy realm for that of humans. Entering that magically anemic place wasn't a pleasant prospect, but it needed doing. Magnus's location had been pinpointed, only the second time that had happened since he'd succumbed to his childish madness and run away. Though leaving her own world meant many of her spells would be rendered useless, she had to take this chance to speak to him herself.

The minion's report of how it had been foiled the first time had been predictably confused—elementals hated admitting to mistakes—but its failure was inarguable. Clearly, messages sent through others would not do. She needed to make her son understand how important it was to her that he come home, how much happier they both would be. Then surely he would see reason.

Beside her, Titania's minion made a snarling, hacking noise that was its idea of a polite cough. Illuminated, quite literally, by her beauty, the elemental was a lumpy fog of darkness wrapped around a sickly, greenish-yellow spark. The creature bowed from a spot that could have been its waist, its cavernous pseudo-eyes rolling upward to watch her face. Its not quite solid nature caused one socket to billow larger than the other.

"Your gloriousness," it said in a rolling profundo bass—but not as if it meant the compliment. "Do you wish me to accompany you into the chamber behind the falls?"

Titania frowned at the elemental, the falseness of its sycophancy making it even uglier to her eyes. Tracking fairies in the human world was difficult, in part because of the magical imbalance, but also because time ran differently between the realms. A delay of moments could mean a chance was missed. This creature had located Magnus, and that ought to have earned it the right to come along, but in Titania's opinion the elementals in her employ spent too much time spying on humans. They were, she had discovered, beginning to ape them in little ways—this less than perfect respect for her supremacy being one of them.

"Thank you for offering," she said. It would have been better to use the creature's name, more binding, but unfortunately all her minions looked the same to her. "I prefer privacy tonight."

The minion bowed even deeper and backed away, its smokey, amorphous face shading into an expression that could have been a smirk. Possibly it knew how little she was looking forward to the task ahead.

Titania pretended not to see the reaction, refusing to waste time quibbling with his sort. The elemental was her creature, magically bound to her will. That was all she needed to know.

In any case, this was *her* door. The elementals had their ghostly hot spots to work their mischief through, and that was more than good enough for them. As queen, no one but she had the right to access this ancient entryway. Had she been able, she would have barred it from being used to transfer changelings, but that was an old tradition, a magic set up long before she won the throne. If she discontinued it, the other royals in her realm would be up in arms. They liked adopting humans; said their unpredictability added "spice" to the process of parenting.

Titania snorted to herself. Her own son was pure fairy, descended from the best bloodlines, and in the century or so since he'd been born, she'd found him quite unpredictable enough.

Satisfied that the minion had really left and wasn't lurking disembodied in a shadow, she flicked her hands at the enchanted wall and willed it to collapse. Air rushed inward, carrying the nasty green scent of water that supported too many living things. *Human gardeners have no discipline,* she thought, but a moment later her lip curled even harder in distaste. Hot on the heels of the waters' smell came the even more offensive essence of fairy sweat mingling with human.

Her son *was* here, exactly as the minion said, and he was copulating with a native. Shuddering in disgust, she moved closer to the curtain of falling water. Already, she could feel her queenly magic beginning to leach away. Despite the stay-put spell on her slippers, she almost slid on the wet sandstone.

I will be quick, she promised herself. *One quick preemptive strike to let him know I mean business.*

That she had to be quick before too much of her magic faded she chose not to dwell upon.

With a spine as straight as any queen had ever boasted, Titania took a good grip on a crevice in the rock and leaned through the icy water. She couldn't lean too far because the current was forceful, and, consequently, the mist obscured her vision. Even more annoying was the fact that, with her head in the human realm, she was forced to rely on purely physical sight. These handicaps aside, Titania didn't need her usual 20-200 vision to identify what had been going on.

A human woman straddled her son's loins, blocking Titania's view of his face. Her frizzy black human hair fell in a braid down her slender back. Her shape was pretty from the rear, but nothing said a human couldn't be tolerably attractive. Some of them cleaned up well enough when raised in Fairy.

Titania's mouth formed a thin, hard line as Magnus's hands came up to frame the woman's face. This was a tender gesture, one that spoke of love and care, and Titania knew all too well what sort of weakness "love and care" led to.

A ruler could lose half her world from weaknesses like that.

I can spare you that, my son, she thought, *and by all that's magic I intend to.*

Alex's hands came up to clasp Zoe's face. Even if she didn't love him, he couldn't stand to see her look sad.

"I'm sorry," she said, her lashes falling to hide her eyes. "I should be brave enough to do this."

A pair of high-pitched shrieks stalled his question about what she needed bravery for. The squeals of terror—if that's what they were—seemed to come from the direction of Zoe's purse. Alex couldn't turn very far with his cock still lodged soft and cozy inside her pussy. Reluctant to lose his mooring, if not to admit that he was, he craned around as well as he could. Corky's pointy white-tipped tail was sticking out between the handbag's handles. Though it was twitching unhappily, Alex didn't think that squeal was a sound a kitten could have produced.

"What the hell was that?" he asked.

Zoe covered her mouth. "I think it must have been my fairies."

"Your fairies are *here*? While I am, too?"

This had never happened in all the time he'd known her. In truth, her fairies avoided him so well that Alex wasn't completely sure they were real. His heart pounded harder at the possibility that they were.

"They like Corky," Zoe said, her fingers still to her lips.

"They must like him a lot."

To his amazement, two fat tears rolled from Zoe's eyes.

"Hey," he said, cupping her face again. "I don't think you have to cry about that."

"I'm not," she said in a wobbly voice.

Alex's heart began to break for reasons he couldn't name. "Zoe, it's all right," he said, gently stroking her cheeks. "We had sex. Okay, we had a lot of sex, but it doesn't have to mean any more than that. Not if you don't want it to."

Zoe swiped her forearm across her eyes. "Right. It means whatever we say it does."

"Exactly." His attention narrowed on a spot behind her naked shoulder. "Well. That's different."

"What is?" she asked, having the same trouble turning that he'd had.

"The falls appear to be blowing bubbles."

He saw at least a dozen bobbing in the turbulent air above the fall's green pool—big rainbow-slicked spheres with what looked like oily black smoke curling inside them. He'd seen street performers blow this kind of thing at fairs, but he'd never felt like he wanted to get away from them.

"Hm," he said, unable to push his instinctive aversion off. "Maybe you ought to put your shirt back on."

He helped her rise, wanting to be gentle but wanting to

hurry, too. He winced as his penis lost her body's warmth, then pulled off the rubber with a muffled curse.

It was probably his imagination, but three bubbles looked like they were breaking off from the others to drift toward Alex and Zoe—which was impossible when he thought about it, because wasn't the breeze blowing in the *opposite* direction?

"Here," he said, struggling to free the blanket from under their feet. "If someone's coming, you should wear this."

He was too late. The damn bubbles sped up as if they knew he was trying to shield her. Two burst on her shoulder before he could pull her behind him.

"Ugh," said Zoe as a third actually followed her around him and burst in her face. The smoke clung to her skin for a second, like a ghostly squid had latched onto her. Then—hard as it was to credit—the smoke seemed to disappear into her pores. Zoe scrubbed at her face with the shirt he'd finally handed her.

"Doesn't that figure," she said in a disgusted tone. "Someone blows a bubble full of nastiness, and it breaks on me. My life is just too crappy for words!"

"Of course it's not," Alex said, amazed to hear her speak this way.

Zoe's mouth twisted. "It's true. The world is a dark, dark place. Full of liars and disappointment. Full of more crap than any person should have to take. I don't know why I didn't see it before. I must have been too stupid, too weak and stupid to face the truth. Nobody can help us. Not angels. Not fairies. Assuming they weren't some delusion I made up. Anyway, they don't care. They're hiding in my freaking purse. We're stuck out here in the crap pile all by ourselves."

"Zoe!" Alex said in shock, gripping her shoulders in the hope of shaking her out of whatever strange fit this was. "You know you don't believe that. You always look on the bright side!"

"Puke the bright side," she said.

Alex was trying to get beyond a wordless stammer when every hair on his nape stood up.

It's time to come home, son, said a voice that ran into his ears like acid.

Alex spun in a circle to see where the speaker was, but everywhere and nowhere was the best he could guess. Even Zoe's purse, which was now wriggling in a truly disturbing fashion, didn't seem to be the source of the sound.

"Did you hear that?" he asked Zoe, goose bumps chasing across his skin. "It sounded like someone was talking right in my ear."

Zoe wrinkled her nose and shook her head doubtfully.

You can't keep her, the voice continued. *I'm not going to let this human be the ball and chain that traps you here.*

With no one visible to speak to, Alex turned to the pack of beachball-size bubbles bobbing by the falls. "What the fuck are you talking about?"

Don't bother pretending. I saw the way you touched her. I know you think you care.

"I do care. But I have no idea why you do."

Zoe clutched his arm, her eyes round with a fear that belonged to her no more than her earlier self-disgust. This, after all, was the woman who'd faced a room full of falling rocks without turning a hair. "Alex, who are you talking to?"

"You don't hear that?"

She can't hear what's meant for the ears of our kind alone. Let her go, Magnus, or I'll make sure there's nothing left of her to care about. Take a good look in her eyes. You can see the woman you love is already slipping away. What do you think will happen if I loose the rest of my spells on her? Who will she be when all her confidence is gone?

"No!" yelled a voice so shrill it made his teeth ache. Alex's heart nearly had a spasm. A tiny winged man, no bigger than his finger, had popped into the air in front of him. Alex blinked hard, but he was still there. He was wearing a little green outfit and waving a sword.

"You can't harm our Zoe!" he cried. "Florrie, go call the queen!"

Omigod, Alex thought, staggering back a step from this vision. *They* are *real.*

He had no chance to catch his breath, because an instant later the air was filled with hundreds of fairies, their wings buzzing like a horde of bees as they flew in perfect formation. They all carried tiny swords, as if they'd raided a cocktail party of frou-frou drinks—except that these swords weren't colored plastic. These swords were shining stingers of steel.

"To me!" cried a lovely soprano from the vanguard of the attacking force. "We must break the spell bubbles with our swords."

They dive-bombed the things en masse, darting in and away so quickly not a single fairy was splashed. Despite their success, Alex could see the danger wasn't over. Once the bubbles were broken, the dark smoke remained, coiling together in an angry mass.

An oily claw of vapor reached out for the nearest jewel-colored Tinkerbell, missing her by inches.

"Sing!" ordered the soprano fairy, the queen to judge by her twinkling crown. "Black magic cannot withstand the sound of fairy joy."

At once the fairies burst into song, and it was as if the most beautiful boys and girls choir the universe had ever known were singing the most beautiful music ever composed. Alex began to weep at the sound of it. If the voice he'd heard behind the falls had been acid, this was pure love, the kind of love that didn't know how to be disappointed, the kind that loved for the simple pleasure of being loving, the kind that asked nothing except to be allowed to love more. He found himself wishing his mother were there to hear it. She'd understand why his soul was flying. She'd understand why this felt like home.

He opened his mouth, and a note came out, not a song, just a note that opened his whole body—his throat, his heart, the channels of energy that ran down his legs—as if he'd rooted in the earth and drawn up its power. The tingle of it streaming through him was almost painful.

A screech of outrage cut through the sparkle-clouded air, too harsh to have come from Zoe's fairies.

This isn't over, warned the voice behind the falls. *You won't get away with betraying your liege again!*

Happily, the voice appeared to be mistaken. As the fairies' song continued, the smoke shrank to the size of a pea and then disappeared, which caused a concerted shout of triumph to burst out from Zoe's rescuers. The noise sounded like The Chipmunks winning the Superbowl.

Alex was still reeling from all he'd seen when the fairy with the purple wings and the yellow crown left the celebration to fly up to him.

She hovered no more than a foot away, twinkling like some acid-induced Disney hallucination, studying him with an intensity that left him tongue-tied. His face felt odd where his tears were drying, but he didn't bother to wipe them off, not when his measure was being taken by something that might be able to turn him into Mickey Mouse.

"You sang with us," the fairy finally said in a musing tone. "That was considerate. You may have my name if you like."

"I would be honored," he said a little breathlessly.

Apparently, this was the correct response. She nodded regally. "I am Queen Rajel. You may call on me if you need help."

"I think maybe Zoe does."

Zoe was looking dazed. Queen Rajel flew up and down and

around her body like a dragonfly physician—studying her aura, Alex supposed. Zoe didn't move except to rub her eyes.

"She will recover," the queen pronounced once she was finished. "She didn't soak up enough of the doubt spell for it to last. If she hadn't had a weak spot, it wouldn't have affected her this much." She darted back to Alex's face and peered at him sternly. "You must tell her what the evil one said to you. Our Zoe needs to be warned."

"I will," Alex said, "but who was—"

He was talking to empty air. Every fairy in the glade had vanished simultaneously.

Boy, Alex thought, unable to form a single thought more rational than that.

Zoe tried to remember what had happened after she and Alex made love, but her mind was fuzzy, as if she'd been woken too abruptly from a troubling dream. She remembered seeing the bubbles, and Alex shaking her, and a terrible ache like an unsuspected wound opening in her chest. Hurt had issued from it dark as oil smoke to blot out the sky.

She was a stupid, stupid woman. Couldn't even fall in love with a man who wouldn't break her heart.

"Zoe." Alex squeezed her wrist. They sat in his Audi outside her gallery. Corky was cuddled against her breasts, his cold pink nose tickling her throat. His purr was a low vibration under her stroking fingers, much more comforting than her thoughts. Alex turned off the car's engine.

She didn't remember him driving here. She'd been lost in that awful dream where the whole world seemed horrible. She rubbed one hand uncomfortably down her thigh, like she had something stuck to her energy that needed peeling off.

"You should take a shower," Alex said. "Use that sea salt scrub you used to like."

It was exactly what she'd have thought of if she'd been in her right mind. The crystals in the sea salt cleansed more than the body.

"I will," she said, and began to open the door.

"Wait," said Alex, stopping her. When she settled back in the leather seat, his expression turned sheepish. "Your, um, fairies told me to make sure you knew what I'd heard."

The idea that her fairies had been speaking to him was almost as strange as the tale he told. Zoe felt her eyes getting wider, but at least her amazement was serving to clear her mind.

"You're certain the name the voice called was *Magnus?*"

"I'm certain, and there can't be that many Magnuses here-abouts. She also called him her son."

Zoe pinched her lip. "I don't know if Magnus's mother is alive or dead."

"You think this might be a ghost?"

"I don't know. I didn't think a poltergeist could fill a room with rocks. Maybe I've been underestimating what the local spirits can do."

"Please don't start calling yourself stupid again."

He looked so worried she had to be amused. "I won't. Though I do wish I'd seen Queen Rajel and her troops attack. That must have been a sight with all their little swords."

"It was." He rubbed his chin on the back of his hand. "I feel like I ought to be apologizing. I mean, I always believed you were talking to something when you talked to fairies. I just didn't know they were really . . . *fairies.*"

Zoe smiled at his consternation. "I should go. Take that shower." She hesitated. "Will you and Bryan be okay at the inn?"

Alex's face flushed a shade darker. "Bryan is looking for a new hotel. I told him I'd meet him at the Longhorn Grill after I saw you."

"He's liable to guess what happened between us, you know."

"I know."

"He's also liable not to like it, in case you hadn't figured out how serious he is about you."

Alex gripped the wheel and stared straight ahead. "I know that, too." The skin across his knuckles whitened. "I'm sorry, Zoe. I always seem to get what ought to be simple tangled up."

Zoe sighed quietly. If she'd doubted Alex was hung up on Bryan, too, she couldn't now.

"It's all right," she said, reaching for the door handle. "It's not like I know what I want, either."

By the time Zoe walked back to her own car, she realized there was one thing she knew she wanted: straight answers from her manager.

Refusing to consider whether getting them was a good idea, she drove to Magnus's Earth-friendly earthship house. She'd only been here once before, for a wine and Cheetos party he'd thrown for his protégés. It had been their first Halloween together, about a month after he'd started managing her. Magnus had been a little high on salsa music and Mexican beer. He'd danced with her in the moonlight with the red rocks stretching out on the horizon and the other guests laughing inside. He'd called her a fairy princess and threatened to lock her in a magic pumpkin so he could keep her all to himself. His words had seemed more silliness than flirtation, but if Zoe could date her crush on him to any moment, that was the one. He'd made her feel special. Not strange. Not gifted. Just special.

Of course, it had been some other woman he'd spent the next full moon with.

She tried to wipe the memory from her face as she proceeded up his succulent-lined walk. She didn't need to be thinking about why she was an idiot when she faced him.

His thick front door swung open at her knock. Surprised that he'd be letting his nice cool air out, Zoe called his name and walked into his long glassed hall. The combined living room and kitchen opened to her left, its ceiling slanting up fifteen feet to meet the tall windows. Magnus sat on a bright blue, modern couch in its shadowed rear, his torso canted over his sprawled knees. He looked up as she entered, but didn't speak.

Strangely, Zoe found she couldn't speak, either. Magnus didn't look like himself. Oh, he was still handsome, still sexy enough to make her grind her teeth against the unfairness of the universe, but the crackling energy that made him *him* had obviously sunk to a depressed ebb. As she approached, she saw he was flipping a DVD case for *The Simpsons* over and over in his hands, as if the thought of putting the disc into the player and possibly laughing was too much for him.

Even more telling, a pint of Ben and Jerry's ice cream was melting into soup on the coffee table next to his brass replica of Aladdin's lamp. Magnus was a junk food junkie, but the spoon didn't even look like he'd picked it up.

When she was close enough to have touched him, he sagged back into the couch. His eyes were hollow, his five o'clock bristle way darker than Alex's. Zoe didn't think she'd ever seen him unshaven. Her insides squirmed with interest, which—after the rather remarkable boinkfest she'd had with Alex—made her want to eat that ice cream herself.

No one who'd refused to have actual sex with her should have the right to look that mouth-wateringly masculine.

She supposed her expression wasn't the friendliest. Magnus stared at her for a long, tired moment before his chest lifted on a sigh. "I have nothing to say to you," he said. "I wish I did, but I don't."

"Why don't you wait until I ask my questions first."

"As you wish." He threw *The Simpsons* listlessly onto the cushion beside him, the opposite of an invitation to sit.

"Fine," Zoe said, ignoring the twinge of hurt. "We don't have to pretend this is fun. I simply need to ask you about a weird experience Alex and I had at Fairy Falls."

"A 'weird experience'? Is that what they're calling wild sex these days?"

Zoe's breath caught in her throat, not only at the accuracy of his guess but at the bitterness of the anger flashing in his eyes. "Okay, I'm not going to ask how you know that, or why you think it's your business, but I need to know if your mother is alive or dead, and if she's dead, I need to know if she passed in some gruesome fashion, because if Alex and I met her spirit, it's seriously pissed."

Magnus was on his feet before she'd finished, his hands pressed trembling to either side of her head. "Oh, God," he said. "Are you all right?"

If she'd understood the reason for it, this level of concern might have been flattering.

"I'm fine," she said, shaking him off. Talking about cursed bubbles seemed ridiculous, so she let that lie. "I'm just confused. Why would your dead mother want you to come home, and why is her shade lingering at the falls?"

Magnus's normally high color seemed to have bled right out of his face. "She said she wanted me to come home?"

"Actually, she said she wanted Alex to. We think . . . it doesn't make a lot of sense, but we think she must have mistaken him for you."

"She's nearsighted when she's here," Magnus said in a dazed, faint tone.

"Evidently, since you and Alex aren't exactly twins."

Magnus winced and took her shoulders in his hands, speaking slowly and carefully. "Did my mother say anything to you, Zoe? Did she seem to know who you were?"

Zoe folded her arms, less than pleased to be answering *his* questions. "She seemed to think I was your girlfriend."

"Hellfire." The curse was typical Magnus, but she didn't smile—considering it wasn't the most ingratiating exclamation he could have made. She watched as he shoved his hands in his thick black hair and began pacing his living room. After about half a minute he spun on his heel.

"You have to promise me you won't go back."

"I can't speak for Alex, but it's safe to say Fairy Falls has dropped off my must-see list. I'm beginning to think I'm not cut out for facing everything Fairyville can throw at me."

Magnus's clear green eyes narrowed. "This isn't a joke. It's important that you stay away from there."

Zoe didn't bother to tell him her answer had been serious. "You want to tell me why?"

His face twisted. "I can't."

"You can't."

"Would you rather I invent a lie?"

Zoe stared at him, refusing to acknowledge the plea for mercy shining in his eyes. "No," she said slowly. "I guess you're right about that. I've had enough of being lied to."

He said her name, but she turned away anyway, walking out the way she'd come without a backward glance. The heat that prickled between her shoulder blades didn't matter. Knowing that he was watching her didn't change a thing.

Magnus didn't bother to scream again, though he wanted to. He also didn't throw the couch across the room or shatter a whiskey glass. Now wasn't the time for pointless operatics. Now was the time for action.

Gritting his teeth, he dumped the melting ice cream into the sink and grabbed an apple from his fruit bowl. Magnus's fairy metabolism ensured he didn't have to worry about getting fat, but his brain was feeling in need of vitamins.

As he saw it, he had two problems to attend to. One: Prevent his mother from making Zoe the target of her ire, and two: Keep himself from going stark, raving bonkers over losing the prize that was meant for him to his damn cousin. Of the two dilemmas, he suspected solving the second would have the biggest influence on his effectiveness.

Concentration, and the magic he could work with it, was going to be key.

Thirteen

The moment Bryan caught sight of Alex that night, he knew.

Alex was walking toward him along the sidewalk, half a block from the steakhouse where they'd planned to meet. Bryan had good news about the hotel, and he was feeling happy to see him—a little horny, maybe, but mostly just happy.

Then he noticed the difference in Alex's stride, a stride he hadn't realized he knew so well. The swing of his legs was looser, the easiness of his hips. His hair was mussed in a haphazard way, and his lips were fuller, redder, as if he'd been kissing someone long and hard.

Bryan stopped in his tracks and had the dubious pleasure of watching Alex's steps falter. The air between them seemed to vibrate as they stared at each other. Even at this distance, Bryan saw the guilty rush of blood to his partner's cheeks.

An idiot could have jumped to the right conclusion. Alex had finally fucked Zoe Clare.

The knot in Bryan's throat didn't surprise him, but the slap of anger did. It was close enough to rage to suggest he really had been hoping Alex would get serious about him. The stupidity of that hope only made it worse. Too angry to have any desire to talk the situation through with him—or *not* talk it through, for that matter—Bryan turned around and walked the other way.

"Bryan!" Alex called, but he was smart enough not to follow.

Which figured, when Bryan thought about it. Guys like Alex didn't make wrong moves. Guys like Alex gave idiots like Bryan time to cool off. They waited until the people they'd stepped on in their selfish pursuit of pleasure were ready to crawl back.

That Bryan probably would crawl back was too mortifying to contemplate.

Muttering under his breath, he pushed into the first bar he saw, a dark, sticky-floored place that didn't look like it catered to the tourist crowd. He ordered what they had on tap and carried it to an empty booth. The crowd was mostly male, blue-collar workers with no one in particular to go home to. It would serve Alex right if Bryan picked someone up, but in a straight-arrow bar like this, he might end up on the wrong end of a baseball bat for so much as thinking it.

Alex never said he was only going to sleep with you, Bryan reminded himself. *You knew who he was before you started this.*

He also knew he wouldn't have chosen any differently. After all those years of yearning after his friend, no way would Bryan have missed the chance to be with him.

Which meant he kind of had to understand why Alex had grabbed his chance with Zoe.

"Crap," he said into his half-drunk beer.

A shadow fell over his booth—too tall to be a waitress and too substantial to be Alex. Bryan was too irritated with the world to bother looking up. Whoever it was could damn well write him off as rude and take a walk.

"An Irishman like you might like this better," the shadow

said, placing a bottle of Jameson's on the dark, knife-gouged wood. Two empty glasses followed, set down by a large and well-kept masculine hand. Dark hair shaded the strong forearm above it. Intrigued in spite of himself, Bryan decided it might be worth his while to lift his head.

"I know you," he said, recognizing the man who'd driven Zoe to the Vista Inn—though he looked a lot harder-edged tonight.

"And I know you," said the man, his dry suggestiveness telling Bryan he meant more than just his name.

The instant heat that ignited in Bryan's body did nothing to legitimize the grievances he'd been brooding on. This man, this Magnus Monroe, was enough to give any mostly gay man a hard-on—and probably a few straight ones, too. He was big all over, and gorgeous to boot, with beautiful, dark-lashed green eyes that promised all sorts of dangerous adventures. This was a man who might do anything to his partners—tie them up, fuck them breathless, force them to have sex with exotic toys . . .

Bryan squirmed on the booth's hard bench, his jeans abruptly tighter than they'd been before. He found himself unable to say a word. He was pretty sure he was reading Magnus's signals right, but if he wasn't . . . or even if he was, was he really ready to thumb his nose at Alex?

"Well?" Magnus prompted, his small, knowing smile a wet dream all by itself. Those lips of his were born to do carnal things. "Should I pour you one, or am I drinking alone?"

Bryan shook himself. Oh, yeah, he was reading the signals right. "That would be a shame, considering that's a ten-year-old single malt. I should tell you, though, I'm only half Irish. The rest of me is all Eye-talian."

"Two fine races," Magnus observed. "Known around the world for the charm and lustiness of their men."

Magnus poured for both of them. Bryan sipped, allowing

himself a tiny gasp of appreciation for the fiery nectar. Then he faced his unexpected company.

"Not that I'm complaining, but to what do I owe this honor?"

Magnus smiled, and there was a sweetness to it no amount of ulterior motives could dim. Bryan's cock gave an embarrassingly forceful lurch. "I want something from you."

That was enough to make Bryan cough. "Is it something I'll want to give you?" he rasped once his breath came back.

"Oh, I expect so. Once I sweeten the pot."

"And how are you going to do that?"

"By giving you something you want from me." His eyes seemed to be glowing in the bar's murky atmosphere, two sexy green lasers that sent a fresh wave of fire lapping Bryan's groin.

Bryan found those eyes unnervingly hard to look away from.

Not sure where he wanted this to be going, Bryan took another hit of whiskey, which—thankfully—went down smooth. "Forgive me for asking, but I was under the impression that Zoe was the object of your romantic interest. Won't, um, offering me what I want complicate that?"

"She is a good-looking woman." Magnus leaned back with his glowing, half-lidded eyes. "You think so yourself, don't you?"

Bryan shrugged. "Sure I do."

"And you could get it up for her if you had to."

This conversation was becoming downright surreal, but oddly enough Bryan had no inclination to cut it short. He was feeling a little buzzed, more so than could be accounted for by what he'd drunk. Magnus was radiating some sort of hum, as if sex appeal could be converted to energy.

"Not a problem," Bryan said. "Those legs of hers could get a rise out of a corpse."

This answer seemed to disconcert his companion, but Magnus recovered soon enough. He leaned forward across the table, the tips of his fingers touching Bryan's hand. Bryan fought a shiver. The humming he'd felt before increased with the contact.

"I want you to be my eyes," Magnus said in a hypnotic singsong tone. "My eyes and my ears, my cock and my skin, my proxy for a night of sexual indulgence. I want you to plunge your hardness into Zoe's cunt. I want you to spill your ecstasy inside her over and over. Nothing could be better than taking your pleasure there, and nothing else will fully satisfy you until your cock tastes her sweet pussy."

"Uh," said Bryan. His head felt thick, the images that Magnus described threatening to cloud his reason. Zoe was a hot tamale, and he didn't know why he shouldn't fantasize about fucking her, but surely it couldn't be that easy. "That sounds nice, but how am I supposed to get Zoe to agree to this?"

"When I make you come, I'll loan you a portion of my magic charm."

"You're going to make me come?" Bryan asked, this somehow more startling than the bit about magic charm.

Magnus's longest finger slid between two of Bryan's, tickling the webbing of skin between. "That is what you want to trade, isn't it?"

"Oh, yeah," Bryan said, his cock so hard it was strangling. "I'd love for you to get me off."

"Then that's how we'll seal the deal. You'll be my secret proxy in Zoe's bed, and no one but I will know I'm there."

"No one but you," Bryan repeated, his thoughts running even more sluggishly. He could hardly remember what he was agreeing to, only that it was going to be fantastic.

"Follow me to the men's room," Magnus said. "I'll make sure no one else comes in."

Magnus had almost forgotten what seducing a man was like. Relatively speaking, he hadn't done it often, though fairies were by nature sexually flexible. Charming a man was certainly quicker than charming a woman, even allowing for the potion he'd slipped into Bryan's glass.

Fairy charm didn't create attraction, only amplified it, so Magnus had used the potion to increase the effect. It still wasn't as potent as it would have been in Fairy, but fortunately, Bryan hadn't required much convincing to let the spell bend his will—his consent a necessity if Magnus wished to stay on the "white" side of magical practice.

Given how well he'd done thus far, he was feeling optimistic as he surveyed the men's bathroom. The Ritz it wasn't, but Bryan hadn't had the look of a man who was finicky. He'd had the look of a man who was beating himself up over his heart's mistakes. If that was the case, these less than genteel surroundings ought to suit him fine.

Magnus glared at the single patron who was using the urinals, which encouraged the man to hurry it up admirably. The two graffitied stalls were empty. Rather than expend more magic preventing others from coming in, he searched the supply closet.

The Out of Order sign that fell off a shelf seemed a pleasant wink from the universe.

As Bryan slipped into the bathroom after him, a curl of adrenaline numbed Magnus's fingers—nerves perhaps, or anticipation at being obliged to enjoy a kind of sex he hadn't had in a while. Magnus didn't need sexual variety the way he had when he was younger, but that didn't mean it couldn't get his blood thrumming.

This is for Zoe, he instructed his swelling cock. *You're doing this so you can know how it feels to truly be with her.*

Bryan was eyeing him warily, maybe as nervous as he was, though he didn't look reluctant. If nothing else, Magnus's seductive methods ensured the man's arousal was too high for that. Bryan's chest was rising and falling shallowly, a fine sheen of perspiration glistening on his swarthy skin.

Despite his obvious eagerness, "How would you like to do this?" Bryan asked politely.

Magnus shook his head, silently amused. "This trade is weighted in my favor. You must be the one to say what you want."

"I don't really—"

"You do," Magnus interrupted, pinning him with his most mesmerizing stare. "You know exactly what you want right now."

"To be sucked off," Bryan said, the answer hushed but bursting from him like it had been pulled. His breath came deeper with the true confession. "I want you to wrap that gorgeous mouth around me and take me whole. I want you to suck my seed down your throat like you're starving for the taste of it."

His pupils were huge, showing the influence of Magnus's magic as much as his own lust. This was an act that involved some risk when done between humans. In his normal frame of mind, Magnus was certain Bryan would have offered to wear protection. In need of no such shields, Magnus smiled at this evidence that his control over the man was strong. Spells were tricky in the human realm. You never knew when they might zig instead of zag.

"Would you like to watch me in the mirror?" Magnus offered. "I haven't done this in a while, but I used to be good at deep throating."

"Oh, man," Bryan said, which Magnus took as a yes.

The mirror was a rust-spotted glass bolted to the wall. The second of two sinks hung beside it. Magnus gestured for Bryan to lean against the porcelain, then went to his knees on the floor.

Bryan's fingers were already fumbling with his fly.

Once he had it open, Magnus pulled the denim down his muscular thighs. Bryan's cock bounced out like it was on springs, big and thick and flushed with engorging blood. Magnus caught it, his thumbs tracing gently up the distended veins. Bryan bit his lip with pleasure and tried to fight back a moan.

"You must be quiet," Magnus warned before he went further. "And I suspect we need to be quick. I don't know how long we have before someone checks the door."

"Do it then," Bryan said roughly. "I'm ready to roll."

There was quick and then there was rushing, which no self-respecting fairy was going to do. Magnus cupped Bryan's balls and began with them, sucking one and then the other into his mouth. They were warm and heavy, their sac drawing up as Bryan's excitement rose. When Magnus mouthed both at once and pulled, Bryan rumbled out a groan.

The grateful sound reminded Magnus that what he was doing was intimate—not just in the sexual sense, but in the emotional, as well. No doubt Bryan had been in a reckless mood, but Magnus couldn't shake the feeling that having this man's vulnerability quite literally placed in his hands was an important trust. Bryan was a person, not a pawn, and Magnus had no business forgetting that. Disconcerted, his sucking slowed.

Bryan grabbed his shoulder, his fingers digging in for balance. Magnus pulled away to speak.

"Don't stop," Bryan begged before he could.

The plea sent its own claws into Magnus's loins, pulling his cock longer and thicker. Whatever his purpose, he saw he wasn't going to remain unmoved by this.

"You will be my stand-in," Magnus reminded him, letting the energy of their lust bind them together. "Your eyes will be my window when you pleasure the one I love."

"Yes," Bryan gasped as Magnus dragged his tongue up the thickened ridge that ran beneath his shaft. He jerked when Magnus reached the head. "Whatever you want."

Satisfied that his magic had the permission it required, Magnus tipped Bryan's erection to a better angle and swallowed half.

"Jesus," Bryan groaned at the immediate strength and wetness of his suction. "Mary and Joseph, look at you take me."

Magnus was too busy concentrating to check out the visuals. Relaxing his throat was easy, and ensuring that Bryan was enjoying himself a piece of cake. The challenge lay in forming the tiny ball of consciousness that Bryan would carry inside him. It needed to hold just enough of Magnus's awareness and no more, because Magnus had no desire to make himself a permanent hitchhiker in Bryan's brain. This was a one-shot deal, one night with Zoe and no more. Not that there would be more. Bryan's taste in partners tended too strongly to the male persuasion for Magnus to worry on that score.

Pleased with his choice, he swirled his tongue around the satin of Bryan's glans. Bryan's whimper of need couldn't help but arouse him, but this wasn't about him. Ignoring the intensifying throb at his groin, Magnus dipped his head until his lips hit the other man's abdomen.

This visual was too alluring not to send Bryan through the roof. Completely into it, but too considerate to clutch a stranger's head and risk choking him, his fingernails pricked Magnus through his collar hard enough to hurt. Magnus was both oddly touched and incredibly turned on. Bryan's girth was swelling, his stomach muscles tensing as Magnus pulled his lips tightly up again. When he flicked his tongue across the little slit, a sweet tinge of pre-come spread across his taste buds.

Knowing the end was near, Magnus spun a filament of charm off his own supply. He wrapped it around his proxy spell until the thing began to tug its imaginary tether like a trapped falcon.

His preparations ready, Magnus curled two fingers around the bottom of Bryan's shaft, holding any loose skin taut. The time for deep-throating was over. Now he needed to focus on the more sensitive upper regions of Bryan's cock. Now he needed to bring this magical agreement home. Bryan's hips began to buck against the vigorous tonguing Magnus was giving him, his whimpers speeding up as well. Magnus increased his suction and rubbed Bryan's glans even harder with the flat of his tongue.

Bryan groaned at this sudden increase in stimulation. Politeness forgotten, he began to thrust, the nerve-rich tip of his penis strafing Magnus's palate.

Magnus gripped Bryan's hips, but only to steady him. His responses weren't those of a human, or even a young fairy. Bryan could have shoved his whole cock down Magnus's throat without hurting him, something he was very nearly trying to do.

"God," Bryan said, his voice rising. "God. God. *Fuck.*"

Magnus gave his balls one firm squeeze, and then the man was gone. His energy poured out of him with his seed, blending their life force in a flare of light. Taking both with more enjoyment than he expected, Magnus released his hold on the proxy spell.

The magic orb soared up Bryan's prick, potent enough to make him shudder at its passage. Caught in that pleasure, Bryan took at least half a minute to stop twitching in Magnus's mouth. His limbs were shaking when Magnus let him slip free.

"That was incredible," Bryan murmured. "You got me off in, like, three minutes."

Magnus stood, his knees stiff from the tension of his own arousal. His erection was too big for even Bryan's glazed eyes to miss, but he caught the other man's hand before it could cup him.

"We're finished here," Magnus said, careful to hold his eyes. "When I step out that door, you'll forget what happened between us. All you'll remember is how you'll never be satisfied until you get your hard-on in Zoe's pussy. Once you've had your night of sex with her, the spell that allows me to ride your consciousness will deactivate."

Bryan wet his lips nervously. "What if I can't seduce her?"

"You can," Magnus said, sending him a mental wave of confidence. "Listen for what she wants and hold her gaze. My charm will help you persuade her—guaranteed."

"Right." Bryan stood a little straighter. He didn't appear as convinced as Magnus would have liked, but at least he seemed determined.

This will work, Magnus assured himself.

A shiver of sensation rolled down his spine. He wished he could have said whether fear or anticipation powered it most.

Zoe stood with her feet straddling the track to her sliding doors, watching the steady downpour fall on her deck. Lightning forked over Mitten Butte, approaching Fairyville but not here yet. The monsoons were coming, she supposed, and this was their first salvo. The sound quieted the unrest inside her, the questions she couldn't answer however hard she tried.

Did it really make a difference if she ran away from Alex and Magnus to protect her heart? Or if she let herself plummet without a safety net? Either way, the earth would turn. Heaven would be heaven regardless of whether she was enjoying it.

It's my choice, she thought, which brought her no closer to making one.

The sound of footsteps slapping her wet walkway brought her out of her reverie. She turned her head to find Bryan climbing the wooden stairs to her deck, soaked to the skin in jeans and a black T-shirt. He had muscles on his muscles, big, meaty slabs that wrapped his chest and thighs. His face was beautiful washed in the rain, his cheekbones and jaw as hard as his expression. Seeing him was like having Fate rub her nose in the inevitability of her own downfall. Of course Alex went for Bryan. Anyone who even sort of swung that way would.

"What's wrong?" she asked, though she couldn't muster the concern to go with the words. "Couldn't you and Alex find a new hotel?"

"I found one," he said. "I left a text message on his phone. I expect he's on his way there now."

"You left a text message."

Bryan came to a halt a single step from her. He put his hand on the adobe beside her head. "I figured out what happened between you and him."

"Did you." She couldn't make it a question. Instead, she pressed her lips together and stared at her painted toes. "I don't think what happened means what you guessed."

"He still loves you."

The words stirred a thrill she couldn't repress. "Maybe. But I don't think I'm the only one he feels that way about."

Bryan touched her cheek, his palm rough with calluses that neither Alex nor Magnus had. When Zoe lifted her head, his face was flushed, intent with an emotion that—with any other man— she would have said was desire. His eyes gleamed in the darkness, their black coffee richness touched with a hint of gold. She found it very hard to look away from him.

"I want my own back," he said. "What Alex did hurt me more than I expected, made me angrier. I was thinking—" He drew his hand from her cheek to her throat, skimming her skin with a tingling delicacy. His eyes followed the motion of his fingers to her slight cleavage. She was wearing a camisole and light cotton drawstring pants, both dampened by the rain, both more transparent than she should have been comfortable with. Her nipples tightened as his gaze hit them.

Okay, maybe her radar *was* working, because Bryan swallowed hard before he went on. "I was thinking I would use what Alex did as an excuse to put the moves on you. I thought if there was any good way to hurt him back, that would be it."

"You sound like you've changed your mind."

"I want to do it." He looked at her face again, his gaze as hungry as any she'd ever seen. "I've been thinking I'd like to since I watched you and Alex eat each other up with your eyes while you made that bed."

Her body seemed to be making its own decisions. She turned to him, her hand coming to rest in a gentle cup above his right nipple, not touching it but close. The left was a tiny point beneath his wet black shirt.

"You like women."

"I like them when they don't try to stop me from doing what I want with men."

Despite the coolness of the rain, Zoe's temperature jumped a few degrees. It was difficult to get her next question out. "What are you trying to ask me?"

"I want you," he said. "I want you so bad I could screw you right where you stand."

"But?"

"But I want Alex to watch me fuck you even more. I want him to see my cock push into you. I want him to know he's not the only one who can take pleasure from someone else."

"And what—" She cleared her thickened throat. "While you're 'taking your pleasure,' what would you want Alex to do?"

Bryan leaned in, his bicep bunching as he bent his arm. "I'd make sure he couldn't do anything but watch until his dick was ready to cry. I'd make sure he was so hot he couldn't see straight. And then, when he was an inch away from screaming with frustration, I'd want us both to do him."

"That last part doesn't sound like punishment."

Her hands had slid to either side of his ribs, holding him lightly but not so lightly that she didn't feel his heart thumping hard and quick. He moved his mouth over hers, the feathery touch tingling on her lips.

"It isn't a punishment," he whispered. "It's a fantasy he's never managed to live out."

Zoe's pussy clenched so hard she felt like she was coming.

She was wet, and hoarse, and so ready for sex she could barely breathe. This wasn't just Alex's fantasy, it was hers. To be with him and another man. To have that other man desire her. No doubt her yen to do this was completely screwy, but to her it seemed the ultimate re-empowerment, the ultimate exorcism of the pain he'd caused her all those years ago.

"You forgive him?" she managed to ask.

Their faces were so close that when Bryan shook his head, his nose bumped hers. "I don't know. I only know I can't hate him. I understand what it's like to want and want and finally get the chance to have."

Zoe wet her lips, the tip of her tongue accidentally touching his. He sucked a quick breath and then licked her back, just enough to curve his tongue inside the softness of her upper lip. He was masculine to the nth degree, and yet *she* wanted to capture his mouth and plunder it like a warrior's prize. This aggressive heat she felt for him was crazy, and it only grew with not giving in to it. She wanted it to grow, to blaze so high it incinerated any shred of conscience that could hold her back. Sensing this perhaps, Bryan drew his mouth away.

"Is this something you'd want to do?" he asked raggedly.

She slid her hands down his sides, over the soaking cotton of his shirt, over the dip of his navel and his clinging jeans. Their front was stretched across his erection, a hard, curved ridge that pulsed beneath the heavy drag of her thumbs.

"Yes," she said and watched his eyes flash with fire.

Fourteen

Zoe held off until Friday evening, though her body had been itching to go with Bryan as soon as he'd asked.

"Don't tell Alex what we're planning," she'd pleaded before he left. "I need time to prepare myself."

"Understood," he'd said, his face still dark with arousal, his fingers playing with a curl of her hair. "I hope you realize I'm going to be crazy until I get inside you, because nothing's going to satisfy me short of that."

She'd smiled, flattered by his half-serious claim, and pulled his head down for a deep, wet kiss. This time, he'd let himself really take her mouth, and the kiss had slipped down her pleasure channels a lot more smoothly than she'd expected. Alex's friend kissed hard but nice, and she hadn't been able to keep from speculating what else he might be hard and nice at.

She'd been useless at work all day, actually giving one of her clients a slew of messages from the wrong spirit, until the woman's confused expression clued her in that she wasn't being

her usual accurate self. Zoe apologized and refused to let the
woman pay, but her lack of focus was telling.

As many times as she'd wondered what making love to Alex
would be like, her most powerful fantasies, the ones that stole
into her mind uninvited, didn't involve him and her alone.

It was funny—and possibly disturbing—but in the two years
she'd known Magnus, she'd dreamed of bedding just him much
more often than she'd dreamed of bedding just Alex.

So I'm perverse, she thought, attempting to shrug it off. *It
stands to reason I'd be more exclusively attracted to a man who's
playing hard to get.*

Naturally, this was the moment her contrary brain chose to
send her a clit-scorching image of all *three* men in bed with her.

Giving up, Zoe rescheduled her last appointment, waved
goodbye to Teresa through the café door, and went home early.
If she was going to live out this fantasy, she was going to do it
right. She was going to shower and shave and moisturize every
inch of her tingling skin. She was going to beg Rajel to help with
her hair, and she was going to pack a discreet black bag with toys
she hadn't been able to resist buying, but had always wondered
if she'd ever use.

Fairyville already knew she was eccentric. She saw no reason
why she shouldn't be kinky, too.

Bryan had been kidding about staying hard until he took her,
but the joke hadn't been far off. He found himself unable to
think of anything but Zoe, and while he'd always had a healthy
libido, this intense preoccupation with a woman was unusual.
Alex had been sleeping—or pretending to—when Bryan returned to their new hotel room, this one fitted out with queen-
size beds. Bryan had taken one for himself without a second
thought, though Alex probably would have welcomed the

chance to help him out with a release or two. Maybe the reason was part anger, but Bryan realized he didn't want him to.

He only wanted to fuck Zoe.

Even when Alex padded to the bathroom the next morning with an erection the size of Flagstaff shoving out his briefs, Bryan had pretended not to see. He'd told Alex to visit the newspaper office without him, saying he wanted to check some of their interviewees' backgrounds on the internet. Though he'd meant to do this, he ended up in bed with the porn channel on, stroking his persistent hard-on while he watched the men get busy and imagined all the women as Zoe.

He should have come a hundred times, given how much he'd played with himself, but somehow he couldn't bring himself to push over the brink. He knew what he wanted. When he got it, he wanted to be really revved up for it.

Zoe called the room at five. The sound of her voice was like a million tiny rockets going off underneath his skin. She was ready, she said, but nervous. Would he consider picking her up and driving her?

The idea that she wouldn't bring a getaway vehicle delighted him. He'd have her all night. *They'd* have her all night.

She was waiting in front of her house when he pulled up, clutching a small black satchel to her side. Unable to stay where he was, he got out of the car, pulled her into his arms, and kissed her so deep and long it was like he wanted to fuck her through her mouth.

"Wow," she said when he finally let her breathe.

Her starry-eyed astonishment made him feel like a million bucks—which wasn't to say her side of the kiss hadn't been spectacular. There was nothing quite like being kept up with to bring out the best in a horny man.

"Alex wasn't back yet when I left," he said, his hands enjoying a slide down her silken arms.

"Do you think he will be by the time we arrive?"

"I don't know." His cock thumped harder at the prospect of Alex waiting, of Alex looking up and seeing him with Zoe. Bryan's prick was rigid, absolutely in pain. He wanted to take her now, against the car, in sight of anyone who drove by. She was wearing a stretchy, sleeveless red velvet minidress that plunged over her creamy cleavage and bared her mile-long legs nearly to her cunt. Sensing his rarther obvious interest, she tugged the hem in embarrassment. That drew a growl from low in his chest even as he grinned.

"I don't usually dress like this," she confessed.

He laughed and kissed her mouth quick and hard. "Alex is going to die when he sees those red hooker shoes."

"You really think he'll say yes to watching us?"

Still smiling, Bryan cupped her anxious face, his eyes burning unexpectedly at how sweet she was. "He'll say yes," he assured her, not a doubt in his mind. "He'd have said yes if you'd cut holes in a grocery bag and worn that."

"Well, good," she said, blowing out a shaky breath. "Because maybe we should strategize on the way."

Alex hated empty hotel rooms. An empty house he was used to, but coming back to these uninspired surroundings after spinning his wheels all day felt like a booby prize.

On the bright side, no one at the paper had recognized him, but the stupid *Fairyville Courier* hadn't even had microfiche. He'd be scrubbing newsprint from his nails for days, and all he had to show for his troubles were a handful of crazy interviews some dewy-eyed oral history student had done with a bunch of dotty octogenarians. Wish fulfillment was all they were, mixed with a mishmash of folktale. Fairies were not riding into Fairyville on great white stallions to debauch young women in the woods.

Never mind the strange things he and Zoe had seen at the falls. There was no such thing as fairies. All right, there were the little fairies Zoe was friends with, who were probably some sort of energy that only looked like Tinkerbell because this was what Alex expected. Whatever they were, they weren't lying in wait in the forest for young maidens to happen by.

Even his open mind had to have limits.

This conclusion didn't satisfy him any more than his day had. Uneasy with his thoughts but not wanting to wallow in them, Alex emptied his pockets onto the bed—*his* bed—and stared at the phone. Bryan had booked them into a nice hotel: room service, bellhops, the works. But without Bryan here—even a resentful, cold-shouldering Bryan—none of its amenities appealed.

Seeing as he had no idea what Bryan was up to, room service was probably his best dinner plan. His appetite nonexistent, he stretched out on the mattress instead . . . which let a different sort of unappealing musing in.

Bryan had every right to be upset with him, just like—strictly speaking—Alex had had every right to sleep with Zoe. He and Bryan weren't boyfriends, they were strictly friends with benefits. Sadly, these very reasonable justifications didn't lessen his discontents.

Neither Bryan nor Zoe had checked in with him today. Alex hadn't been what you'd call a people person since he'd left high school, but he was dismayed to discover how much he wanted contact with these two.

He was pressing the heels of his hands into his eye sockets when the door lock clicked and Bryan walked in.

"Hey," he said as Alex sat up with his heart pounding.

"Hey," Alex said back, and then, "*Zoe.*"

Her name came out a little breathless, but he couldn't help that, considering what she had on. He had never, in his life, seen her wear such a blatantly sexy dress. The way it fit her was combustible, cut down to there and up to here and probably grounds for arrest if she lingered in the lobby long.

"You two going out?" he asked, confused but trying not to show it. He took in Zoe's four-inch heels with a silent *ulp*. Women in shoes like that were a weakness he didn't need right now. "If you are, I think Bryan might have to play bodyguard."

Zoe smiled, just a little, so she and Bryan probably hadn't made a secret pact to do away with him.

"We're not going out," she said, dropping her little satchel on the foot of his bed. "If you agree to our proposition, we're staying in."

"Proposition?" He wasn't sure it was possible for a man to croak more foolishly. A proposition meant sex, right? That you'd been forgiven and were about to get lucky?

He looked to Bryan for confirmation but found only a seraphic smile.

"Bryan wants his pound of flesh," Zoe explained, "and he's decided the particular pound he wants belongs to me."

Alex blinked. This didn't sound like what he'd been hoping for. It sounded like Bryan wanted to get horizontal with Zoe.

"Oh," he said, realizing he was in no position to object. Yes, the idea that Bryan wanted Zoe surprised him a bit, but he'd slept with both of them, and he could see this had a certain vengeful symmetry. "I'll, uh, just clear out and leave you two alone."

"No." Bryan's gentle smile broadened. "We've decided we want you to watch."

"To watch?"

"We know that will be hard for you," Zoe said, "given how you like to be in the driver's seat, but I brought something to make it easier."

His jaw dropped when she pulled a pair of shiny handcuffs from her leather bag. Zoe owned handcuffs? *His* Zoe? His face grew hot as he realized she meant to use them on him. Alex had been known to play at bondage, but never, ever on the receiving end.

"You could sit in that chair," she continued, nodding at the nearest one as if she weren't threatening to turn his personal erotic world on its head. "We'd cuff your wrists to the arms and drag it nice and close to us."

His hands had curled into fists. "I can't," he said, though his cock was thickening up enough to put the lie to that.

"You can," Zoe said, sweet and low. "It would wipe the slate clean for all of us. No more recriminations. No hard feelings. I'd really like to, Alex, and so would Bryan. Don't you think he deserves a chance to cheat on you?"

With all the blood surging to his cock, Alex's synapses weren't firing too quickly. "I didn't make Bryan watch," was all he could think to say.

Zoe's smile was as angelically wicked as Bryan's had been. "Maybe you didn't make him watch because you two have different hot buttons."

Alex opened his mouth to argue, but Bryan cut him off.

"Get in the chair," he ordered in his intimidate-the-suspect voice. "Unless you'd rather I do her where you can't see."

A tiny shiver shook Alex's shoulder blades. He didn't want to be handcuffed; didn't want to give up control. But to *not* watch Bryan do Zoe, to *not* see him shove that hard, muscled body into and over her, suddenly seemed worse. Bryan had a hard-on to beat all hard-ons as he stood there challenging him, his legs planted wide, his eyes glittering like ink in his angry face.

Seeing him, his testosterone on full display, Alex didn't know how he'd kept his hands off him for so long.

He came unsteadily to his feet. "You want me dressed or naked?" he asked as calmly as he could.

"Naked," the conspirators chimed in unison.

"Right," Alex said on a nervous huff. "I don't suppose she could leave those shoes on then . . ."

For days, Magnus had been listening for the ping in his brain that would say his spell was in play. He'd been expecting it since he'd left Bryan in the bar. Magnus's compulsions weren't known to work slowly, and after a full twenty-four hours had passed, he'd begun to wonder if the thing had really taken root. He'd convinced himself it was for the best if it hadn't. Maybe he'd be better off not seeing Bryan take Zoe, even if it would sate his craving to know how she felt.

And then the mental nudge came at last. Magnus was in his bedroom, fresh from a shower with a towel wrapped around his waist. In three long waves, his cock surged up and tented it.

Evidently, his few last doubts weren't going to take the edge off of his excitement.

He settled onto his back on the bed, wishing he felt more prepared. It would have been more ideal to do this from his secure bunker, but there wasn't time to relocate. The psychic houselights were dimming, ready or not.

"Showtime," he murmured huskily to himself.

He closed his eyes as the metaphorical curtain rose. When he saw what it revealed, he almost opened them again.

There was one more participant in this drama than Magnus had been planning on. Apparently, Bryan had added his own twist to the fuck-her spell.

Bryan wanted in Zoe so badly he was shaking—not just his cock but every inch of him. She was laid out lengthwise on Alex's bed, a feast in pink and cream. Wearing only the high-heeled shoes, she had one knee bent and wagging, while the other draped the edge of the mattress. Aroused but nervous, her fingers played up and down the smooth-shaven thigh she'd raised. The plump folds of her slit were glistening in the little flashes she was giving him. The shoes were enough to crank him up—his tastes running in line with Alex's there—but it was the sight of her wetness that stretched him to the bursting point.

This was trust she was showing him, a friendship he hadn't earned. Her lips were parted with anticipation, and the contrast between her lashes and her eyes transformed them to lustrous jewels. Her gaze was fastened on his, telling him more than words could that the next move was up to him.

Of course, it wasn't only her rapt attention that got Bryan going.

The chair they'd handcuffed Alex to was close enough for his shins to touch the bed next to Zoe's leg. The knowledge that he could also see Zoe creaming made Bryan's testicles ache. Even though he'd agreed to go along with this, Bryan still had trouble believing Alex had actually let them restrain him.

"For God's sake," his friend said now, the exclamation hoarse. "You've got me where you want me. Go ahead and take her."

Bryan lifted Zoe's second leg until the sole of that shoe lay on the mattress, too. Then he raised both legs to wrap his waist. Finding the bed too low, he grabbed a pillow for her hips. As he worked it under her, Zoe's hands slid up his arms, her fingers admiring the contours of his muscles. Her palms were warm and a little sweaty. Bryan's lungs began to fill faster as he lowered himself. His chest met the slightly cooler softness of her breasts, and she buried her face in his shoulder.

"You're so thick," she whispered, not an observation likely to calm him. "Please don't go too fast right away."

"Guide me in," he whispered back. "I want to feel your hands on me."

He flinched when she touched his shaft. As ready as he was, the gentle pressure of her fingers was almost too good to stand. A second later, her opening wrapped him in sultry warmth. That steadied him, oddly enough. He might be thick, but he knew his tip was formed for smooth entry—more bullet-shaped than crested. He tried to remember how many times he'd done this: no more than a dozen, he didn't think, but the bliss of it came back quick. As much as he liked men, as much as he needed them, women were a unique pleasure. He pushed, and her flesh gave way, smooth and hot and growing creamier as he eased in.

He found himself wanting to memorize every sensation.

She moaned, gripping his elbows, and he swelled thicker. She was right about him needing to go slow. His teeth gritted at her snugness, his thigh muscles flexing harder to get him in. It must have been a bit of a show. Alex choked out a sound beside him, but Bryan didn't look at him. He was almost there, almost surrounded . . .

And then he was there, his hipbones grinding greedily against hers.

Zoe made a husky noise and opened her eyes.

"Okay?" Bryan asked, his voice nearly suffocated by how good this felt. Either her pussy was sweeter than other women's or he was going to have to reassess some of his choices.

She smiled at his breathless question, or maybe at the way his cock pulsed wildly in her stretched tissues. "It's better than okay. It's almost perfect."

"Almost?"

"It'll be perfect when you start to move."

The jump his pulse gave damn near did him in. "All right, sweetheart," he said. "I'm gonna start real easy. You tell me when you want to finish, and I'll speed up then."

"I love it slow," she warned him. "With nice, long strokes that last forever."

Bryan gave her what she asked for, dragging out to her brink before pushing slowly, heavily back in. His gentleness didn't surprise her, but his adeptness did. He had a knack for rolling his hips as he entered, shifting the pressure with each inch gained. Zoe's hands were soon fisted on his ropy back. What he was doing was too delicious not to have to fight her own urge to speed things up.

"Tell me when," he panted like he wanted it to be soon.

Rather than give in, she dropped the leg closest to Alex from Bryan's waist, splaying her thigh to give him the clearest possible view of Bryan sliding into her.

Alex made a noise like he'd been kicked, the handcuffs clinking against the chair as he tugged at them. Her pussy tightened at the evidence of his distress.

"Oh-kay," Bryan said, obviously seeing what she was aiming at. "Maybe I *could* keep this up a while longer."

Alex knew he shouldn't have agreed to this. They were trying to kill him, making him watch Bryan take her so slow and long. He knew how much Zoe loved that, and would have known it even if she hadn't begged him to do it at the falls. Her skin was flushed all over, her trembling breasts tipped with rosy spikes.

Bryan's shaft gleamed with her juices, so red it ought to have been steaming. Alex wanted nothing more than to lean close enough to lick it. He fought the cuffs, but it did no good.

Please, he thought, his cock hard enough to split. Pre-come slid down it in warm trickles, copious and steady, as if his body were as good at getting wet as Zoe's. *Please, God, finish this.*

Zoe heard the chair creak as Alex gripped it in a sudden upsurge of need. Both she and Bryan turned to look. Blood suffused Alex's face, the muscles twisted and sweating with erotic strain. His cock was straining, too, its tip running with desire. He was glaring at them, his eyes hot blue fire.

He looked ready to pull the chair apart.

Maybe it wasn't nice of her to enjoy his suffering, but Zoe's sheath fluttered in reaction, letting down a sluice of moisture that made Bryan gasp.

When he twitched and lengthened, she knew she'd had enough.

"All right," she said, her throat thick with excitement. "You can push me over now."

Magnus expected her to go quickly, but it didn't take more than three hard plunges to trigger Zoe's climax. His cock forgot it wasn't inside her, jerking as she moaned and trying its damnedest to come with her. He could feel Bryan pumping faster, could sense his balls tightening. She was honeyed inside and hot, and Magnus licked his lips at the feel of her. So sweet. So perfect. But Bryan was better at this than he should have been. Magnus knew he had to be seconds from blasting off, but he hung on well enough to increase the pressure on her G-spot.

Zoe screamed when she came this time, her thighs clutching like a vise, her pussy flooding him with wetness. Bryan's cock slid faster, slicker, jolts of sensation sparking down his nerves with each contraction of her vagina. He strained for his finish with a hunger magnified to desperation by the fuck-her spell.

He'd die if he couldn't come. Just . . . plain . . . die.

Lungs that felt like Magnus's sucked in air, but only Bryan's seed jetted like a fountain when Zoe's sex squeezed again.

Bryan's body jammed against Zoe's as if all of him could join his cock.

Me now, Alex thought, his brain reduced to its most primitive condition. It repeated the demand as Bryan rolled off Zoe. She looked at Alex, her gaze hot enough to burn, trailing down his body to the evidence of how successfully they'd tormented him. Alex's cock was pounding harder than his heart. He shouldn't have neglected it just because Bryan was mad at him. At the least, he should have jacked off in this morning's shower. Now he was paying the price for his misguided sense of restraint.

Zoe seemed to know it. Her smile was slow enough, and more than devilish enough, for her to have read his mind.

Too bad he didn't think her smile meant relief was near.

"You'll like this next bit," she said, and dug into her black satchel.

"Jesus," Alex swore, though he'd intended to remain silent.

She held a molded "jelly" dildo, bright blue, with tiny bubbles glittering inside. She tapped her pouting lips with it, drawing Bryan's eyes to the thing as surely as Alex's. When she licked it, both men shuddered.

"Eight long inches," she said archly, "but I think we know Bryan is man enough to take that."

That pulled Bryan's gaze to Alex's erection, shining clearly with its own wetness. Alex knew how big he was, how red and angry and stiff. Bryan's breathing had been settling after his explosive climax, but now it reversed course.

"Hm," said Zoe. "I was worried this toy might be a little thick, but the girth looks like a good match, too."

Alex couldn't help himself. He tugged wildly at the hand-cuffs, a growl rising in his chest his pride couldn't stop. "You are *not* going to make me watch you fuck him with that."

"Why, Alex, you sound possessive."

He growled at her again, but she only smiled.

"You've always been a good sport," she said. "Which is why I know I *am* going to fuck him, and you *are* going to watch."

Magnus groaned as the dildo breached him, the bound-aries between him and Bryan blurring as this night went on. Zoe had lubed it, but—by all that was magic—the thing was big. He and Bryan were on hands and knees, their muscles shaking, their throat tight with pleasure and panic mixed. This had been so much easier when they were in charge. Did she know what she was doing? Would she hurt them accidentally? The puckered ring of muscle that stretched around the toy burned with ecstasy. Magnus hadn't had this done to him very often, and never by a neophyte. The opening was incredibly sensitive, jumping and tingling as she slowly pushed past its nerves.

As if to soothe their worry, she kissed their rump, her little tongue coming out to lick.

She nipped it, too, like she couldn't quite help herself.

"Stroke him," Alex said in a voice like broken concrete. "Give him a distraction so he can relax."

Her hand wrapped their dick, then pulled down the shaft to its tip, making it sing with the stimulation of her warm fingers. This they could tell she was practiced at. They relaxed with a moaning sigh, their entrance giving to her intrusion. The dildo slid farther, farther, warming with each gentle, rocking push.

It felt so good they knew they wanted to let more in.

"Harder," they begged and—bless her—she knew they meant for her to work their cock with more force.

"Tell me when I hit the good spot," she whispered.

She'd hit quite a few already, but then—oh, Lord, *then*—the dildo reached their prostate and fireworks went off. Magnus's previous partners must not have been very skilled. This was the closest thing he knew to coming without actually spilling seed.

"Oh, God," he groaned, or would have if he'd had control of their mouth. Fortunately, Bryan wanted exactly what he did.

"Move," he barked, "under me. I'm gonna die if I don't get my cock inside you."

Alex groaned at the picture the two of them made, at the heavy thump of the headboard against the wall. Zoe rocked the dildo against Bryan's prostate while he fucked her like a lust-crazed beast. Her motions were far from smooth, the limits of her reach and her extreme arousal precluding grace. Alex doubted Bryan cared. Hard and fast seemed to be all he wanted, and that she was supplying—from either side. Bryan was whining in his throat, his God-I-need-to-come pre-orgasmic sound. Alex clenched his jaw so hard his teeth ached, in perfect sympathy with his urgency.

Those gorgeous legs were climbing Bryan's back, their clenching calves and thighs the sexiest thing he'd ever seen on a woman—the sexiest thing he'd ever seen on a man being the knotted muscles of Bryan's ass. Bryan was close. Alex knew the signs. His friend's throat arched back on a strangled moan, his Adam's apple standing out like stone.

Higher, Alex thought, his nails biting into his palms with his need to be where Bryan was. He could hardly stand not being in control of this. "Pull her leg higher."

Bryan glanced sideways at him, startled, but a second later he yanked Zoe's foot to his shoulder. She still wore the red fuck-me shoes, though how hard her toes were curled seemed to be all that held them on. The change in angle pulled her tighter against him, letting her feel each hard stroke hit the subtle pressure point near her womb.

Alex knew this was what she needed. She wailed in reaction, her orgasm grabbing her violently. Bryan barely had time to plough back inside her before he went, too. He cried out at the sudden climax, both their bodies straining to stay close.

Alex had to close his eyes. Their expressions were too naked, too electrified by pleasure. Even without a view, it was bad enough. Their throaty cries grew softer, slower as the peak played out. Finally, silence fell except for their panting, except for the sucking click of their decoupling.

Bryan sighed as he pulled out, repletion and regret mingling in the sound. Alex heard a condom hit the trash can, like a slap to his neglected cock.

He wondered how much longer they were going to torture him. Oh, he understood why they wanted to. He just didn't think he could sit here a second longer without going mad.

"Okay," Zoe said into the quiet. "Give us a minute to catch our breaths, and we'll take care of you."

He should have been elated, but he could hardly move when they unlocked the cuffs. He'd spent his strength struggling against them. They had to help him to the bed and lay him down.

"Please don't make me wait," he begged them both, his lust stronger than his pride. "I want your hands on me. I need to come so bad I could scream."

"Shh." Zoe kissed the marks his fight had left on his wrists. "Bryan and I are going to make it all better."

Fifteen

Alex was no stranger to strong desires, but if he'd ever needed release this badly, he couldn't remember it. He felt more at Zoe and Bryan's mercy than when he'd been handcuffed to the chair. The touch of their hands dragged helpless moans from him, and he didn't even care whose hands they were.

"Shh." Bryan echoed Zoe's soothing as Alex thrashed. Kneeling up by the headboard, he used his weight to pin Alex's wrists apart, which allowed Zoe to kiss a teasing path down his sweat-streaked chest. Alex's skin was starved for touch and, in that way, he felt as if she saved his sanity, but—God—she was too gentle. After what they'd put him through, he needed so much more than that.

His wish burst out when she licked a circle around his navel. "I want both of you," he ground out. "I want both of you to suck me off."

Zoe looked up his body, her eyes two gray stars. Her hand

steadied his beating shaft mere inches from her soft pink mouth. "Both of us at once?"

He nodded, swallowing, not sure how this request would be received. Zoe turned her gaze to Bryan, who quirked his brows. "There does appear to be room," he remarked dryly.

Alex's lust broke its bounds even before their heads found space to maneuver on either side of his groin. He gripped the sheets and gasped for control as Bryan's tongue swept wetness across his crown. Zoe's mouth went lower, latching and suckling beneath the rim. The intensity of his excitement had him in knots. He could be quick on the trigger when he was made to wait, not a problem when you were as multiorgasmic as he was— or not usually. The sensation of two mouths, two tongues, and four hands worth of fingers probing the sweet spots around his cock was too good to relinquish a second before he had to.

Alex wanted to roll in the feelings, to memorize each suck and squeeze—and never mind the enthrallment of just watching what they were doing. Those two dark heads . . . those naked bodies . . . each a perfect example of its sex—these were images he'd fantasize to for years. The realization that Bryan and Zoe likely would as well came all too close to doing him in. He hung by his nails for minutes, then tens of minutes, delirious with pleasure even as he shuddered with his grinding need to let go.

"You now," Zoe said to Bryan as her mouth released his prick. "I want to see how deep you can swallow him."

Her curls pulled off him like a warm blanket. She and Bryan had been switching places for the last few minutes, one mouth replacing the other, a trade that not only kept them from tiring but seemed to goad both on. Spots of color burned on their cheeks, proof of how worked up they were. Seeing the matched display, Alex knew he wouldn't survive this next alternation, no matter how much he wished he could.

He tried to brace as Bryan took Zoe's place. His mouth was

stronger, bolder. He took almost all of Alex in the first dip. Tension coiled in his muscles until they ached. Zoe murmured something comforting, her slender hand pressing his now-tender balls up into his groin. Her breath fanned hot against the crease between his leg and torso, and suddenly he couldn't stand it anymore. Giving in to desperation, he released his stranglehold on the sheets to grab Bryan's head.

"Oh, God," he gasped as Bryan's mouth sank down for another pull. His tongue was wet, his lips tight and hard where they wrapped his teeth. Bryan didn't have to deep-throat Alex to get him to see stars. He was a fucking Hoover vacuum of oral sex, sucking like he was trying to force the orgasm out. The pressure hurt for a second, and then he went.

Light flashed behind his eyes as a searing wave of feeling rolled through his limbs. It was too good. Too much. He came like a dam breaking, burst after burst until he thought he'd die if it didn't end.

And then it did end, lassitude spreading through him like a steaming bath.

"There," Zoe said. "That's got to feel better."

She crawled up beside him and kissed his cheek. "Want to rest a minute, or shall Bryan and I get started on your next climax?"

"My next?" he said through his gasping breaths.

"We know how many you can take." Bryan's hand slid up his lax inner thigh. "We've agreed we're not going to stop until you're worn out."

Alex was speechless. Bryan moved up and kissed him just as sweetly as Zoe had. The touch of his tongue sent a tiny sparkler down through his cock. This was too good an offer for a man like him to turn down.

"Now," Alex said, rolling toward Bryan and his muscled thigh. "I'm ready for everything now."

He was ready but not prepared. Alex had been with many partners who desired him, but he'd never been with two people who both knew and cared about him. Certainly, he'd never been with anyone who only wanted to see to him. Maybe his need to be in charge had stopped the others, but he honestly couldn't remember anyone trying hard.

Bryan and Zoe weren't just trying, they were overwhelming him with their determination to bring him every possible sensual delight, until he could hardly process them all. When Zoe rode him, Bryan caressed his legs. When Bryan pulled him to his shaky knees and fucked him, Zoe bent down in front and mouthed his cock. Their hands went everywhere, the contrast between their male and female bodies touching off desires he had no defense against. He came until he was hoarse from crying out in ecstasy. Only then did their touch grow gentler, kinder, tweaking here and there in pinches to wake his nerves from their sweet stupor.

Most devastating of all was that Bryan and Zoe fed off each other, stealing each other's tricks with a sense of play he hadn't expected.

They weren't rivals. They were a team.

"Show me that tongue thing," Bryan demanded, trying to master a flutter Zoe had used to bring his spine off the bed.

"Only if you tell me what you were doing with your fingers."

"Oh, God," Alex said, because he knew exactly what technique she meant. It had involved Bryan sliding two lubed fingers inside his anus, and then opening and closing them like a pair of slowly beating wings.

Bryan laughed at his alarm. "Oh, yeah," he said. "Let me show you that one first."

With her smaller hands, Zoe needed three fingers to have the same effect, but the mere fact that she was willing to perform this act had him moaning just as loudly.

"Shall I suck you now?" Bryan offered, the same as if Alex still had the power to speak.

"I think that groan means yes," Zoe said for him.

Alex was on his side, unable to do more than twitch between them. Bryan lifted Alex's thigh over his shoulder, spreading him wide. One of Zoe's hands massaged the ridge of his perineum, while Bryan's wonderfully hard mouth surrounded him in warmth. Alex was trapped, but this time only by pleasure.

One more, he begged his weary body, the coil of need beginning to tighten. *Let me have one more.*

The soles of his feet were tingling, the palms of his hands. Heat lapped his body from either side where Zoe and Bryan worked their magic. Zoe's breasts were soft against his back, Bryan's penis hard against his shin. Alex was almost coming, almost toppling over the wall. Bryan reached up his chest to tweak his nipple . . . and all the skeins of feeling wound together in a blissful ball. Like the final sweet that capped a feast, his ejaculation came in slow pulses, each wrenched from exhausted but willing nerves.

His every cell sighed with completion.

"Enough," he said, and for the first time in his life he honestly meant it.

Zoe laid her head beside his hip and let out her breath, but Bryan dragged himself up the bed until they could hug. Though he barely had strength to move, Alex's throat was tight.

"Thank you," he said, the words inadequate but all he had. "That meant more to me than I can say."

Bryan slid his arm under Alex's neck, his bicep a hard but warm pillow. "You're welcome, buddy."

He was grinning just a little, those near-black eyes so gentle it was impossible to believe him capable of cuffing anyone to a chair.

"This was your idea," Alex whispered, his voice failing him. "You knew this was my fantasy."

"I knew," Bryan agreed.

Alex felt Zoe move away from them to sit up, but he couldn't look away from Bryan. This night had been a gift Alex doubted he would have had the generosity of soul to give—especially if his affections had been involved the way Bryan's were. Alex was humbled by what he'd done, not just grateful but awed.

Then, as if his subconscious had been waiting for his guard to fall, a rusty blade of loneliness jabbed his heart. He'd never had a night this sweet, but he'd had many just as daring, and none of those partners were now a part of his life. Alex didn't think he could bear losing Bryan, too.

He touched his friend's face and kissed him, gentle but deep. He couldn't say he loved him, not when he wasn't sure what he meant, or how Bryan would interpret it. He felt it, though, with a fullness words couldn't touch.

Whatever the nature of his feelings, he had no trouble conveying their intensity. The kiss went on and on—though it was never anything but tender. Each time it seemed it might end, one of them would turn his head a fraction, and their tongues would slide against each other, and they'd have to explore the charm of the new angle.

They couldn't let go. They were holding something to them so it couldn't fray. Bryan's hands moved up and down Alex's back, slow, soothing passes of his callused palms. Alex was vaguely aware that Zoe wasn't touching them, wasn't participating in what they were doing like she had before.

It was this that finally made him pull away from Bryan.

He turned to her, his head swimming slightly from the lengthy kiss. She was sitting cross-legged on the mattress, watching them quietly.

"Zoe," he said, his hand sliding up her arm.

She shook her head as if her name had been a question. Wondering if she felt left out, he squeezed her shoulder.

"No," she said. "I don't want you to kiss me now. That's how tonight should end. Watching you two was . . . really special."

Despite her apparent calm, her voice choked up on the final words.

"Zoe." He swept his thumb over her clavicle.

She covered his hand with a shaky laugh. "I'm sorry. I'm not upset, not the way you think. I . . . just love the way you look at him. I love the way you look at each other. I thought it would hurt if I ever saw that, but it doesn't."

Alex sat up, needing to hold her no matter what she said. "Something hurts, or you wouldn't be fighting tears."

Her forehead rolled against his chest. "Watching you and Bryan made me realize something I wasn't ready to face."

"I haven't stopped loving you, Zoe. I never will."

She pulled back to smile softly. "And I'll never stop loving you, but we're not in love with each other anymore. I think we turned the last page in that chapter back at the falls."

Was she saying she thought he was in love with Bryan? Alex didn't know how to parse feelings the way she did. He opened his mouth but could think of nothing appropriate to let out.

"Watching you made me ache," she said, lightly touching her breastbone. "But not with jealousy. There's someone I want to open my heart to the way you and Bryan have. It's stupid, I guess. I feel safe with him, even though I know I'm not." She shook her head at herself. "I'm actually glad I'm in love with him. I'm just pretty sure he doesn't feel the same way."

Zoe might not have been jealous, but Alex was small enough to experience a bite of anger when she spoke of loving someone else. "It's that bastard Magnus, isn't it?"

Her smile tugged ruefully higher on one side. " 'Fraid so."

"How can he not feel the same?" Bryan blurted out. "You're really great."

Zoe laughed at that and wiped the corners of her eyes. "Thank you, but Magnus has a lot of women to choose from, and a lot of secrets—neither of which he wants to give up for me."

"Secrets," Alex said, his brain eager to sharpen on a problem it could actually do something about. "If it's secrets you need to uncover, you went to bed with the right two men."

Magnus's eyes blinked open and immediately stung with sweat. His skin throbbed all over, as if every inch of his body were about to spasm in climax. He shoved his hand under the towel to make it happen, then realized his energy was already blazing like a sun. If he worked himself to release, he'd as good as turn on a search light for his mother's minions to follow. No way could they miss the galaxy-sized flare of ecstasy he'd sent up.

He forced his trembling hand away from his erection and sat up, wincing as his balls shifted position.

He hadn't planned on being reminded what a fairy orgy was like, nor would he have guessed two humans could jog his memory. The strength of the urge surprised him, but part of him wanted to drive to that hotel and take them all himself, just let loose of everything but being satisfied. He'd been careful for so long, concerned about sparing Zoe's feelings. But if tonight were any indication, she might like that side of his nature.

Magnus thrust his hands into his hair and groaned. If anyone had told him he could want Zoe more, he would have sworn it was impossible. He'd never get her out of his system now, never stop wanting to explore every twist and turn of her fantasies. She was his match in so many ways. Even the thrill she found in pleasing another he understood. The thought that they could never truly be together nearly drove him mad.

Zoe was enough to be an orgy all by herself.

And then a smile broke across his face, as unstoppable as sunrise.

She was in love with him. Magnus hated that Alex was going to poke into his secrets, though chances were his safeguards would hold against the changeling's untrained powers. What mattered was that Zoe was in love with *him*. His grin stretched wide enough to bare his molars. Regardless of how he'd disappointed her, she wanted to open her heart to him.

The Will-Be shimmered on the edge of vision like a heat mirage. Magnus hadn't called it consciously. It was simply drawn to his joy and eager to deliver some unmet desire. Even as he wondered what freak of fortune might unfold, a loud crash from his yard brought him to his feet. Not with fear, though. Nothing bad could happen if Zoe loved him, especially if she loved him better than her old boyfriend.

Indulging in a chuckle that was purely male, he went outside to see what had transpired.

He found a pizza delivery car smashed into his scrubby yard's one large rock. The dazed but unharmed young driver was scratching his head over the wreck.

"Dude," he said on seeing Magnus, not seeming to register that his clothing consisted of a towel. "I don't even know how I did that. My radio is, like, totally crushed."

"You can use my phone," Magnus offered. "Call your boss and a tow truck."

"That'd be good," said the teenager, still sounding spaced. He looked at Magnus. "I don't suppose you're hungry, 'cuz I'm, like, never gonna make these deliveries now. No charge, of course."

Magnus let out a startled laugh. Clearly, this was the Will-Be's idea of making up for his missed pizza night at Zoe's.

"As a matter of fact, pizza is my favorite midnight snack." He smiled at the boy, knowing he probably deserved some recompense for being yanked into this. "Why don't you come inside, and I'll tell you a few of my secrets for getting anything you want while working half as hard."

"Cool," said the boy. "Just, you know, put on some pants."

Magnus swallowed the last bite of pizza-with-everything and slid the other two pies the delivery boy had given him into his fridge. He'd enjoyed playing magical mentor to the laid-back lad, who probably didn't suspect half the value of what he'd been told. His stomach full, his cheer restored, Magnus felt more himself than he had in days. He even had pizza for breakfast to look forward to. With that prospect before him, any problem seemed solvable.

Hadn't he learned that nothing was impossible to a man who believed? Magnus didn't have to know *how* he'd be with Zoe, he simply had to know he would. With that assurance trembling to be born inside him, all was right with his world.

Or almost right.

"Ahem," said a high-pitched female voice from a spot above his right ear. "The universe has a message for Magnus Monroe."

Magnus's mood was too good not to smile. Despite the officiousness his invisible visitor was trying to put on, he knew it represented neither the "universe" nor his mother.

"Ah," he said, closing the refrigerator door. "Are you certain this message doesn't come from a small fairy? Maybe one who's too proud to admit she's deigning to speak to me?"

The air vibrated with a tense silence.

"The reason I ask," he continued casually, "is because if my honored guest were a small fairy, I'd feel obliged to tell her I mean her and her kind no harm. As an emigre myself, naturally I respect her choice to live in the human realm."

The air hummed a little harder. "Titania's blood has been known to lie, Big One."

"True," Magnus admitted. "But many say my father's blood runs truer in my veins." He turned to face the almost-glow in the air, catching an elusive hint of purple wings. "Come on, Rajel. I've seen you already, when you were hovering over Zoe's kitten. Why not show yourself and say what you came here for?"

The queen of Zoe's fairies blinked into visibility with her arms already folded across her chest. "Don't imagine we've forgotten your shameless ploy to suck up to us."

"Careful," Magnus teased. "You stay that grumpy long, and some more mirthful member of your flock is liable to steal your throne."

"As if!" Rajel exclaimed, demonstrating an admirable command of human attitude. "We all think this matter is serious."

"Tell me what it is then, queen, and maybe I'll think it's serious too."

Rajel squinted suspiciously at him, her wings beating so hard her sparkly yellow crown slid over one eye. She pushed the headgear level with one tiny hand. Finally, she huffed and landed on his countertop.

"I hope you think it's serious," she said. "Because if you don't sever your ties to Zoe, your mother is determined to do her harm."

"Zoe told me she showed up at the falls."

"She didn't just show up, Big One, she attacked Zoe with a self-doubt spell. If my flock and I hadn't saved her, Zoe would be a mass of insecurities the Will-Be couldn't do nice things for. Why, she might have gotten so bad she'd forget to believe in us!"

Magnus's face went cold. "Zoe didn't tell me that."

"She didn't know how dangerous it was."

Shaken, Magnus pulled a chair out from his kitchen table and sat. Zoe's confidence was an integral part of who she was. He couldn't imagine her without it and frankly didn't want to try. "We can't let my mother attack again."

"*You* can't let your mother attack." Rajel flew off the counter to land on his knee. Though she wasn't made of matter, her magic gave the impression that she weighed as much as his cell phone. "*You're* the reason Zoe is in danger."

"I can't return to Fairy," Magnus said. "And that's the only thing that would convince Titania to back off."

"You wouldn't go home even to save Zoe?"

"It's not that simple. My mother wants me under her thumb to solidify her position with the other nobles. If I refuse, she'll consider it an act of war. I saw what happened when my father tore the realms apart. I don't want our people to suffer that again."

Her Lilliputian size notwithstanding, Rajel understood a ruler's responsibility to protect her own. Her little face was sober.

"Then you need another plan," she said. "Zoe doesn't understand your mother's brand of magic. She won't know how to defend herself."

The answer came to him between one breath and another, no doubt the lingering effect of his recent attunement with the Will-Be.

"I have a plan," he said. "But it's going to require your help."

Zoe was as interested in Magnus's secrets as anyone, but after the night she'd spent, she needed shower time more. Leaving Bryan and Alex to their detecting, she grabbed her purse and shut the door. The solitude was immediately comforting. She'd made a choice tonight, possibly a choice that wasn't going to work out, but just knowing for sure what her heart desired was a relief. If nothing else, tonight proved she could be brave if she wanted to.

She felt renewed by the time she'd rinsed the last of the hotel's spicy soap down the drain—which was when the love-birds, Samuel and Florabel, apparated in the middle of the spray.

"Hey!" she said, covering her breasts.

"Outside the curtain!" Florabel scolded, pointing her finger firmly at her new boyfriend. "Remember your boy-girl human etiquette!"

Florabel didn't seem to realize Zoe might want privacy from *her*. Resigned, she asked the obvious. "Why are you here?"

"We need a curl of your hair. Please cut one off for us."

If this was an example of Florabel's communication skills, Zoe understood why her toaster still didn't work. "Am I allowed to know why?"

"We need it for a private bit of magic we can't talk about."

"A private bit of magic."

"It's *very* important."

"You're sure you're not going to use it to turn me into a toad?

"Zoe!" Samuel cried from outside the curtain. His agitated shadow buzzed closer. "You are our human. We wouldn't harm you no matter what."

No matter what suggested their patience might have been tempted these last few days. Zoe supposed she ought to be glad they were talking to her at all.

"Fine," she said. "I guess I owe you for saving me and Alex at Fairy Falls."

"That invokes no debt," Samuel said with chivalrous outrage.

"Saving you was our honor," Florabel added.

"We'll take that curl, though. At least three inches, if you please."

Zoe stifled a sigh. She had a pair of scissors in her sewing kit. She still had no idea why they wanted a lock of hair, but her fairies had done so much for her, she couldn't start doubting them now.

Sixteen

Alex got his room service after all. He ordered steaks and baked potatoes for him and Zoe and a garden salad for Bryan. Bryan tended to get nervous if he'd recently eaten anything he liked too much. Alex figured he had one more day of watching his partner munch lettuce before his post-pizza guilt wore off.

Alex was looking forward to that. Bryan barely looked up from his laptop when Alex set his plate on the desk. Apparently, a pile of romaine and vinaigrette wasn't worth interrupting his Internet search on Magnus for. He only grunted when Alex asked how it was going, so Alex returned to the white-clothed table the waiter had set up.

His food, he decided, was worth paying attention to.

He was sighing over his perfect steak when Zoe emerged from her marathon shower. Wrapped in a big bath towel, she looked like the little mermaid with her curls damp and hanging down. Alex liked seeing her in that intimate, comfortable state—probably more than someone who, according to her, wasn't "in love" with her should. It felt good that she wasn't self-conscious around him.

"Yum," she said, inhaling the aroma of charbroiled meat.

"I got you what I have," Alex assured her, but her eyes had already left the table. She was staring at the corner of the room behind him, her gaze unfocused, her attention caught. A chill prickled over Alex's scalp. He remembered that look of hers from high school.

"Um, Alex?" she said, still not facing him. "Do you have an Uncle Harry or maybe Harvey who passed when you were pretty young?"

"My father had a best friend whose name was Henry," he said unsurely. "He was close to all us kids. Sometimes he'd tease and call himself our favorite uncle."

"Well, he's showing me his shoes." A grin flickered over her face a second before she laughed. "They're very blue. Like, glowing neon blue. He's saying, 'Remember Elvis. Remember the radio.' "

"Oh, my God," Alex breathed, the hair on his arms standing up in waves. "Elvis's *Blue Suede Shoes*. That was Uncle Henry's personal theme song. Every time it came on the oldies station, he'd turn it up so loud us kids would cover our ears and scream. I'd forgotten that completely until just now."

"He's talking really loudly, too," Zoe said, laughing. "Like he's got a bullhorn. Let me give you his message before my ear falls off. He says . . . excuse me, he's insisting I repeat it at his volume. He says, *Stop worrying about your heart!* He says there's nothing wrong with it, it's just big. Nobody on the other side would judge you for how many folks you love. He says as long as you do love, when you cross over you won't have regrets."

She turned to Alex then, her affection shining so brightly it brought a burn to his eyes. "He says he's going to start talking to you directly when this is over, so you better get ready to not pee your pants. He says he's been watching over your family like a guardian angel, but his job would be easier if he had you to pass messages."

"Me?" Alex was so startled he dropped the fork he hadn't remembered he was holding. "I'm not psychic."

"He says you are, Alex, and he's showing me a big heap of presents, like for a birthday. No . . ." She paused for a moment, her head tilted to the side. "He says these were gifts you were *born* with, this giant heap up to the ceiling, and you've only opened a few. He says you need to start tearing off the wrapping, 'cause they're all for you."

"That's crazy," Alex said, his breath coming like he'd run up a flight of stairs.

"Henry doesn't think so. He's nodding at me emphatically. He says I said what he meant just right. And now he's crossing his forearms over his heart to say he loves you, and he's going now."

Zoe crossed her arms over her chest just like Alex had seen his father's friend do a thousand times. If he hadn't been sitting already, he would have had to then. Every muscle in his legs was trembling. Zoe had never done a reading for him before. If this was how her clients felt when they got one, it was no wonder they were impressed. His head was floating, and every color in the room seemed impossibly beautiful and bright. Zoe herself looked as if rays of sunshine were shooting out of her skin.

I could forgive myself for what I did, he thought, the moment of clarity extraordinary. *And then it wouldn't matter what anyone in this town thought.*

The idea almost frightened him.

"Wow," he said, incapable of uttering another word.

Zoe took the chair next to him and squeezed his hand. "That was good. Your uncle really came through clear."

"I can't believe he took the trouble to talk to me."

"Oh, you're worth more trouble than that," Zoe teased. "Especially since it sounds like he plans to try again later."

Alex shivered involuntarily, and Zoe laughed.

"You're in for it now, buddy. At least, when whatever he meant by 'when this is over' happens."

Alex glanced at Bryan to see what he made of this. To his surprise, Bryan was engrossed in working on his laptop. He appeared not to have noticed his and Zoe's exchange.

"Find something?" Alex asked.

"Hm?" said Bryan as he read whatever he'd called up.

"Magnus Monroe? What have you turned up?"

Bryan shook himself. "Lived at his current address eight years, owns the house and the land, no mortgage. Two years before that, his residence was an apartment."

"His business is doing well," Zoe said. "So that no mortgage thing isn't strange."

She grimaced when Alex lifted a brow at her. She must have realized she'd come off like she was defending him. Rather than apologize, she tucked her towel more firmly beneath her arms.

"Criminal record?" Alex asked, since he had no reason to defend her would-be boyfriend.

"Not that I can find."

"And where was he before ten years ago?"

"Dunno yet," Bryan said.

"What about incorporation?" Alex suggested, determined to find something. "If he runs his business that way, the Secretary of State website will have records."

Bryan gave him a look like, *Who's got their fingers on these keys?*, but he did as Alex asked.

"No luck," he said a minute later. "We'll have to track his earlier history some other way."

"You know where he went to college?" Alex asked Zoe.

Zoe looked embarrassed. "He never mentioned it."

Her acting like it was her fault she didn't know this joker better stole the last of his patience.

"Let me," he said to Bryan, dragging the chair back with him in it. Bryan ceded his place with an eye roll that Alex ignored. Maybe his gut couldn't be trusted in this particular instance, and maybe Zoe liking Magnus more than Alex thought she should wasn't a real basis for mistrust. All the same, it had struck him from their first meeting that there was something off about the guy. Magnus was too damn big and smiley to be for real.

He cracked his knuckles and set to work, his fingers flying as deftly over the keys as they'd once sent passes spiraling down the football field. Voter registration was kind enough to supply Magnus's Social Security number, always a useful snippet for a search. Then Alex thought, *What does it mean when you can't trace someone's history more than ten years?*

Maybe that they used to be someone else.

Grinning to himself, he pulled up Social Security's Master Death File. What he found there was exciting enough to have him splitting his browser's screen. Muttering to himself, he took a little jaunt through an old DMV database. When the license he wanted finished loading, and he compared the pages side by side, he knew he'd scored a Hail Mary.

"Gotcha!" he crowed. "Take a look at this, guys. The real Magnus Monroe was a skinny carrottop who died in 1992. The one you know is a fake!"

He remembered a little too late that Zoe might not be as happy as he was to hear this news. With an effort, he dialed back the cheer in his voice.

"I need a current picture of him," he said to Zoe, who was gaping at him from the table. "Maybe our contact at the FBI can find a match for his face."

"The FBI?" Bryan put his hand on Alex's shoulder, pulling

his gaze back to him. "Alex, I know you don't like this guy, but I can't let you mislead Zoe this way."

"What are you talking about? I've got him. The real Magnus Monroe is dead. Zoe's friend could be anyone."

"Alex, the screen says 'record not found.' "

His tone was so certain and his eyes so sad that Alex had to check the laptop again. The incriminating and slightly pop-eyed picture of the red-haired man remained exactly where he'd left it. Alex's neck prickled for the third time that evening.

"What's wrong with you?" he asked Bryan. "It's right there as plain as day. The Social Security record. The DMV photo."

Zoe came over to see for herself.

"It's right there," Alex assured her, as if she, too, might deny its reality.

Zoe bent close to read the screen, then turned to Bryan. "It *is* right there. Why would you want to hide this from me?"

Bryan began to look confused. "It's blank. I swear, you two, Magnus Monroe is exactly who he says he is."

Then he backed away from them and sat on the bed.

"I don't think he's joking," Zoe said. "I think he really can't read the screen."

"But why wouldn't . . ." Alex trailed off, his brain slowing to a crawl, until he almost heard the *tock, tock, tock* of its gears turning. He'd been trying to push the incident from his mind, but the voice at the falls came back to him, the one that had mistaken him for Magnus and told him to come home. Fairy Falls had figured heavily in the dotty old lady stories that he'd read at the *Courier*. If the fairies weren't galloping out of the falls on their white stallions, they'd been haunting the woods nearby. He hated to admit it, but maybe Fairy Falls was more than a name. Maybe real live fairies were traveling back and forth.

And maybe Magnus was one of them.

"Oh, God," he said, his face gone hot with embarrassment, though he hadn't said one crazy thought out loud.

Except . . . someone had cast some sort of spell on Zoe at the falls, and if not a fairy, then what? Maybe Magnus had found a similar magical means of protecting his bogus records from inquiring eyes, and maybe he and Zoe were immune because they were Fairyville natives.

Alex had seen a little fairy at the falls, complete with wings. Possibly it had been part delusion, but could he truly be certain big fairies weren't real?

"Oh, God," he said, this time just to Zoe. "I so don't want to share my theory about this . . ."

At some point during Alex's story, Zoe sat beside Bryan on the bed. This tale was too wild to take standing up.

"If Magnus really is a fairy," she said, the words faltering a little on their way out, "wouldn't someone have noticed? Wouldn't being a magical creature make him stand out?"

"People find ways to account for what they don't understand. If his power is making people *not* see things . . . I mean, how can you explain Bryan thinking that screen is blank? And you said yourself his business is successful. Maybe he's working some sort of money mojo, too."

"He's very charming," Zoe justified.

"And what if it's *fairy* charm? Look, I know this sounds crazy, but you of all people know the value of an open mind."

Zoe did know. She simply wasn't comfortable admitting the world might be even stranger than she'd given it credit for. She smoothed the towel down her thighs, wishing she'd put on something more armorlike. Sighing, she asked what she had to.

"What exactly did the newspaper stories say?"

Alex handed her a sheaf of copies, which he'd probably

sweet-talked some intern to make for him. "Here," he said. "These are the original transcripts of the interviews. Basically, these old ladies are repeating stories from when Fairyville was more like a ghost town, about how handsome men used to ride out of Fairy to seduce young girls."

"On the full moon," Zoe said, skimming down the page. "It says here they had to win a maiden's heart, and if they did, they could remain in the forest, dallying with their new girlfriend for the full month."

Oh, Lord. Her back tightened as if it wanted to shiver but couldn't quite. Was this the reason Magnus slept with a different woman on each full moon? Could it really be as simple and as insane as that?

She had to admit him being a fairy would explain some of his quirks.

Alex reached over to flip through the stack for the page he wanted. "One of the old ladies says that if the parents of the girl came to look for her, the fairies could make themselves invisible. The girls could still see them, but the parents couldn't. It was like they'd been hypnotized."

Zoe's eyes refused to focus on the passage he'd pointed out, though she didn't doubt what he said was there. "Why haven't *my* fairies mentioned this? Surely they can spot an imposter."

Alex shrugged. "I don't know. Bad blood maybe. Your fairy queen did call Magnus's mother 'The Evil One.' And if his mother isn't a ghost but actually a fairy, that would probably make him one, too."

"Jesus," Zoe said, which showed how flummoxed she was. She'd never liked taking that name in vain.

"Guys," Bryan interrupted in a firm but patient tone. "The. Screen. Is. Blank."

Zoe knew she couldn't leave him in his confusion.

"Come back and look again," she said. "With me this time."

She pulled him gently behind her, coaxing his arms around her waist until his body touched hers above the towel. He and Alex had only pulled on their trousers, and his upper body was bare. It was odd to feel his warm skin and chest hair in this context, but she pushed off the distraction. Closing her eyes, she imagined her aura getting bigger and brighter and blending with Bryan's. It was a trick her old mentor had taught her to goose up another person's psychic sensitivities—assuming they had a few to start with.

"Look over my shoulder," she said, hoping this would work for Bryan. "Tell me what you see now."

"It's still showing no—" Suddenly Bryan stiffened. "Shit." He blinked so hard she heard his eyelids click. "It's there. Magnus Monroe *is* a fraud."

Zoe didn't want to say it, but she did. "We have to call him on this."

Bryan's arms were still circling her. They tightened comfortingly. "The explanation might not be as bad as you think."

He didn't sound like he believed it, but he was sweet. Alex rubbed his hand up and down Bryan's muscled arm. Oddly enough, Zoe got the impression that he was trying to reassure her, too.

"It's nearly midnight," her old boyfriend said. "Nobody's going to call anybody on anything until tomorrow."

The men exchanged glances, then looked at her.

"You'll stay here tonight," Alex said, not letting it be a question.

Zoe flushed. Maybe this discovery should have changed her feelings about Magnus, and maybe she wouldn't have minded playing a bit more with Alex and Bryan, but what would she think of herself if she let her heart's decision be so easily swayed?

It hadn't swayed anyway. Scary though it was, when she looked inside herself, it was still Magnus she yearned for.

"I don't think—" she began, and then Bryan silenced her with a gentle hug.

"Just stay to snuggle," he said. "No night as special as we had should end with bad feelings."

Seventeen

Magnus needed a couple of cooperative ghosts to finish baiting the trap he was constructing in his faux sweat lodge. Calling spirits wasn't his area of expertise, nor was he certain ten in the morning was the best time for it, so luckily he had Zoe's hair to act as his lure. If the personal essence of a top-notch medium couldn't bring ghosts out of the ethers, he didn't know what would.

"You're too tense," the boy fairy, Samuel, critiqued from his seat on Magnus's left shoulder. "Zoe's always more relaxed than this."

Magnus opened one eye to glare at him. It hadn't been his idea to have company, but "Samuel the Stubborn," as the green-clad fairy had dubbed himself, was doing his best to live up to his name.

"Zoe's had years of practice," Magnus pointed out. "And I doubt she's ever tried to open up a hot spot for infernal beings to attack her through."

Unimpressed by the complaint, Samuel swung his feet against Magnus's collarbone. "You've already decided to do it, and you know all the reasons why. It's pointless to drag your heels because you're pretty sure it won't be fun."

Magnus was unable to argue that. This wasn't going to be fun, but it was necessary, and if Magnus did it right, it would get his mother off Zoe's case for good. With that to brace him, he drew a slow, deep breath and tried to relax.

"Oh, for magic's sake," Samuel cried, jumping up before Magnus had a chance to fully blow out the breath. "I'll do it."

Samuel's idea of doing it was crying "Here, ghosties!" at the top of his little lungs. "Send messages to your loved ones! Tell them you forgive them and you're all right! Arizona's hottest medium is here for you!"

"You're lying to them," Magnus hissed, taken aback. His plan had been to enlist willing participants.

"Oh, boo hoo," Samuel shot back in an undertone. "We're only going to get a bunch of stupid newbies. They haven't got anything important to say anyway."

With barely a pause, he filled his diminutive chest with air and continued his shrieking pitch. "No waiting! No being pushed aside like a pesky fly! All chatty ghosties will get their say!"

Apparently "Samuel the Shrill" was capable of piercing multiple dimensions with his fairy call. Magnus had just long enough to contemplate plugging his ears when at least a dozen wavering spirits showed up in a clump in his lodge's dome, every one talking at top speed. Magnus couldn't make out a single word, but that didn't discourage them. In half a minute their combined spectral force had dropped the temperature ten degrees.

"There," Samuel said, swiping his palms against each other in satisfaction. "Now just let them go on for about five minutes.

Their vibrations will create a thin spot a baby minion could get through."

Magnus eyed the nattering ghosts uneasily. He had a feeling letting them talk long enough wasn't going to be the issue.

Titania sat at the dragonbone desk beside the window in her private tower. Outside, the sun was setting over her realm, its picture-perfect hills and castles bathed in scarlet and tangerine. She was mulling over the entertainment for her upcoming new moon ball. Normally, this would have soothed her. Six young fairies were coming into their full power tonight. Given the aptitude of her line for using charm in bed, she ought to be able to seduce a couple during the festivities. One could never have too many carnally enchanted allies, and if they sprang from the next generation, all the better.

It went without saying that Titania's rule was supreme, but that didn't mean she could ignore the rising grumbles of discontent from those nobles who—like her—numbered their centuries and not their years. Young flesh was more amenable to influence, if only because it required so much sex to be satisfied. Sadly, the thought of enjoying that flesh tonight did not improve her mood. She was a queen, and her crown lay heavy. Mere physical pleasure could not lighten it, not when her foolish son hadn't been spotted in three whole months.

At her flare of anger, a tiny crack sizzled across the nearest windowpane.

Somehow, her sister Elena had found out about Titania's unsuccessful attempt to woo Magnus through the portal. Now she was spreading the story of Titania's failure to all her friends—including the fact that it was Magnus's love for a human female that kept him there. Elena had the gall to declare her opinion that this was romantic, though this wouldn't surprise anyone. Ever since her adoption of a changeling boy, Titania's sister had been soft in the head.

The sound of further crackling drew her attention to the network of jagged lines now riddling the window glass. Titania waved her fingers at it impatiently, but was interrupted before her magic could mend the damage. One of her minions was materializing in a smoky mass above her black mirrored floor.

Hoping it wouldn't take forever, Titania turned in her chair.

"Your Luminescence," it said unctuously once its mouth had formed. "We have good news."

"You had better," she snapped. "Otherwise, I may rethink my policy of not sending servants to my torturers."

This policy had been honored in the breach more than once—as her minions had cause to know.

"Your Gloriousness," this one said with a fawning bow. "We elementals would rather serve our queen in hell than any empress in heaven."

"Of course you would. Now tell me where you've found my son."

The minion's billowing body drew back slightly. "Er," it said. "Bodacious One, it is not your son we've found, but the deceitful human woman who stole his loyalty."

Titania narrowed her eyes. She didn't like being contradicted any more than she liked being given indecipherable human compliments. Nervous, the minion bared the white razor teeth that always looked too solid to belong to it.

"If you cannot part your son from her," it suggested, "surely you can part her from him."

"And how do you propose I do that? Considering my doubt spell worked so well last time."

"The little fairies were protecting her. This time she is alone.

We were hoping . . . that is, we think it might be advisable if you gave us leave to play hardball."

"Hardball?" she repeated, frowning at what was probably human slang.

"A more final solution," the minion translated delicately.

Titania pushed from her gilded chair. This euphemism she understood. She pressed steepled fingers before her mouth. Her soul ought to be quailing. Murder was serious business even for her. Then again, given the superiority of fairy lovers, this human might cling to Magnus even under torture—and who knew when another chance to get her alone would come?

She paced to the ancient tapestry that hung on her tower's curved wall, a masterpiece whose tiny figures moved and danced when she drew near. It had been created by the little fey, former subjects who now defended this woman.

Was it really murder if her victim was a human? And was it really wrong if it saved her son?

As queen, Titania enjoyed not only her personal power but the power that passed with the throne. Once upon a time, her husband's defection had threatened her position, but she had recovered, and in the years that followed she had arranged this realm exactly as she liked. Today, everyone else's magic was subordinate to hers. She might hate to admit it, but her son's support was becoming necessary to sustain that state of affairs. His philosophical oddities aside, Magnus was strong—both in magic and in character. The nobles would never dare band against her if he stood with her.

That he would stand with her she had no doubt. Her son had forgone his chance to abandon her when Jovian left—and he hadn't stayed just because his friends were, like some people said. Once Titania removed his human distraction, Magnus was bound to remember how devoted he was to her.

Really, once she weighed all the factors, her decision was easy. She turned back to the waiting minion.

"Torture the woman first," she said. "Then, if she persists in refusing to give up my son, you may execute your 'final solution.' I'll watch you from my scrying pool."

The minion bowed deeply. "My queen," it said with seemingly genuine respect. "Obeying your orders will be our pleasure."

The attack came fast and furious, the minions having learned their lesson from their earlier misfire at the Vista Inn. Magnus thanked the Will-Be that the last ghost had been shooed in time, because he got no warning that his attackers were on their way. The minions were simply there in the thin spot the ghosts had made, lobbing fear spells and insults with equal glee. Zoe would be given no opportunity to muster angelic resources—or in this case, Magnus impersonating Zoe with the help of her lock of hair.

The disguise was so good it could have fooled him. Knowing his limits, Magnus had to wonder if Samuel had broken the little fairy pact about not working magic for their former oppressors. Either that, or desperation had sharpened his skills. When he gasped out his feigned confusion at what was going on, he could have sworn Zoe's voice issued from his throat.

For the first ten minutes, he put up a show of resistance. Not only would his mother mistrust a speedy victory, but it would insult Zoe to suggest she'd give up easily.

Then again, "easy" wasn't what he'd call this experience. The fear spells were just as skin-crawlingly awful as he remembered from boyhood punishments. It wasn't until the rain of rocks began, however, that he realized he might have underestimated his mother's zeal for scaring Zoe off.

"Wait!" he cried in his beloved's voice, his fear not as pretend as it had been before. "Can't we talk about this? Maybe I could just see Magnus on weekends."

"No you couldn't!" three minions roared in unison.

Their native realm was a hell dimension, neither Earth nor Fairy. Where they'd gathered, a flaming void had opened in his bunker's dome. To make the thin spot more inviting, Magnus had scraped away its protective layer of amethysts. The sound that rumbled steadily from the hole was like an evil electrical generator, and it wasn't long before he wished he'd made the opening smaller. He could see new elementals arriving by the minute, flashing their razorlike white teeth as their bloodlust rose. If Magnus didn't find a way to calm them, they were going to do more damage than he could heal. Already he was bleeding from a dozen wounds, his concentration strained from fighting off the artificial terror.

Had Zoe truly been here, she would have been scarred.

"All right," he said, judging the time had come for capitulation. "I *will* give Magnus up. No man is worth this much grief."

"We don't believe you," the minions chortled, a sound more like rusty chains than laughter. "We can smell fear, and you're not half as afraid as you ought to be!"

Magnus was wishing for his own "in" with Zoe's angels then. Sweat was rolling down him in the now airless atmosphere, stinging everywhere the rocks had broken skin.

"I don't need to be more afraid," he said. "I'm smart enough to cut my losses."

"We'll show you losses," the minions said just as something small and silver flashed through the air.

Magnus raised his forearm defensively. The flash came from an arrow tipped with fairy steel, a metal native to his homeland. He barely registered the slice it made before a second volley of shafts followed. Magnus was stronger than most humans and could heal quickly, but this particular metal penetrated his defenses. Where he'd been trickling blood before, now it poured.

Dizziness rose with alarming swiftness. His legs gave way and dropped him to the fluorite floor. The size of the puddle his knees squelched in wasn't comforting.

"Stop," he gasped. "You don't have to do this."

The minions laughed uproariously. "Where are your big stuff angels now?" they said. "Don't you humans know other tricks?"

Help, Magnus thought, though he doubted any was coming. He'd made Samuel cross his heart and promise to stay away, unsure how safe the little fey would be. Now he saw that might have been a mistake. His vision had begun to fade, darkening around the edges like a tunnel contracting.

The lead minion looked behind its own foggy shoulder, the other elementals parting so it could see. A mirror seemed to hang in the flames behind it, its surface rippling like water. Magnus's stomach did an unpleasant flip. He recognized his mother's scrying pool.

"Your Graciousness," the minion said as Titania's always lovely image appeared. "The human's strength is flagging. Do you want us to finish her?"

Magnus had a heartbeat to identify himself. He doubted his mother would kill him. Even the hope of his support strengthened her power base. But if he told her, she'd never let Zoe be. He had to keep up this pretense, even if it cost him his life.

His mind became very calm. He was aware that Zoe wouldn't thank him for doing this. Her heart was so big, so forgiving that she wouldn't wish her worst enemy to sacrifice himself for her— much less someone she loved. The truth was, though, that this wasn't a sacrifice for Magnus. He knew as clearly as Zoe did that death was only a change of state. He'd lived many years on the material plane and had fulfilled more dreams than he could count. Zoe was a baby compared to him. She deserved to finish what she'd come here for, whatever that was . . . *with* whomever she chose.

Love expanded inside him until his heart seemed ready to burst his ribs. His natural possessiveness fell away like some old suit he had no use for. He wanted Zoe happy. He wanted her well. And he'd never felt so purely joyous as the moment he decided to give up everything for her. In the beautiful hum of his elation, he barely heard his mother's words.

"Do it," she said.

A second later, the tunnel of his vision shrank to black.

Eighteen

He's not here," Bryan said, having peered in all the windows of Magnus's house.

Zoe should have been glad to put off what was sure to be an awkward—not to mention bizarro—confrontation. Instead, she felt like something painful had squeezed her heart, like more than her romantic prospects depended on finding Magnus soon. She found herself wishing they hadn't slept so late. Saturday or not, her instincts told her this couldn't wait.

"He has a sweat lodge on his property," she said. "We should check that."

"It's ninety degrees out," Bryan objected. "Although, who knows how hot *fairies* like to be. Sheesh." He ran both hands through his rumpled hair. "I just wanna tell you guys, I'm not ready for more weird stuff."

Unable to promise this visit would be weirdness-free, Zoe pointed out the beehive dome of Magnus's getaway. It stuck out of the ground maybe thirty yards away from where they stood.

The three of them set off, each with a private sigh. Alex's face was stiff and Bryan's weary. Zoe didn't even want to know how bedraggled she looked tramping across the desert in her short red dress and her hooker shoes.

Halfway there, vertigo kicked her in the small of her back. She stumbled and went down, saved from pitching on her face by Alex grabbing her elbow.

"Hey," said Bryan, beside her, too. "You okay?"

"Too much sun," she mumbled, though they'd only been in it a few minutes. "I'm okay. We need to keep going."

Alex gave her a look that said he knew something was up, but he hauled her onto her feet all the same. The closer they got to the sweat lodge, the worse she felt, hot and cold and like she was seconds from passing out. All her brain would focus on was that she needed to reach that lodge.

"Let me carry you," Alex said the third time she tripped. "Bryan, you get the door."

"Are you sure?" Bryan asked. "She looks like she'd be better off waiting in the car with the AC on."

"Call Michael," Zoe begged in a whisper against Alex's neck. "Call him like you know he's going to come for you."

"*Archangel* Michael?" Alex's eyes were round, and Zoe knew he was going to balk.

"Call your Uncle Henry then. He'll pass the message to anyone you want."

Alex set his jaw, but this help he could believe in. "Uncle Henry," he said firmly. "We need assistance. Angels, please, if you can get them to come."

Bryan had been tugging ineffectually at the sweat lodge's door. At Alex's words it burst open.

"Shit," he said. "More damn rocks."

"Carry me down there," Zoe said to Alex. "We'll be okay. I can feel the angels surrounding us."

"Guys!" Bryan called from the belowground chamber in a strange, tense voice. "I think you need to see this."

Alex carried her down the steps into the dimness. At first, all she could see was the flickering hellfire up in the ceiling. That was startling enough, but then she noticed the slim, still figure lying on its side on the rock-strewn floor.

That sight clutched her throat in a fist of ice.

"It's you," Bryan said, gasping a bit in the stifling air. "That body looks just like you."

Zoe scrambled out of Alex's hold. No matter how the body looked, she'd recognize that energy signature anywhere. She fell to her knees beside it, dimly registering the odd flooring. The figure who resembled her was bloodied all over, its skin ghostly pale in the daylight slanting down the steps from outside. Arrows bristled from its front like a pincushion.

"Magnus," she said, somehow finding the strength to lift his shoulders onto her lap. "Oh, God, what have you done?"

The moment she pressed her lips to his forehead, his disguise shivered and fell away.

"No," said a shocked female voice. "*No!* You didn't make me attack my son!"

Whoever the voice belonged to, Zoe didn't need the angels to banish it. It disappeared with a cry of aggravated horror, taking the circle of hellfire along with it.

At the moment, Zoe was too worried to be grateful.

"I feel a pulse," Alex said, crouching on Magnus's other side to press two fingers to his neck. "I think we got here in time."

Magnus's body shuddered like an earthquake.

"You did," he croaked. His lashes were stuck together, and his eyes struggled to open. When they did, they shone green as emeralds in his bloody face. Zoe gasped, the glow of his irises too bright to be imagination. The light turned the red that painted his features to a brutal mask, though it left his beauty oddly undimmed. Seeing her amazement, Magnus swallowed painfully. "I guess maybe you have a few questions about this."

"Hush," Zoe urged, not daring to stroke his cheek, he was so cut up. Her heart was breaking for his injuries; to have him hurt was to hurt herself. Tears began to roll unstoppably down her face. "Alex figured out you were a fairy. He found some old newspaper stories about men riding through the falls. You just lie still, and we'll call for help."

Bryan was already digging out his cell phone.

"No," Magnus said in a voice so firm it caused all of them to blink. "I can heal this quicker with no doctors watching. All I need is rest and orange juice. And to get these arrows out."

"I'll get the juice from your house," Bryan said, obviously eager to be out of there. "And a blanket in case you're in shock."

Magnus *was* shivering in her lap, his torso as heavy as a load of bricks. He closed his eyes and got heavier. "I can't believe you found me."

"I can't believe you were trying to convince your mother you were me! That is what you were doing, isn't it?"

His hand found her upper arm and squeezed. "You deserve more of this lifetime, love. You've hardly made a dent in it."

That made her cry harder. "You're an idiot. I have defenses."

"Not against my mother. She's rather more bloodthirsty than you're used to."

"No kidding." Zoe sniffed and dashed her tears away angrily. "Tell me the truth now, Magnus—no stories. Is your being from Fairy the reason you and I couldn't . . . be intimate the way I wanted to?"

He opened his eyes to smile at her with them, seeming relieved to be asked. "I made a magical agreement, so I could stay in the human realm. I had to win a new heart with each full moon and then give it back. I knew if I took yours, I'd want to keep it. I knew I'd never want to sleep with anyone but you. I would have been sent home as soon as the month ran out. I might never have seen you again."

"So when I thought you didn't trust me, that you didn't love me—"

Magnus took her face between hands that were sticky with his own blood. "I'm so sorry that's what you thought, so sorry I caused you a moment's pain. My heart was yours the day I laid eyes on you. Those other women were all that allowed me to be close to you."

"You could have told me the truth!"

"And risk enraging my mother?" Magnus shook his head. "I can't regret anything I did to keep you from facing her."

Zoe had to bite her lip to still its trembling. Maybe it was too soon, but the words *I love you* were an explosion waiting to break free. Magnus saw them in her expression, and his smile deepened. His beautiful, glowing eyes said everything she'd ever longed to hear from him. He loved her, too. No matter what appearances had suggested, it was there in his warm green gaze.

"Not to break this up," Alex said in an acid tone, "but what are the chances your mother is going to try for Zoe again?"

Magnus waited a beat before shifting his gaze to him. "I don't know. Realizing she almost killed her son may shock her out of more attempts for a while."

"For a while." Alex shook his head, his sea-blue eyes as hard as Zoe had ever seen them. "I'm sorry, Mr. Fairy Guy, but that's unacceptable."

"Zoe is as protected as any human can be."

"And you wouldn't, oh, I don't know, just go home like your mother wants?"

"Alex!" Zoe's cry drew neither of the men's attention from their stare off. "Magnus almost died for me."

"Magnus put you in danger in the first place."

"It's all right," Magnus said, touching her arm before she

could speak again. "He deserves an answer more than most. I don't go home because my mother wants me to shore up her shaky rule. One faction would love that. Another hopes I'll depose her—preferably violently. The remainder would like it if I magically split the realm so that nobody ever has to meet anyone who disagrees with them. That was my father's choice, and, given the current situation, I can't say it worked. People simply find new things to fight about. At the moment, I appear to be the only one who knows the cure for Fairy lies not with me, but within each individual fairy heart."

"Which means what?" Alex said, his arms flexing with muscle as they crossed atop his navy polo shirt.

Magnus seemed to recognize the posturing for what it was. The corners of his mouth curved up. "It means magic should be shared and not hoarded. The universe makes room for every fairy's wishes to come true. If everyone understood that, Fairy could support a hundred thrones, including my mother's. But they'd rather believe one person or philosophy must reign supreme, and so they split into parties and sharpen their swords. Live and let live is not a model they understand."

Wincing slightly, Magnus shifted until he sat higher in her lap. With a grunt of effort, and a ruthlessness that made Zoe blanch, he pulled the most uncomfortable of the arrows from the ridged belly muscle where it had lodged. He panted for a moment before continuing. "I cannot rule my people because, in my heart, the only person I believe I have the right to rule is me."

"You could tell them that," Zoe said.

"Love," Magnus said gently, "I lived in my homeland for centuries. Everything I've told you, my people have heard from me and others more eloquent. Change will come one fairy at a time, when and if each chooses."

"A convenient attitude," Alex observed, but not as confidently as he had before. It was, after all, difficult to scold a man who looked more like St. Sebastian than the poster boy for selfishness.

Magnus smiled as gently at Alex as he had at her. "Perhaps we should table this debate for another time. I doubt any of us want to be here if those minions return."

The debate was tabled altogether, it being all too obvious that Zoe and Magnus wanted to be alone. Alex drove himself and Bryan back to their new hotel, where his grumpiness was not improved by what they encountered in the blandly modern lobby.

Admittedly, Alex's last progress report had been a little vague—and wasn't likely to get clearer, given today's events—but he hadn't expected to find Mrs. Pruitt lying in wait for them. She looked ten years older than when they'd seen her last, and she hadn't been her freshest then. Circles shadowed eyes that were tired beyond what sleeplessness could cause, and her clothes—jeans and a pastel sweater set—were creased from traveling. The only real snap of life about her was her thin-lipped frown. She was pissed, Alex saw, and gearing up to get pissier.

Far more troubling than her mood was little Oscar's presence. Mother and son both slid from the lobby's blockish ecru chairs when they caught sight of him and Bryan.

"About time," huffed Mrs. Pruitt, as if he and Bryan were late for an appointment.

"Mrs. Pruitt," Alex said, going into soother mode.

"Oh, can it," said Mrs. Pruitt. "Your nicey-nice *GQ* manners are about as much use to me as that damn report."

"Your case is hardly straightforward," Alex reminded her. "We're doing what we can."

"What you can!" she repeated, the words sharp enough to catch the attention of nearby guests. She lowered her voice, though her temper clearly remained at full volume. "And while you do *what you can*, what am I supposed to do with him? Ever since we went to you for help, he's been worse than ever. Yesterday, he rolled my grocery cart to the ice cream section without touching it. People were staring. I thought I was going to die!"

"I didn't mean to," little Oscar whispered. "You said I could have a Fudgsicle."

It was such a typical kid complaint, Alex almost smiled. He lost the urge when Mrs. Pruitt closed her eyes and began to shake.

"Maybe we should take this conversation to our room," Bryan suggested, seeing that, for whatever reason, the end of Mrs. Pruitt's rope had been reached.

Oscar's mother fisted her hands a little tighter. "No," she said, firm and low. "I'm not going one step farther with this freak of nature. You think my life is straightforward? You try living yours with him around your neck."

"Mommy!" Oscar gasped, almost as shocked as Alex and Bryan.

Mrs. Pruitt flinched, not quite as hard-hearted as she appeared. She knelt before the boy.

"It will be all right," she said, smoothing her hands down his Superman T-shirt. "These nice men are going to take care of you. Don't give them any trouble, and you'll be fine."

Two fat tears rolled down Oscar's cheeks.

"Shit," said Bryan. "Mrs. Pruitt, you really can't do this."

Her lips were shaking, but her eyes were as cool as Siberia. "Watch me," she said, and strode stiffly to the revolving door.

"Stop her," Bryan pleaded, but Alex took one look at Oscar and decided he'd better not.

The boy was trembling worse than his mother, his gaze glued to his Wile E. Coyote sneakers, his breath hitching as he fought not to cry harder than he was. Those yellow shoes didn't look so bad to Alex today. They looked like something you might *want* to wear, if you needed cheering up.

"I'm sorry," Oscar said in a quavery voice. His big blue eyes spilled over as they met Alex's. "I tried to stay happy, I really did, but I just can't do it anymore."

Alex scooped him up and held him tight against his shoulder.

"She can't just *leave* him," Bryan murmured, though she obviously had. His hand came to rest beneath where Alex's was rubbing Oscar's back. "What are we supposed to do with him?"

"Keep him safe," Alex answered. "For as long as we have to."

Oscar's head bobbled back to look at him, his tears beginning to dry as he decided whether he ought to believe this assurance. Alex felt like he was staring into a blurred mirror. How had this kid kept it together? How had he stayed happy when the person whose love he should have been able to take for granted kept telling him he was unlovable?

"You're a good kid," Alex said. "I know you are."

Oscar gnawed his lip and nodded unsurely. Alex prayed he wasn't going to cry again. Alex was the youngest in his family. Child care really wasn't in his box of tricks.

"Do you like kittens?" he asked, inspiration—or possibly desperation—striking out of the blue. "Because one of my good friends has a kitten, and I bet she'd love to meet you."

"His good friend also has a kitchen," Bryan added wryly, "and a guest room with an empty bed."

Alex and Bryan exchanged rueful looks. No matter what else was going on, they knew Zoe would help them. She was much too tenderhearted to turn a boy like Oscar away.

Magnus drank a pint of orange juice, ate three Pop Tarts, then took a rather gruesome shower, during which he pulled out the remaining arrows. Zoe sat on the toilet lid while he did this, incapable of helping except to wince and make sure he didn't slip or faint. The swiftness of his recovery amazed her. By the end of the shower he was no longer bleeding, and could walk—albeit slowly—under his own power. Despite him seeming to be out of danger, she knew she wouldn't relax until she had him out of his home and into hers.

Magnus didn't protest her nesting impulse, just handed her the keys to his 4x4 and let her drive.

Once she had him at her place, she settled him on the over-stuffed saddle leather couch in her living room, covering him with one of the quilts her Nana Sonia had stitched. He smiled through her fussing, his eyes sleepy but fond, his big, smooth muscles looking relaxed.

Seeing a nap was about to happen, and not wanting to miss out, Corky scrambled up the quilt to join him.

"I'd sleep better with my head in your lap," Magnus pointed out, his hand swallowing the kitten as he petted it.

"Oh, would you?" Zoe said, but she didn't mind scooting onto the couch under him.

He had his shirt unbuttoned and, though none of his wounds still bled, he was all over bruises, as if his body were a steak someone had been trying to tenderize. Zoe traced the edges of his wounds with her fingertips, aghast at the thought of what she'd almost lost. If they'd arrived a minute later . . . If she'd let Bryan convince her to return to the car . . .

An unexpected moan had Zoe pulling back her hand.

"Sorry," she said. "I didn't mean to hurt you."

"You didn't." Amused lines fanned around his eyes. "It's just, if you keep touching me like that, I'm going to have more aches than I already do." He lifted his hips in explanation, drawing her eyes to the not-so-subtle hump forming under the quilt.

"Oh," she said. Heat lapped through her in a torrid wave. "I would have thought you'd be too . . ."

He pressed her hand to a spot just beneath his ribs, keeping it in place with his. "Fairies like a lot of sex, Zoe. Need it, if it comes to that. We have a saying that if a fairy on his deathbed can't get it up, you know he's truly passed."

"But I thought—" She wasn't sure what she thought, because her head wasn't really working. Luckily, Magnus understood.

"Zoe, had it been possible, I would have happily, gratefully, delightedly spent every urge I had on you. You are the only woman I want in my bed."

"So when you only had sex once a month—"

"I was holding back."

"Because of me. Because you didn't want to hurt me by having sex as often as you normally would."

"Yes," he said solemnly.

Zoe fought not to squirm beneath him. Her sex was pulsing inappropriately, hot and wet and ready for action.

"How often?" she burst out.

Magnus laughed and circled her wrist with stroking fingers. "Oh, half a dozen times a day would be sufficient. More for young fairies."

"Half a dozen!" Her jaw had fallen. "But that's— No wonder you always went all night when you finally took someone!"

Magnus's eyes were hot green fire. "I'd go all week if it were possible to make love the way I want with you." He winced and shifted, and Zoe realized this conversation hadn't helped his condition.

"Let me," she said, reaching under the quilt for the well-strained fastening of his jeans. Undoing it, she lowered the zipper carefully and reached in. The minute she had his hot, smooth thickness wrapped in her palm, she forgot she'd been intending to relax him.

"Oh, God," Magnus said, his hips surging up at her. "I think I have to put Corky back on the floor."

It was all she could do not to gasp at the size of him, and he grew more aroused with every pulse. Alex wasn't this long, nor Bryan this thick. Helpless to stop herself, she eased him fully out and stroked him from balls to tip, marveling at his steely vitality. His veins were so swollen they resisted pressure almost as well as the rest of him.

"Zoe," he said, a moan of praise and relief. "Every morning, I wake up like this, hard and aching from knowing I'll be seeing you. It makes me happy just to be with you, just to look forward to your company."

"Me, too," she murmured, adoring the abandoned way his body rolled. "I've been in love with you a long time."

He stilled at her words, making her realize what she'd admitted. She believed he loved her back, but he'd never said it in so many words. Before she could grow embarrassed, he put his hand over hers. His eyes were very serious.

"You don't know how happy I am to hear that, but this isn't going to be easy just because the truth is in the open now. The terms of my magical visa haven't changed. If I want to stay here, the ritual demands that a woman and I come together as if we were going to procreate. It demands that I spill my pleasure inside of you. Then I have to return the heart I've won." He offered her a crooked smile. "That's the part that trips me up with you. I don't think I could bear for you to be merely fond of me."

He'd mentioned this before, but only now did understanding dawn. "That's why none of the others hate you. Because you don't keep their hearts."

He nodded, the worry in his expression telling a tale she had no trouble deciphering. He thought she'd give him up if she had to share.

She watched the throbbing flesh she held, only her thumb moving on his shaft. He was bruised here, too, though he hadn't stopped her from caressing him. A drop of fluid beaded from his slit, crystal on his lust-flushed skin. She knew he'd taken pleasure from those other women; knew he had to like them at least a bit, or they'd never have fallen for him. Despite this knowledge, her decision came without effort.

"I want you to stay," she said. "I've never felt so connected to anyone, so safe and right and able to be myself. I can learn to live with the other women, if I know it's me you love most."

When she looked at him, his eyes gleamed with emotion. "Oh, love, I'm not sure *I* can live with hurting you."

Zoe bit her lip, then blurted out the truth. "Last night I slept with Alex and Bryan."

Magnus seemed strangely unsurprised by her confession, his smile so understanding, it made her heart wrench even worse with guilt.

Then he dropped his bombshell.

"I know," he said. "I was there."

Nineteen

When Zoe opened the door to Alex's knock, she had the flushed and frazzled look of a woman who'd been arguing, crying, and being kissed—not necessarily in that order. Alex told himself it wasn't childish to hope the arguing had come last.

Whether it had or not, Zoe wasn't ready for visitors.

"Hello," Oscar said shyly from his perch on Alex's hip. "I'm Oscar. We're here to see Corky."

That earned him a smile and Alex an inquiring look.

"Our client had to leave Oscar in our care for a while."

"Mommy wanted me to hang around *their* necks," Oscar said helpfully.

"I see," said Zoe, and Alex could tell she did. She laid her hand on Oscar's dark-blond hair. "You must be the boy who makes paper fly. You're in luck, as it happens. Corky is home and always happy to have a new playmate."

Alex set the five-year-old down so he could run after her into the living room, his yellow shoes pattering across the terra cotta floors. Oscar jerked to a halt when he found Magnus sitting up on Zoe's saddle leather couch. The man looked awfully healthy wrapped in her quilt—a little pale, but not like a guy who'd been bleeding to death an hour ago. The kitten was stretched beside him like a tiny sphinx, his ears alert and interested.

Oddly enough, Magnus seemed to fascinate Oscar more.

"Hey," said the boy in a tone of discovery.

"Hey," Magnus said back.

Oscar took a few steps closer and pointed. "You have the same shoes as me."

Magnus looked down at them and smiled. "So I do."

Goose bumps climbed Alex's arms, a reaction he was beginning to tire of. Something was going on here, something more than Magnus being a natural with kids. Alex and Bryan had paused at the end of the front hallway. Alex put his hand on Bryan's arm before he could step farther and interrupt.

"Can you make things move without touching them?" Oscar was asking his new friend.

"If I concentrate. But my specialty is spells and wishes."

"What kind of wishes?"

"Good wishes. I'm strictly a white fairy."

Oscar snickered. "You're too big to be a fairy."

"Fairies come in different sizes. Some aren't any smaller than you."

Bryan's hand took a sudden death grip on Alex's. "He can't be saying what I think he is."

But Alex was pretty sure he was. He watched as Magnus lifted Oscar onto the couch. The kitten immediately bounced across Magnus's lap to sniff at the boy.

"Where are your wings?" Oscar asked, giggling as the kitten tickled him with his whiskers.

Rather than answer, Magnus turned to Alex and Bryan. "Why is this boy with you?"

"His mother thinks he's not her son," Bryan said simply.

Magnus hummed. "That doesn't happen often."

Alex couldn't stand it anymore. He left the entry hall and stepped onto the rug. "You think Oscar is a fairy, too."

Magnus put his arm around Oscar's shoulders. "Not just a fairy: a changeling."

Despite all he'd seen, Bryan still managed to be amazed. "You mean Mrs. Pruitt was right? Somebody did steal her son?"

"*Your* people stole her son," Alex said pointedly. He was angrier than he could account for, rage flooding his veins in a hot, dark tide. Magnus tilted his head at him.

"It isn't stealing when the parties agree."

"Mrs. Pruitt didn't agree."

"Not consciously," Magnus conceded without rancor. "The contract would have been negotiated in her dreams."

"Why would any woman agree to give up her child?"

Magnus's eyes seemed to burn straight into Alex's soul. Alex's chest was tight, his breath coming so fast you'd have thought the other man's stare posed a fatal threat.

"A woman might agree," Magnus said, "if that was the only way to save her baby's life. What medicine can't heal, magic often can."

"Oscar's heart murmur!" Bryan cried. "The doctors thought he was going to die."

Magnus nodded, his eyes remaining on Alex. "Fairies like to help in such situations. They find humans interesting to raise."

Oscar's head had been turning back and forth like a tennis fan's. "Is that why you have my shoes? Because we're both fairies?"

Magnus ruffled his hair. "Most likely. No matter how far apart they live, fairies share a special bond. They can sense each other, even if they don't know what the feeling means."

"So I really don't belong to my mommy?"

"You do," Magnus said. "She just . . . temporarily forgot she promised to love you."

Oscar didn't seem content with this answer, and Alex knew how he felt. "This isn't going to satisfy our client, assuming we could get her to believe it. Lizanne Pruitt wants her real son back."

For some reason, Magnus burst out laughing. He stopped when Oscar gaped at him.

"Forgive me. I was amused because her son isn't what she expects anymore. Perhaps—" He rubbed the annoyingly heroic blade of his jaw. "Perhaps if she met her son, as he is now, it would reconcile her to raising the boy she has. She'd have to be sworn to secrecy, of course, but I believe I could concoct a strong enough spell to enforce that."

"Great," Alex said. "Set it up."

Again Magnus smiled. "It's not that simple. Changelings have the power to travel back and forth to Fairy, but only one member of the pair can be in any realm at once. Oscar is too young to go by himself. He'll need an adult fairy to escort him."

Alex folded his arms.

"It can't be me," Magnus said, reading his body language flawlessly. "Oh, I could take Oscar in, but my travel pass only runs one way. Oscar needs someone who can get him there and out again. Oscar needs a grown-up changeling."

"Well, where are we going to find a—" Bryan cut off his own protest. "Oh," he said, looking at Alex in a whole new way. "Boy, would that explain a few things!"

"No," said Alex, his heart filling up his throat. "I'm not."

"Come on," Magnus coaxed. "Weren't you a sick infant, too? Wasn't there some childhood illness that made your mother fear she'd lose you?"

"You did buy the shoes," Bryan said, "even if you threw them out as soon as you could."

Alex gritted his teeth harder. "I don't do psychic stuff. I don't move objects without touching them."

"Not all changelings' powers develop," Magnus said. "Human parents don't give them the training they need for that."

"Your uncle did say you had unopened gifts," Zoe added, joining the chorus. "And it would explain why you—" She glanced sideways at Oscar, conscious of his innocent ears. "Magnus says younger fairies have especially strong needs."

"My mother loves me!" Alex blurted out.

"Of course she does," Magnus said, his eyes more sympathetic than they had any right to be, considering how Alex felt about him. "That's how the switch is supposed to work. Like an adoption. Trust me, the woman who raised your mother's biological son loves him just as much as yours loves you."

Magnus said this like he knew, like he'd actually met the other him. Alex shook his head, but the denial wasn't working the way it should.

"You're fey," Magnus said. "And if you perform this service for Oscar, you'll have an almost unheard of chance to investigate your heritage. Most changelings never figure out who they are."

Zoe had moved behind the couch, her hands on Magnus's shoulders. She squeezed them now to get his attention. "Won't this be dangerous?"

"Normally, yes. In this instance, however, Alex's biological mother is one of the few people in Fairy who can protect them from my mother. She's my aunt: Titania's sister."

"You *know* her?" To the relief of Alex's bruised temper, Zoe looked appalled by this. "You knew who Alex was, and you didn't say?"

"This isn't a secret you blurt out for no good reason."

"But surely he had a right to know!"

"No," Alex interrupted, his anger fading unexpectedly. "I wouldn't have wanted to know before. I hardly want to now."

He looked at Oscar, who slid off the couch and came hesitantly toward him as he crouched down. Reluctant as he was to admit it, he did feel a bond with the boy, and a sense of responsibility. Maybe Alex would be happier if he stopped wishing he could be normal. Maybe he needed to face who he was. Steadying Oscar by the shoulders, he met his serious young eyes.

"What do you say?" he asked the boy. "Should we go to Fairy and see what it's like? Should we let your mother meet her real son?"

Oscar wiggled his jaw in thought. "I don't think she's going to be happy until she does."

"Then we'll do it," Alex said, his heart abruptly racing like a rabbit's. "Assuming Mr. Magnus can teach us how."

There wasn't any point in putting off the journey another day. That would only give Magnus's mother time to regroup. Bryan handled calling Mrs. Pruitt, while Magnus grabbed a few supplies. Then they all drove to Fairy Falls.

Because Oscar and Alex had no experience with meditation, Magnus made them a pair of amulets to help focus their intentions. The little drawstring bags contained some crystals for protection, a lock of Magnus's hair to push them into Fairy, and—since it had already proven powerful—a lock of Zoe's hair to draw them back. Operating on the assumption that the Will-Be knew what it was doing, Magnus loaned Alex his yellow high-tops, and put a stay-put spell on both his and Oscar's shoes.

Alex pulled a face as he tied the laces beside the falls, but he'd need the extra traction to cross the slippery rocks.

"She looks worried for him," Zoe said, nodding at Oscar's mother. Mrs. Pruitt was biting her thumbnail and pacing across the grass. "I'm not sure how much Bryan explained, but she turned her car around the minute he phoned her cell. Maybe she's having second thoughts about abandoning her son."

Magnus glanced at her doubtfully. Maybe she was having second thoughts, but they weren't strong enough to stop the exchange. Truth be told, Zoe's fears concerned him more. She was hooked into the forces that arranged this world more than most, and, consequently, her faith or lack thereof affected the outcome.

"Alex's opposite will know he's coming," Magnus said, hoping to assuage her anxiety. "He'll have known the moment Alex made up his mind. I'm sure he's informed his mother. She'll be waiting on the other side when Alex and Oscar cross."

Zoe nodded and bit her lip, watching Alex with worried eyes.

Magnus stroked the bend of her arm to bring her gaze back to him. "It's important that you believe they'll return safely. Like when you call your angels. You know they're coming to help you, and you know you're worthy."

"You're right." She squeezed his fingers. "Your aunt is going to look out for them, and they're going to come back fine."

"You want a crystal to calm you?" he offered.

Zoe shook her head and smiled. "Your hand is touchstone enough for me."

He had to kiss her for that, brushing it soft and gentle across her lips.

Alex cleared his throat as he approached. "I think we're ready," he said. He was holding little Oscar's hand. Both changelings looked steady—wired but not frightened. Magnus experienced a flash of respect for Zoe's old boyfriend. When Alex made a decision, he didn't second guess himself.

"I have one more charm for you," Magnus said, reaching into his breast pocket. "This watch is spelled to keep human time. Don't wind it and don't lose it. It will track how long you've been gone."

Alex accepted the timepiece, flicking it open and checking it against the modern watch he wore.

"They match," he said, which Zoe took as her cue to kneel and hug Oscar.

"Don't go falling in love with any girl fairies," she said. "Corky and the rest of us want to see you again."

Oscar squeezed her neck and giggled. When Zoe rose, Alex didn't pull her to him but only touched the side of her face.

"That advice goes for you, too," she tried to whisper.

"No worries," he said with a slanted smile. "Those fairies have a few hard acts to follow."

Bryan was waiting a stone's throw away, closer to the rocks that led to the falls. Magnus watched Zoe watch the men embrace and slap each other's backs.

"He'd better come back," she said, one hand pressed to her throat. "That man loves the heck out of him."

Something in her voice said she was saying goodbye to him in a deeper way. Though she'd already told Magnus she loved him, her willingness to release Alex caused his eyes to sting. Alex was a good man. He could have won her again. Magnus wrapped his arm around Zoe's shoulder and squeezed just a little bit.

Oscar's goodbyes were shorter. From a distance, he looked at his mother, clearly not waiting for her to hug him. Her arms wrapped her upper body as if she feared she would fly apart: eagerness and fear and guilt practically screaming from her expression.

Then Alex and Oscar were ready to go.

"Hold tight to my belt," Alex told the boy. "I'll lead the way across the stones."

The time Magnus had spent practicing magic in the human realm seemed to have paid off. The stay-put spells were effective. Alex and Oscar climbed like papa and baby mountain goats up the boulders toward the ledge.

Perhaps the portal knew they were approaching. Dusk was falling, but the curtain of water began to glitter so brightly it was hard to look at without shading their eyes.

"Ooh," Zoe said, her breath catching. "Those are the lights I saw above the falls when Oscar was born."

Magnus could just see them, faint spheres of illumination in every color of the rainbow. "They're spirit guardians for changelings. Probably cousins to your angels."

Zoe's hold tightened on his waist in acknowledgment. They couldn't hear Alex or Oscar over the sound of the falls, but they saw Alex's lips move. He stood at the edge of the roaring curtain, at the mouth of the cave beyond. Oscar reached up with both hands and let Alex lift him in. They both ducked as the water struck their heads. The glitter of the falls flared blindingly, like a sun exploding in the wooded glade. Too solid-seeming to be mere light, the wave struck them silently.

When it passed, Magnus's ears rang for a few seconds.

"Hey," he heard Bryan say over the hum. "Someone is coming out of the falls."

They all leaned forward to see. Two someones were coming, two tall, athletic young men who clambered down the rocks like they'd been doing it all their lives. They were garbed in flowing cambric shirts and chamois leather trousers—classic hunting clothes in Fairy.

Seeing them, Mrs. Pruitt covered her mouth.

"Where's my son?" she demanded, her voice rising. "You promised I'd see my son!"

The taller of the two young men leaped lightly from the final boulder onto the grass, dripping water and laughing. His shoulder-length, wavy hair was a beautiful honey-brown, his eyes the same sky-blue as Mrs. Pruitt's.

Stopping a step away from her, he put his hands on his waist and grinned. "Madame," he said, "I am your son."

"Oh, dear," Zoe murmured as Mrs. Pruitt gasped. "I see what you meant about him not being what she expects."

Before Zoe could go to Oscar's mother to offer support, the glen seemed to explode with fairies—tiny ones.

In the gathering darkness, their colorful glows made it look like a party was starting. The two young men exclaimed with awe, as if they'd never seen such a marvelous sight. Where they'd all come from Zoe didn't know, but she supposed Rajel's crew couldn't have been the only little fey who'd escaped Fairy.

"Rajel is the queen of queens," Magnus said, seeing her confusion. "All the human flocks owe her allegiance."

"Really?" Zoe wondered what she'd done to rate such an important mini-godmother. She spotted a few more crowns among the crowd, but Rajel's did appear to be the sparkliest. "It looks like she's called out the fairy National Guard."

"Yes," Magnus said, a hint of musing in his tone.

As he rubbed his jaw, a trio Zoe recognized flew up to them. Samuel wasted no time revealing what was up.

"We want to go back to Fairy!" he declared, hovering side by side with Florabel.

"Go?" Zoe's question broke in the middle as Magnus pulled her closer to his side.

Samuel's little chest puffed up, but it was Queen Rajel who addressed her next. She flew a bit above and behind the lovebirds, her face beaming with a joy Zoe hadn't seen on it since Alex blew into town.

"Yes," said the queen of queens. "If a five-year-old child and an ignorant fairy changeling are willing to dare the Evil One's wrath, my people can do no less."

But . . . what about me? Zoe thought.

"We want to see if what he says is true," Rajel continued,

jerking her head toward Magnus. "Much time has passed since the last of us fled Fairy. We want to know if there are other big ones like him, who wouldn't make slaves of us, who believe their only right is to rule themselves."

"You heard that?" Zoe said, remembering Magnus's speech to Alex at the sweat lodge.

Samuel zipped a dizzying circle around her head. "We hear everything that concerns our human."

Zoe swallowed the lump in her throat. She'd always liked being called "their" human. "You don't need my permission to go," she said huskily. "But you have my blessing if you want it."

Florabel flew to Zoe's ear. "The queen would like a confidence spell," she whispered so loudly that Zoe winced. "The opposite of what *that one's* mother tried to put on you. *He* knows her magic. *He* can guarantee we stay brave."

This request gave Zoe an even higher estimation of Magnus's abilities. Her fairies were nothing if not magically gifted. Not knowing what to say, she turned to him helplessly.

He was smiling with red-rimmed eyes.

"Queen Rajel," he said, his formal tone causing the fairy's beaming to falter as she flew to him.

"Prince," she responded, curtseying in the air. "Since you obviously heard that, my people and I humbly request your aid."

"You would have it if you needed it, little queen, but you require my help no more than you did Zoe's permission. You are free will fairies. You reclaimed that title the moment you decided to escape to the human realm."

"But your magic has grown strong here," Rajel said, "among the slow and heavy Earth ethers."

"So has yours," Magnus assured her. "Didn't you fight off my mother when she threatened Zoe the other day?"

Queen Rajel's face twisted. "That was quick," she said. "Too quick to give us time to be afraid. *And* the ignorant changeling sang with us—which means honor obliges us to protect him now."

Magnus put out his hand, allowing the queen to flutter warily to his palm. "You are brave, Rajel, the bravest queen the little fey have ever known. Being a tiny bit afraid won't change that. All that my good wishes can give, you have, but I cannot steal your victory from you. I *know* your courage is up to this challenge. You can do what you wish without any help from me."

He seemed a prince as he said this, quietly sure of himself and her. For the first time, Zoe could believe he'd lived for centuries. Rajel also seemed impressed—if a tad suspicious. She stared at him, weighing his words. Then she squared her shoulders and put up her chin.

"Very well," she said, lifting off his hand. "We shall follow the path we've chosen on our own steam." She turned in the air to the horde of fairies who flew behind her, her next words ringing. "We go, my beloved subjects, with our honor bright and our hearts strong!"

"For honor!" Florabel echoed.

"For fun!" Samuel chimed in.

"Before the portal closes!" Rajel urged.

They zoomed away en masse, sparkling like multicolored confetti in the darkening air. The instant they disappeared through the water, Zoe had to hide her face in Magnus's chest.

Thankfully, he understood.

"Don't worry," he soothed, rubbing her back to comfort her. "Those little buggers might not realize it yet, but they wield more power than the rest of my kind combined. I predict they're not going to have any trouble once they're home."

Zoe nodded but couldn't loosen her grip on him. The fairies had been with her since she was a baby. They'd been her most constant and sometimes her only friends. It didn't seem fair that they were leaving only minutes after she'd said goodbye to Alex.

"You'll be all right," Magnus promised. "Neither your power nor your happiness came from them. Okay, maybe your good hair days did, but you'll find a way to compensate."

Zoe couldn't laugh at his joke. "I'm going to be sad for a while," she warned him. "I can't help it."

"I understand," he said, and even as his eyes crinkled in amusement, one tear slipped from them for her sake.

Zoe didn't miss her fairies any less at seeing that, but the bands of longing that had tightened around her chest loosened just a little to know she was loved by him.

Twenty

I know you don't remember," Mrs. Pruitt's grown son was telling her, "but we all agreed to this."

Mrs. Pruitt had collapsed back against a tall red boulder that was probably going to ruin her sweater set. She was clutching Zoe's hand hard enough that Zoe's fingers were going numb. The other Oscar knelt before her and spoke gently. He was a pleasant, late twenty-ish young man—though his adroitness at avoiding being sucked into Mrs. Pruitt's hysterics suggested more years than that. His smiling calm reminded Zoe of Magnus, and she wondered if Fairy might be nicer place than its queen's habits suggested.

If it was, that had to be good news for Alex and Oscar.

"I wouldn't have done that," Mrs. Pruitt said, swiping at her nose with the tissue Zoe had given her. "I never would have agreed to give up my son."

"You did it to save my life," the other Oscar said, "and in return, you promised to love the boy you have as if he were your own. My fairy foster mother showed me the dream where we all decided. You said you wanted to experience unconditional love from the inside out. You said your mother had never loved you like that, and you wanted to be different."

Mrs. Pruitt's gasp of recognition was a sound Zoe had heard before. Her clients did the same thing each time her ghosts found the right detail to convince their loved ones that they were real.

"Mother always said my sister was the smart one," Mrs. Pruitt exclaimed. "She said it was lucky I married because I'd never make it on my own the way Corrine did."

"You see," said the other Oscar, laying his hands gently on her knees.

"But you left me!" Mrs. Pruitt teared up again. "You went to live with some other woman, and she watched you grow up!"

"I went because I knew your Oscar would love you even better than I could. He's a wise old soul, Mother, and this is the first Earth life he chose. He promised to see your true heart, no matter how you acted. From what I was able to see through my foster mother's scrying glass, he kept his word—though all he remembers from his lives in Fairy is a bit of his old magic."

Mrs. Pruitt covered her face in shame. "You saw me? You saw how I treated him?"

"I've learned some magic myself," the other Oscar said, "and I can see your true heart, too. I know you wanted to love him. You simply got caught up in worrying about other people, about what they'd think because he was different."

Mrs. Pruitt quieted at his words, finally letting go of Zoe's hand. Her fingers lifted to almost touch her real son's honey-gold hair. "You're a good boy. Your . . . other mother raised you right."

"You still have your chance," her son pointed out. "You could still watch your Oscar grow into a man. He trusted you to be his mother for a reason, just as I trusted the fairies."

Mrs. Pruitt pressed her fingers to her trembling mouth. "Do you think he could forgive me?"

"I'm sure he can," the other Oscar said. "And it will be easier for you now, knowing you weren't crazy, knowing why you took him in."

"Will I ever see you again?"

"When your Oscar gets older, he and I will be able to go back and forth as we like. It's our right as changelings."

Mrs. Pruitt rolled her lips together and nodded. "I'd like that. And I *do* want him back. I'll be braver this time, now that I know."

The grown-up Oscar grinned so blindingly with approval that Mrs. Pruitt had to smile. "Good. Because I really want to come back and have a chance to drive a human car!"

"You're just like your father," Mrs. Pruitt laughed. "He spends every spare minute tinkering in the garage." Her laughter faded as she took the other Oscar's face in her hands. "You've given me a gift by coming here today. I don't know how to thank you."

"We have a little longer," said her son. "I can't sense the others coming back just yet."

Judging it was safe to leave Mrs. Pruitt and her son alone, Zoe moved quietly away. To her surprise, the other Alex was talking with Magnus beneath a tree, looking casual and at ease.

Magnus's aunt raised this Alex, Zoe reminded herself. *They have no reason not to be friendly.*

Both men turned as she approached. She was wearing the jeans and sneakers she'd changed into before they left. Despite the absence of her short red dress, there was a flicker of male admiration in the other Alex's eyes, one that said his taste in women wasn't that different from his counterpart's.

"Milady," he said when she was close enough for him to bow

over her hand. "The prince informs me that you are acquainted with my opposite."

"I am," she said, tempted to grin at his courtly manners—and at Magnus being called a prince.

"I wonder if you'd allow me to walk apart with you."

Magnus shrugged his eyebrows when she looked at him. Apparently, he considered the other Alex a harmless companion. Or maybe he was counting on him being too polite to hit on the "prince's" girl.

"I'd be happy to walk with you," she said, "and, please, call me Zoe."

They walked away from the others down a path into the trees. Moonlight filtered through the leaves to guide their way.

"You want to know about your twin," she guessed.

"Yes. It's strange to feel him so much a part of my life and yet to know we'll never meet. I share his dreams sometimes." The other Alex's shoulders lifted and fell. Though she knew it probably wasn't the case, he seemed younger than the Alex she knew, more comfortable with himself but less tried. "Perhaps he's shared my dreams as well without knowing it. I've sensed he's troubled, that this world hasn't treated him as kindly as it might."

"Maybe not, but he's made a place in it I think he likes."

"He's a good man?"

"Very." She said it without hesitation, and meant it more than she expected.

"He treats my birth mother well?"

"He adores her. They adore each other."

His head turned in surprise. "You know her?"

"Yes. She would adore you, too. She's a special woman. She stayed in touch with me even after Alex and I broke up."

"You are in love with Prince Magnus now."

Zoe heard an amusing hint of Alex's knee-jerk rivalry in his voice, or maybe it was protectiveness toward his counterpart.

"I am," she said, "though it's strange to hear you call him by that title."

"The prince is well respected in Fairy. He is older than I, of course, and ran with a different circle, but I met him on occasion, at hunts and other events. My mother and he get on. He is fair, I think, and never cheats at games."

The grudging praise amused her—though she wasn't convinced Magnus had treated Bryan with complete fairness. She shifted her gaze toward the bubbling brook that the falls ran into. This was an argument she'd agreed to drop. She didn't think it would benefit Bryan to know that he'd been spelled to sleep with her, or that Magnus had been a party to the encounter. Her own reaction was a mix of outrage and arousal. To think of Magnus participating in that night, feeling everything Bryan did . . .

"I'm a bit surprised by his restraint," the other Alex observed, calling her back from her distraction. "He hasn't charmed you. Your aura shows no signs of tampering."

She realized then that it had never occurred to her to wonder if Magnus had tampered magically with her. That omission frightened her for a moment before it fell away. It seemed she could trust her instincts—no bad thing to have confirmed.

"You can see auras?" she said aloud. "Despite being human?"

The other Alex grinned, and the expression was so like the Alex she knew that her heart squeezed tight. "You're human, aren't you? And you see them."

"Yes, but—I suppose your parents raised you to believe in magic."

"And trained me to use it." He hesitated, as if he wasn't sure he should say what he was going to. "Your Alex won't come back the same, milady. Fairy changes everyone."

*   *   *

The hour that had passed since Alex and Oscar disappeared into the falls felt like an eternity to Bryan. Magnus had explained that time would move differently in Fairy. Bryan tried not to turn each imagined minute into a nightmare, but when little Oscar's not-so-little twin lifted his head and said, "They're coming," his already anxious heart just about thumped through his ribs.

Alex's double seemed to be connected to the same psychic news wire. He emerged at a run from the trees where he'd gone with Zoe, not even seeing Bryan as he leaped, gazelle-like, up the boulders to the falls.

"Goodbye," he cried from the ledge, waving to Alex's old girlfriend. "Best fairy wishes to you all!"

The grown-up Oscar took a moment to hug his mother and then followed. Both men seemed eager to go home, clapping each other's shoulders as they ducked under the water. Bryan supposed Fairy was like a lot of places here on Earth. No matter who was in charge, people found a way to enjoy their lives.

Those two don't know us, he told himself, fighting his hurt at having been ignored. *All their ties lie elsewhere. The real Alex isn't going to forget you.*

This time, the falls only brightened a little for the exchange—more like moonlight than sun. Through the blue-white glow, the two figures he'd been waiting for clambered out.

"We're back!" Oscar shouted, not needing help to climb down. "We're safe and sound!"

Bryan's breath caught in his throat as they came closer. Oscar was noticeably taller, as if he'd been away a year instead of an hour, and Alex—Alex was smiling, so relaxed and easy he might have returned from a good vacation. Bryan's friend paused to watch Oscar and his mother hug, the pair looking a good deal warmer toward each other than they had before. Seeing they were well, Alex turned and headed for Bryan.

"I've learned new tricks!" Bryan heard Oscar announce to his mother. "And how not to do them by accident."

Mrs. Pruitt murmured her approval, for which Bryan was glad, but the lion's share of his attention was on his friend.

Alex's eyes shone like lasers as he approached, his ribs going in and out faster than normal. Bryan ordered himself not to make a scene, but when Alex stopped in front of him, when Alex looked into his eyes and held out his arms, it was hard not to.

"Hey, buddy," Alex said, pulling Bryan close with one hand cupping his head. "You have no idea how much I missed you."

Bryan squeezed him back and tried not to let his tears roll free. Alex felt so good—so warm and hard and *him*. "I love you," he said, unable to keep it in. "I'm glad you're all right."

Alex kissed his ear. "I love you, too," he whispered, then pulled back to look at him. "I have some things to tell you, but maybe they can wait until we're alone."

"I'm not sure they matter compared to you saying the *L* word."

Alex laughed, and that same easiness Bryan had noticed when he emerged from the water was in the sound. "Jeez, it's good to see you and, yes, I mean the *L* word the way you hope. A lot has happened. I had a chance to grow up and, well, sow my oats, I guess you'd say. I realized how important really connecting to someone is. I can't promise—" His eyes glowed blue as his hand stroked roughly down Bryan's face. "I can't promise you'll always be my only, but I'm pretty sure I can promise to put you first. That is, assuming you'd be interested in an arrangement like that."

His unexpected shyness made Bryan bark out a laugh. "You've only been gone an hour. It'd take longer than that for me to lose my interest in being number one on your list."

It was hard to tell in the moonlight, but Bryan thought Alex blushed.

"Come with me," he said, slinging his arm around Bryan's shoulder. "I have things to say to Magnus and Zoe."

Zoe held Magnus's hand feverishly tight as the men approached. To Magnus, the chemistry between Bryan and Alex was obvious, their bodies leaning against each other with every stride. He rubbed Zoe's knuckles in the hope of easing her tension. Alex had been a big part of her life. No matter how long he'd been gone from it, no matter how much she loved Magnus, seeing Alex as half of a couple that didn't include her had to be difficult.

"Hey you," Alex said, bending down to kiss her cheek.

Magnus needed no special powers to see Alex's sojourn in Fairy had altered him. His face and manner said he'd made peace with who he was—and with at least trying to let Zoe go.

That he'd been gone a year and had only gotten up to *trying* was a worry for another day.

"You look good," Zoe said, a little teary as she touched his jaw. The touch, or maybe the tears, inspired a flare in Alex's aura, but he shook it off.

"Do I look magic?" he asked, wagging his brows.

"Should you?" she said, falling in with his playfulness. "Because I might need time to adjust to you being a *psychic* detective."

"Oh, God," Bryan moaned, and everyone laughed.

"I have news for you," Alex said to Magnus. "From your aunt."

Alex's self-esteem wasn't the only thing that had changed during his absence. His rancor toward Magnus was also gone. He seemed both more respectful and more confident—as if they were equals now.

"There's been a coup," Magnus said, knowing it was true the moment the words came out.

"Yes," Alex said. "Very nearly bloodless. Your mother has been deposed and stripped of the power that came with the throne, which doesn't leave her with enough to cause trouble, as I understand. Evidently, relying so heavily on black magic drained the stores she was born with. Your aunt rules unopposed, thanks in part to Zoe's fairies."

"To my fairies!" she exclaimed, her hand to her breast.

"They'd been in exile so long, their return impressed everyone. When the little fey threw in their lot with Queen Elena, people decided she must be destined to wear the crown. Queen Rajel and her troops barely had to swing their swords."

"Oh, my," Zoe breathed.

"Oh, my, indeed," Alex agreed. "You should have seen the party they threw afterward. Lasted for weeks." He turned again to Magnus. "Your aunt charged me to tell you that you're welcome to serve on her cabinet any time—should you wish to return."

Magnus chuckled. His aunt was wise enough to know he wouldn't want the throne, and ambitious enough not to volunteer to give it up. "I'm sure she'll find good advisors on her own."

"So . . . then you're a prince," Bryan said to Alex. "Because this Queen Elena is your birth mother."

Alex hooked his arm around his lover's neck and grinned. "I'm no prince here," he said, "but if you wanted to bow occasionally, just for fun, I'd allow it."

They'd taken an hour to get out of the grove, letting everyone say goodbye to everyone else, making sure Oscar had all their e-mails—and an open invitation to visit. Mrs. Pruitt seemed a little startled by how affectionate they were toward her son, but Magnus suspected this was good for her. Raising Oscar was a privilege she was only beginning to appreciate.

As much as Magnus had enjoyed witnessing the happy resolution of these issues, he was even more relieved to return with Zoe to her home. He had resolutions of his own to contemplate.

They were very much on his mind as he gazed into the starry sky that stretched above Zoe's deck. Tonight's moon was a bright half circle—a waning one.

One quarter gone, he thought, his hands gripped tight to the wood railing. *Three more to go before I have to cheat on her again.*

Zoe stood within his arms, her slight weight leaning warmly on his chest. It felt wonderful to hold her, to think of her as his—but maybe that was selfish. Maybe he should have let Alex win her, the way he'd decided to when he was dying. From the looks of it, she'd probably have to share him with Bryan, but would that really be worse than what Magnus was offering?

Uncomfortable with the question, he shifted on his feet. The movement roused Zoe.

"The stars are beautiful," she said. "Like someone flung a million diamonds against the black."

He kissed the top of her head, thankful for the reminder that tomorrow wasn't now, and that now held plenty of treasures.

Sensing something of his mood, Zoe turned in his arms and looked up at him. He could just make out her face, its delicate features so dear to him his throat tightened. A furrow formed between her brows.

"Something's been bothering me," she said. "You said you lived in Fairy for centuries. Does that mean you're immortal?"

He'd been wondering when she'd think to ask that. "In this realm, I'm only immortal in the sense that all conscious beings are. I expect I'll live a slightly longer than average life span, age gracefully, and leave when I'm ready to." He pinched the tip of her nose. "I also expect I can teach you what little you need to do the same. Humans are just beginning to realize how much in control of their lives they are."

To his surprise, her brow creased harder. "You're saying you would have been immortal if you hadn't come here?"

"Relatively immortal. Even fairies don't live forever."

"But you gave up a relatively eternal life to be with me."

Magnus had to smile at her shock. "You of all people know every soul is eternal."

"Yes, but I'm still impressed!"

His smile turned into a laugh. "I hope you stay impressed. Maybe we'll have many lifetimes together after this one."

"I'd like that," she said, her cheek pressed against his chest. "Almost more than I can say."

His heart turned over as he hugged her back. He reacted to her closeness; he couldn't not. He wanted so badly to have her in all the ways their bodies were meant to join. Despite this longing, tenderness ruled his response. The feel of her slender strength, the scent of her, the crazy curling mass of her hair—all tangled together inside his soul. She was it for him, the partner he'd been looking for all his life without knowing it. Breaking her heart would destroy his own. Aching, he kissed her temple and drank in her warmth.

I'm going to have to go home.

The recognition dropped like an anvil inside his mind. He could return to Fairy now that Titania had been deposed. His aunt wouldn't use him the way his mother had wanted to. What he couldn't do was keep taking other lovers, never knowing which would be the one Zoe discovered she could not forgive.

He thought of Teresa, Zoe's best friend from the café, whom he'd always avoided for that reason. Steering clear of her hadn't kept him safe. That silly waitress from the Longhorn

Grill had come close enough to being a last straw. Even if Zoe knew why he slept around, Magnus couldn't keep cheating his own heart. He would take his month with her. He would make the best of it.

And then he would let her go.

The atmosphere seemed to thicken and vibrate as he made his choice. He filled his lungs with breath to share it with her—only to realize that the tingling running through him wasn't the effect of nerves.

"Felicitations!" cried a small, high voice a second before Zoe's deck came alive with hundreds of fairies. "Best fairy wishes to the big people!"

The voice belonged to Samuel, who set himself off from the glittering crowd by zipping like a maniac around their heads.

"Oh!" Zoe cried as if she were about to weep. "You're back!"

Queen Rajel fluttered more sedately into the space between them. "We're commuting," she said, her face serene, her little body glowing with happiness. "In return for our support, Queen Elena has agreed to give us unlimited access to her portal. We get to keep our humans *and* our home."

"Oh, how wonderful!" Zoe said. "I wanted you to be happy, but I was going to miss you so much."

"I'm Samuel the Secretary of State now!" the boy fairy burst in, having flown himself to actual breathlessness. "I'm the liaison between big and small."

"Congratulations," Zoe laughed. "I'm sure you'll be marvelous."

"I'm helping!" Florabel cried. "I'm the official Party Planning Fairy."

"A crucial post," Zoe concurred, her eyes twinkling.

"Peace," said the queen, flying at Samuel and Florabel to herd them back. "We have an important message to deliver."

Her fairies quieted down to a chitter, and then to actual silence. Queen Rajel cleared her throat and turned to Magnus.

"We owe you an apology, Big One. We misjudged you, thinking you were like your mother and the other bad big fey. We did our best not to help you win our human, but you have proven yourself a true friend to fairies—"

"—and kittens—" Samuel interrupted.

"—and Zoe," Florabel piped last.

"Especially to Zoe," Rajel agreed. "You didn't simply wish to win her heart, you gave her yours. Consequently, we must share the truth about the magic that brought you here."

"You know the terms of my visa?" The sudden pounding of his heart stole Magnus's breath. Had the little fairies found a loophole? Was he going to be able to keep Zoe and have her the way he craved? His cock hardened instantly, straining so painfully against his zipper that it was an effort to focus on the queen.

Luckily, she gave him a moment to collect himself.

"The small fey know the underpinnings of all the best magic," she said, her fists planted proudly on her tiny waist, "and we've found the secret clause. Because you have given your heart to Zoe, and have asked nothing in return, you do not have to win a new heart every month. You only have to re-win hers."

Zoe and Magnus began to speak at once. Rajel hushed them by holding up her hand.

"This is not as easy as it sounds. You will have to be thoughtful with each other—"

"—and playful—" Samuel chimed in.

"—and not let silly arguments grow into big ones. Zoe, you will have to truly value this big one's presence in your life, because if you don't love him when each full moon sets, the magic that lets him stay here will yank him back."

Magnus could hardly credit her scolding tone. The queen

sounded like she was protecting him. Zoe heard the change as well, but she only smiled.

"I will heed your warning," she said, her skin delightfully flushed, "and I thank you for your wisdom."

"Good," said Rajel. "Now take this big one to your bedroom and treat him as he deserves."

Twenty·one

Zoe doubted either of them needed Rajel's encouragement. Their hands found each other, their breath coming faster at the instantly explicit thoughts that streaked through their heads. Zoe had never seen anything so arousing as the flush that suffused Magnus's face. His fingers were hot as they twined with hers. They could be together the way they wanted. They didn't have to say goodbye.

And, boy, did they have time to make up for!

Zoe didn't notice when the queen and her court vanished, only that Magnus's eyes were glowing like green lasers.

"If we don't get inside soon," he said, husky and low, "I'm going to make love to you up against the side of your house."

Zoe grinned. "You say that like it would be a bad thing."

Feeling bolder than she ever had, she peeled her plain white T-shirt over her head. She was right not to worry over Magnus's reaction. He swallowed at the sight of her naked breasts. Her nipples were already tight, and they tightened more in the cool night air. Magnus's hands curled into fists with his effort not to reach for them.

"I know you like to start slowly," he said, his voice so throaty it was hard to hear. "I need to lay you down for that."

"Lay me down here. Under the stars."

He stared at her, deciding, then began to attack the buttons of his Western shirt. Zoe was far from jaded by this procedure. She knew what glories lay under that pale-blue cotton.

"All your clothes have to go," he said, toeing off his shoes hurriedly. "I'll take as long with you as you like, but I want you naked fast."

As ultimatums went, she didn't mind this one. She pulled off everything for him, reveling in his moan when she shucked her panties down with her jeans. Goggling at her legs and various other bare parts distracted Magnus from his undressing. Trying to hide her amusement, Zoe lowered herself to the deck's smooth cedar planking, leaned back on her elbows, and let her knees swing wide. When she played her fingers down her belly, skimming the crisp black edge of her pubic thatch, Magnus shook himself.

"Two weeks," he warned her. "Then *maybe* I'll let you out of bed."

This reminded him he was supposed to be naked, too. He finished the task with flattering speed, but Zoe still got her ogling in. His body was a god's, his big, long muscles silvered by the quarter moon. They bunched and flexed with every movement, but even they could only hold her gaze so long. His hugely erect cock thrust up from its nest of curls like some ancient worshiper's wish fulfillment. It jerked when her eyes lit on it, so formidable in its arousal that she bit her lip.

This was enough to get him to his next mark. He fell over her in one smooth motion, his palms slapping the decking, his torso crowding hers in primal male display. His heat washed over her in waves.

"You like the size of me a bit too much," he growled. "I'm beginning to think that's all you want me for."

Zoe reached down his body to caress the hard, satiny length. "It's not just the size I like, big guy. It's the fact that this"—he shuddered as she squeezed it—"belongs to you."

He captured her mouth and kissed her, so deep, so hungry, that she momentarily forgot what she was holding. When her faculties returned to her, she was flat on her back with her hands stretched above her head, both her wrists captured in one of his hands. He wasted no time taking advantage of her vulnerability, rubbing his big hard torso slowly against hers. This close, the size of his body simply overwhelmed. His erection blazed against her inner thigh, a long-awaited present just out of reach.

Its skin was slightly damp with sweat.

"No fair," she said, writhing beneath him as all her insides tried to strain toward him. "I know you fairies like control, but I want to touch you, too."

The tiny points of his nipples dragged sparks of fire across her breasts.

"You are touching me," he whispered.

He was doing something with his energy, causing it to lick over her skin, to curl into her quivering pussy. She gasped as one hot flare reached inside her, touching nerves her flesh should have protected. Fluid welled from her walls and ran out as the agonizing sweetness probed deeper.

"Oh, God," she cried. "Magnus!"

Her clit throbbed frantically at the hidden touch. She realized he'd done this before: first when she'd introduced him to Alex, and later when he'd taken her anally in her bed. Then the effect had been possible to dismiss as imagination. Now the sensations were so sharp she both wanted and didn't want to go over the edge from them.

"Don't," she finally begged. "I want to come with you inside me, from the *physical* feel of you."

He nuzzled her neck and sent a tendril of energy curling further in. Zoe jerked helplessly. It felt like her very womb was being caressed.

"This is only a fairy tease," he murmured, "to make sure you're ready to take all of me."

"I've been ready for the last two years!"

He chuckled at her hoarse complaint. "Patience," he said. "We only have one first time."

Zoe understood his position, even agreed, but her body had no patience left. She nipped his shoulder in answer, which startled him enough to release her hands.

"Fair is fair," she said, running them down his back and purring with enjoyment. His skin was velvet over hard muscle, so smooth she marveled that she'd ever thought him like other men. He was wonderfully different, that skin of his luring her to explore all the curves and creases that she could reach.

He had a pair of sweet ones under the shadow of his rear.

"Zoe," he cautioned even as his eyes glowed with arousal.

"Tease me all you want," she said. "Just know I'm going to tease you back."

The hand he'd trapped her wrists with slid over and cupped one breast, its thumb circling her nipple until it ached—which, for her, took all of two seconds. He watched the little hardness darken, then looked back at her.

"You won't let me have my traditional masculine advantage?"

"No," she said very firmly. "You and I are going to give as good as we get."

His expression lifted in a wicked grin. "I should warn you I know a lot of tricks."

"Yeah, but I'm a quick learner."

He laughed and kissed her, more warmth than finesse in it. Grabbing his head, Zoe flicked and sucked his tongue until a hungry sound broke in his throat. He must have guessed what she was pretending she was sucking. His hips ground reflexively against her before he tore away.

"All right," he said breathlessly. "I'm ready to give you what you've asked for."

For all his braggadocio, his hands were shaking as he parted her folds. She immediately saw another advantage to his smooth fey skin. One big finger slid inside her sheath like a sexy dream.

"Just to be sure," he rasped when she whimpered. "I want you to be wet enough for me."

She was more than wet, she was soaking, her juices running down his finger as it eased into her. Her body arched without her controlling it, her spine stretching as it tried to pull the luscious feelings he was creating all the way in.

Her reaction siderailed his good intentions.

"Hellfire," he cursed. "I'm sorry, Zoe. I know I promised to take you, but I have to give you one kiss first."

He moved down her with the easy grace he seemed to have brought with him out of Fairy. His mouth settled over her clitoris with unerring aim. She could feel the little organ swelling, growing more sensitive as he sucked it voluptuously. His tongue licked slow and hard up the tiny rod. Despite her desire to come with him inside her, her hands clutched his thick, dark hair. She was so close she was panting. Once more he licked her, bottom to top, the finger he'd pushed inside her giving her a dangerously sweet hardness to squeeze around.

Then he lifted his head and released her.

"Now?" he asked harshly.

Zoe could only nod and loll her legs wider.

His flush of anticipation was unmistakable, and the gleam of his hot, green eyes. He took his cock in hand, the thing standing so high he had to tilt it down for the right angle. Heat radiated outward from her pussy, like an oven door opening. He touched her with the head of him, parting hot, lust-slicked lips. The broad upper curve lodged just inside her, too big to slip free. His mooring secure, he propped himself over her on his arms. His head dropped so he could see the place they would join. She guessed he liked the visual. His chest went in and out, and then his eyes rose to hers.

"I love you," he said. "I hope I get the chance to love you forever, but however our lives unfold, you'll always be the dearest partner I ever had."

Her throat choked with tears as she clasped his handsome face in her hands. "Magnus, I'd trust you with my forever. I'd trust you with my soul."

They both knew what she was saying, maybe better than any other two people would.

"Love," he said, his voice as husky as hers. "You honor me."

She smiled and slid her hands down his solid chest. "Why don't you honor me with your body?"

His erection leaped like an eager horse at a starting gate. His breath rushed into his lungs, and then he cocked his hips and pushed—one slow, silky glide that filled her and filled her until she moaned and had to lift her knees to give him room. His thickness, his heat, the sense that he was truly claiming her, was heaven come to earth for her. With him, she only had to be herself. No hiding, no apologies. Given how important that was to her, seeing how much this act meant to him brought her to the stinging edge of tears.

Neither of them would ever forget this.

He shuddered with pleasure, the involuntary motion shaking her hands as she rubbed his back.

"Oh, God," he gasped, catching one of her knees to urge it even higher. "You feel better than you did for—"

He cut himself off, but Zoe guessed what he'd been about to say. "Better than I did for Bryan?"

"Yes," he admitted, the shudder wracking him again.

"You're bigger than he is," she suggested, unable to resist teasing. "Maybe you like a closer fit."

Magnus groaned and swelled impossibly thicker. "Fairy nerves are different." He reset his knees and gave an actual, grunting shove. "We feel things more."

"I feel *you* more."

"My energy might—" He shoved again and gained a millimeter. "It might be sensitizing you."

If it was, it felt fabulous. Her entire body tingled with pleasure, from her fingertips to her toes. She wrapped her legs around his waist and tightened their muscles. "You'll have to teach me how to do that."

"You feel so good already, you'd probably kill me if you learned." With another pull, she almost took all of him. His hand clamped her buttock to lift her to him, his breath coming quick and rough. "It's a good thing you like the first stroke slow. I don't think we could—"

And then he was there, fully surrounded, fully home. He closed his eyes and sighed, positively beatific. Zoe couldn't have asked for a better gift than to have put that look on his face. Add that to the pleasure she herself was feeling, and it was no wonder they moaned and squirmed at the same time.

"Three weeks in bed," he panted, "and maybe time out for meals."

She was laughing when he began to stroke, which effectively transformed her laughter to a pleasured cry. At once, she realized Bryan wasn't the only man of her acquaintance with superior aim. Magnus knew just how to roll his hips into her, just where to linger and press harder—and the size he put behind the pressure sent her into the stratosphere. His thrusts were strong and steady:

deep, long motions that surged in and out. In spite of the delight they brought, they weren't altogether what she wanted—nor what he did, to judge by the tension he was fighting.

She didn't want him to fight anything, not when they'd both been waiting so long.

"More," she pleaded, pushing up at him from her hips. "Please, Magnus, take me the way you want."

He panted down at her. "Zoe, I want to ravage you."

"Then do it," she urged with her body as well as her voice. "That's what I want, too."

"Okay then." His expression hardened. "I will."

When he let go, it was like trying to hold a tornado within her arms. He had so much power, so much control, and under that a wildness no mere human could have contained. He didn't just *have* sex, he embodied it, like the gods of folklore must have done. He didn't hurt her, he simply sent her up in flames. She had an instant to wonder if Alex had learned to do this while he was in Fairy, and then the funnel sucked her up, her orgasm an incredible, squeezing pressure that exploded from her in a help-less wail.

"Again." Magnus breathed in ragged bursts against her hair. "Go up for me again."

She went up even higher and felt his hardness twitch inside her tugging contractions.

"No," he gritted out, maybe to himself. "I'm not going yet."

He sank onto his elbows, one corded forearm shoving under her neck. "Is this all right?" he asked, his hips working more em-phatically into her, as if he couldn't help but go harder. "I don't want to hurt you."

His thrusts did hurt now, just a little, but she was groaning over yet another stupendous orgasm and couldn't really com-plain. When she came out of it, the ache of his pounding felt even better.

"Magnus," she gasped, her nails digging into his big shoulders. "Please, don't stop what you're doing."

She heard his teeth grind together, felt his muscles bunch for more power. He shoved her into another climax so quickly she didn't have time to prepare herself for how good it was. She wasn't even sure it was one climax. It seemed more like a chain of throbbing peaks, each pulsing with violent sweetness until the next one seized and shook her.

She knew he reveled in doing this to her, but Magnus could only stand feeling her clench around him for so long.

"That's it," he said, his thrusts utterly savage now. "Grab it. I can't— Oh, God—"

He slammed into her, hard and deep, his eyes blind with pleasure, his mouth slack as he went over. She felt him come inside her, a jet of force that was more than seed—though there was plenty of that. It felt as if his soul were bursting through its barriers, joining hers, loving hers. Ecstasy sang through her body and melted it away. She was light and joy in a humming silence bigger than the world.

Best of all, *he* was there, with the same tender, awestruck emotions beating in him.

She didn't have to give him her heart. He was her heart, and she was his. In this shining moment, there were no differences between them: no regret, no fear, just a love that loved for the pleasure of letting that delicious energy run through their consciousness. They would never lose each other, because they would always know this was the truth within each of them.

She felt him sigh a thought that might have been her name. There was wonder in it, and she knew that however many women he'd shared pleasure with, he'd never reached this pinnacle with them. The place they dwelt was so lovely, its peace so profound, that it almost didn't matter if he had.

Still, it was nice to know she was the only one.

She found herself back in her body a blink later. He had collapsed on top of her, but now he rolled to the side, pulling her with him to snuggle close.

She was almost afraid to speak. Instead, she pressed her lips to his pounding heart and stroked her hand down his side. He was summer-warm, like a big, cuddly radiator. It seemed magical to be lying here in the open, totally comfortable, with the stars wheeling over them.

"Sleep," he said, his hand gentle on her curls. "I'm going to see if I can remember a healing spell."

Zoe slung her leg over his thigh and hummed happily. She hoped he could remember. Pummeled though her pussy was, she was looking forward to trying that again.

Zoe had always wondered what it would be like to go all night with Magnus.

They did make it into the house before she found out, the noise of their entry sending Corky scurrying under her bed. Fortunately, the kitten wasn't permanently traumatized. When they finally quieted again, he crawled out and mewed for Magnus to pick him up. Magnus petted him no more than half a dozen times, and Corky collapsed into kitty dreamland, actually purring a bit in his sleep.

If Zoe's heart hadn't belonged to Magnus already, it would have then.

"You *are* a true friend to kittens," she joked.

"This pussy certainly seems to think so."

Zoe smiled. A brand new day was dawning outside. The sliver of orangey-pink sun looked pretty nice seen over his shoulder.

"I have something to ask you," she said, "which seems a little silly now. What is your name really?"

"Oh," he said, then chuckled. "It's really Magnus Monroe. I

was able to steal the identity of someone with the same name—
which seemed a lucky break at the time. I knew I'd have to keep
secrets if I stayed, and I wanted my name to feel like me."

"And Bryan couldn't see through your falsified records because he's not psychic?"

Magnus shifted higher on his elbow, his face serious. He
seemed to hear the words she didn't say. "I didn't force him to
want you, Zoe. My spell only broke down his hesitation to pur-
suing you."

Zoe stroked his strong forearm. "I'm not sure that makes me
more comfortable. You saw me with him and Alex."

"Are you upset because I intruded on your privacy?"

"I don't know. I—" She stopped, not wanting to spoil their
morning, not when their night had been perfect.

"Whatever it is, Zoe, you can tell me. I know more about the
twists and turns desire can take than most people."

She knew he did, and it was one of the qualities she loved
most. *Start the way you mean to go on,* she thought. *If it's important to you, you need to talk it out.*

"I know Alex loves Bryan," she said, "and I'm glad for them.
The thing is, there was something in Alex's eyes last night when
he looked at me, even after he came back from Fairy." She hesitated, but Magnus's look was kind. "I don't think he's completely over me, or at least not completely over needing more
than one lover. I want him and Bryan to make it."

Magnus stroked a tumbled curl out of her face. "You want
your old love to be happy . . . and maybe you'd like a little of his
happiness to come from you."

He was so perceptive he scared her. "I love you, Magnus,"
she said, wanting to be very clear. "You are my choice, completely. I know it's not my responsibility, or even my business,
but I can't help wanting him to be content."

Magnus was silent for a moment, his gaze thoughtful. He

ran one finger gently down Corky's tail. "Suppose we help them out?"

Zoe blinked at him. "How do you mean?" she asked carefully.

"Well, you're right that Alex probably isn't ready to be monogamous. If he develops like the average fairy, he has a decade or so before his heart, and his body, can really settle on one person. We could, if you wanted, provide him the variety his fairy constitution needs without endangering his bond with Bryan. I don't mean to sound arrogant, but I doubt Bryan or Alex would kick me out of bed any sooner than they'd kick you."

Zoe hadn't been this surprised when she found out he was a fairy. "You'd do that for them? For me?"

"I would do anything to bring you pleasure. But perhaps you'd find it easier not to see Alex with his new lover?"

Zoe took a couple swallows to find her voice. "I think . . . I have to admit, I liked seeing them together. I found it . . . exciting."

Magnus's smile was sly. "You aren't the first woman to like watching men."

"Did you, um, like being in Bryan's head when he took Alex?"

His laugh was low and wicked. "I'm fey, Zoe. We like almost everything."

"Oh, my." Zoe's hand pressed her breast. "Just hearing you say that makes me wet again."

He leaned over Corky to kiss her lips deep and soft. When he pulled away, despite how vigorously they'd attempted to sate themselves, an ember of carnal interest glowed in his eyes. She had to press her thighs together at the new flutter that inspired.

"I want you to know you'd be enough for me," he said.

"I feel the same," she responded shyly. "But if we *could* have more, now and then . . ."

"Now and then would be lovely—as long as the rest of the time you're mine."

He'd cupped her breast in his hand, a physical claiming to match his verbal one. His possessiveness pleased her in a deep and feminine way. She grinned to camouflage how much. "I like your idea of compromise."

"I won't compromise on your marrying me," he warned. "As soon as you're ready, I'm calling the priest."

He took her breath away and made her laugh at the same time. She hadn't been thinking of marriage, but—boy—did she discover she wanted it!

"Oh, what female tears will fall in Fairyville," she cried, "the day Magnus Monroe walks down the aisle with me!"

"And I hope you enjoy every one," he said, "for my pride's sake, if nothing else." He smiled at her, his eyes so radiant with love her own grew hot. "There's one last thing I should tell you. When fairies are particularly happy, good fortune has a way of . . . magnetizing itself to them. If you and I get married, I can't predict what stroke of luck might burst into our lives."

"Hm," said Zoe, giving in to temptation to cruise her hand slowly down his chest. "I guess we'll have to make the best of that."

Alex and Bryan drove back to Phoenix the next morning. Oscar and his mother were staying another day, because, as Mrs. Pruitt put it, "My son has a lot of stories to tell me before we go home."

Bryan and Alex could have stayed as well. They were both a bit bleary-eyed, having fucked like bunnies the whole night through. Despite their sensual exhaustion, both had wanted to get on the road early, as if what had developed between them wouldn't be official until they got home.

It was a beautiful—and predictably sunny—Arizona day, with a sky like a window straight into heaven. Bryan felt like a different person, or maybe like the same person, simply living in a different world. He couldn't stop looking at Alex while he drove, trying to measure how much his friend had changed in his year away.

Had he learned things from the fairies besides a touch of psychicness? Last night they'd just gone at it like they were starved, but might Alex have new bed tricks he'd want to try?

That titillating thought led him inexplicably to one of Magnus. Bryan didn't know why, but ever since Zoe had slept with him and Alex, he'd felt connected to the man, as if seducing Zoe had somehow been the same as seducing him. He could imagine Magnus sucking him off so clearly it seemed like it had happened, like Bryan knew how those gorgeous lips of his would feel around his cock. If Bryan tried, he could even picture a seedy men's room where it would take place.

He shifted on the seat at his rising hard-on, half hoping it would go away but suspecting not. It wasn't really wrong to lust after another man, as long as he didn't act on it. And Alex, of all people, would understand.

Alex, of all people, seemed not to have lost his radar for arousal. Bryan nearly jumped out of his skin when Alex reached across the seat to squeeze his thigh.

"Oh, boy," he said, chuckling. "That guilty start tells me you're not fantasizing about me."

"Shit," said Bryan, which made Alex laugh harder.

"Spill," said Alex, "or I'll winkle it out of you with my fairy charm."

"Oh, hell," Bryan said. "I know I'm probably the last person who should be suggesting this, but do you think Zoe and Magnus would ever want to . . ."

"Want to what?" Alex asked.

Bryan shook his head, amazed he'd even had the nerve to think of it. Alex had agreed to make their relationship a priority. Bryan shouldn't be trying to complicate his own dream-come-true.

"Ignore me," he said aloud. "Just a crazy idea."

"Ohh," said Alex, maybe calling on his new gifts. "*That* kind of crazy idea."

Bryan blushed harder, but Alex only looked back at the highway and grinned.

"You never know what might happen," he said, his hands sliding caressingly on the wheel. "Fairies and their partners do love adventuring."